W9-BCW-525

SPRIG MUSLIN

WITH A FOREWORD BY LINDA LAEL MILLER

This Large Print Book carries the
Seal of Approval of N.A.V.H.

Sprig Muslin

WITH A FOREWORD BY LINDA LAEL MILLER

Georgette Heyer

THORNDIKE PRESS

A part of Gale, Cengage Learning

Detroit • New York • San Francisco • New Haven, Conn • Waterville, Maine • London

GALE
CENGAGE Learning™

LIBRARY OF CONGRESS CATALOGING-IN-PUBLICATION DATA

Heyer, Georgette, 1902–1974.
    Sprig muslin / by Georgette Heyer ; with a foreword by Linda Lael Miller.
        p. cm. — (Thorndike Press large print clean reads)
    ISBN-13: 978-1-4104-0833-4 (alk. paper)
    ISBN-10: 1-4104-0833-7 (alk. paper)
    1. Large type books. I. Title.
PR6015.E795S67 2008
823'.912—dc22   2008021658

Published in 2008 by arrangement with Harlequin Books S.A.

Printed in the United States of America
1 2 3 4 5 6 7 12 11 10 09 08

FOREWORD

It's hard to believe, but somehow, for all my voracious reading over the years, I missed Georgette Heyer. What can I say? The library in my hometown was open only on Tuesday afternoons, and the books were all donated. What a happy circumstance that Harlequin is reissuing a great selection of her work — now I can catch up! And what a joy to discover a "new" old author.

I read *Sprig Muslin* on an airplane, and what a delightful distraction it was. I was so absorbed in this largely comical story that I missed the peanut-and-pretzel portion of the trip entirely, with no regrets at all. I laughed aloud several times, no doubt drawing the concerned attention of other passengers, but not to worry. I was in Heyerland, and enjoying every moment.

Come and meet, as I did, this splendid crop of well-spoken characters, each one distinct enough to walk right off the page and buckle himself — or herself — into the seat next to you.

First there is Sir Gareth Ludlow, a noble and quick-witted hero, a hunk with a brain. I was in love with him from word one. Dashing and a real hand with the horses, and with a good tailor, to boot. Yum.

In the beginning of the story, our Sir Gareth, better known as Gary, is on his way to Brancaster, family seat of Lord Widmore, "not many miles from Chatteris, in the heart of the fens," much to the chagrin of his spirited sister, Beatrix (aka Trixie), to offer for Lady Hester Theale, a scatterbrained character who has been on the shelf for too long. A timid creature, our Lady Hester, but don't give up on her too soon. She's an "out-and-outer," and you'll like her, especially in the end, when she drops the mousy act, braces up and shows her true colors.

The story takes off right away. As the whole thing comes into vivid focus, I swear it's like watching a movie in my head. Gary has just stopped at an inn, to rest the horses and maybe throw back some grog, when Miss Amanda "Smith" blows into his life like the proverbial storm. She's young and innocent, but definitely a lady who knows her own mind. She's a splendid liar, telling all manner of tales, but no fool our Sir Gareth. Since it's the only thing to do, he appoints himself her protector, over her loud protests, and the merry romp begins. Gary takes her firmly in hand and, being too much a gentleman to leave her in a public inn where she might fall under the spell of scurrilous influences, he escorts (drags) her to Brancaster, hoping to palm her off on someone respectable. Like the woman he hopes to marry, for instance.

That would be Lady Hester. Being a shy soul, and thinking him still in love with his long-dead fiancée — who was a pistol herself, by the by — she rejects his suit, much to the irritation of her impoverished and highly abrasive family, who hoped for access to Gary's sizable fortune. Gary is disappointed to be spurned, however politely, but undaunted, too, in true hero fashion, and is prepared to press on the next morning and deliver Amanda to someone respectable for safekeeping, until her family can be identified and contacted. (She cannot stay at Brancaster, after all, for various good reasons.) Gary soon learns, however, that the vixen has escaped in the wee small hours, in the dubious company of Lady Hester's "aging roué" of an uncle, who has been known to frequent "the petticoat line."

Here's a deuced snarl, and the chase is on!

Amanda is a consummate stinker, but she's a clever bit of baggage, and she soon catches on to the uncle's unsavory plans for her delectably spunky little self, and gives him the slip, hiding out in a farmer's cart. At this point she's planning a career as a milkmaid, while she waits for her grandfather to come to his senses and let her have her way.

Good thing she wasn't holding her breath.

Gary, meanwhile, is hot on her trail, and a fine figure of a man he is, too. How I love books with a chase scene, and this one is a dandy. It doesn't hurt that Gary isn't merely hot on the trail — he's just plain hot!

He catches up with Amanda, though it takes considerable doing, after convincing her present besotted keepers that she's prone to engage in farafiddles (love that word) and grand bouncers. (That's a lie, for those of you who are as yet uninitiated.) Heyer's writing is full of such lively terms and, for a lover of language such as yours truly, that alone would be reason enough to savor the book, but happily, the story is a kick, as well. No sooner do you get out of a twist than you're careening into a turn.

Alas, Amanda is captured, and her claims

that Gary is a scoundrel, abducting her for nefarious purposes, fall on deaf ears.

On the road again. Gary is still trying to find out who she is — "Smith" being an obviously made-up name — and though he gets some of the truth out of her, he still has no idea where or to whom she belongs, and she isn't about to tell him.

Skulduggery ensues, despite Gary's manly efforts to keep his charge from rushing headlong into certain disaster and social ruin, if there's a difference. (Our Amanda, we have learned, is in love with a certain soldier, a member of the Horse Guards, and is determined to hook up with him, live in Spain and wring the necks of chickens, all over the strenuous objections of her grandfather.) They stop at another inn, where Amanda soon catches the fancy of young Hildebrand Ross (now, there's a name you can chew on, and it's only one of a dozen), who is on his way to join some buddies for a hike in Wales. Amanda persuades the poor fool that her virtue is in the very gravest peril from Sir Gareth and she must, simply *must* escape his dastardly clutches in all haste.

Being a sucker, though an appealing one, Hildebrand buys into the ruse and cooks up one of the most harebrained and entertaining schemes I have ever come across. I just wish I'd thought of it! Since I don't want to spoil the adventure for you, I won't tell you what happens, but you must read it. Here's a hint, though — there's a swooning highwayman involved.

Quite by accident, tragedy occurs — I guarantee it will tug at your heartstrings, but only after making you laugh like a maniac — and Amanda does some fast growing up. The princess of bouncers gets her comeuppance big time, and *begins* to see the error of her impulsive ways. You've got to hand it to this girl: she's persistent, and her imagination just doesn't quit.

Gary has been grievously injured, due to Amanda's foolish but irrepressible mischief, and even though you know all the time that he's going to make it, you can't help being touched by the pathos of the situation. Hildebrand, thinking himself a murderer, is inconsolable. Amanda, heretofore the bane of Sir Gareth's existence, becomes his champion, and proves herself to be a handy in a pinch. Lady Hester is summoned to the inn to nurse our hero back to health, and considering that she'd be in therapy today for borderline agoraphobia, not to mention a terminal case of ditzy-ism, her speedy departure from the hallowed halls of

Brancaster is a stirring example of good, old-fashioned courage.

Well, things are in a tangle, I'll tell you. The sensitive Hildebrand, a budding playwright, is fearful of ending up in Newgate for his inadvertent crime. The innkeeper's wife, a testy sort, thinks they're all a bunch of hoodlums, and you wouldn't let the village nurse take care of your pet rock, let alone a prime example of the masculine persuasion like Sir Gareth. Amanda, though good in a crisis, is out of her depth when it comes to tending a delirious patient and battling a fever, and forces are starting to converge in Town, though she has no way of knowing that. In other words, the jig is up.

Enter Lady Hester, who promptly, if shyly, takes charge. The wallflower turns out to be a creditable nurse, and the old one is sent packing. She was more interested in laying Gary out for burial than saving him, anyway.

Meanwhile, back in London, soldier Neil gets wind of his youthful and winsome lady love's "abduction" and goes straight to Amanda's grandfather with the news. In Western vernacular, he's loaded for bear. Her grandfather is beside himself, having looked everywhere for his lost darling, and has even engaged the Bow Street Runners to search high and low for the troublesome

11

little minx, all to no avail. Amanda and Neil want to be married — the whole reason for her flight in the first place — but her grandfather is having none of that. Neil might be on the up-and-up, but he's not good enough for Amanda, and that's that.

Nonetheless, Neil is not about to be left behind, twiddling his thumbs. He has a distressed damsel to rescue. The two of them get a fix on Amanda's location, breathlessly certain that she is being ravished on a daily basis by the demonic Sir Gareth Ludlow, and rush to her aid.

To make already complicated matters more so, Lady Hester's family has discovered her deception — naturally, she couldn't just say she was going off to an inn to nurse a naked man back from the brink of death, that being a serious breach of etiquette — and her father and the tiresome family chaplain track her down, lest she be besmirched.

Both factions beat feet to the countryside and arrive to find Sir Gareth idling under a tree, mending fast but still with his arm in a sling. Drat. It wouldn't be British to demand a duel of a wounded man, but heated words are spoken. Not by Sir Gareth, however — he's wryly amused (another trait I love in a hero) and you will be, too, as you watch this comedy of errors unfold to its pleasing denouement.

Thanks to Neil, who is serious but also brave, thrifty, loyal and true, Amanda, the little termagant, gets a dressing-down to remember. Heyer's handling of the resolution is satisfying, funny and moving.

Take my advice. Buy this book. A few nibbles and you'll find yourself gobbling whole chapters. Will *Sprig Muslin* change your life? No. Will it change your afternoon or evening? Indubitably. You will relish the clever dialogue, the constant action and the skillfully drawn characters, each one with a clear and distinctive voice.

As for me, well, I'm on to the next Heyer book.

Cheerio, old bean, and don't spare the horses.

Linda Lael Miller

CHAPTER ONE

Mrs. Wetherby was delighted to receive a morning call from her only surviving brother, but for the first half hour of his visit she was granted no opportunity to do more than exchange a few commonplaces with him over the heads of her vociferous offspring.

Sir Gareth Ludlow had arrived in Mount Street just as the schoolroom party, comprising Miss Anna, a lively damsel within a year of her débût, Miss Elizabeth, and Master Philip, were returning from a promenade in the park under the aegis of their governess. No sooner did these delicately nurtured children catch sight of their uncle's tall, elegant figure than they threw to the winds every precept of gentility, so carefully instilled into their heads by Miss Felbridge, and, with piercing shrieks of: "Uncle Gary, Uncle Gary!" raced helter-skelter down the street, to engulf Sir Gareth on their doorstep. By the time Miss Felbridge, clucking but indulgent, had overtaken them, the butler was holding open the door, and Sir Gareth was being borne into the house by his enthusiastic young relatives. He was being pelted with questions and confidences, his eldest niece hanging affectionately on one arm, and his youngest nephew trying to claim his attention by tugging violently at the other, but he disengaged himself for long enough to offer his hand to Miss Felbridge, saying with the smile which never failed to set her heart fluttering in her chaste bosom: "How do you do? Don't scold them! It is quite my fault — though why I should have this shocking effect upon them I can't conceive! Are you quite well again? You were suffering all the discomfort of a bad attack of rheumatism when last we met."

Miss Felbridge blushed, thanked, and disclaimed, thinking that it was just like dear Sir Gareth to remember such an unimportant thing as the governess's rheumatism. Any further interchange was cut short by the arrival on the scene of Mr. Leigh Wetherby, who erupted from the library at the back of the house, exclaiming: "Is that Uncle Gary! Oh, by Jove, sir, I'm devilish glad to see you! There's something I particularly wish to ask you!"

16

The whole party then swept Sir Gareth upstairs to the drawing-room, all talking at the tops of their voices, and thus deaf to a halfhearted attempt on Miss Felbridge's part to restrain her charges from bursting in upon their mama in this very irregular fashion.

It would have been useless to have persisted, of course. The young Wetherbys, from Leigh, undergoing the rigours of coaching to enable him to embark upon a University career later in the year, to Philip, wrestling with pothooks and hangers, were unanimous in giving it as their considered opinion that nowhere was there to be found a more admirable uncle than Sir Gareth. An attempt to whisk the younger members off to the schoolroom could only have resulted in failure, or, at the best, in a fit of prolonged sulks.

In the well-chosen words of Mr. Leigh Wetherby, Sir Gareth was the most bang-up fellow that ever drew breath. A noted Corinthian, he was never too high in the instep to show a nephew aspiring to dandyism how to arrange his neckcloth. Master Jack Wetherby, unconcerned with such fopperies as this, spoke warmly of his openhandedness and entire comprehension of the more urgent needs of young gentlemen enduring the privations of life at Eton College. Miss Anna, by no means out yet, knew no greater source of joy and pride than to be taken up to sit beside him in his curricle for a turn or two round the Park, the envy (she was convinced) of every other, less favoured, damsel. As for Miss Elizabeth, and Master Philip, they regarded him as a fount of such dizzy delights as visits to Astley's Amphitheatre, or a Grand Display of Fireworks, and could perceive no fault in him.

They were not singular: very few people found fault with Gareth Ludlow. Watching him, as he contrived, while displaying over and over again for the edification of little Philip the magical properties of his repeating watch, to lend an ear to the particular problem exercising Leigh's mind, Mrs. Wetherby thought that you would be hard put to it to find a more attractive man, and wished, as she had done a thousand times before, that she could discover some bride for him lovely enough to drive out of his heart the memory of his dead love. Heaven knew that she had spared no pains during the seven years that had elapsed since Clarissa's death to accomplish this end. She had introduced to his notice any number of eligible females, several of them as witty as they were beautiful, but she had never been able to detect in his gray eyes so much as a flicker of the look that had warmed them when they had rested on Clarissa Lincombe.

These reflections were interrupted by the entrance of Mr. Wetherby, a dependable-looking man in the early forties, who grasped his brother-in-law's hand, saying briefly: "Ha, Gary! Glad to see you!" and lost no time in despatching his offspring about their several businesses. This done, he told his wife that she shouldn't encourage the brats to plague their uncle.

Sir Gareth, having regained possession of his watch and his quizzing-glass, slipped the one into his pocket, and hung the other round his neck by its long black riband, and said: "They don't plague me. I think I had better take Leigh along with me to Crawley Heath next month. A good mill will give him something other to think of than the set of his coats. No, I know you don't approve of prize-fighting, Trixie, but you'll have the boy trying to join the dandy-set if you don't take care!"

"Nonsense! You don't wish to burden yourself with a scrubby schoolboy!" said Warren, imperfectly concealing his gratification at the invitation.

"Yes, I do: I like Leigh. You needn't fear I

shall let him get into mischief: I won't."

Mrs. Wetherby broke in on this, giving utterance to the thought in her mind. "Oh, my dear Gary, if you knew how much I long to see you with a son of your own to indulge!"

He smiled at her. "Do you, Trixie? Well, as it chances, it is that subject which has brought me to see you today." He saw the look of startled consternation in her face, and burst out laughing. "No, no, I am not about to disclose to you the existence of a lusty love-child! Merely that I believe — or rather, that I hope — I may shortly be demanding your felicitations."

She was for a moment incredulous, and then cried eagerly: "Oh, Gary, is it Alice Stockwell?"

"Alice Stockwell?" he repeated, surprised. "The pretty child you have been throwing in my way? My dear! No!"

"Told you so," remarked Mr. Wetherby, with quiet satisfaction.

She could not help feeling a little disappointed, for Miss Stockwell had seemed to be of all her protégées the most eligible. She concealed this very creditably, however, and said: "I declare I have not the least guess, then, who it may be. Unless — oh, do, pray, tell me at once, Gary!"

"Why, yes!" he replied, amused at her eagerness. "I have asked Brancaster's leave to address myself to Lady Hester."

The effect of this announcement was somewhat disconcerting. Warren, in the act of taking a pinch of snuff, was surprised into sniffing far too violently, and fell into a fit of sneezing; and his lady, after staring at her brother as though she could not believe her ears, burst into tears, exclaiming: "Oh, Gary, *no!*"

"Beatrix!" he said, between laughter and annoyance.

"Gareth, are you hoaxing me? Tell me it's a take-in! Yes, of course it is! You would never offer for Hester Theale!"

"But, Beatrix — !" he expostulated. "Why should you hold Lady Hester in such aversion?"

"Aversion! Oh, no! But a girl — *girl?* She must be nine-and-twenty if she's a day! — A woman who has been on the shelf these nine years, and more, and never *took,* or had *countenance,* or the least degree of modishness — You must be out of your senses! You must *know* you have only to throw the handkerchief — Oh, dear, how could you do such a thing?"

At this point, her helpmate thought it time to intervene. Gareth was beginning to look

21

vexed. A charming fellow, Gary, with as sweet a temper as any man alive, but it was not to be expected that he would bear with complaisance his sister's strictures on the lady whom he had chosen to be his bride. Why, from amongst all the females only too ready to receive the addresses of a handsome baronet of birth and fortune, he should have selected Hester Theale, who had retired after several unsuccessful seasons to make way for her more marriageable sisters, was certainly a baffling problem, but not one into which Warren thought it seemly to enquire. He therefore cast an admonitory look at his wife, and said: "Lady Hester! I am not particularly acquainted with her, but I believe her to be an unexceptionable young woman. Brancaster accepted your offer, of course."

"Accepted it?" said Beatrix, emerging from her handkerchief. "Jumped at it, you mean! I imagine he must have swooned from the shock!"

"I wish you will be quiet!" said Warren, exasperated by this intransigent behaviour. "Depend upon it, Gary knows what will suit him better than you can! He is not a schoolboy, but a man of five-and-thirty. No doubt Lady Hester will make him an amiable wife."

"No doubt!" retorted Beatrix. "Amiable, and a dead bore! No, Warren, I will not hush! When I think of all the pretty and lovely girls who have done their best to attach him, and he tells me that he has offered for an insipid female who has neither fortune nor an extraordinary degree of beauty, besides being stupidly shy and dowdy, I — oh, I could go into strong hysterics!"

"Well, if you do, Trixie, I give you fair warning that I shall empty over you the largest jug of water I can find!" responded her brother with unimpaired cordiality. "Now, don't be such a goose, my dear! You are putting poor Warren to the blush."

She sprang up, and grasped the lapels of his exquisitely cut coat of blue superfine, giving him a shake, and looking up into his smiling eyes with the tears still drowning her own. "Gary, you do not love her, nor she you! I have never seen the least sign that she regards you even with partiality. Only tell me what she has to offer you!"

His hands came up to cover hers, removing them from his lapels, and holding them in a strong clasp. "I love you dearly, Trixie, but I can't permit you to crumple this coat, you know. Weston made it for me: one of his triumphs, don't you think?" He hesitated, seeing that she was not to be diverted; and then said, slightly pressing her hands: "Don't you understand? I had thought that you would. You have told me so many times that it is my duty to marry — and, indeed, I know it is, if the name is not to die with me, which I think would be a pity. If Arthur were alive — but since Salamanca I've known that I can't continue all my days in single bliss. So — !"

"Yes, yes, but why *this* female, Gary?" she demanded. "She has nothing!"

"On the contrary, she has breeding, and good manners, and, as Warren has said, an amiable disposition. I hope I have as much to offer her, and I wish that I had more. But I have not."

The tears sprang to her eyes again, and spilled over. "Oh, my dearest brother, *still?* It is more than seven years since —"

"Yes, more than seven years," he interrupted. "Don't cry, Trixie! I assure you I don't grieve any longer, or even think of Clarissa, except now and then, when something occurs which perhaps brings her to my memory. But I have never fallen in love again. Not with any of the delightful girls you have been so obliging as to cast in my way! I believe I could never feel for another what I once felt for Clarissa, so it seems to

24

me that to be making a bid for the sort of girl you would wish me to marry would be a shabby thing to do. I have a fortune large enough to make me an eligible suitor, and I daresay the Stockwells would give their consent, were I to offer for Miss Alice —"

"Indeed they would! And Alice is disposed to have a *tender* for you, which you must have perceived. So, why — ?"

"Well, for that very reason, perhaps. Such a beautiful and spirited girl is worthy of so much more than I could give her. Lady Hester, on the other hand —" He broke off, the ready laughter springing to his eyes. "What a wretch you are, Trix! You are forcing me to say such things as must make me sound like the veriest coxcomb!"

"What you mean," said Beatrix ruthlessly, "is that Lady Hester is too insipid to like anyone!"

"I don't mean anything of the sort. She is shy, but I don't think her insipid. Indeed, I have sometimes suspected that if she were not for ever being snubbed by her father, and her quite odious sisters, she would show that she has a lively sense of the ridiculous. Let us say, merely, that she has not a romantic disposition! And as I must surely be considered to be beyond the age of romance, I believe that with mutual liking to help us we may be tolerably comfortable together. Her situation now is unhappy, which encourages me to hope that she may look favourably upon my proposal."

Mrs. Wetherby uttered a scornful exclamation, and even her stolid spouse blinked. That he rated his very obvious attractions low was one of the things one liked in Gary, but this was coming it a trifle too strong. "No doubt of that," Warren said dryly. "May as well wish you happy at once, Gary — which I'm sure I hope you will be. Not but what — However, it is no business of mine! You know best what will suit you."

It was not to be expected that Mrs. Wetherby could bring herself to agree with this pronouncement; but she appeared to realize the futility of further argument, and beyond prophesying disaster she said no more until she was alone with her husband. She had then a great deal to say, which he bore with great patience, entering no caveat until she said bitterly: "How any man who had been betrothed to Clarissa Lincombe could offer for Hester Theale is something I shall never understand — nor anyone else, I daresay!"

At this point, Warren's brow wrinkled, and he said in a dubious tone: "Well, I don't know."

"I should think not, indeed! Only consider

how lovely Clarissa was, and how gay, and how spirited, and then picture to yourself Lady Hester!"

"Yes, but that ain't what I meant," replied Warren. "I'm not saying Clarissa wasn't a regular out-and-outer, because the lord knows she was, but, if you ask me, she had too much spirit!"

Beatrix stared at him. "I never heard you say so before!"

"Haven't said it before. Not the sort of thing I should say when Gary was betrothed to her, and no use saying it when the poor girl was dead. But what I thought was that she was devilish headstrong, and would have led Gary a pretty dance."

Beatrix opened her mouth to refute this heresy, and shut it again.

"The fact is, my dear," pursued her lord, "you were in such high gig because it was your brother who won her that you never could see a fault in her. Mind, I'm not saying that it wasn't a triumph, because it was. When I think of all the fellows she had dangling after her — lord, she could have been a duchess if she'd wanted! Yeovil begged her three times to marry him: told me so himself, at her funeral. Come to think of it, it was the only piece of good sense she ever showed, preferring Gary to Yeovil," he added thoughtfully.

"I know she was often a little wild, but so very sweet, and with such engaging ways! I am persuaded she would have learnt to mind Gary, for she did most sincerely love him!"

"She didn't love him enough to mind him when he forbade her to drive those grays of his," said Warren grimly. "Flouted him the instant his back was turned, and broke her neck into the bargain. Well, I was devilish sorry for Gary, but I don't mind owning to you, Trix, that I thought he was better out of the affair than he knew."

Upon reflection, Mrs. Wetherby was obliged to acknowledge that there might be a certain amount of justice in this severe stricture. But it in no way reconciled her to her brother's approaching nuptials to a lady as sober as the dead Clarissa had been volatile.

Seldom had a betrothal met with more general approval than that of Gareth Ludlow to Clarissa Lincombe, even the disappointed mothers of other eligible damsels thinking it a perfect match. If the lady was the most courted in town, the gentleman was Society's best liked bachelor. Indeed, he had seemed to be the child of good fortune, for he was not only endowed with a handsome competence and an impeccable lineage, but possessed as well as these essentials no common degree of good looks, a graceful, well-built frame, considerable proficiency in the realm of sport, and an open, generous temper which made it impossible for even his closest rivals to grudge him his success in winning Clarissa. Sadly Mrs. Wetherby looked back to that halcyon period, before the fatal carriage accident had laid Clarissa's charm and beauty in cold earth, and Gareth's heart with them.

He was thought to have made an excellent recovery from the blow; and everyone was glad that the tragedy had not led him to indulge in any extravagance of grief, such as selling all his splendid horses, or wearing mourning weeds for the rest of his life. If, behind the smile in his eyes, there was a little sadness, he could still laugh; and if he found the world empty, that was a secret he kept always to himself. Even Beatrix, who adored him, had been encouraged to hope that he had ceased to mourn Clarissa; and she had spared no pains to bring to his notice any damsel who seemed likely to captivate him. Not the mildest flirtation had rewarded her efforts, but this had not unduly depressed her. However modest he might be, he could not but know that he was regarded as a matrimonial prize of the first rank; and she knew him too well to suppose that he would raise in any maidenly breast expectations which he had no intention of fulfilling. Until this melancholy day, she had merely thought that she had not hit upon the right female, never that the right female did not exist. Her tears, on hearing his announcement, had sprung less from disappointment than from the sudden realization that more than Clarissa's loveliness had perished in that fatal accident of seven years ago. He had spoken to her as a man might who had put his youth behind him, with all its hopes and ardours, and was looking towards a placid future, comfortable, perhaps, but unenlivened by any touch of romance. Mrs. Wetherby, perceiving this, and recalling a younger Gareth, who had seen life as a gay adventure, cried herself to sleep.

So, too, when the news of Sir Gareth's very flattering offer was later made known to her, did the Lady Hester Theale.

CHAPTER TWO

The Earl of Brancaster's family seat was situated not many miles from Chatteris, in the heart of the fens. The mansion was as undistinguished as the surrounding countryside, and, since his lordship's circumstances, owing to his strong predilection for gaming, were straitened, it bore a good many signs of neglect. In theory, it was presided over by his lordship's eldest daughter, but as his son and heir, Lord Widmore, found it expedient to reside, with his wife and growing family, under his father's roof, the Lady Hester's position was, in fact, little better than that of a cipher. Upon the death of her mama, several years previously, persons who were not particularly acquainted with the Earl had thought that it was fortunate, after all, that she had been left on the shelf. She would be able, said the optimistic, to comfort her stricken parent, and to take her mama's place as the mistress of Brancaster

Park, and of the house in Green Street. But as the Earl had disliked his wife he was by no means stricken by her death; and as he was looking forward to an untrammelled single existence he regarded his eldest daughter not as a comfort but as an encumbrance. Indeed, he had been heard to say, when in his cups, that he was no better off than before.

His feelings, when, recovering from a momentary stupefaction, he realized that Sir Gareth Ludlow was actually soliciting permission to marry his daughter, almost overcame him. He had given up all hope of seeing her respectably married: that she should achieve a brilliant match had never for an instant occurred to him. An unwelcome suspicion that Sir Gareth must be a trifle bosky crossed his mind, but there was nothing in Sir Gareth's manner or appearance to lend the slightest colour to it, and he banished it. He said bluntly: "Well, I should be very pleased to give her to you, but I'd better tell you at the outset that her portion isn't large. In fact, I shall be devilish hard put to it to raise the wind at all."

"It is really quite immaterial," responded Sir Gareth. "If Lady Hester will do me the honour to accept me, I shall of course make whatever settlement upon her that our attorneys think proper."

Greatly moved by these beautiful words, the Earl gave Sir Gareth's suit his blessing, invited him to Brancaster Park the following week, and himself cancelled three sporting engagements, leaving London on the very next day to prepare his daughter for the singular stroke of good fortune which was about to befall her.

Lady Hester was surprised by his sudden arrival, for she had supposed him to be on the point of going to Brighton. He belonged to the Prince Regent's set, and in general was to be found, during the summer months, residing in lodgings on the Steyne, or at the Pavilion itself, where it was his affable practice to share in all his royal friend's more expensive pastimes, and to play whist, for extremely high stakes, with his royal friend's brother of York. Such female companionship as he sought in Brighton had never included that of his wife, or of his daughter; so, at the end of the London Season, Lady Hester had removed, with her brother and her sister-in-law, to Cambridgeshire, whence, in due course, she would proceed on a round of yearly and very dull visits to various members of her family.

Her amiable parent, having informed her

that it was a father's concern for her welfare which had brought him, at great inconvenience, to his ancestral home, said, by way of preamble to the disclosure he was about to make, that he hoped she would furbish herself up a trifle, since it would not do for her to receive guests in an old gown, and a Paisley shawl.

"Oh, dear!" said Hester. "Are we to have visitors?" She focused her slightly myopic gaze upon the Earl, and said, with more resignation than anxiety in her voice: "I do hope no one whom I *particularly* dislike, Papa?"

"Nothing of the sort!" he replied testily. "Upon my soul, Hester, you are enough to try the patience of a saint! Let me tell you, my girl, that it is Sir Gareth Ludlow whom we are to entertain here next week, and if you dislike him you must be out of your senses!"

She had been somewhat aimlessly disposing the despised shawl about her shoulders, as though, by rearranging its shabby folds, she could render it less objectionable to her father, but at these words she let her hands fall, and said incredulously: "*Sir Gareth Ludlow,* sir?"

"Ay, you may well stare!" said the Earl. "I daresay you will stare more when I tell you why he comes!"

"I should think it very likely that I should," she agreed, in a reflective tone. "For I cannot imagine what should bring him here, or, indeed, how he is to be entertained at this season."

"Never mind that! He is coming, Hester, to make you an offer!"

"Oh, is he?" she said vaguely, adding, after a thoughtful moment: "Does he want me to sell him one of Juno's pups? I wonder he should not have told me so when we met in town the other day. It is not worth his while to journey all this distance — unless, of course, he desires first to see the pup."

"For God's sake, girl — !" exploded the Earl. "What the devil should Ludlow want with one of your wretched dogs?"

"Indeed, it has me quite in a puzzle," she said, looking at him enquiringly.

"Paperskull!" said his lordship scathingly. "Damme if I know what he wants with you! He's coming to offer for your *hand!*"

She sat staring at him, rather pale at first, and then flushing, and turning away her face. "Papa, pray — ! If you are funning, it is not a kind jest!"

"Of course I'm not funning!" he answered. "Though it don't surprise me you should think so. I don't mind owning to you,

Hester, that when he broke it to me that it was my permission to address you that he was after I thought either he was foxed, or I was!"

"Perhaps you were — both of you!" she said, trying for a lighter note.

"No, no! No such thing! But for him to be taking a fancy for you, when I daresay there are a dozen females trying to fix his interest, and every one of 'em as well-born as you, besides being younger, and devilish handsome into the bargain — well, I never was nearer to being grassed in all my life!"

"It isn't true. Sir Gareth never had a fancy for me. Not even when I was young, and, I think, quite pretty," said Hester, with the ghost of a smile.

"Oh, lord, no! Not *then!*" said his lordship. "You were well-enough, but you couldn't have expected him to look at you when the Lincombe chit was alive."

"No. He didn't look at me," she agreed.

"Well, well!" the Earl said tolerantly. "She had 'em all beaten to flinders. By all accounts, he never cast so much as a glance at any other girl. And I've made up my mind to it that that's why he's offered for you." He saw that she was looking bewildered, and said with some impatience: "Now, don't be a pea-goose, girl! It's as plain as a

36

pikestaff that what Ludlow wants is a quiet, well-bred female who won't have her head stuffed with romantic nonsense, or expect him to be thrown into a transport of passion. The more I think of it, the more it seems to me that he's acting like a man of sense. If he's still hankering after Clarissa Lincombe, it wouldn't suit him at all to offer for some out-and-outer who would expect him to be dangling after her for ever, carried away by the violence of his feelings, or some such flummery. At the same time, it's his duty to marry, and you may depend upon it he made up his mind to that when that brother of his got himself killed in Spain. Well, I don't scruple to tell you that I never thought to see such a piece of good fortune befall you, Hester! To think that you should make a better match than any of your sisters, and at your age, too! It is beyond anything great!"

"Beyond anything — oh, beyond *anything!*" she said, in a queer voice. "And he is coming here, with your consent! Could you not have asked me first what my sentiments were? I do not wish for this splendid match, Papa."

He looked as though he could hardly credit his ears. "Don't wish for it?" he repeated, in a stupefied tone. "You must be out of your senses!"

"Perhaps I am." The ghostly smile that was at once nervous and mischievous again flitted across her face. "You should have warned Sir Gareth of it, sir. I am persuaded he cannot wish to marry an idiot."

"If," said his lordship awfully, "you fancy that that is a funny thing to say, let me tell you that it is not!"

"No, Papa."

He eyed her in uncertainty, feeling that in some strange way she was eluding him. She had always been an obedient, even a meek, daughter, but he had several times suffered from the uncomfortable suspicion that behind the cloud of gentle compliance there existed a woman who was quite unknown to him. He saw that it behoved him to tread warily, so he curbed his exasperation, and said, with a very fair assumption of paternal solicitude: "Now, what maggot has got into your head, my dear? You won't tell me you don't wish to be married, for every female must wish that!"

"Yes, indeed!" she sighed.

"Can it be that you dislike Ludlow?"

"No, Papa."

"Well, I was sure of *that!* I daresay there isn't a better liked man in England, and as for you ladies — ! The caps that have been set at him! You will be the envy of every unmarried woman in town!"

"Do you think so indeed, Papa? How delightful that would be! But perhaps I might feel strange, and unlike myself. It wouldn't be comfortable, not to be acquainted with myself."

This baffling and (he considered) very nonsensical observation threw him out of his stride, but he persevered, saying with as much patience as he could command: "Well, never mind that! To be sure, I never thought he was trying to fix your interest, but I am sure I have seen him stand up with you at balls a hundred times! Ay, and sit talking to you, when one might have supposed that he would have been making up to one of the beauties that have been hanging out lures to him for ever!"

"He is very civil," she agreed. "He was used to talk to me of Clarissa, because I knew her too, and no one else would ever mention her name within his hearing."

"What, is he still doing so?" exclaimed the Earl, feeling that here must be the clue to the mystery.

"Oh, no!" she replied. "Not for a long time now."

"Then why the devil, if he don't want to talk of the Lincombe Beauty, should he seek you out?" he demanded. "Depend upon it, it has been to attach you!"

"He does not precisely seek me out," she responded. "Only, if we meet at parties, he is too kind, and, I think, too great a gentleman, to pass me by with no more than a common bow." She paused, and sighed, blinking at her father. "How silly! I expect you are quite right, and he has had this notion of offering for me ever since Major Ludlow was killed."

"Of course I am right, and a fine compliment he is paying you!"

"Oh, no!" she said, and relapsed into silence, gazing thoughtfully before her.

He began to feel uneasy. It was impossible to read her countenance. It was mournful, yet tranquil; but in the tone of her voice there was an alarming note which recalled to his mind her contumacious behaviour when he had disclosed to her the only other offer he had ever received for her hand. He remembered how meekly she had borne every manifestation of his wrath, how dutifully she had begged his pardon for disobliging him. That had been five years ago, but here she was, still a spinster. After eyeing her for a moment or two, he said: "If you let this chance of achieving a respectable alliance slip, you are a bigger fool than I take you for, Hester!"

Her eyes came round to his face, a smile quivered for an instant on her lips. "No, how could that be, Papa?"

He decided to ignore this. "You and he are both past the age of romantical high-flights," he urged. "He is a very agreeable fellow, and I don't doubt he'll make you a kind husband. Generous too! You will have enough pin-money to make your sisters stare, a position of consequence, and you will be mistress of a very pretty establishment. It is not as though your affections were engaged otherwhere: of course, if that were so, it would be another matter; but, as I told Ludlow, though I could not answer for your sentiments upon this occasion, I could assure him that you had formed no other attachment."

"But that was not true, Papa," she said. "My affections were engaged many years ago."

She said this so matter-of-factly that he thought he must have misunderstood her, and demanded a repetition of the remark. She very obligingly complied, and he exclaimed, quite thunderstruck: "So I am to believe that you have been wearing the willow, am I? Fudge! It is the first I have ever heard of such a thing! Pray, who may this man be?"

She got up, drawing her shawl about her shoulders. "It is of no consequence, Papa. He never thought of me, you see."

With that, she drifted away in the indeterminate way which was peculiarly her own, leaving him baffled and furious.

He did not see her again until the family assembled for dinner; and by that time he had discussed the matter at such length with his son, his daughter-in-law, and his chaplain, and with such sublime disregard for the ears of his butler, two footmen, and his valet, all of whom at some time or another came within hearing, that there was hardly a soul in the house unaware that the Lady Hester had received, and meant to decline, a very flattering offer.

Lord Widmore, whose temper was rendered peevish by chronic dyspepsia, was quite as much vexed as his father; but his wife, a robust woman of alarmingly brusque manners, said, with the vulgarity for which she was famed: "Oh, flimflam! Mere flourishing! I'd lay a monkey you crammed her, sir, for that's always your way. Leave it to me!"

"She's as obstinate as a mule!" said Lord Widmore fretfully.

This made his lady laugh heartily, and beg

him not to talk like a nodcock, for a more biddable female than his sister, she said, never existed.

It was perfectly true. Except in her inability to attract eligible suitors to herself, Hester was the sort of daughter with whom the most exacting parent might have been pleased. She always did as she was told, and never argued about it. She indulged neither in sulks nor in hysterics; and if she was unable to attract the right men, at least she had never been known to encourage the wrong ones. She was a good sister, too; and could always be relied upon to take charge of her young nephews and nieces in times of crisis or to entertain, uncomplainingly, the dullest man invited (willy-nilly) to a dinner-party.

The first person to discuss Sir Gareth's proposal with her was not Lady Widmore, but the Reverend Augustus Whyteleafe, the Earl's chaplain, who seized the earliest opportunity that offered of conveying to her his own reflections upon the occasion.

"You will not object, I know, to my adverting to the topic, painful though it must be to you," he stated. "His lordship, I should perhaps mention, did me the honour to admit me into his confidence, feeling, I collect, that a word from a man in my position might bear weight with you."

"Oh, dear! I am sure it ought to," said Hester, in a conscience-stricken tone.

"But," said Mr. Whyteleafe, squaring his shoulders, "I found myself obliged to inform his lordship that I could not take upon myself the office of Sir Gareth Ludlow's advocate."

"How very brave of you!" Hester said, sighing. "I am so glad, for I don't at all wish to discuss it."

"It must indeed be repugnant to you. You will allow me, however, to tell you that I honour you for your decision, Lady Hester."

She looked at him in mild surprise. "Good gracious, do you? I can't think why you should."

"You have had the courage to spurn a match of mere worldly brilliance. A match which, I daresay, would have been welcome to any lady less high-minded than yourself. Let me venture to say that you have done just as you should: nothing but misery, I am persuaded, could result from an alliance between yourself and a fashionable fribble."

"Poor Sir Gareth! I fear you are right, Mr. Whyteleafe: I should make him such an odiously dull wife, should I not?"

"A man of his frivolous tastes might think so," he agreed. "To a man of more serious disposition, however — But on this head I must not, at present, say more."

He then made her a bow, looking at her in a very speaking way, and withdrew, leaving her hovering between amusement and consternation.

Her sister-in-law, who had not failed to mark the exchange, from the other end of the Long Gallery, where the party had assembled after dinner, did not hesitate, later, to ask her what had been said. "For if he had the effrontery to speak to you about this offer your papa has received, I hope you gave him a sharp set-down, Hetty! Such presumption! But there! I don't doubt your papa egged him on. I promise you I made no bones about telling him that capping hounds to a scent won't do in this case."

"Thank you: that was kind. But Mr. Whyteleafe didn't try to persuade me. Indeed, he said that he had told my father he would not, which I thought very courageous in him."

"Ay, that was what made Lord Brancaster as sulky as a bear. I'll tell you what, Hetty: you'll do well to accept Ludlow's offer before Widmore puts it into your father's head that you mean to have a beggarly parson for your husband."

"But I don't," said Hester.

"Lord, I know *that!* But I have eyes in my head, and I can see that Whyteleafe is growing extremely particular in his attentions. The devil of it is that Widmore has seen it too, and you know what a slowtop he is, my dear! Your father's another. I don't doubt he said something to put you in a tweak."

"Oh, no!" Hester said calmly.

"At all events, he told you Ludlow was still moping for that girl he was betrothed to the deuce knows how many years ago!" said Lady Widmore bluntly. "If you take my advice, you won't heed him! I never saw a man less in the dumps than Ludlow."

"No, indeed. Or a man less in love," remarked Hester.

"What of it? I can tell you this, Hetty: it ain't so often that persons of our station marry for love. Look at me! You can't suppose I was ever in love with poor Widmore! But I never took, any more than you did, and when the match was proposed to me I agreed to it, because there's nothing worse for a female than to be left on the shelf."

"One grows accustomed to it," Hester said. "Can you believe, Almeria, that Sir Gareth and I should — should suit?"

"Lord, yes! Why not? If the chance had been offered to me, I should have jumped out of my skin to snatch it!" responded

Lady Widmore frankly. "I know you don't love him, but what's that to the purpose? You think it over carefully, Hetty! You ain't likely to receive another offer, or, in any event, not such an advantageous one, though I daresay Whyteleafe will pop the question, as soon as he gets preferment. Take Ludlow, and you'll have a handsome fortune, a position of the first consequence, and an agreeable husband into the bargain. Send him to the rightabout, and you'll end your days an old maid, let alone be obliged to listen to your father's and Widmore's reproaches for ever, if I know anything of the matter!"

Hester smiled faintly. "One grows accustomed to that too. I have sometimes thought that when Papa dies I might live in quite a little house, by myself."

"Well, you won't," said Lady Widmore trenchantly. "Your sister Susan will pounce on you: I can vouch for *that!* It would suit her very well to have you with her to wait on her hand and foot, and very likely act as governess to all those plain brats of hers as well! And Widmore would think it a first-rate scheme, so you'd get no support from him, or from Gertrude or Constance either. And it's not a particle of good thinking you'd stand out against 'em, my dear, for you haven't a ha'porth of spirit! If you want a home of your own, you'll take Ludlow, and bless yourself for your good fortune, for you won't get one by any other means!"

With these encouraging words, Lady Widmore took herself off to her own bedchamber, pausing on the way to inform her lord that provided he and his father could keep still tongues in their heads she rather fancied she had done the trick.

The Lady Hester, once her maid was dismissed, the candles blown out, and the curtains drawn round her bed, buried her face in the pillow and cried herself quietly to sleep.

CHAPTER THREE

Three days later, Sir Gareth, in happy ignorance of the wretched indecision into which his proposal had thrown his chosen bride, left London, and pursued a rather leisurely progress towards Cambridgeshire. He drove his own curricle, with a pair of remarkably fine match-bays harnessed to it, and broke the journey at the house of some friends, not many miles from Baldock, where he remained for two nights, resting his horses. He took with him his head groom, but not his valet: a circumstance which disgusted that extremely skilled gentleman more than it surprised him. Sir Gareth, who belonged to the Corinthian set, was always very well dressed, but he was quite capable of achieving the effect he desired without the ministrations of the genius who had charge of his wardrobe; and the thought that alien hands were pressing his coats, or applying inferior blacking to his Hessian boots, caused him to feel no anguish at all.

He was not expected at Brancaster Park until the late afternoon, but since the month was July, and the weather sultry, he set forward for the remainder of the journey in good time, driving his pair at an easy pace, and pausing to bait, when some twenty miles had been accomplished, in the village of Caxton. The place boasted only one posting-house, and that a modest one; and when Sir Gareth strolled into the coffee-room he found the landlord engaged in what appeared to be a somewhat heated argument with a young lady in a gown of sprig muslin, and a hat of chip-straw, which was tied becomingly over a mass of silken black locks.

The landlord, as soon as he perceived an obvious member of the Quality upon the threshold, abandoned the lady without ceremony, and stepped forward, bowing, and desiring to know in what way he might have the honour of serving the newcomer.

"It will be time enough to serve me when you have attended to this lady," replied Sir Gareth, who had not failed to remark the indignant expression in the lady's big eyes.

"Oh, no, sir! No, indeed! I am quite at liberty — very happy to wait upon your honour immediately!" the landlord assured him. "I was just telling the young person that I daresay she will find accommodation at the Rose and Crown."

These words were added in a lowered voice, but they reached the lady's ears, and caused her to say in a tone of strong disapprobation: "I am not a young person, and if I wish to stay in your horrid inn, I shall stay here, and it is not of the least use to tell me that you have no room, because I don't believe you!"

"I've told you before, miss, that this is a posting-house, and we don't serve young per — females — who come walking in with no more than a couple of bandboxes!" said the landlord angrily. "I don't know what your lay is, nor I don't want to, but I haven't got any room for you, and that's my last word!"

Sir Gareth, who had retired tactfully to the window-embrasure, had been watching the stormy little face under the chip-hat. It was an enchantingly pretty face, with large, dark eyes, a lovely, wilful mouth, and a most determined chin. It was also a very youthful face, just now flushed with mortification. The landlord plainly considered its owner to be a female of no account, but neither the child's voice nor her manner, which was

51

decidedly imperious, belonged to one of vulgar birth. A suspicion that she was a runaway from some seminary for young ladies crossed Sir Gareth's mind: he judged her to be about the same age as his niece; and in some intangible way she reminded him of Clarissa. Not that she was really like Clarissa, for Clarissa had been divinely fair. Perhaps, he thought, with a tiny pang, the resemblance lay in her wilful look, and the tilt of her obstinate chin. At all events, she was far too young and too pretty to be going about the country unattended; and no more unsuitable resting-place than the common inn to which the landlord had directed her could have been found for her. If she were an errant schoolgirl, it clearly behoved a man of honour to restore her to her family.

Sir Gareth came away from the window, saying, with his attractive smile: "Forgive me, but can I perhaps be of some assistance?"

She eyed him uncertainly, not shyly, but with speculation in her candid gaze. Before she could answer, the landlord said that there was no need for the gentleman to trouble himself. He would have expanded the remark, but was checked. Sir Gareth said, quite pleasantly, but on a note of authority: "It appears to me that there is considerable need. It is quite out of the question that this lady should spend the night at the Rose and Crown." He smiled down at the lady again. "Suppose you were to tell me where you want to go to? I don't think, you know, that your mama would wish you to stay at any inn without your maid."

"Well, I haven't got a mama," replied the lady, with the air of one triumphing in argument.

"I beg your pardon. Your father, then?"

"And I haven't got a father *either!*"

"Yes, I can see that you think you have now driven me against the ropes," he said, amused. "And, of course, if both your parents are dead we shall never know what they would have felt about it. How would it be if we discussed the matter over a little refreshment? What would you like?"

Her eyes brightened; she said cordially: "I should be *very* much obliged to you, sir, if you would procure a glass of lemonade for me, for I am excessively thirsty, and this odious man wouldn't bring it to me!"

The landlord said explosively: "Your honour! Miss walks in here, as you see her, wanting me to tell her when the next coach is due for Huntingdon, and when I say there won't be one, not till tomorrow, first she asks me if I'm needing a chambermaid, and when I tell her I'm not needing any such thing, she up and says she'll hire a room for the night! Now, I put it to your honour —"

"Never mind!" interrupted Sir Gareth, only the faintest tremor in his voice betraying the laughter that threatened to overcome him. "Just be good enough to fetch the lady a glass of lemonade, and, for me, a tankard of your home-brewed, and we will see what can be done to straighten out this tangle!"

The landlord started to say something about the respectability of his house, thought better of it, and withdrew. Sir Gareth pulled a chair out from the table, and sat down, saying persuasively: "Now that we are rid of him, do you feel that you could tell me who you are, and how you come to be wandering about the country in this rather odd way? My name, I should tell you, is Ludlow — Sir Gareth Ludlow, entirely at your service!"

"How do you do?" responded the lady politely.

"Well?" said Sir Gareth the twinkle in his eye quizzing her. "Am I, like the landlord, to call you miss? I really can't address you as ma'am: you put me much too strongly in mind of my eldest niece, when she's in

54

mischief."

She had been eyeing him rather warily, but this remark seemed to reassure her, which was what it was meant to do. She said: "My name is Amanda, sir. Amanda S-Smith!"

"Amanda Smith, I regret to be obliged to inform you that you are a shockingly untruthful girl," said Sir Gareth calmly.

"It is a very good name!" she said, on the defensive.

"Amanda is a charming name, and Smith is very well in its way, but it is not your surname. Come, now!"

She shook her head, the picture of pretty mulishness. "I shan't tell you. If I did, you might know who I am, and I have a particular reason for not wishing anyone to know that."

"Are you escaping from school?" he enquired.

She stiffened indignantly. "Certainly not! I'm not a schoolgirl! In fact, I am very nearly seventeen, and I shall shortly be a married lady!"

He sustained this with no more than a blink, and begged pardon with suitable gravity. Fortunately, the landlord returned at that moment, with lemonade, beer, and the grudging offer of freshly baked tarts, if

Miss should happen to fancy them. Judging by the hopeful gleam in Amanda's eyes that she would fancy them very much, Sir Gareth bade him bring in a dish of them, adding: "And some fruit as well, if you please."

Quite mollified by this openhanded behaviour, Amanda said warmly: "Thank you! To own the truth, I am excessively hungry. Are you really an uncle?"

"Indeed I am!"

"Well, I shouldn't have thought it. Mine are the stuffiest people!"

By the time she had disposed of six tartlets, and the better part of a bowl of cherries, cordial relations with her host had been well-established; and she accepted gratefully an offer to drive her to Huntingdon. She asked to be set down at the George; and when she saw a slight crease appear between Sir Gareth's brows very obligingly added: "Or the Fountain, if you prefer it, sir."

The crease remained. "Is someone meeting you at one of these houses, Amanda?"

"Oh, yes!" she replied airily.

He opened his snuff-box, and took a leisurely pinch. "Excellent! I will take you there with pleasure."

"*Thank* you!" she said, bestowing a brilliant smile upon him.

"And hand you into the care of whoever it is who is no doubt awaiting you," continued Sir Gareth amiably.

She looked to be a good deal daunted, and said, after a pregnant moment: "Well, I don't think you should do that, because I daresay they will be late."

"Then I will remain with you until they arrive."

"They might be *very* late!"

"Or they might not come at all," he suggested. "Now, stop trying to hoax me with all these faradiddles, my child! I am much too old a hand to be taken in. No one is going to meet you in Huntingdon, and you may make up your mind to this: I am not going to leave you at the George, or the Fountain, or at any other inn."

"Then I shan't go with you," said Amanda. "So then what will you do?"

"I'm not quite sure," he replied. "I must either give you into the charge of the Parish officer here, or the Vicar."

She cried hotly: "I won't be given into anyone's charge! I think you are the most interfering, odious person I ever met, and I wish you will go away and leave me to take care of myself, which I am very well able to do!"

"I expect you do," he agreed. "And, I very

much fear, I am just as stuffy as your uncles, which is a very lowering reflection."

"If you knew the circumstances, I am persuaded you wouldn't spoil everything!" she urged.

"But I don't know the circumstances," he pointed out.

"Well — well — if I were to tell you that I am escaping from persecution — ?"

"I shouldn't believe you. If you are not running away from school, you must be running away from your home, and I conjecture that you are doing that because you've fallen in love with someone of whom your relations don't approve. In fact, you are trying to elope, and if anyone is to meet you in Huntingdon it is the gentleman to whom — as you informed me — you are shortly to be married."

"Well, you are quite out!" she declared. "I am *not* eloping, though it would be a much better thing to do, besides being most romantic. Naturally, that was the first scheme I made."

"What caused you to abandon it?" he enquired.

"He wouldn't go with me," said Amanda naively. "He says it is not the thing, and he won't marry me without Grandpapa's consent, on account of being a man of honour.

He is a soldier, and in a *very* fine regiment, although not a cavalry regiment. Grandpapa and my papa were both Hussars. Neil is home on sick leave from the Peninsula."

"I see. Fever, or wounds?"

"He had a ball in his shoulder, and for *months* they couldn't dig it out! That was why he was sent home."

"And have you become acquainted with him quite lately?"

"Good gracious, no! I've known him for ever! He lives at — he lives near my home. At least, his family does. *Most* unfortunately, he is a younger son, which is a thing Grandpapa quite abominates, because Papa was one too, and so we both have very modest fortunes. Only, Neil has every intention of becoming a General, so that's nothing to the purpose. Besides, I don't want a large fortune. I don't think it would be of the least use to me, except, perhaps, to buy Neil's promotion, and even that wouldn't answer, because he prefers to rise by his own exertions."

"Very proper," Sir Gareth said gravely.

"Well, I think so, and when we are at war, you know, there is always a great deal of opportunity. Neil has his company already, and I must tell you that when he was obliged to come home he was a Brigade-

Major!"

"That is certainly excellent. How old is he?"

"Twenty-four, but is he quite a hardened campaigner, I assure you, so that it is nonsense to suppose he can't take care of me. Why, he can take care of a whole brigade."

He laughed. "*That,* I fancy, would be child's play, in comparison!"

She looked mischievous suddenly, but said: "No, for I am a soldier's daughter, and I shouldn't be in the least troublesome, if only I could marry Neil, and follow the drum with him, and not have to be presented, and go to horrid balls at Almack's, and be married to an odious man with a large fortune and a title."

"It would be very disagreeable to be married to an odious man," he agreed, "but that fate doesn't overtake everyone who goes to Almack's you know! Don't you think you might like to see a little more of the world before you get married to anyone?"

She shook her head so vigorously that her dusky ringlets danced under the brim of her hat. "*No!* That is what Grandpapa said, and he made my aunt take me to Bath, and I met a great many people, and went to the Assemblies, in spite of not having been presented yet, and it didn't put Neil out of my head at all. And if you think, sir, that perhaps I was not a success, I must tell you that you are quite mistaken!"

"I feel sure you were a success," he replied, smiling.

"I was," she said candidly. "I had *hundreds* of compliments paid me, and I stood up for every dance. So now I know all about being fashionable, and I would liefer by far live in a tent with Neil."

He found her at once childish and strangely mature, and was touched. He said gently: "Perhaps you would, and perhaps you will, one day, live in a tent with Neil. But you are very young to be married, Amanda, and it would be better to wait for a year or two."

"I have already waited for two years, for I have been betrothed to Neil since I was fifteen, secretly! And I am not too young to be married, because Neil knows an officer in the 95th who is married to a Spanish lady who is *much* younger than I am!"

There did not seem to be anything to say in reply to this. Sir Gareth, who was beginning to perceive that the task of protecting Amanda was one fraught with difficulty, shifted his ground. "Very well, but if you are not at this moment eloping, which, I

61

own, seems, in the absence of your Brigade-Major, to be unlikely — I wish you will tell me what you hope to gain by running away from your home, and wandering about the countryside in this very unconventional manner?"

"That," said Amanda, with pride, "is Strategy, sir."

"I am afraid," said Sir Gareth apologetically, "that the explanation leaves me no wiser than I was before."

"Well, it *may* be Tactics," she said cautiously. "Though that is when you move troops in the presence of the enemy, and, of course, the enemy isn't present. I find it very confusing to distinguish between the two things, and it is a pity Neil isn't here, for you may depend upon it he knows exactly, and he could explain it to you."

"Yes, I begin to think it is a thousand pities he isn't here, even though he were not so obliging as to explain it to me," agreed Sir Gareth.

Amanda, who had been frowning over the problem, said: "I believe the properest expression is a plan of campaign! That's what it is! How stupid of me! I am not at all surprised you shouldn't have understood what I meant."

"I still don't understand. What *is* your

plan of campaign?"

"Well, I'll tell you, sir," said Amanda, not displeased to describe what she plainly considered to be a masterpiece of generalship. "When Neil said that on no account would he take me to Gretna Green, naturally I was obliged to think of a different scheme. And although I daresay it seems to you pretty poor-spirited of him, he is *not* poor-spirited, and I don't at all wish you to think such a thing of him."

"Set your mind at rest on that head: I don't!" replied Sir Gareth.

"And it isn't because he doesn't wish to marry me, for he does, and he says he is going to marry me, even if we have to wait until I am of age," she assured him earnestly. She added, after a darkling pause: "But, I must say, it has me quite in a puzzle to understand how he comes to be a very good soldier, which everyone says he truly is, when he seems to have not the least notion of Surprise, or Attack. Do you suppose it comes from fighting under Lord Wellington's command, and being obliged to retreat so frequently?"

"Very likely," responded Sir Gareth, his countenance admirably composed. "Is your flight in the nature of an attack?"

"Yes, of course it is. For it was *vital* that

something should be done immediately! At any moment now, Neil may be sent back to rejoin the regiment, and if he doesn't take me with him I may not see him again for years, and years, and years! And it is of no avail to argue with Grandpapa, or to coax him, because all he does is to say that I shall soon forget about it, and to give me stupid presents!"

At this point, any faint vision, which Sir Gareth might have had, of a tyrannical grandparent, left him. He said: "I quite expected to hear that he had locked you in your room."

"Oh, no!" she assured him. "Aunt Adelaide did so once, when I was quite a little girl, but I climbed out of the window, into the big elm tree, and Grandpapa said I was never to be locked in again. And, in a way, I am sorry for it, because I daresay if I had been locked in Neil would have consented to an elopement. But, of course, when all Grandpapa would do was to give me things, and talk about my presentation, and send me to parties in Bath, Neil couldn't perceive that there was the least need to rescue me. He said that we must be patient. But I have seen what comes of being patient," Amanda said, with a boding look, "and I have no opinion of it."

"What *does* come of it?" enquired Sir Gareth.

"Nothing!" she answered. "I daresay you might not credit it, but Aunt Adelaide fell in love when she was quite young, like me, and *just* the same thing happened! Grand-papa said she was too young, and also that he wished her to marry a man of fortune, so she made up her mind to be patient, and *then* what do you think?"

"I haven't the remotest guess: do tell me!"

"Why, after only two years the Suitor married an odious female with ten thousand pounds, and they had seven children, and he was carried off by an inflammation of the lungs! And none of it would have happened if only Aunt Adelaide had had a grain of resolution! So I have quite made up my mind not to cultivate resignation, because although people praise one for it I don't consider that it serves any useful purpose. If Aunt Adelaide had been married to the Suitor, he wouldn't have contracted an inflammation of the lungs, because she would have taken better care of him. And if Neil is wounded again, I am going to nurse him, and I shall not permit *anyone,* even Lord Wellington himself, to put him on one of those dreadful spring-wagons, which was harder to bear than all the rest, he told me!"

"I'm sure it must have been. But none of this explains why you ran away from your home," he pointed out.

"Oh, I did that to compel Grandpapa to consent to my marriage!" she said brightly. "And also to show him that I am *not* a child, but, on the contrary, very well able to take care of myself. He thinks that because I am accustomed to be waited on I shouldn't know how to go on if I had to live in billets, or perhaps a tent, which is absurd, because I should. Only it never answers to *tell* Grandpapa anything: one is obliged to *show* him. Well, he didn't believe I should climb out of the window when I was locked into my room, though I warned him how it would be. At first I thought I would refuse to eat anything until he gave his consent — in fact, I did refuse, one day, only I became so excessively hungry that I thought perhaps it wasn't such a famous scheme, particularly when it so happened that there were buttered lobsters for dinner, and a Floating Island pudding."

"Naturally you couldn't forgo two such dishes," he said sympathetically.

"Well, no," she confessed. "Besides, it wouldn't have shown Grandpapa that I am truly able to take care of myself, which is, I think, important."

"Very true. One can't help feeling that it might have put just the opposite notion into his head. Now tell me why you think that running away from him will answer the purpose!"

"Well, it wouldn't; not that part of it, precisely. *That* will just give him a fright."

"I have no doubt it will, but are you quite sure you wish to frighten him?"

"No, but it is quite his own fault for being so unkind and obstinate. Besides, it is my campaign, and you can't consider the sensibilities of the enemy when you are planning a campaign!" she said reasonably. "You can have no notion how difficult it was to decide what was best to be done. In fact, I was *almost* at a stand when, by the luckiest chance, I saw an advertisement in the *Morning Post*. It said that a lady living at — well, living not very far from St. Neots, wished for a genteel young person to be governess to her children. Of course, I saw at once that it was the very thing!" A slight choking sound made her look enquiringly at Sir Gareth. "Sir?"

"I didn't speak. Pray continue! I collect that you thought that you might be eligible for this post?"

"Certainly I did!" she replied, with dignity. "I am genteel, and I am young, and, I assure you, I have been *most* carefully educated. And having had several governesses myself, I know exactly what should be done in such a case. So I wrote to this lady, pretending I was my aunt, you know. I said I desired to recommend for the post my niece's governess, who had given *every* satisfaction, and was in all respects a most talented and admirable person, able to give instruction in the pianoforte, and in water-colour painting, besides the use of the globes, and needlework, and foreign languages."

"An impressive catalogue!" he said, much struck.

"Well, I do think it sounds well," she acknowledged, accepting this tribute with a rosy blush.

"Very well. Er — does it happen to be true?"

"Of course it's true! That is to say — Well, I am thought to play quite creditably on the pianoforte, besides being able to sing a little, and sketching is of all things my favourite occupation. And naturally I have learnt French, and, lately, some Spanish, because although Neil says we shall be over the Pyrenees in a trice, one never knows, and it might be very necessary to be able to converse in Spanish. I own, I don't know if

I can *teach* these things, but that doesn't signify, because I never had the least intention of being a governess for more than a few weeks. The thing is that I haven't a great deal of money, so that if I run away I must contrive to earn my bread until Grandpapa capitulates. I have left behind me a letter, you see, explaining it all to him, and I have told him that I won't come home, or tell him where I am, until he promises to let me be married to Neil immediately."

"Forgive me!" he interpolated. "But if you have severed your lines of communication how is he to inform you of his surrender?"

"I have arranged for that," she replied proudly. "I have desired him to insert an advertisement in the *Morning Post*! I have left nothing to chance, which ought to prove to him that I am not a foolish little girl, but, on the contrary, a most responsible person, quite old enough to be married. Yes, and I didn't book a seat on the stage, which would have been a stupid thing to do, on account of making it easy, perhaps, for them to discover where I had gone. I hid myself in the carrier's cart! I had formed that intention from the outset, and that, you see, was what made it so particularly fortunate that the lady who wished for a governess lived near to St. Neots."

"Oh, she did engage you?" Sir Gareth said, unable to keep an inflexion of surprise out of his voice.

"Yes, because I recommended myself very strongly to her, and it seems that the old governess was obliged to leave her at a moment's notice, because her mother suddenly died, and so she had to go home to keep house for her papa. Nothing could have fallen out more fortunately!"

He was obliged to laugh, but he said: "Abominable girl! What next will you say? But if you are now on your way to take up this desirable post, how come you to be trying to hire yourself as a chambermaid at this inn, and why do you wish to go to Huntingdon?"

The triumphant look in her eyes was quenched; she sighed, and said: "Oh, it is the shabbiest thing! You would hardly believe that my scheme could miscarry, when I planned it so carefully, would you? But so it was. I am not on my way to Mrs. — to That Female. In fact, quite the reverse. She is the horridest creature!"

"Ah!" said Sir Gareth. "Did she refuse after all to employ you?"

"Yes, she did!" answered Amanda, her bosom swelling with indignation. "She said I was by far too young, and not at all the

70

sort of female she had had in mind. She said she had been quite deceived, which was a most unjust observation, because she said in the advertisement that she desired a *young* lady!"

"My child, you are a shameless minx!" said Sir Gareth frankly. "From start to finish you deceived this unfortunate woman, and well you know it!"

"No, I did not!" she retorted, firing up. "At least, only in pretending I was Aunt Adelaide, and saying I had been my own governess, and *that* she didn't know! I am truly able to do all the things I told her I could, and very likely I should be able to teach other girls to do them too. However, all was to no avail. Unreasonable, too, for in the middle of it her eldest son came in, and as soon as he heard who I was he suggested that his mama should engage me for a little while, to see how I did, which was most sensible, I thought. But it only made her crosser than ever, and she sent him out of the room, which I was sorry for, because he seemed very amiable and obliging, in spite of having spots." She added, affronted: "And I do not at all understand why you should laugh, sir!"

"Never mind! Tell me what happened next!"

"Well, she ordered the carriage to take me back to St. Neots, and while it was being brought round she began to ask me a great many impertinent questions, and I could see she had an extremely suspicious disposition, so I thought of a splendid story to tell her. I gave myself an indigent parent, and *dozens* of brothers and sisters, all younger than I am, and instead of being sorry for me, she said she didn't believe me! She said I wasn't dressed like a poor person, and she would like to know how many guineas I had squandered on my hat! Such impudence! So I said I had stolen it, and my gown as well, and really I was a wicked adventuress. That, of course, was impolite, but it answered the purpose, for she stopped trying to discover where I had come from, and grew very red in the face, and said I was an abandoned girl, and she washed her hands of me. Then the servant came to say that the carriage was at the door, and so I made my curtsy, and we parted."

"Abandoned you most certainly are. Were you driven to St. Neots?"

"Yes, and it was then that I hit upon the notion of becoming a chambermaid for a space."

"Let me tell you, Amanda, that a chambermaid's life would not suit you!"

"I know *that,* and if you can think of some more agreeable occupation of a gainful nature, sir, I shall be very much obliged to you," she responded, fixing him with a pair of hopeful eyes.

"I'm afraid I can't. There is only one thing for you to do, and that is to return to your grandpapa."

"I won't!" said Amanda, not mincing matters.

"I think you will, when you've considered a little."

"No, I shan't. I have already considered a great deal, and I now see that it is a very good thing Mrs. — That Female — wouldn't employ me. For if I were a governess in a respectable household Grandpapa would know that I was perfectly safe, and he would very likely try to — to starve me out. But I shouldn't think he would like me to be a chambermaid in an inn, would you?"

"Emphatically, no!"

"Well, there you are!" she said triumphantly. "The instant he knows that that is what I am doing, he will capitulate. Now the only puzzle is to discover a suitable inn. I saw a very pretty one in a village, on the way to St. Neots, which is why you find me in this horrid one. Because I went back to it, after the coachman had set me down, only they didn't happen to need a chamber-maid there, which was a sad pity, for it had roses growing up the wall, and six of the dearest little kittens! The landlady said that I should go to Huntingdon, because she had heard that they needed a girl to work at the George, and she directed me to the pike-road, and that is why I am here!"

"Are you telling me," demanded Sir Gareth incredulously, "that you bamboozled the woman into believing that you were a maidservant? She must be out of her senses!"

"Oh, no!" said Amanda blithely. "I thought of a splendid story, you see."

"An indigent parent?"

"No, much better than that one. I said I had been an abigail to a young lady, who most kindly gave me her old dresses to wear, only I had been turned off, *without* a character, because her papa behaved in a very improper way towards me. He is a widower, you must know, and also there is an aunt — not like Aunt Adelaide, but more like Aunt Maria, who is a very unfeeling person —"

"Yes, you may spare me the rest of this affecting history!" interrupted Sir Gareth, between amusement and exasperation.

"Well, you *asked* me!" she said indignantly. "And you need not be so scornful, because I took the notion from a very improving novel called —"

"*Pamela*. And I am astonished that your grandfather should have permitted you to read it! That is to say, if you have a grandfather, which I begin to doubt!"

She showed him a shocked face. "Of course I have a grandfather! In fact, I once had *two* grandfathers, but one of them died when I was a baby."

"He is to be felicitated. Come, now! Was there one word of truth in the story you told *me,* or was it another of your splendid stories?"

She jumped up, very much flushed, and with tears sparkling on the ends of her long eyelashes. "No, it was not! I thought you were kind, and a *gentleman,* and now I see I was quite mistaken, and I wish very much that I *had* told you a lie, because you are *exactly* like an uncle, only worse! And what I told those other people was just — just make-believe, and *that* is not the same thing as telling lies! And I am excessively sorry now that I drank your lemonade, and ate your tarts, and, if you please, I will pay for them *myself!* And also," she added, as her misty gaze fell on an empty bowl, "for the cherries!"

He too had risen, and he possessed himself

of the agitated little hands that were fumbling with the strings of a reticule, and held them in a comforting clasp. "Gently, my child! There, there, don't cry! Of course I see just how it was! Come! Let us sit on this settee, and decide what is best to be done!"

Amanda, tired by the day's adventures, made only a token of resistance before subsiding on to his shoulder, and indulging in a burst of tears. Sir Gareth, who had more than once sustained the impassioned and lachrymose confidences of an ill-used niece, behaved with great competence and sangfroid, unshaken by a situation that might have cast a less experienced man into disorder. In a very few minutes, Amanda had recovered from her emotional storm, had mopped her cheeks, and blown her diminutive nose into his handkerchief, and had offered him an apology for having succumbed to a weakness which, she earnestly assured him, she heartily despised.

Then he talked to her. He talked well, and persuasively, pointing out to her the unwisdom of her present plans, the distress of mind into which a continuance of them must throw her grandfather, and all the disadvantages which must attach to a career, however temporary, as a serving-maid in a public inn. She listened to him with great docility, her large eyes fixed on his face, her hands folded in her lap, and an occasional sob catching her breath; and when he had finished she said: "Yes, but even if it is very bad it will be better than not being allowed to marry Neil until I come of age. So will you please take me to Huntingdon, sir?"

"Amanda, have you attended to one word I've said to you?"

"Yes, I attended to all of them, and they were exactly the sort of things my own uncles would say. It is all propriety and nonsense! As for grieving Grandpapa, it is quite his own fault, because I warned him that he would be excessively sorry if he didn't give his consent to my marriage, and if he didn't believe me he deserves to be put in a pucker for being so stupid. Because I always keep my word, and when I want something very much I get it."

"I can well believe it. You must forgive me if I tell you, Amanda, that you are a shockingly spoilt child!"

"Well, that is Grandpapa's fault too," she said.

He tried another tack. "Tell me this! If he knew of your exploit, do you think your Neil would approve of it?"

She replied unhesitatingly: "Oh, no! In

fact, I expect he will be very angry, and give me a tremendous scold, but he will forgive me, because he knows I would never serve *him* such a trick. Besides, he must perceive that I am doing it all for his sake. And I daresay," she added reflectively, "that he won't be so very much surprised, because he thinks I'm spoilt, too, and he knows *all* the bad things I've done. Indeed, he has often rescued me from a fix, when I was a little girl." Her eyes brightened; she exclaimed: "Why, that would be the very thing! Only I think it ought to be a dire peril this time. Then he can rescue me from it, and restore me to Grandpapa, and Grandpapa would be so grateful that he would be obliged to consent to the marriage!" She frowned in an effort of concentration. "I shall have to think of a dire peril. I must say, it's very difficult!"

Sir Gareth, who experienced no difficulty at all in thinking of it, said in a damping voice that by the time she had contrived to advise Neil of her danger it might be too late for him to effect a rescue.

She rather regretfully acknowledged the justice of this observation, further disclosing that she was not perfectly sure of Neil's direction, since he had gone to London, for a medical inspection, after which he would report at the Horse Guards. "And goodness knows how long that will take! And the dreadful part of it is that if the doctors think him quite well again, he may be sent back to Spain almost immediately! That is why it is *imperative* that I should lose not a moment in — in prosecuting my campaign!" She jumped up, saying with a challenging look: "I am very much obliged to you, sir, and now, if you please, we will part, for I believe Huntingdon is almost ten miles away, and if there is no stage, and you don't wish to take me there in your carriage, I shall have to walk, so that it is high time I was setting forward."

She then held out her hand, with all the air of a great lady taking gracious leave of an acquaintance, but upon Sir Gareth's not only taking it in his, but maintaining a firm hold on it, her grandeur abruptly deserted her, and she stamped her foot, and commanded him to let her go instantly.

Sir Gareth was in a dilemma. It was plainly useless to continue arguing with Amanda, and he had seen enough of her to be tolerably sure that an attempt to frighten her into disclosing her grandfather's name and direction would fail. If he carried into execution his threat to hand her into the charge of the Parish officer, nothing was more certain than that she would give this worthy the slip. Leave her to her own absurd devices? No: it was impossible, he decided. Headstrong and, indeed, extremely naughty she might be, but she was as innocent as a kitten, and by far too lovely to be allowed to wander unescorted about the country.

"If you don't let me go this instant, I shall bite you!" stormed Amanda, tugging fruitlessly at his long fingers.

"Then not only will you not be offered a seat in my curricle, but you will get your ears soundly boxed into the bargain," he replied cheerfully.

"How *dare* you —" She broke off suddenly, stopped clawing at his hand, and raised a face alight with joyful expectation. "Oh, *will* you take me up in your curricle, sir? *Thank* you!"

He would not have been in the least surprised had she flung her arms round his neck in her transport of gratitude, but she contented herself with squeezing his hand tightly between both of hers, and bestowing upon him a rapturous smile. Registering a silent vow not to let so trusting a damsel out of his sight until he could restore her to her proper guardian, he put her into a chair, and went off to inform his astonished groom that he must relinquish his seat in the curricle to a lady, and stand up behind as best he might.

Trotton thought it a strange start, but when, a few minutes later, he clapped eyes on the unexpected passenger, the disturbing suspicion that his master had run mad darted into his mind. There were plenty of gentlemen in whom such conduct would have seemed natural, but Sir Gareth, in Trotton's experience, had never been one to fall into the petticoat line. Sir Gareth had not told any member of his household what his errand was to Brancaster Park, but all his servants, from his butler down to the kitchen porter, had guessed what it must be, and it seemed to Trotton the height of insanity for him to succumb just at this moment to the lures thrown out by the pretty bit of muslin he was handing up into his curricle. A nice setout it would be if he were to be seen driving such a prime article as that down the road! He wondered whether perhaps his master had a touch of the sun, and was trying to remember what ought to be done for sufferers from sun-stroke when Sir Gareth's voice recalled his wandering wits.

"Are you deaf, Trotton? I said, let 'em go!"

CHAPTER FOUR

A couple of miles beyond the cross-road from Cambridge to St. Neots the road forked. Sir Gareth took the right fork without hesitation. His youthful companion, who had (as she artlessly informed him) hitherto travelled in no more sporting vehicle than a gig, which Grandpapa sometimes permitted her to drive, was hugely enjoying herself, and was too ruthlessly intent on discovering whether her protector was a whip celebrated enough to merit the title of Nonesuch to notice a weatherbeaten signpost which bore, in faded lettering, the simple legend: *To St. Ives*. It was otherwise with the faithful henchman. Standing precariously behind his master, and maintaining his balance by a firm grip on the curricle's lowered hood, he ventured to intervene. He had gathered, from Amanda's prattle, that Sir Gareth had engaged himself to drive her to Huntingdon, and he considered it his duty to point out to Sir Gareth that he had taken the wrong fork.

Restraining an impulse to curse his too-helpful retainer, Sir Gareth said calmly: "Thank you, Trotton. I know the road."

But the mischief was done. Bristling with suspicion, Amanda demanded: "Is this not the road to Huntingdon?"

It had been Sir Gareth's intention to postpone for as long as possible the disclosure that he was taking Amanda not to Huntingdon but to Brancaster Park; but thus directly questioned he saw nothing for it but to tell her the truth. He replied: "No, but I have a better plan for you."

"You promised you would drive me to Huntingdon!" she cried hotly.

"Oh, no, I didn't! I offered you a seat in my curricle: no more than that! You cannot have forgotten that I told you I would for no persuasion leave you in a public inn."

"Stop! Set me down at once!" she ordered. "I won't go with you! I was never so taken in! Why — why, you are nothing but an *abductor!*"

He could not help laughing at this, which naturally made her very angry. She raged at him for several minutes, but as soon as she paused for breath he said soothingly: "If you will be quiet for a moment, and listen to what I have to say, I'll tell you where I *am* taking you."

"It is not of the slightest consequence, because I won't go with you *anywhere!* You are a deceiver, and a wicked person, and very likely you mean to murder me!"

"Then you are now in dire peril, and what you should do is to summon your Brigade-Major to the rescue immediately," he returned. "A message to the Horse Guards will undoubtedly find him. Tell me his name, and I will engage not only to bring him to you with all possible speed, but also to refrain from murdering you in the meantime."

"I hope very much that *he* will murder *you!*" she declared through shut teeth. "And I expect he will, when he knows how treacherously you have behaved to me!"

"But you can't expect him to murder me if you don't tell him of my treachery," he pointed out, in a very reasonable way. "If I were you, I would lose not a moment in summoning him to your side. Trotton shall travel post to London with a message for him. I shouldn't be astonished if I were a dead man within two days."

From the sparkling look in her eyes, it was to be inferred that the prospect strongly attracted her. It seemed, for a moment, as though she were on the point of divulging her Brigade-Major's name, but just as Sir Gareth was silently congratulating himself on the success of his tactics, she said suddenly: "I see what it is! It is all a trick, so that you may discover where I live, and ruin my scheme! Well, I shall not send a message to Neil!"

"You know, Amanda," he said seriously, "you may just as well tell me what I wish to know, because I am going to discover it, whether you do or whether you don't."

"No! How can you?" she demanded.

"If you force me to do so, I shall pay a visit to the Horse Guards, and enquire of them there if they can furnish me with the direction of a captain of infantry, a Brigade-Major, sent home from the Peninsula with a ball in his shoulder, but now in hourly expectation of rejoining. I expect they will be able to help me, though I can't but feel that Neil would infinitely prefer to be discovered in a rather more private style. That is for you to decide."

She did not speak for several moments; then she said, in a gritty little voice: "You think you've worsted me, but you have not! I shan't tell you anything, and I promise you I — I shall come about!"

"Very well," he replied equably.

"I believe," said Amanda, after another seething pause, "that kidnappers are sent to prison, or even *transported!* You would not like that, I daresay!"

"No, indeed!"

"Well! I am just warning you!" she said.

"Thank you! I am very much obliged to you."

"And if *you*," declared Amanda, bethinking herself of the groom, and twisting round to address him, "had one grain of manliness, you would not permit your master to carry me off!"

Trotton, a deeply interested audience, was unprepared for this attack, and nearly lost his balance. Much discomposed, he could only stammer an unintelligible answer, and glance imploring at Sir Gareth's back-view.

"Oh, you mustn't blame Trotton!" said Sir Gareth. "Consider how difficult is his position! He is obliged to obey my orders, you see."

"He is not obliged to assist you in kidnapping people!" she retorted.

"I engaged him on the strict understanding," said Sir Gareth firmly, "that that would form an important part of his duties."

"I w-wish you will not be so absurd!" said Amanda, struggling to suppress a giggle.

He turned his head to smile down at her.

"That's better!"

She laid a mittened hand on his sleeve, directing a beseeching look up at him. "Oh, will you *please* let me go? You are ruining everything!"

"I know I am, and I do beg your pardon. I must be quite the most abominable marplot imaginable."

"Well, you are! And I thought you were so very agreeable!"

"I too have been badly deceived in myself," he said, shaking his head. "Would you believe it? — I had no notion that I was such a monster of inhumanity as I have proved myself to be."

"Well, it is being a monster to betray me, and then to try to roast me!" she said, turning away her flushed countenance, and biting her lip.

"Poor Amanda! You are perfectly right: it is a great deal too bad of me, and I won't roast you any more. Let me tell you instead where I am taking you!"

"I shan't listen to a word you say," she informed him coldly.

"That will teach me a lesson," he observed.

"I think you are the horridest creature!" she exclaimed. "Yes, and now I come to think of it, if you are taking me to your own home, it is most improper, and far worse than letting me go to an inn!"

"It would be," he agreed. "But my home isn't in this part of the country. I am taking you to Brancaster Park, where I think you will find a very kind hostess in Lady Hester Theale."

Upon hearing these words, Trotton, who was much attached to his master, very nearly allowed a protest to escape him. If Sir Gareth meant to arrive at Brancaster Park with this dazzling young beauty on his arm, he was unquestionably out of his senses, and ought to be restrained. But it was not the business of his groom to point out to him the unwisdom of introducing his chance-met bit of muslin to the Lady Hester. Trotton dared do no more than give a warning cough, to which Sir Gareth paid no heed at all.

Sir Gareth stood in no need of a warning. Had any other solution for the safe disposal of Amanda occurred to him, he would have seized it, for he was well aware that to present himself at Brancaster Park, with the declared intention of proposing marriage to Lady Hester, accompanied by Amanda must be as prejudicial to his interests as it was ludicrous. But he believed that he could rely on Hester to receive Amanda kindly;

and he hoped that she would understand that he had no other choice than to bring that headstrong damsel to the shelter of her home.

Amanda, meanwhile, was demanding to be told who lived at Brancaster Park. When she learned that she was to be the uninvited guest of Lord Brancaster, and of his daughter, she protested vehemently, saying that so far from being anxious to regain possession of her, her grandfather would in all probability be delighted to know that she was a guest in an Earl's country seat. Sir Gareth suggested helpfully that she should prevail upon Lady Hester to hire her as an abigail.

Amanda audibly ground her teeth. "If you force me to go there with you, I shall make you very, very sorry!" she warned him.

"I expect you will, and am already in a quake of terror," he agreed.

"I *trusted* you!" she said tragically. "Now you are going to betray my confidence, besides ruining all my schemes!"

"No, I won't betray your confidence, except, I think, to Lady Hester. When you have met her, you won't, I fancy, object to her knowing the truth. I shall desire her not to divulge it to her father, or — if they should happen to be at Brancaster — to her brother and his wife."

She was quick to catch a certain inflexion in his voice, and lifted her eyes to his profile, saying: "I can tell you don't like them above half, sir. Are they horrid?"

He smiled. "No, not horrid. I daresay very worthy people, but it so happens that they are not particular friends of mine."

"Oh! Is Lord Brancaster a particular friend of yours, sir?"

"Well, he is considerably older than I am," he temporized.

She digested this, enquiring presently: "Is Lady Hester a particular friend of yours, then?"

"Why, yes! She and I have been good friends for many years now."

He was prepared for even more searching questions, but she relapsed into silence. After several minutes, he said: "I have been wondering what I should tell Brancaster, and the Widmores, and I am strongly of the opinion, Amanda, that you are the daughter of some acquaintances with whom I have been staying, at Baldock. You are on your way to visit relations at — Oundle, perhaps — and from some cause or another I offered to take you with me as far as to Huntingdon, where these relations had engaged themselves to meet you. Unhappily, there must have been a misunderstanding, for no carriage awaited you there. Being pledged to present myself at Brancaster Park today, what was I to do? Why, take you along with me, to be sure, with the intention of conveying you to Oundle tomorrow! How does that suit your notion of a splendid story?"

"It is quite untrue," she said primly.

"I wonder why I should have thought that that would have recommended it to you?" he murmured.

The only reply he got to his sally was a dagger-glance. He said, over his shoulder: "I trust you heard that, Trotton?"

"Yes, sir."

"Well, don't forget it!"

"Pray have the goodness to inform me, sir," said Amanda, with awful civility, "where you have the intention of taking me tomorrow?"

"I hope, to your grandfather."

"No!"

He shrugged. "As you wish."

Intrigued, she demanded: "Where, then?"

"That, my child, you will see, in good time."

"I believe you are at a stand!" she challenged him.

"Not a bit of it!"

Conversation languished after that, Amanda occupying herself for the remainder of the journey in turning over in her mind various plots for Sir Gareth's discomfiture, and returning only monosyllabic replies to his occasional remarks.

They reached Brancaster Park as the shadows were beginning to lengthen, passing through impressive lodge-gates, and driving for some way up an avenue which had been allowed to deteriorate into something akin to a cart-track. The trees, growing rather too thickly beside it, rendered it both damp and gloomy; and when the pleasure gardens came into sight these too bore unmistakable signs of neglect. Amanda looked about her with disfavour; and, when her eyes alighted on the square, grey mansion, exclaimed: "Oh, I wish you had not brought me here! What an ugly, disagreeable house!"

"If I could have thought of any other place for you, believe me, I wouldn't have brought you here, Amanda!" he said frankly. "For a more awkward situation I defy anyone to imagine!"

"Well, if it seems so to you, set me down now, while there is still time!" she urged.

"No, I am determined not to let you escape me," he replied lightly. "I can only hope to be able to pass you off with some credit — though what the household will think of a young lady who travels with her belongings contained in a couple of band-boxes heaven only knows! I trust at least that we may not find the house full of guests. No, I fancy it won't be."

He was right, but his host, who did not scruple to exaggerate in moments of acute vexation, had been so describing it ever since the unwelcome arrival, earlier in the day, of the Honourable Fabian Theale.

Mr. Theale was his lordship's brother, and if he had been born with any other object than to embarrass his family, his lordship had yet to discover it. He was a bachelor, with erratic habits, expensive tastes, and pockets permanently to let. His character was volatile, his disposition amiable; and since he had a firm belief in benevolent Providence neither duns nor impending scandals had the power to ruffle his placidity. That it was first his father, and, later, his elder brother, who enacted the role of Providence troubled him not at all; and whenever the Earl swore that he had rescued him for the last time he made not the slightest effort either to placate his brother or to mend his extremely reprehensible ways, because he knew that while the Earl shared many of his tastes he had also a strong prejudice against open scandals, and could always be relied upon, whatever the exigencies of his own situation, to rescue one of his name from the bailiff's clutches.

At no time was his lordship pleased to receive a visit from Mr. Theale; when that florid and portly gentleman descended upon him on the very day appointed for Sir Gareth's arrival he so far forgot himself as to say, in front of the butler, a footman, and Mr. Theale's own valet, that no one need trouble to carry the numerous valises upstairs, since he was not going to house his brother for as much as a night.

Mr. Theale, beyond enquiring solicitously if his lordship's gout was plaguing him, paid no attention to this. He adjured the footman to handle his dressing-case carefully, and informed the Earl that he was on his way to Leicestershire.

The Earl eyed him with wrath and misgiving. Mr. Theale owned a snug little hunting-box near Melton Mowbray, but if he was proposing to visit it in the middle of July this could only mean that circumstances had rendered it prudent, if not urgently necessary, for him to leave town for a space. "What is it this time?" he demanded, leading the way into the library. "You haven't come home for the pleasure of seeing me, so out with it! And I give you fair warning,

Fabian —"

"No, no, it's no pleasure to me to see you, old fellow!" Mr. Theale assured him. "In fact, if I weren't in the basket I wouldn't have come here, because to see you fretting and fuming is enough to give one a fit of the dismals."

"When last I saw you," said the Earl suspiciously, "you told me you had made a recover! Said you had had a run of luck at faro, and were as fresh as ever."

"Dash it, that was a month ago!" expostulated Mr. Theale. "You can't expect it to be high water with me for ever! Not but what if you could trust to the form-book I ought to be able to buy an abbey by now. But there it is! First there was the Salisbury meeting — by the by, old fellow, did you lay your blunt on Corkscrew? Got a notion I told you to."

"No, I didn't," replied the Earl shortly.

"Good thing," approved Mr. Theale. "Damned screw wasn't placed. Then there was Andover! Mind you, if I'd followed my own judgment, Whizgig would have carried my money, and very likely I wouldn't be here today. However, I let Jerry earwig me into backing Ticklepitcher, so here I am. I hear you was at the July meeting at Newmarket, and came off all right," he added dispassionately.

"As to that —"

"Three winners, and a devilish long price you must have got on True-blue, my boy! If I were half as tetchy as you are, I should take it mighty ill that you didn't pass me the word."

"I'll grease you in the fist on one condition!" said the Earl brutally.

"Anything you please, dear boy!" said Mr. Theale, impervious to insult. "Just tip over the dibs!"

"I have Ludlow coming here today, on a visit, and I shall be glad if you will take yourself off!"

"Ludlow?" said Mr. Theale, mildly surprised. "What the devil's he coming here for?"

"He's coming to offer for Hester, and I don't want him to hedge off, which I don't doubt he will, if you try to break his shins!"

"Well, by God!" exclaimed Mr. Theale. "Damme if ever I thought Hester would contract an engagement at all, let alone catch a man like Ludlow on her hook! Well, this is famous! I wouldn't put his fortune at a penny less than twelve thousand pounds a year! Very right to warn me, dear boy: fatal to borrow any money from him until you have the knot safely tied! Shouldn't dream of making the attempt. I hope he means to come down handsome?"

"Will you," said the Earl, controlling his spleen with a visible effort, "take yourself off to Leicestershire?"

"Make it a monkey, old fellow, and I'll be off first thing in the morning," said Mr. Theale obligingly.

With this promise the Earl had to be content, though he made a spirited effort to improve the terms of the bargain before at last agreeing to them. Nothing, it was clear, would avail to dislodge his brother until the following day, Mr. Theale pointing out very reasonably that it was rather too much to expect that he would set forth on his travels again before he had recovered from the exhaustion entailed by a journey of more than sixty miles. It had taken him two days to achieve this prodigious distance, travelling at a sedate pace in his own carriage, with his valet following behind in a hired coach with all his baggage. "And even with my own fellow to drive me I felt queasy," he said. "Mind, if I had the sort of stomach that didn't turn over on me when I'm being jolted and rocked over these devilish bad roads I'd pack up and be off this instant, because I can see we're bound to spend a damned flat evening here. Wouldn't do to hook Ludlow in for a rubber or two, for though I don't doubt you and I, Giles, if we played together, which could be arranged, would physic him roundly, it would be bad policy! Besides, we should have to hook in Widmore to make a fourth, and there's no sense in winning his money, even if he could be got to sport a little blunt, which I've never known him do yet. Of course, you're his father, but you must own he's a paltry fellow!"

So the Earl was forced to resign himself, which he would have done more easily had not Mr. Theale's family loyalty prompted him to lend his aid to the preparations in train for the entertainment of the expected guest. Since this took the form of an invasion of the kitchens, where he maddened the cook by freely editing the dinner to be set before Sir Gareth; and a voyage of exploration to the cellars, whence he brought to light several crusted bottles which the Earl had been jealously preserving, it was not long before his brother's little stock of patience was exhausted. Forcefully adjured to cease meddling, he was obliged to seek diversion in other fields, with the result that a young housemaid, unused to the ways of the Quality, was thrown into strong hysterics, and had to have her ears boxed before she could be induced to stop screeching that she was an honest maid, and desired instantly to return to her mother's protection.

"And very stupid it was of Mrs. Farnham to send that girl of all others to make up Fabian's bed!" said Lady Widmore, in her customary forthright style. "*She* must know what your uncle is!"

By the time Sir Gareth and his protégée were ushered into the Grand Saloon the only members of the family, gathered there, whose sensibilities had not been in some way or other ruffled were Mr. Theale, and Lady Widmore. The Earl was on the one hand uncertain what his daughter's answer was going to be, and on the other he had been reduced to a state of impotent fury by his brother's activities; Lord Widmore shared his parent's misgivings, and was very much put out by the discovery that five hundred pounds, urgently needed on the estate, had been bestowed upon his uncle; and Lady Hester, exhorted and commanded to the point of distraction, was looking positively hagged. A gown of lilac silk, with a demi-train, three rows of flounces, a quantity of ivory lace, and knots of violet velvet ribbons enhanced her pallor; and her abigail, in her anxiety to present her mistress at her best, had slightly over-crimped her soft brown hair. Lately, she had adopted a cap, but although this circumstance had apparently escaped the notice of her relations for several weeks it had today come in for such unmeasured censure that she had wearily removed the wisp of lace.

"And let me tell you, Hetty, that a stupid sort of indifference is by no means becoming in you!" said her father severely. "These dawdling and languid airs are enough to give Ludlow a disgust of you."

"Now, don't fidget the girl!" recommended Mr. Theale. "Ten to one, Ludlow won't notice she ain't in spirits, because what with you in one of your distempered freaks, and Widmore looking as sulky as a bear, he'll have enough to frighten him off without looking at Hester. In fact, it is just as well I took it into my head to visit you. You can't deny I'm a dashed sight better company than the rest of you."

The Earl's retort was cut short on his lips by the opening of the double-doors into the saloon.

"Miss Smith!" announced the butler, in the voice of one heralding disaster. "Sir Gareth Ludlow!"

CHAPTER FIVE

"Eh?" ejaculated the Earl, in a sort of bark, wheeling round, and staring with slightly protuberant eyes at the vision on the threshold.

Amanda, colouring deliciously under the concentrated scrutiny of so many pairs of eyes, lifted her chin a little. Sir Gareth went forward, saying easily: "How do you do? Your servant, Lady Widmore! Lady Hester!" He took the cold hand she had mechanically stretched out to him, lightly kissed it, and retained it in his. "May I present Miss Smith to you, and solicit your kindness on her behalf! I have assured her that she may depend on *that.* The case is that she is the daughter of some old friends with whom I have been staying, and I engaged myself to conduct her to Huntingdon, where she was to be met by some relations. But either through a misunderstanding, or some mishap, no carriage had been sent to meet her there, and since I could not leave her in a public inn, there was nothing for it but to bring her here."

Every vestige of colour had drained away from the Lady Hester's cheeks when she had looked up to perceive the lovely girl at Sir Gareth's side, but she replied with tolerable composure: "Of course! We shall be most happy." She drew her hand away, and went to Amanda. "What a horrid predicament! I am so glad Sir Gareth brought you to us. I must make you known to my sister-in-law, Lady Widmore."

Amanda raised her brilliant eyes to Lady Hester's gentle gray ones, and suddenly smiled. The effect of this upon the assembled gentlemen caused Lady Widmore's already high colour to deepen alarmingly. Mr. Theale, who had been regarding the youthful beauty with the eye of a dispassionate connoisseur, sighed soulfully; the Earl's indignant stare changed to one of reluctant admiration; and Lord Widmore was moved to adjust his neckcloth, throwing out his narrow chest a little. However, as he caught his wife's fulminating eye at that moment, he was speedily recalled to a sense of his position, and altered a somewhat fatuous smile to a frown.

"An awkward situation indeed!" agreed

Lady Widmore, subjecting Amanda to a critical scrutiny. "But you have your abigail with you, I must suppose!"

"No, because she fell ill, and, besides, there was no room for her in the curricle," replied Amanda, with aplomb.

"In the curricle?" exclaimed Lord Widmore, looking very much shocked. "Driving with Ludlow in a curricle, without some respectable female to chaperon you? Upon my soul! I do not know what the world is coming to!"

"Now, don't talk like a nick-ninny, Cuthbert!" begged his uncle. "Damme if I see what anyone wants with a chaperon in a curricle! If it had been a chaise, it would have been another matter, of course."

"If Miss Smith was travelling in Sir Gareth's charge, sir, she had no need of her abigail to take care of her," interposed Hester, her tone mildly reproving.

"No," said Amanda gratefully. "And I had *no* desire to go with him, either, and am very well able to take care of myself!"

"You have had your hands full, I collect!" Lady Widmore said, putting up her sandy brows at Sir Gareth.

"Not at all!" he retorted. "I have had a charming companion, ma'am!"

"Oh, I don't doubt *that!*" she said, with a

laugh. "Well, child, I suppose I had best take you upstairs! You will wish to change your dress before dinner. I daresay they will have unpacked your trunk by now."

"Yes," said Amanda doubtfully. "I mean — that is —" She stopped, blushing and looking imploringly towards Sir Gareth.

He responded at once to this mute appeal, saying, with the flicker of a reassuring smile: "That is the most awkward feature of the whole business, isn't it, Amanda! Her trunk, ma'am, I must suppose to be at Oundle, for it was despatched by carrier yesterday. We could find room only for a couple of bandboxes in my curricle."

"Despatched yesterday?" said the Earl. "Seems an odd circumstance, then, that these relations of hers shouldn't have kept their engagement to meet her! What the devil should she send her trunk for, if she didn't mean to follow it?"

"That, sir," said Sir Gareth, quite unshaken, "is what makes us fear some mischance."

"I expect it has been delayed," said Lady Hester. "How vexing! But not of the least consequence."

"Lord, Hetty, what an addle-brained creature you are!" remarked Lady Widmore, with good-natured contempt. "If it ain't of any consequence, it ain't vexing either!"

"How silly of me!" murmured Hester, accepting this rebuke in an absentminded way. "Will you let me take you upstairs, Miss Smith? Don't put yourself about, Almeria! I will attend to Miss Smith."

Amanda looked rather relieved; and Sir Gareth, who had moved to the door, said, under his breath, as Hester paused beside him to let her guest pass before her out of the room: "Thank you! I knew I might rely on you."

She smiled a little wistfully, but said nothing. He closed the door behind her, and she paused for a moment, looking at Amanda, and blinking as though in an attempt to bring that enchanting face into focus. Amanda gave her back stare for stare, her chin well up, and she said, in her shy soft voice: "How *very* pretty you are! I wonder which room Mrs. Farnham has prepared for you? It must be wretchedly uncomfortable for you, but pray don't heed it! We will think just what should be done presently."

"Well," said Amanda, following her to the staircase, "for my part, I can see that it is most uncomfortable for you to be obliged to receive me when I haven't an evening-gown to wear, and as for Sir Gareth, it is all his fault, and he told you nothing but the most shocking untruths, besides having abducted me!"

Hester paused, with her hand on the banister-rail, and looked back, startled. "Abducted you? Dear me, how excessively odd of him! Are you quite sure you are not making a mistake?"

"No, it is precisely as I say," replied Amanda firmly. "For I never set eyes on him before today, and although at first I was quite deceived in him, because he looks just like all one's favourite heroes, which all goes to show that one shouldn't set any store by appearances, I now know that he is a most odious person — though still very like Sir Lancelot and Lord Orville," she added conscientiously.

Lady Hester looked wholly bewildered. "How can this be? You know, I am dreadfully stupid, and I don't seem able to understand at all, Miss Smith!"

"I wish you will call me Amanda!" suddenly decided that damsel. "I find I cannot *bear* the name of Smith! The thing is that it was the only name I could think of when nothing would do for Sir Gareth but to know who I was. I daresay you know how it is when you are obliged, on the instant, to find a name for yourself?"

"No — that is, I have never had occasion

— but of course I see that one would think of something very simple," Hester replied apologetically.

"Exactly so! Only you can have no idea how disagreeable it is to be called Miss Smith, which, as it happens, was the name of the horridest governess I ever had!"

Utterly befogged, Hester said: "Yes, indeed, although — You know, I think we should not stay talking here, for one never knows who may be listening! Do, pray, come upstairs!"

She then led Amanda to the upper hall, where they were met by her abigail, a middle-aged woman of hostile aspect, whose devotion to her mistress's interests caused her to view Amanda with suspicion and dislike. The news that Sir Gareth Ludlow had arrived at Brancaster with a regular out-and-outer on his arm had rapidly spread through the house; and Miss Povey knew just what to think of beauties who possessed no other luggage than a couple of bandboxes, and travelled unattended by their abigails or governesses. She informed Lady Hester that the Blue bedchamber had been prepared for the Young Person: an announcement that brought Lady Hester's eyes to her face, a tiny frown in them. "What did you say, Povey?" she asked.

The tone was as gentle as ever, but Miss Povey, permitting herself only the indulgence of a sniff, lost no time in altering her phraseology. "For the young lady, I *should* say, my lady."

"Oh, yes! The Blue bedchamber will be just the one. Thank you: I shan't need you any longer."

This dismissal by no means pleased the handmaiden. On the one hand, she was extremely reluctant to wait upon Amanda, and would, indeed, have bitterly resented a command to do so; but, on the other, she was agog with curiosity. After a brief struggle with her feelings, she said: "I thought, my lady, being as how Miss hasn't brought her own abigail, she would like me to dress her hair, and that."

"Yes, presently," said Hester. "And perhaps, since Miss Smith's trunk has gone to Oundle, you could bring that pink gown of mine to her room." She smiled diffidently at Amanda, adding: "Should you object to wearing one of my dresses? I think it would become you, for it is too young for me, and I have not worn it more than once."

"No, not at all. In fact, I shall be excessively obliged to you," replied Amanda warmly. "For the only other gown I have with me is another morning one, and I daresay it will be odiously crumpled. And this one is very dirty, through my having walked a great distance in it, besides being in the carrier's cart, though I took the greatest care to wrap my cloak round me."

"Muslin seems to pick up the dirt so *easily!*" agreed Hester, accepting the carrier's cart as the merest commonplace. "But Povey will wash and iron it for you to wear again in the morning."

With these calmly uttered words, she led Amanda into her allotted bedchamber, firmly closing the door on her scandalized abigail.

The bandboxes had been unpacked, and Amanda's few possessions disposed in the appropriate places. That damsel, after a comprehensive survey of the apartment, awarded it her approval, adding candidly: "And Sir Gareth was quite right: I *do* like you very much, ma'am, though I quite thought I should not!"

"I am so glad," murmured Hester. "Do let me untie the strings of your hat!"

"Yes," said Amanda, submitting to this, "but I must warn you, because I *never* tell lies to people I like, that I do not at all wish to visit an Earl!"

"I expect you have been brought up on revolutionary principles," said Hester wisely. "I do not, myself, know very much about it, but I believe that many people nowadays —"

"Oh, no! But the thing is that I particularly wish to establish myself in the sort of situation from which one's relations are bound to rescue one. And if it had not been for Sir Gareth I daresay I might have done it. I was never so taken-in! He said he would take me to Huntingdon, where I had every expectation of being hired as a chambermaid at the George — at least, that is what I thought he said he would do, only I soon discovered that it was all a hoax — and then, when he had lured me into his curricle, he brought me here instead!"

Lady Hester, quite bewildered by this recital, sat down a little weakly, and said: "I don't think I *perfectly* understand, Amanda. I expect it is because I am being stupid, but if you could tell it all to me from the start I am persuaded I shall. But not, of course, if you don't wish! I don't care to ask you questions, for there is nothing more disagreeable than to be obliged to listen to questions, and scoldings, and good advice." Her sudden smile, which betrayed a gleam of shy mischief in her eyes, swept across her face.

"You see, I have suffered from that all my life."

"Have you?" said Amanda, surprised. "But you are quite old! I mean," she corrected herself hastily, "you — you are not under age! I wonder you should not tell people who scold you to go about their business."

"I am afraid I have not enough courage," said Hester ruefully.

"Like my aunt," nodded Amanda. "She has no courage, either, and she lets Grandpapa bully her, which puts me out of all patience, because one can always get one's own way, if only one has resolution."

"Can one?" said Hester doubtfully.

"Yes, though sometimes, I own, one is forced to take desperate measures. And it is of no use to tease oneself about propriety," she added, with a touch of defiance, "because it seems to me that if you never do anything that is not quite proper and decorous you will have the wretchedest life, without any adventures, or romance, or *anything!*"

"It is very true, alas!" Hester smiled at her again. "But not for you, I think."

"No, because I have a great deal of resolution. Also I have made a very good plan of campaign, and if you will faithfully promise not to try to overset it, I will tell you what it is."

"I shouldn't think I could overset anyone's plans," said Hester reflectively. "Indeed, I promise I won't try!"

"Or tell those other people?" Amanda said anxiously.

"My family? Oh, no!"

Reassured, Amanda sat down beside her, and for the second time that day recounted the tale of her adventures. Lady Hester sat with her hands lightly clasped in her lap, and her eyes fixed wonderingly on the animated little face beside her. Several times she blinked, and once a little trill of laughter was surprised out of her; but she did not make any comment until Amanda reached the end of her recital, and then she only said: "How very brave you are! I hope you will be able to marry your Brigade-Major, for I am sure you must have been made to be a soldier's wife. I should think, you know, that your grandfather would give his consent if only you could be content to wait for a little while longer."

"I have waited a very long time already, and now I am determined to be married, so that I can accompany Neil to Spain," stated Amanda, looking mulish. "I daresay you think it is very wrong of me, and that I ought to obey Grandpapa, and so it may be — only I don't care for anything except Neil, and I won't go meekly home, whatever anyone says!"

This was uttered very challengingly, but all Hester said was: "It is very difficult to know what would be the best thing to do. Do you think, perhaps, you should send for Neil?"

Amanda shook her head. "No, because he would take me back to Grandpapa, and there's no depending on Grandpapa's being grateful enough to give his consent to our marriage. In fact, he would very likely think I had plotted it all with Neil, which would be fatal! That is what he is bound to think, at the outset, but when he discovers that Neil knows no more than he does where I am, he will see that it is not so. And besides that he will be in a much worse pucker about me, which would be a good thing."

This ruthless speech moved Hester to make a faint protest, but it was cut short by a tap on the door. Povey came in, with a dress of pink silk over her arm, and an expression of long-suffering on her face; and Hester got up, saying: "We are very much of a height, I believe, and I am quite sure that that gown will become you very much better than it becomes me. Will you put it on, and then, if it needs some little adjustment, Povey will arrange it for you?"

Amanda, whose eyes had sparkled at sight of the dress, said impulsively: "Thank you! It is most obliging of you, and exactly the sort of gown I wish for! I have never worn a silk one, because my aunt has the stuffiest notions, and she will not buy anything but muslin for me, even when she took me to the Bath Assemblies."

"Oh, dear!" said Hester, looking conscience-stricken. "She is perfectly right! How shatterbrained of me! Never mind! The dress is not cut very low, and I will lend you a lace shawl to put round your shoulders."

She then drifted away to find the shawl, but before she had reached her own room she heard her name spoken, and turned to see that Sir Gareth had come out of his bed-chamber.

He had changed his driving-dress for knee-breeches and silk stockings, an elegant waistcoat of watered silk, and a swallow-tailed coat of black cloth; and no one, observing the exquisite set of that coat across his shoulders, and the nicety with which his starched neckcloth was arranged, could have supposed that he had effected this transformation with extreme rapidity, and without the assistance of his valet.

He came across the hall, saying, with his delightful smile: "I have been lying in wait for you, hoping to exchange a word with you before we go downstairs again. Has that absurd child told you the truth about herself? I warned her that I should! How good it was of you to accept her without a murmur! But I knew you would. Thank you!"

She returned his smile, but nervously. "Oh, no! Pray do not! There is not the least need — I am only too happy — ! She has told me how she came to meet you. You did very right to bring her here."

"Were you able to discover her name?" he demanded.

"No — but, then, I did not ask her to tell me. I expect she would rather not disclose it."

"I am well aware of that, but this grandfather of hers must be found. Good God, she cannot be permitted to carry out her outrageous scheme!"

"It does seem very hazardous," she agreed.

"Hazardous! Quite foolhardy! With that face, and no more worldly wisdom than a baby, how can she escape running into danger? She is as confiding as a kitten, too. Did she tell you I had abducted her? Well, I might have done so, you know! She hopped up into my curricle in the most trusting way imaginable."

"I expect she knew she could trust you," she replied. "She is quite innocent, of course, but not, I think, stupid. And so courageous!"

He said, after a tiny pause: "Yes — a headstrong courage, an enchanting way-wardness which could so easily be her undo-ing. When I first saw her, I was reminded — I hardly know by what! — the tilt of her chin, perhaps, and a certain look in her eyes —" He broke off, as though he regretted his words.

"I, too," she said, in her quiet voice. "I expect it was that resemblance which drew you to her."

"Perhaps. No, I don't think it was. She was plainly a gently-bred child in difficul-ties: I could do no less than go to the rescue."

"I am afraid she is not very grateful to you," she said, with a glimmer of a smile.

"Not a bit!" he said, laughing. "She has promised to make me very sorry, and I dare-say she'll do it, for she is the naughtiest little wretch I ever encountered. My dependence is on *you!* If you can prevail upon her to disclose her grandfather's name —"

"Oh, but I can't!" she interrupted apologetically. "You see, I promised I wouldn't try to overset her plan of campaign. So even if she were to tell me who she is I couldn't betray her confidence, could I?"

He said, between amusement and exasperation: "In such a case as this? I hope you could, for most certainly you *should!*"

"I think she ought to be allowed to marry her soldier," she said thoughtfully.

"What, at her age to be allowed to throw herself away on a needy young officer, and to undergo all the hardships of a life spent following the drum? My dear Lady Hester, you can have no notion of what it would be like! I am entirely at one with the unknown grandfather on that head."

"Are you?" She looked at him in her shortsighted way, and sighed. "Yes, perhaps. I don't know. What shall you do?"

"If she can't be persuaded to let me escort her to her home, I must find out this Brigade-Major of hers. That should not prove to be a difficult task, but it will mean my posting back to London tomorrow. I see nothing for it but to take her with me, and to place her in my sister's charge. It is really the most abominable coil!"

"Would you like to leave her in my charge?" she asked doubtfully.

117

"Of all things!" he replied. "But I am reasonably certain that she would run away as soon as my back was turned! Nor do I think that your brother and his wife would welcome her as a guest here."

"No," she admitted. She raised her eyes to his face, and said, with an unhappy little smile: "I beg your pardon: I am being so very unhelpful! But I could not compel Amanda to remain here, or, I am afraid, prevent Almeria's saying cutting things to her. Excuse me! I have to fetch a shawl for her to wear!"

"Must you do so immediately?" he asked, putting out his hand. "We have spoken of nothing but Amanda, and it was not, I assure you, to talk about a troublesome schoolgirl that I came to Brancaster."

She seemed to shrink into herself, and said quickly: "It is almost time for dinner! I would so much rather — indeed I must not stay!"

She was gone on the words, leaving him to look after her in some little surprise. He knew her to be very shy, but it was not like her to betray agitation; and he had believed himself to be on such easy terms with her as must preclude her receiving his proposal with embarrassment. But embarrassed she undoubtedly was; and she had certainly shrunk from him. A suspicion that she was being coerced into accepting his offer crossed his mind, and brought a frown into his eyes; but that she meant to refuse it he could not believe, not deeming it possible that Lord Brancaster would have permitted him to come to Brancaster only to be rebuffed.

It was a reasonable belief, and one shared by Mr. Theale; but no sooner had Sir Gareth left the saloon to change his dress than his lordship had exclaimed: "That's knocked everything into horse-nails! What the devil made him bring that chit here? Just when I was in hope Hester meant to have him after all! Depend upon it, she'll shy off!"

"Eh?" said Mr. Theale. "Pooh! Nonsense! She wouldn't be such a fool!"

"You know nothing of the matter!" snapped the Earl. "She never had a grain of commonsense!"

"Lord, Giles, she'd enough to jump at the chance of making such a match! She won't cry off just because Ludlow has a nonpareil in his charge: not the sort of girl to take a pet, though I own I wouldn't have thought Ludlow was the man to do such a daffish thing."

"Well, she didn't jump at the chance!" said the Earl angrily. "Said she didn't wish for the marriage! Almeria thought she would come round to it, but I'll go bail she wasn't bargaining for this mischance!"

"Well, by God!" ejaculated Mr. Theale. "Do you mean to tell me you let the poor fellow come all this way when you ain't sure Hester means to have him? Well, damme, what a backhanded turn to serve him!"

"Oh, stuff!" said Lady Widmore, in her strident voice. "Let him go the right way to work with her, and she'll have him! But I'll see to it that that little baggage is sent packing in the morning! Daughter of some old friends, indeed! Fine friends, to be sending their daughter about the country with no respectable female to look after her! Coming it very much too strong, I make bold to say!"

"I should not have thought it of Ludlow," said her husband. "Who that young female is, or what she is, I do not pretend to know, but I am very much shocked by the whole affair."

"Don't talk like a fool!" said his father irritably. "For anything I know, Ludlow may have half a dozen mistresses in keeping, but if you imagine he would bring some fancy-piece here you must be a bigger bottlehead than ever I guessed! *That* ain't what's worrying me!"

"Well, it ought to worry you," observed his brother. "I'm not a worrying man myself, but if I'd sired such a pea-goose as Widmore it would keep me awake at night, I can tell you that."

This ill-timed facetiousness enraged the Earl so much that he looked to be in danger of bursting several blood-vessels. Before he could command his voice sufficiently to deal with Mr. Theale as he deserved, his daughter-in-law, who had accorded the pleasantry a hearty laugh, intervened, saying: "Now, you hold your tongue, Fabian, do! I know what's worrying you, sir, and small blame to you! If Hetty don't snap Ludlow up while she has a chance to do it, he'll be head over ears in love with that girl, and you may kiss your fingers to him. I don't say she's his mistress, but I'd lay you odds she's up to no good. What's more, she's a beauty — if you like those bold eyes, which, for my part, I don't, though it's easy to see they're exactly to Sir Gareth's taste! Well, what I say is that to set poor Hetty beside *that* bird of paradise is to ruin any chance she might have had!"

The truth underlying these blunt words was forcibly brought home to the company, when, just before dinner was announced, Hester led Amanda into the room.

Had Lady Widmore given way to impulse at that moment, she would have boxed her sister-in-law's ears. One glance at the radiant vision on the threshold was enough to inform her that Hester, like the hen-witted female Lady Widmore had for long considered her to be, had lent one of her own gowns to the interloper. Its rose-pink sheen had never become Hester, but it was fair to say that it might have been created especially to show Amanda off to the best advantage. The chit looked dazzlingly lovely, her great eyes sparkling with pleasure in her first silk gown, her cheeks a little flushed, and her lips just parted in a smile at once shy and triumphant. Small wonder that all the gentlemen were staring at her, like dogs at a marrowbone! thought her ladyship bitterly.

Amanda was in fine fettle, and had been peacocking in front of the mirror for several minutes, admiring herself, and playing at being a grand lady. She expected to stun all beholders by so much magnificence, and she was pleased to perceive that she had done it. A month at Bath had by no means inured her to admiration, but it had taught her a good deal about the ways of fashionable beauties. To Sir Gareth's appreciative amusement, she began to play off all the tricks she had observed, flirting with the fan

Hester had given her, and making shameless use of her brilliant eyes. Nothing, he thought, could more surely have betrayed her extreme youthfulness. She was like a child, allowed to dress-up in her elder sister's clothes, and doing her best to ape the ways of her seniors. He could picture his niece, who always became alarmingly grown-up if ever he took her for a drive round the Park, play-acting in just such a style; and he knew exactly how to apply a damper to spirits mounting too high. Well, if she became too outrageous he would apply that damper; but if she kept within bounds he would let her enjoy herself: it might keep her from hatching plans of escape from him.

At that moment, she caught his eye, and threw him a look so saucy and full of challenge that he nearly laughed out. It was at this precise instant that Mr. Whyteleafe entered the saloon.

Mr. Whyteleafe came prepared to meet Sir Gareth, but he was by no means prepared for Sir Gareth's travelling companion, and the sight of Amanda exchanging what he afterwards described as a very Speaking Look with Sir Gareth held him transfixed for several moments. His startled eyes rolled towards Lady Hester, and she, perceiving him, kindly presented him to Amanda.

Amanda, flattered by the attentions of Mr. Theale, was civil, but unenthusiastic. Clergymen, in her view, were sober persons who almost always disapproved of her; and this one, she thought, wore an even more disapproving expression than the Rector at home. She made no effort to engage him in conversation but turned back to the practised gallantries of Mr. Theale.

Mr. Whyteleafe, who, to do him justice, had no desire to converse with a young female whom he had instantly perceived to be fast, made his way to Lady Widmore's side, and begged her, in an undervoice, to tell him who Amanda might be.

"Don't ask *me!*" she replied, shrugging up her shoulders. "All I can tell you is that Sir Gareth brought her here."

He looked very much shocked, and could not forbear to cast a glance towards Lady Hester. She did not appear to be in any way discomposed, nor did it seem as though she were offended with Sir Gareth. She was, in fact, smiling faintly at him, for he had crossed the room to her side, and had just thanked her for her kindness in providing Amanda with a dress to wear.

"Oh, no! I am so glad I had one that

becomes her so well. How very beautiful she is!"

"Little monkey! You will own, however, that it would be a sin to permit her to cast herself away on her Brigade-Major before she has had a chance to set the town ablaze! Give her a year to find her balance, and I promise you she will."

"Yes, I suppose she would."

"Unconvinced?" he said quizzically.

"I don't know. She is a very unusual girl."

"Yes, something quite out of the ordinary — but too inexperienced yet to settle upon a husband."

She was silent for a moment, her eyes lifted to his profile. He was watching Amanda, but as though he was conscious of Hester's regard, he turned his head, and smiled down at her. "Don't you agree?"

"Perhaps you are right," she said. "Oh, yes, I expect you must be! She will very likely change her mind."

CHAPTER SIX

By the time dinner came to an end, several persons at the table were fully persuaded that however innocent the relationship between Sir Gareth and Amanda might be, Sir Gareth was far more interested in that lively damsel than was at all seemly in one on the verge of proposing marriage to another lady. He was placed between Hester and Lady Widmore, on the opposite side of the table to Amanda, and while he conversed with easy good manners with both of these ladies, it was noticed that his attention was seldom wholly distracted from Amanda. What no one could have guessed from his demeanour was that his interest was not at all pleasurable, or that this informal dinner-party would live in his memory as the most nerve-racking function he had ever attended.

That he must keep a watchful eye on Amanda had been decided at the outset,

when he saw her, after doubtfully considering the wine the butler had poured into her
glass, take a cautious sip. Probably one glass
would do her no harm, but if that fool of a
butler tried to refill it, intervene he must.
She was behaving with perfect propriety,
but she was undoubtedly flown with pink
silk and compliments, and was receiving
every encouragement from Fabian Theale
to overstep the bounds of decorum. Sir Gareth was not particularly acquainted with
Mr. Theale, but he knew him by reputation.
Ten minutes spent in listening with half an
ear to Mr. Theale's conversation confirmed
his belief in all the most scandalous stories
he had heard of that enterprising gentleman, and imbued him with a strong desire
to plant him a flush hit with a right justly
famed in Corinthian circles.

But Amanda was not unacquainted with
middle-aged roués who adopted a fatherly
air in their dealings with her; and Amanda,
however elated, had by no means lost her
head. She was prepared to enjoy to the full
a slightly intoxicating evening undimmed
by the repressive influence of a careful aunt,
but not for one moment did she forget the
end she meant to achieve. She had passed
the entire company under review, and had
rapidly reached the conclusion that the only

possible ally was Mr. Theale. While her face wore an expression of flattering interest in what he said to her, and her pretty lips formed appropriate answers, her brain was busy with the problem of how to turn him to good account.

For his part, Mr. Theale was bent on discovering, before the evening was out, in what relation she stood to Sir Gareth. A worldly man, he agreed with his brother in thinking it in the highest degree unlikely that Ludlow would have brought a little barque of frailty to Brancaster; on the other hand, he could see that Ludlow was keeping a jealous eye on her, and it was entirely beyond his comprehension that he might be doing so from altruistic motives. The story of the relations at Oundle he had disbelieved from the outset; and since, in his experience, no young lady of gentle birth was ever permitted to walk abroad unattended, he was much inclined to think that Amanda was not the schoolroom miss she appeared to be, but, on the contrary, a remarkably game pullet. If that were indeed the case, he would be strongly tempted to take her off Sir Gareth's hands. She was as pretty as she could stare: just the type of ladybird he liked. Young, too, and inexperienced, which would make a pleasant change from the harpy lately living under his protection. Probably she would be grateful for little trumpery gifts, not, like the high flyers, always keeping her fingers crooked into his purse.

These ruminations were interrupted by the departure of the ladies from the dining-room. The cloth was removed, and the decanters set upon the table, but the Earl, contrary to his usual custom, did not encourage his guests to linger over the port. In his opinion, the sooner Sir Gareth was given the opportunity to pop the question to Hester the better it would be. He might not be a paragon amongst fathers, but he was not so improvident as to run the risk of allowing his daughter's suitor to present himself to her in a slightly bosky condition. So, at the end of half an hour, he said that they must not keep the ladies waiting, and rose from the table. He wondered whether it would be well to detach his prospective son-in-law from the rest of the party, and to thrust him and Hester into some room apart, but decided that it would probably be wiser to leave Sir Gareth to make his own opportunity for private speech with Hester. He led the way, therefore, to one of the suite of saloons ranged along the south side of the house. These opened on to a broad terrace, commanding views of the pleasure-gardens, and a small lake; and, since the evening was sultry, the long windows had not yet been closed against the night air.

Strains of Haydn greeted the gentlemen, when the Earl threw open the door into the drawing-room, and Amanda was discovered, seated at the pianoforte, and playing a sonata with considerable verve, if not with strict accuracy.

For this, Lady Widmore had been responsible. Upon first entering the room, she had supposed, with the too evident intention of discomfiting the unbidden guest, that Miss Smith was proficient upon the instrument, and had begged her to indulge her with a little music. As her ladyship was almost tone-deaf, she might have been said to have been rightly served for her malice, since Amanda, instead of being obliged to confess ignorance of an accomplishment indispensable to any female with the smallest claim to gentility, had, in the most complaisant way imaginable, instantly embarked on a very long and dull sonata.

Mr. Theale, sharing her ladyship's dislike of chamber music, and prohibited by his brother's violent disapproval from indulging one of his favourite vices within the walls of Brancaster, slid unobtrusively away to enjoy a cigarillo in the moonlit garden; but the other gentlemen bravely entered the drawing-room, and disposed themselves about it, Mr. Whyteleafe, to the Earl's annoyance, nimbly appropriating a chair at Lady Hester's elbow. Sir Gareth walked over to the window, and stood leaning his shoulders against the frame, his eyes on the fair performer.

"I am at a loss for words," whispered Mr. Whyteleafe, "to convey to you my sentiments upon this occasion, Lady Hester. I can only say that if I am not surprised I am profoundly shocked. *Your* feelings I can readily imagine!"

"Oh, no, I don't think you can," she responded, with a gleam of amusement. "But pray hush! You must not talk just now, you know."

He relapsed into silence, and his resolve to address such words to Lady Hester as must fortify her against the ordeal of having her hand solicited by one whom he clearly perceived to be a libertine of the most unblushing order was frustrated by Lady Widmore, who, as soon as Amanda stopped playing, began at once to make loud plans for the further entertainment of the company, and commanded him to set out a card-table. Breaking in with the rudeness for which she was famed on the compliments being paid to Amanda, she announced that a rubber of casino would be just the thing, adding, with a jolly laugh, as she caught the Earl's starting eye, that she knew better than to expect him or Fabian to take part in this amusement.

"And Hester doesn't care for cards, so if you and Fabian choose to play piquet, as I don't doubt you will, Sir Gareth must entertain her, and that will leave four of us to make up a snug game," she said.

Even her husband, who was inured to her ways, felt that this attempt to provide Sir Gareth with an opportunity to propose to Hester was rather too blatant to be encouraged; and the Earl, mentally apostrophizing her as a cowhanded thruster, considered it enough to put up the backs of both interested parties. While her ladyship bustled about the room, directing the reluctant chaplain where to place the table, and searching for a couple of packs of cards in various chests, both he and Lord Widmore endeavoured to dissuade her from these exertions. Lady Hester, murmuring that she rather thought that the cards had last been used by the nursery party, went away to retrieve them; and Amanda, snatching the chance offered by the preoccupation of her hosts, slipped out on to the terrace, saying in a fierce whisper as she went past Sir Gareth: "I wish to speak to you *alone!*"

He followed her beyond the range of the window, but said, as soon as he came up with her: "Take care, Amanda! You will set the household by the ears by such improper conduct as this. Do remember that you are the daughter of a friend of mine, who is by far too well brought-up to indulge in anything so fast as a tête-à-tête in the moonlight!"

"I am *not* the daughter of any friend of yours, and I have a very good mind to tell Lord Brancaster so!" she said crossly.

"I don't think I should, if I were you. Is that what you wished to tell me?"

"No, it is not!" She paused, and then said airily: "In fact, I don't wish him to know the truth, because it so chances that Lady Hester has very kindly invited me to remain here for a visit, and I have made up my mind to do so."

He laughed. "Have you, indeed?"

"Yes, so you may be quite at your ease, and not tease yourself about me anymore," Amanda said kindly.

"Now, that," said Sir Gareth, much moved, "is a singularly beautiful thought! Tell me, by the way, what put the notion into your head that you had to deal with a flat?"

"I do not understand what you mean," replied Amanda, with dignity.

"A flat, my child, is one who is easily duped."

"Well, I don't think you that, at all events! In fact, quite the reverse, because first you duped me, and then you duped all these people! And if you try to carry me off by force tomorrow, I shall tell Lord Brancaster just how you have deceived him."

"I hope you won't!" he said. "I fear his lordship, whose mind is not elastic, wouldn't believe a word of your story, and then what a pickle we should be in!"

"It was abominable of you to have brought me here!"

"Yes, I fancy that opinion is shared by several other members of the party," he observed. "At least I won't aggravate the offence by leaving you here! No, don't begin scolding again! I know exactly what's in your foolish head: you are bent on giving me the slip, and you know you cannot do it while my eye is upon you, and so you hope to make me believe that you are willing to remain here, like the good little girl you most emphatically are not. But as soon as my back was turned you would be off —

and you may make up your mind to this, Amanda: I may wish you at Jericho, but I am not going to let you escape from me! Yes, I'm well aware that I am a deceiver, an abductor, and wholly contemptible, but really you will be much better off with me than seeking menial employment, for which, believe me, you are not in the least suited! I'll let you scold tomorrow as much as you choose, but in the meantime come back into the drawing-room, and play casino!"

"I won't!" she declared, on an angry sob. "You may tell that odious Lady Widmore that I have the headache! And though you may think you have me in your power, you will find that you have not, and at all events you can't force me to play casino, or any other horrid game."

With these words, she retired to a stone seat at the far end of the terrace, and sat down with her face averted. Sir Gareth, well aware of the folly of arguing with damsels in a passion of fury, left her to sulk herself back to good humour, and strolled into the house again to make her apologies. He also offered to deputize for her at the card-table, but the Earl said hastily: "Pooh! Nonsense! No one wants to play a rubbishy game of casino! Come along to the library: I daresay we shall find my brother there!"

He then drew Sir Gareth out of the room, and was just wondering where the devil Hester had taken herself off to, and why the wretched girl could never be where she was wanted, when she came out of the morning-room on the opposite side of the hall, looking harassed, and saying in a distracted way that she could not imagine what the children had done with the cards.

At any other time the children's fond grandparent would have favoured her with his unexpurgated opinion of persons besotted enough to allow a pack of brats to roam at will over the house, picking up anything that chanced to take their fancy, but on this occasion he refrained, even saying benignly that it was of no consequence. "I'll tell Almeria they can't be found!" he added, with a flash of inspiration, and went back into the drawing-room, and firmly shut the door.

Lady Hester looked after him in helpless dismay, the colour rushing to her cheeks. She glanced deprecatingly at Sir Gareth, and saw that his eyes were brimful of laughter. He said: "Shall we see how many shifts your father and sister-in-law have in store to detach us from the rest of the company? It is extremely diverting, but, for myself, I confess I have been hoping for the opportunity to talk to you ever since I arrived at Brancaster."

"Yes," she said unhappily. "I am aware — I know that it is only right that I should — Oh, dear, I am saying such foolish things, but if you knew how painful it is to me you would forgive me!"

He had taken her hand in his, and he could feel how wildly her pulse was fluttering. He drew her towards the morning-room, and gently obliged her to enter it. It was lit only by an oil-lamp, a circumstance for which Hester disjointedly apologized.

"But, Hester, what is it?" he asked, his eyes searching her face. "Why do you tremble so? Surely you are not shy of me, such old friends as we are!"

"Oh, no! If we can but remain just that!"

"I think you must know that it is my very earnest wish to become more than your friend."

"I do know it, and indeed I am very much obliged to you, and truly sensible of the honour you do me —"

"Hester!" he expostulated. "*Must* you talk such nonsense?"

"Not nonsense! Oh, no! You have paid me a great compliment, and journeyed all this distance, which quite sinks me with shame, for I daresay it was most inconvenient — yet how could I write to you? I am aware that it *should* have been done — it makes it so excessively disagreeable for you! But indeed I told Papa at the outset that I didn't wish for the match!"

He was perfectly silent for a moment, a tiny crease between his brows. Perceiving it, she said despairingly: "You are very angry, and I cannot wonder at it."

"No, I assure you! Only very much disappointed. I had hoped that you and I might have been happy together."

"We should not suit," she said faintly.

"If that were so, it must be my fault — and I would do my best to mend it," he replied.

She looked startled, and exclaimed: "Oh, no! Pray do not — I did not mean — Sir Gareth, indeed you must not press me! I am not the wife for you."

"Of that you must let me be the judge. Are you trying to tell me civilly that I am not the husband for you? But I would do my best to make you happy."

She slid away from the question, saying only: "I don't think of marriage."

He came up to her, and again possessed himself of her hand. "Think of it now! If I don't remotely resemble the man you dreamed you would marry, how many of us marry our dreams? Not many, I think — yet we contrive to be happy."

She said mournfully: "So very few! Alas, my dear friend, *you* did not!"

His clasp tightened on her hand, but he did not answer her immediately. When he spoke again, it was with a little difficulty. "Hester, if you are afraid that — if you are afraid of a ghost — you need not be! It is all so long ago! Not forgotten, but — oh, like a romantic tale, read when one was very young! Indeed, my dear, I haven't come to you, dreaming of Clarissa!"

"I know — oh, I know!" she said, in a shaking voice. "But you don't care for me."

"You are mistaken: I have a very great regard for you."

"Ah, yes! And I for you," she said, with a pitiful attempt at a smile. "I think — I hope — that you will meet someone one day whom you will be able to love with all your heart. I beg of you, say no more!"

"I am not taking my rejection as I should, am I?" he said wryly.

"I am so very sorry! It is dreadfully mortifying for you!"

"Good God, what does that signify? But there is one thing I must say before we leave this. We are such old friends that you will let me speak frankly, I believe. Do you not think that even though we haven't tumbled into love, headlong, as we did when we were very young, we might yet be very comfortable together? If I can't give you romance, there are other things I can give you. No, I don't mean riches: I know they would not weigh with you. But your situation is not happy. Forgive me if this gives you pain! You are not valued as you should be; neither your comfort nor your sensibility is a matter of concern to any member of your family. Indeed, it has frequently seemed to me that your sisters regard you as a convenient drudge! As for your sister-in-law, the tone of her mind is such that I am tolerably convinced that to live under the same roof with her must be a severe penance! Well! I can offer you a position of the first consequence. You would be at no one's beck and call, you would be your own mistress — with a husband who, I promise you, would not make unreasonable demands of you. You may be sure that I should always attend to your wishes, and hold you in respect as well as affection. Would that not mean a happier life than the one you now lead?"

Her face was very white; she pulled her hand away, saying in a stifled voice: "No — *anguish!*"

This seemed so strange a thing for her to have said that he thought he could not have heard her aright. "I beg your pardon?" he said blankly.

She had moved away from him in some agitation, and said now, with her back turned to him: "I didn't mean it — don't heed it! I say such foolish things! Pray forgive me! I am so deeply grateful to you! Your wife will be the happiest of females, unless she is a monster, and I do *hope* you won't marry a monster! If only I could find my *handkerchief!*"

He could not help smiling at this, but he said soothingly: "Take mine!"

"Oh, thank you!" she said, clutching it gratefully, and drying her cheeks with it. "Pray forgive me! I can't think what should possess me to behave like a watering-pot. So inconsiderate of me, when I daresay there is nothing you dislike more!"

"I dislike very much to see you in distress, and still more do I dislike the knowledge that it is my fault."

"Indeed it is not! It is nothing but my own folly, and perhaps being a little tired tonight. I am better now. We must go back to the drawing-room."

"We will do so, but presently, when you are more composed," he replied, pulling forward a chair. "Come, sit down! It won't do for you to show that face to your family,

141

you know." He saw that she was reluctant, and added: "I am not going to say anything to distress you further, I promise you."

She took the chair, murmuring: "Thank you! Is my face quite blotched?"

"A very little: nothing to signify. Are you fixed at Brancaster for the whole summer?"

This calm, conversational gambit did much to restore her tranquillity; she replied with tolerable composure: "No, I shall be visiting my sisters, and one of my aunts. When my brother and his wife remove to Ramsgate, with the children. My little nephew is inclined to be sickly, and it is thought that sea-bathing may be of benefit to him."

They discussed sea-bathing, and childish ailments, until suddenly Hester laughed, and exclaimed: "Oh, how absurd this is! I am very much obliged to you: you have made me quite comfortable again. Is my face fit to be seen? I think we should go back: Almeria is disposed to be uncivil to Amanda, I am afraid, and although I dare-say Amanda is very well able to take care of herself, I do think it would be better that they should not quarrel."

"Undoubtedly! But when I left Amanda she was indulging a fit of the sullens on the terrace, and had no intention of returning to the drawing-room."

"Oh, dear! It will be very awkward if she won't be in the same room with Almeria," said Hester, looking harassed. "You see, I asked her if she would not like to remain with me, instead of seeking employment at an inn — which I *cannot* think at all suitable — and I fancy she will do so."

"So she informed me, but I disbelieved her. Thank you: it was kind of you to invite her, but I wouldn't for the world impose so much upon your good-nature. If she remained with you, which I doubt, she would very soon have the whole house in an uproar. Indeed, I shudder to think of the battle royal which would rage between her and Lady Widmore! You would be utterly crushed between them!"

"I don't suppose I should," she said reflectively. "I find I don't notice things as much as perhaps I ought. I daresay it is through being pretty well accustomed to living with peevish persons. And I have my dogs, you know. Perhaps Amanda would like to have one of Juno's pups. I thought that you wished for one but it turned out otherwise."

"Not at all!" he responded promptly. "I should be delighted to have one of Juno's pups!"

The fugitive smile lit her eyes. "No, you wouldn't. You are not at all the sort of man who would wish to have a pug at his heels. Do you think that Amanda would run away from Brancaster?"

"I am perfectly sure that she would. Not, I fancy, while I am on the premises, for she's no fool, and she must know she could not hope to get more than a mile or two away before I should have overtaken her. She doesn't yet know how far it is to Chatteris, or what coaches go there, or even where to find a convenient carrier, but you may depend upon it that it would not take her long to discover these things. She would then hatch some scheme fantastic enough to baffle all conjecture, and by the time I had returned with her Brigade-Major she would have hired herself out as a washerwoman, or thrown in her lot with a band of gypsies."

"I expect she would like to become a gypsy," agreed Hester, apparently deeming this a reasonable ambition. "But I believe there are none in the neighbourhood just now. Of course, no one could wonder at it if she thought this a sadly dull house, but I do think that she would be more comfortable here than at an inn, particularly if she were employed at the inn in a menial capacity."

He laughed. "Most certainly she would! But she won't care a button for that, you know. I'm afraid the blame is mine: I was foolish enough to tell her that I should discover the Brigade-Major's name and direction at the Horse Guards, which must scotch any hope we might otherwise have nursed of inducing her to remain under your protection. Really, I can't think how I came to be so corkbrained, but the mischief is done now, and the only thing I can do is to carry her to my sister's house."

She got up, making an ineffectual attempt to straighten the lace shawl she wore over her shoulders. Sir Gareth took it out of her hands, and disposed it becomingly for her, which made her say, with a gleam of fun: "Thank you! You see how unhandy I am: I should be *such* a trial to you!"

He smiled, but only said: "You know, Hester, I am very much afraid that your father will be displeased with the outcome of this interview. Is there any way in which I can shield you?"

"Well, you *could* say that it was all a fudge, and what you really wish for is one of Juno's pups," she offered.

"No, that I most assuredly could *not* say!"

"Never mind!" she said consolingly. "I shall be quite in disgrace, I daresay, but it is not of the least consequence. I must find poor Amanda."

"Very well. Unless she has recovered from the sulks, she is seated at the end of the terrace, plotting vengeance on me," he replied, holding open the door for her.

But Amanda was no longer on the terrace. No sooner had Sir Gareth left her than Mr. Theale, an interested and shameless eavesdropper, had risen from the rustic bench immediately below the parapet, where he had been enjoying his cigarillo, and mounted the broad stone steps to the terrace. What he had heard had resolved his doubts: he was now assured that Sir Gareth had had the effrontery to introduce his particular into the chaste precincts of Brancaster Park. Mr. Theale had not previously held him in much esteem, but he was obliged to own now that he had underrated the fellow: such audacity commanded his instant respect. He wondered what peculiar concatenation of circumstances had rendered it necessary for Ludlow to adopt such a desperate course, and reflected that it all went to show how unwise it was to judge a man by the face he showed to the world. One would have supposed Ludlow to be the last man alive to desire a reluctant mistress, yet here he was, plainly determined not to let this little bird of paradise escape him. Mr. Theale sympathized with him, but could not forbear chuckling to himself. He rather fancied that he had the poor fellow at a disadvantage, for however infuriated he might be at having his mistress filched from him he would be obliged to accept the situation with apparent complaisance. Damn it, thought Mr. Theale, he can't so much as mention the matter to me, let alone call me out! I'm poor Hetty's uncle! He may be brazen, but he won't kick up such a dust as that!

Fortified by this conviction, he threw away the butt of his cigarillo, and made his way towards the end of the terrace.

Amanda watched his advance with the light of speculation in her eye. He might be a fat old man, doddering on the brink of the grave, but he was clearly disposed to admire her, and might, with a little ingenuity, be turned to useful account. She smiled upon him, therefore, and made no objection to his seating himself beside her, and taking her hand between both of his.

"My dear little girl," said Mr. Theale, in a voice of fatherly benevolence, "I fear you are in some trouble! Now, I wonder if I might be able to help you! I wish, my dear, that you would confide in me!"

Amanda drew a long breath of sheer ecstasy. Mr. Theale mistook it for a sigh, and patted her hand, saying fondly: "There, there! Only tell me the whole!"

"I am an orphan," said Amanda, adding tragically: "Cast upon the world without the means to support myself!"

"My poor child!" said Mr. Theale. "Have you no kindred to care what becomes of you?"

"No, alas!" said Amanda mournfully.

"Let us take a turn in the garden!" said Mr. Theale, much heartened by this disclosure.

CHAPTER SEVEN

It could not have been said, when Amanda came to the end of her imaginative confidences, that Mr. Theale perfectly understood all the ramifications of her story. Certain features, such as the precise nature of the circumstances which had drawn Sir Gareth into her life, remained obscure, but this did not greatly trouble him. One thing was quite plain to him: Sir Gareth had hideously mangled a promising situation, which, reflected Mr. Theale, was a further example of the unwisdom of trusting to appearances. One wouldn't have suspected that a fellow with such address, and such easy, pleasant manners, would have so grossly mishandled a shy filly whom anyone but a cod's head must have guessed would respond only to a very light hand on the bridle. That Amanda had disliked him from the outset Mr. Theale did not for a moment believe, for the particular story Amanda had selected for his edification was the one she owed to the pen of Mr. Richardson. Sir Gareth had recognized the provenance, and had very unkindly said so; Mr. Theale, whose reading did not embrace the works of novelists admired by his parents, did not recognize it. Broadly speaking, he accepted the story, but the construction he put upon it was scarcely what the fair plagiarist would have desired. No doubt the little lovebird had encouraged the widowed parent of her young mistress to make up to her: probably, thought the cynical Mr. Theale, she had hoped to lure him into proposing marriage. That would account for the apparent inhumanity of the gentleman's sister in turning her out of doors incontinent. Just how much time had elapsed, or what had happened, between this heartless eviction and Amanda's arrival at Brancaster under Sir Gareth's protection, Mr. Theale neither knew nor troubled to discover. She had said that she had met Sir Gareth for the first time on the previous day, but that, naturally, was a lie. Understandable, of course, but Mr. Theale was rather too downy a one to accept it. On his own admission, Sir Gareth had lingered on the road from London. He had pitched them a Canterbury-story about a visit to old friends in Hertfordshire: in Mr. Theale's view, it had been a young friend who had detained him, and had succeeded in fixing his interest so securely that rather than lose her he had adopted the perilous course of bringing her to Brancaster. Mr. Theale considered it a bold stroke, but a trifle harebrained: ten to one that had been when the chit had taken fright. When all was said and done, he thought, preening himself, an experienced man of fifty, even though he had become a little portly, could give Ludlow points, and beat him. A handsome face and a fine figure were very well in their way, but what was needed in this case was delicacy.

Mr. Theale, in the most delicate fashion imaginable, offered Amanda an asylum. He did it so beautifully that even if she had been attending closely to him she must have found it difficult to decide whether he was inviting her to become an inmate of his hunting-box in the guise of a maidservant, or in that of an adopted daughter. In the event, she paid very little heed to his glibly persuasive periods, being fully occupied in considering how, and at what stage of the journey to Melton Mowbray, to dispense with his further escort.

On one point, Mr. Theale failed to re-assure her. So great was her dread of Sir

Gareth that nothing served to convince her that he would not, as soon as her flight was discovered, pursue her relentlessly, probably springing his horses in a very reckless way, and quite certainly, unless she had several hours' start of him, overtaking her, and snatching her back into his power.

"No, no, he won't do that!" Mr. Theale said comfortably.

"Well, I think he will," replied Amanda. "He is determined not to let me escape: he said so!"

"Ay, I heard him," said Mr. Theale, chuckling to himself. "He was bamming you, my dear. The one thing he can't do is to get you away from me. He's been hoaxing you more than you knew. I'll go bail he hasn't told you what brought him here, has he?"

"No," admitted Amanda. "But —"

"Well, he's come to offer for my niece," disclosed Mr. Theale.

"For Lady Hester?" gasped Amanda, roundeyed with surprise.

"That's it. Sets him at a stand. A nice dust there would be if the truth of this business were to become known! Bad enough to have brought you here in the first place. The tale will be that I've taken you to those relations of yours at Oundle. Of course, he'll know I haven't done any such thing, because he knows there ain't any relations at Oundle, but he won't dare say so; and as for trying to get me to hand you over to him — well, if he's got as much effrontery as that, he's got more than any man that ever existed!"

"I think," said Amanda firmly, "that we should fly from this place at dawn."

"No, we shouldn't," replied Mr. Theale, even more firmly. "Not at dawn, my dear."

"Well, very early in the morning, before anyone is out of bed," she conceded.

Mr. Theale, although not addicted to early rising, agreed upon reflection that it would be desirable to have left Brancaster before Sir Gareth had emerged from his bedchamber. He could not be induced to favour so ungoldly an hour as that suggested by Amanda, but after some argument a compromise was reached, and they parted, Mr. Theale repairing to the library, where he was later discovered, apparently sleeping off a liberal potation of brandy; and Amanda seating herself under a fine yew-tree on the lawn. Here she was found by Lady Hester, who begged her to come back into the house before she contracted a chill. Amanda, who had been pondering the astonishing intelligence conveyed to her by Mr. Theale, would dearly have liked to have asked her whether she really was about to become affianced to Sir Gareth. The question was on the tip of her tongue when she reflected that if the story were untrue Lady Hester might be put out of countenance by such a question. In her youthful eyes, Hester was long past the marriageable age, but she approved of her, and was inclined to think that she would be just the wife for a gentleman also stricken in years. The unexpected streak of maturity which underlay her childish volatility made it possible for her to understand, in the light of Mr. Theale's disclosure, the hitherto incomprehensible hostility of Hester's abigail; and although she was not much given to considering any other interests than her own she did feel that it would be a great shame if, through her unwitting fault, the match came to nothing. This led to the comfortable conviction that in leaving Brancaster without the formality of bidding farewell to her kind hostess she was acting almost entirely in Hester's interests. So she accompanied Hester back to the drawing-room with all the good-humour engendered by the agreeable feeling of having decided to adopt a very unselfish course of action. She was only sorry that it was impossible to guess, from either Hester's demeanour or Sir Gareth's, whether they were, in fact, betrothed, or whether the story was nothing but a hum.

An even strong desire to know what had happened in the morning-room burned in the breasts of the other members of the party. Nothing was to be read in either of the principals' countenances, but the Earl, trying unavailingly on several occasions to catch Sir Gareth's eye, was despondent.

It was not until some time after the ladies had retired for the night that the truth was out. Mr. Theale, mounting the stairs on his way to bed, reached the upper hall just as Lady Widmore, her colour considerably heightened, emerged from Hester's room, shutting the door behind her with a distinct slam. Perceiving Mr. Theale, she ejaculated with all the exasperation of one whose worst fears had been realized: "She rejected him!"

"Tell her not to make a cake of herself!" recommended Mr. Theale.

"Lord, do you think I haven't? Mind, I hold him entirely to blame! What possessed the man to bring that girl here?" Mr. Theale closed one eye in a vulgar wink. "You don't say so!" her ladyship exclaimed. "The devil take him! Upon my soul, if that ain't the biggest insult — yes, but she don't believe it, Fabian! That's what puts me out of all patience with her. You needn't doubt I told her there was nothing in it, though from the

way he kept his eyes on the little baggage —
well! But Hester is such a zany! 'Take it from
me, my dear,' I said, 'he's no more in love
with her than Cuthbert is!' And what do
you think she said to that? I declare I could
have boxed her ears! *You* know that way she
has of answering you as though she hadn't
heard above half you had said to her! 'No,'
she said, *'not yet!'* I'm sure I don't know
how I kept my temper, for if there's one
thing I can't abide it's people who go off
into a daze, which, let me tell you, is what
Hester does! *Not yet,* indeed! 'Pray, what do
you mean by that?' I asked her. So then she
looked at me, as if I were a hundred miles
away, and said: 'I think perhaps he will be.'
You know, Fabian, there are times when I
can't but wonder whether she's queer in her
attic! Depend upon it, I told her pretty
roundly that if that was what she thought
she'd best snap the man up before the
mischief was done. All she had to say to that
was that she didn't think she would, for all
the world as though I had offered her a slice
of cake, or some such thing. I've been talking to her for ever, but if she listened to
anything I said it's more than I bargain for!
Well, I've no patience with her, and so I
have told her! To be whistling Ludlow down
the wind at her age, and affairs here in the

case they are, makes me angry enough to burst my stay-laces! He was prepared to come down devilish handsomely, you know. Well, I don't say Hester hasn't often vexed me to death, but I declare I never thought she would behave so selfishly! What his lordship will have to say about it I hope *I* don't have to listen to! I shall have enough to bear from Widmore, for this news will be bound to turn his stomach sour on him, you mark my words if it don't!"

"You know what, Almeria?" interrupted Mr. Theale, a look of profound concentration on his florid countenance. "I believe she has a *tendre* for him!"

Lady Widmore stared at him in contempt and suspicion. "I suppose you are top-heavy," she remarked.

Not for the first time, Mr. Theale wondered what had possessed his nephew to marry this coarse-tongued and unattractive female. "No, I'm not," he said shortly.

"Oh, beg pardon! But what made you say such a daffish thing, if it wasn't brandy?"

"It ain't daffish, but I daresay it may seem so to you. There isn't one of you here who can see what's dashed well under your noses. It occurred to me when I saw Hester look at Ludlow."

"I'll swear she has never given the least

sign of such a thing!" she said incredulously. "What the deuce can you possibly mean?"

"Just a certain look in her eye," said Mr. Theale knowledgeably. "No use asking me to explain it, because I can't, but I'd lay you odds she'd have had him if he hadn't walked in with that little ladybird on his arm."

"I could wring her neck!" exclaimed Lady Widmore, her cheeks reddening angrily.

"No need to do that: I'm going to take her off your hands first thing in the morning. To those relations at Oundle," he added, with another of his vulgar winks.

She regarded him with great fixity. "Will she go with you?"

"Lord, yes! Do anything to get away from Ludlow. The silly fellow seems to have frightened her, poor little soul."

"She! I never saw anyone less frightened in my life!"

"Well, it don't signify. The point is, I'm going to take her away. Ludlow will be obliged to put a good face on it, and I shouldn't be surprised if once Amanda is out of his eye he'll see what a cake he's been making of himself, and try Hester again."

"If he can be persuaded to remain here," she said. "Does he know?"

"Of course he doesn't! Doesn't even know *I'm* leaving tomorrow. I stayed behind after he'd gone up to bed, and told my brother I meant to be off early, and would carry Miss Smith to Oundle."

"What did he say?"

"Didn't say anything, but I could see the notion took very well with him. If you want to be helpful, you'll see to it no one hinders the child from joining me in the morning. I've ordered the carriage for seven o'clock. Breakfast in Huntingdon."

"I'll tell Povey!" said Lady Widmore, a scheming light in her eye. "My woman has been saying that she's as mad as fire with that chit, for coming here and spoiling Hester's chances. Would you believe Hester could be such a ninny? She has invited the wretched wench to remain here for a week! You may lay your life Povey will take care no one stops her from going with you. I suppose there's no fear Ludlow will go after you?"

"Lord, you're as bad as Amanda!" said Mr. Theale impatiently. "Of course there's no fear of it! He'd have to tell the truth about her if he did that, and that's the last thing he's likely to do."

"Well, I hope you may be right. At all events, it will do no harm if Povey tells Hester the girl's still abed and asleep at breakfast-time. I wouldn't put it beyond

159

Hester to *send* Ludlow after her!"

"What the devil should she do that for?" demanded Mr. Theale. "She'll think I'm taking the girl to her relations!"

"I'll do my best to make her think that," retorted Lady Widmore grimly, "but ninny though she may be, she knows you, Fabian!"

He was not in the least offended by this insult, but went chuckling off to bed, where, like Amanda, he enjoyed an excellent night's repose.

They were almost the only members of the party to do so. Not until the small hours crept in did sleep put an end to Lady Hester's unhappy reflections; her father lay awake, first dwelling on her shortcomings, then blaming Sir Gareth for her undutiful conduct, and lastly arguing himself into the conviction that it formed no part of his duty to interfere with whatever plan Fabian had formed; Lady Widmore was troubled by bad dreams; and her husband, as she had prophesied, succumbed to an attack of acute dyspepsia, which caused him to remain in bed on the following day, sustaining nature with toast and thin gruel, and desiring his wife not — unless she wished to bring on his pains again — to mention his sister's name within his hearing.

Lady Widmore was the first person to put

in an appearance at the breakfast-table. She, alone amongst the family, had attended the service Mr. Whyteleafe held daily in the little private chapel. The Earl was always an infrequent worshipper, but it was rarely that Lady Hester rose too late to take part in the morning service. This morning, however, she had been an absentee. Sir Gareth, confidentially informed overnight by his host that the chaplain was employed for the edification of the servants and the ladies of the family, had not felt it to be incumbent upon him to attend either; but he was the second person to enter the breakfast-parlour.

Lady Widmore, after bidding him a bluff good-morning, told him bluntly that she was sorry his suit had not prospered.

"Thank you: I too am sorry," replied Sir Gareth calmly.

"Well, if I were you I wouldn't give up hope," said her ladyship. "The mischief is that Hester's the shyest thing in nature, you know."

"I do know it," said Sir Gareth unencouragingly.

"Give her time, and I dare swear she'll come round!" she persevered.

"Do you mean, ma'am, that she might be scolded into accepting me?" he asked. "I trust that no one will make the attempt, for however much I must hope that her answer to me last night was not final, I most certainly don't wish for a wife who accepted me only to escape from the recriminations of her relatives."

"Well, upon my word!" ejaculated Lady Widmore, her colour rising.

"I know that your ladyship is an advocate of plain speaking," said Sir Gareth sweetly.

"Ay, very true!" she retorted. "So I will make bold to tell you, sir, that it's your own fault that this business has come to nothing!"

He looked coolly at her, a hint of steel in his eyes. "Believe me, ma'am," he said, "though you may be labouring under a misapprehension as little flattering to yourself as it is to me, Lady Hester is not!"

Fortunately, since her temper was hasty, the Earl came in just then, with his chaplain at his heels; and by the time he had greeted his guest, with as much cheerfulness as he could muster, and had expressed the conventional hope that he had slept well, she had recollected the unwisdom of quarrelling with Sir Gareth, and managed, though not without a severe struggle with herself, to swallow her spleen, and to call upon her father-in-law to persuade Sir Gareth not to curtail his visit to Brancaster.

The Earl, while responding with a fair assumption of enthusiasm, privately considered that it would be useless for Sir Gareth to linger under his roof. His daughter, he had decided, was destined to remain a spinster all her days; and he had formed the intention, while shaving, of putting the whole matter out of his mind, and losing no time in repairing to the more congenial locality of Brighton. He had been prepared to perform his duties as a host and a father while Hester mooned about the gardens with her affianced husband, but if this very easy way of entertaining Sir Gareth failed, as fail it assuredly must, he wondered what the devil he was to do with the fellow for a whole week in the middle of July.

"Thank you, sir, you are very good, but I fear it is not in my power to remain," replied Sir Gareth. "I must convey my charge to Oundle — or even, perhaps, back to her parents."

"Oh, there is not the smallest need for you to put yourself about!" struck in Lady Widmore. "Fabian was saying to me last night that he would be pleased to take her up in his carriage as far as to Oundle, for he goes to Melton today, you know, and it will not carry him far out of his way."

"I am very much obliged to him, but must not trespass upon his good-nature," replied Sir Gareth, a note of finality in his voice.

"No such thing!" said Lady Widmore robustly. "It can make no difference to Fabian, and I am sure I know not why you should be dancing attendance upon a schoolgirl, Sir Gareth!"

There was a challenge in her eye, but before Sir Gareth could meet it, Mr. Whyteleafe said with precision: "I must venture to inform your ladyship of a circumstance which cannot but preclude Mr. Theale's being able to offer his services to Miss Smith. Mr. Theale's travelling carriage, closely followed by the coach containing his baggage, passed beneath my window at fourteen minutes past seven o'clock exactly. I am able, I should explain, to speak with certainty on this point because it so chanced that, being desirous of knowing the hour, I was at that instant in the act of consulting my watch."

The Earl had never liked his chaplain, but he had not hitherto considered him actively malevolent. He now perceived that he had been cherishing a viper. Sir Gareth was of course bound to discover the truth, but it had been his lordship's intention to have taken good care that he should not do so in his presence. The more he had considered the matter, the stronger had become his conviction that the disclosure would lead to an awkward scene, and the avoidance of awkward scenes was one of the guiding principles of his life. In an attempt to gloss over the perilous moment, he said: "Yes, yes, now you put me in mind of it, I recall that my brother said he rather thought he should make an early start. Doesn't like travelling in the heat of the day," he added, addressing himself to Sir Gareth.

The door opened, and Lady Hester came into the room. Sir Gareth, as he rose to his feet, pushing back his chair, saw with concern that she was looking pale, and rather heavy-eyed.

"Good-morning," she said, in her soft voice. "I am afraid I am shockingly late this morning, and as for Miss Smith, my woman tells me that she is still asleep."

"Lady Hester, have you yourself seen Amanda?" Sir Gareth asked abruptly.

She shook her head, looking enquiringly at him. "No, I didn't wish to disturb her. Ought I to have? Oh, dear, you don't think she can have — ?"

"Yes, I do think that she can have," said Sir Gareth. "I have just learnt that your uncle left Brancaster two hours ago, and nothing appears to be more likely than that he took Amanda with him."

"Well, what if he did?" demanded Lady Widmore. "Very obliging of him, I should call it, and nothing to make a piece of work about! To be sure, it is excessively uncivil of her to have gone off without bidding anyone goodbye, but I, for one, am not amazed."

"I will go up to her room immediately," Lady Hester said, ignoring her sister-in-law.

She found Amanda's bedchamber untenanted. A note addressed to herself lay on the dressing-table. As she was reading the few lines of apology and explanation, Povey came in, checking at sight of her, and saying in some confusion: "I beg pardon, my lady! I was just coming to see if Miss was awake!"

"You knew, Povey, when you told me that Miss Smith was asleep, that she had left the house," said Hester quietly. "No, do not try to answer me! You have done very wrong. I don't wish to talk to you. Indeed, I don't feel that I shall be able to forgive you."

Povey instantly burst into tears, but to her startled dismay her tenderhearted mistress seemed quite unmoved, leaving the room without so much as another glance thrown in her direction.

Lady Hester found Sir Gareth awaiting

her at the foot of the stairs. She put Amanda's note into his hand, saying remorsefully: "It is just as you suspected. I have been dreadfully to blame!"

"You! No, indeed!" he returned, running his eye over the note. "Well, she doesn't tell you so, but I imagine there is no doubt she went away with your uncle." He gave the note back to her, saying, as he saw her face of distress: "My dear, don't look so stricken! There is not so very much harm done, after all. I own, I wish I knew where Theale is taking her, but I daresay they will not be difficult to trace."

"It is quite *shameful* of Fabian!" she said, in a tone of deep mortification.

He replied lightly: "For anything we yet know she may have prevailed upon him to take her to Oundle, where, I don't doubt, she will try to give him the slip."

"You say that to make me feel more comfortable, but pray don't!" she said. "There can be no excuse for his conduct, and the dreadful thing is that there *never* is! Even if she made him think she indeed had relations at Oundle, he cannot have thought it proper to remove her from Brancaster in such a way. And I very much fear that he has not taken her to Oundle. In fact, it would be much more like him to carry her off to his hunting-box, which I should have no hesitation in saying is what he has done, only that he must know that is the first place where you would look for her."

"Well, if we are to speak frankly of your uncle, I will own that that is precisely what I fear he may have done," said Sir Gareth.

"Oh, yes, pray say what you like! I assure you, none of us would disagree with you, however badly you think of him, for he is almost the most severe misfortune that ever befell us. But it would be quite foolhardy of him to have taken her to Melton Mowbray!"

"I suspect that he thinks I shan't attempt to follow him," replied Sir Gareth dryly. "Your brother and his wife certainly believe me to have brought my mistress to Brancaster, and your uncle's conduct now leads me to suppose that they are not alone in that belief."

"I don't know very much about such matters," said Hester thoughtfully, "but I shouldn't have thought you would do that."

"You may be perfectly sure I would not!"

"Oh, yes, I am! I told Almeria so. I cannot but feel that it would be such a *silly* thing to do!"

"It would also be an extremely insulting thing to do," he said, smiling at her tone of serious consideration. "How Theale came to credit me with so much ill-breeding is something that perhaps he will explain to me presently."

"Well," said Hester, wrinkling her brow, "I think it is just the sort of thing he would do himself, which would account for it. But what has me in a puzzle is why you should think he would not, in that event, expect you to follow him. I should have thought it quite certain you would do so — unless, of course, not pursuing people who steal your mistress is one of those rules of *gentleman*'s etiquette which naturally I know nothing about."

"No," he answered, laughing, "it is not! But if I had been so lost to all sense of propriety as to have brought my mistress with me, when my errand was to beg you to honour me with your hand in marriage, I must indeed have found it an awkward business — to say the least of it! — to recover Amanda from your uncle."

"Yes, so you must!" she agreed, pleased to have the problem elucidated. "Dear me, how excessively shabby of Fabian to try to take advantage of your position! You know, whenever he is in a scrape, one always hopes that he has gone his length, but he seems never to be at a loss to think of something worse to do. How very vexing it is for you!

What shall you do?"

"Try to discover which road he took when he left this house, and go after him. What else can I do? I made myself responsible for Amanda, and although she deserves to be well spanked I can't let her run into mischief that might so easily mean her ruin. I have already desired your butler to send a message to the stables." He held out his hand, and she put hers into it, looking fleetingly up into his face. "I owe you an apology," he said. "Believe me, if I had guessed how troublesome she would be, I would not have burdened you with Amanda." He smiled suddenly. "*One* advantage, however, must have been gained. I was obliged to tell your father the truth — or some part of it, and as he plainly considers me to be touched in the upper works I imagine he will congratulate you on your good sense in refusing to have anything to do with me!"

She flushed, and very slightly shook her head. "Don't let us speak of that! I wish I might be of some assistance to you now, but I cannot think of anything I could usefully do. If Fabian has gone to Melton, he will have taken the road to Huntingdon, because although the more direct way is through Peterborough the road from Chatteris to Peterborough is very narrow and

170

rough, and he will never venture on to it for fear of being made to feel ill. He is a very bad traveller." She paused, and seemed to reflect. "Will you feel obliged to call him out? I don't know what may be the proper thing for you to do, and I don't wish to tease you, but I can't help feeling that it would be more comfortable if you did not."

His lips quivered, but he replied with admirable gravity: "Just so! I shan't go to such desperate lengths as that, and although I own it would give me a good deal of pleasure to draw his cork — I beg your pardon! make his nose bleed! — I daresay I shan't even do that. He is too old, and too fat — and heaven only knows what tale Amanda may have beguiled him with! I only wish I may not figure as the villain of it."

"Now, that," said Hester, roused from her gentle tolerance, "would be really *too* naughty of her, and quite beyond the line of what is excusable!"

He laughed. "Thank you! I must go now. May I write to tell you the outcome of this nonsensical adventure?"

"Yes, indeed, I hope you will, for I shall be very anxious until I hear from you."

He raised her hand to his lips, and kissed it, pressed it slightly, and then released it, and went away up the stairs. Lady Hester remained for a moment or two, staring absently at nothing in particular, before going slowly back into the breakfast-parlour.

CHAPTER EIGHT

The first check to Amanda's new plan of campaign was thrown in the way by Mr. Theale, who disclosed, when midway between Brancaster Park and Huntingdon, that he had ordered his coachman to drive straight through that town to the village of Brampton, where, he said, they would pause for breakfast and a change of horses. He did not tell her that he preferred, on the whole, not to be seen in her company in a town where his was naturally a familiar figure; but was prepared, if questioned, to dilate upon the excellencies of the posting-house at Brampton: a hostelry which had never, as yet, enjoyed his patronage. But she did not question him. Successful generals did not allow their minds to be diverted by irrelevancies: they tied knots, and went on.

The set-back was not as severe as it might have been, had she been still adhering to her plan of seeking employment at one of

173

the town's chief posting-houses. This scheme she had abandoned, knowing that the George, the Fountain, and no doubt the Crown as well, would be the first places where Sir Gareth would expect to find her. But she had ascertained from the obliging Povey that stage-coaches to various parts of the country were to be boarded in Huntingdon, and it had been her intention to have bought herself a ticket on one of these, to some town just far enough away from Huntingdon to have baffled Sir Gareth. A village situated two miles beyond Huntingdon would not suit her purpose at all: it might be hours before a coach passed through it; if she succeeded in escaping from Mr. Theale there, and walked back to Huntingdon, she would run the risk of meeting Sir Gareth on the road, or find, when she reached the coach-office, that he had been there before her, and had directed the clerk to be on the watch for her. Mr. Theale's society, she decided, would have to be endured for rather longer than she had hoped.

How to give Mr. Theale the slip had become the most pressing of the problems confronting her, for however easy a matter it might have been in a busy country-town, it was not going to be at all easy in some small village. Artless questioning elicited the information that the next town on their road was Thrapston, which was some fifteen miles distant from Brampton. Mr. Theale said that by nursing the horses a little they could very well make this their next stage, but Amanda had a lively dread that long before his leisurely carriage, with its odiously conspicuous yellow body, had reached Thrapston, it would be overtaken by Sir Gareth's sporting curricle: and she realized that as soon as she was far enough from Huntingdon she must part company with her elderly admirer.

She would do this without compunction, too, but with a good deal of relief. At Brancaster, fortified by the scarcely acknowledged protection of Sir Gareth in the background, she had thought Mr. Theale merely a fat and foolish old gentleman, whom it would be easy to bring about her thumb; away from Brancaster, and (it must be owned) Sir Gareth's surveillance, although she still thought him old and fat, she found, to her surprise, that she was a little afraid of him. She had certainly met his kind before, but under her aunt's careful chaperonage no elderly and amorous beau had ever contrived to do more than give her hand a squeeze, or to ogle her in a very laughable way. She had classed Mr. Theale with her grandfather's friends, who always petted her, and paid her a great many extravagant compliments; but within a very short time of having delivered herself into his power she discovered that, for all his fatherly manner, he was disquietingly unlike old Mr. Swaffham, or General Riverhead, or Sir Harry Bramber, or even Major Mickleham, who was such an accomplished flirt that Grandpapa scolded him, saying that he was doing his best to turn her head. These senile persons frequently pinched her cheek, or chucked her under the chin, or even put their arms round her waist, and gave her a hug; and old Mr. Swaffham invariably demanded a kiss from her; so why she should have been frightened when Mr. Theale's arm slid round her was rather inexplicable. She had stiffened instinctively, and had had to subdue an impulse to thrust him away. He seemed to want to stroke and fondle her, too, and as her flesh shrank under his hand the thought flashed suddenly into her mind that not even Neil, who loved her, petted her in just such a fashion. Certain of her aunt's veiled warnings occurred to her, and she began to think that possibly Aunt was not quite as foolish and old-fashioned as she had supposed her to be. Not, of course, that she was not well able to take care of herself, or at all afraid of her aged protector: merely, he made her feel uncomfortable, and was such a dead bore that she would be glad to be rid of him.

This desire, however, carried with it no corresponding wish to see those match-bays of Sir Gareth's rapidly overtaking her; and she scarcely knew how to contain her impatience while Mr. Theale, very much at his ease, selected and consumed a lavish breakfast. Her scheme for the subjugation of her grandfather had by this time become entangled with a clenched-teeth determination to outwit and wholly confound Sir Gareth. His cool assumption of authority had much incensed a damsel accustomed all her short life to being tenderly indulged. Only Neil had the right to dictate to her, and Neil never committed the heinous sin of laughing at her. Sir Gareth had treated her as though she had been an amusing child, and he must be shown the error of his high-handed ways. At the same time, he had succeeded in imbuing her with a certain respect for him, so that, although the clock in the inn's coffee-room assured her that it was in the highest degree unlikely that he had yet emerged from his bedchamber, she could not help looking anxiously out of the window every time she heard the sound of an approaching vehicle. Mr. Theale, observing these signs of nervous apprehension, called her a silly little puss, and told her that she would be quite safe in his care. "He won't chase after you, my pretty, and if he did I should tell him to go to the devil," he said, transferring a second rasher of grilled ham from the dish to his plate, and looking wistfully at a cluster of boiled eggs. "No, I shan't venture upon an egg," he decided, with a sigh of regret. "Nothing is more prone to turn me queasy, and though I am in a capital way now, we have a longish journey before us, and there's no saying that I shan't be feeling as queer as Dick's hatband before we come to the end of it."

Amanda, who was breakfasting on raspberries and cream, paused, with her spoon halfway to her mouth, a sudden and brilliant notion taking possession of her mind. "Do you feel unwell in carriages, sir?" she asked.

He nodded. "Always been the same. It's a curst nuisance, but my coachman is a very careful driver, and knows he must let the horses drop into a walk if the road should be rough. Ah, that makes you think me a sad old fogey, doesn't it?"

"Oh, no!" said Amanda earnestly. "Because it is exactly so with me!"

"God bless my soul, is it indeed? Well, we are well suited to one another, eh?" His gaze fell on her brimming plate; he said uneasily: "Do you think you should eat raspberries, my dear? I should not dare!"

"Oh, yes, for I assure you I feel delightfully this morning!" she replied, pouring more cream over the mound on her plate. "Besides, I am excessively partial to raspberries and cream."

Mr. Theale, watching with a fascinated eye, could see that this was true. He hoped very much that Amanda was not misjudging her capacity, but he felt a little anxious, and when, half an hour later, her vivacious prattle became rather forced, he was not in the least surprised. By the time they reached the village of Spaldwick, it had ceased altogether, and she was leaning back against the elegant velvet squabs with her eyes closed. Mr. Theale offered her his vinaigrette, which she took with a faintly uttered word of thanks. He was relieved to see that the colour still bloomed in her cheeks, and ventured to ask her presently if she felt more the thing.

"I feel very ill, but I daresay I shall be better directly," she replied, in brave but faltering accents. "I expect it was the raspberries:

they always make me feel like this!"

"Well, what the devil made you eat them?" demanded Mr. Theale, pardonably annoyed.

"I am so *very* partial to them!" she explained tearfully. "Pray don't be vexed with me!"

"No, no!" he made haste to assure her. "There, don't cry, my pretty!"

"Oh, don't!" begged Amanda, as he tried to put his arm round her. "I fear I am about to swoon!"

"Don't be afraid!" said Mr. Theale, patting her hand. "You won't do that, not while you have such lovely roses in your cheeks! Just put your head on my shoulder, and see if you don't feel better in a trice!"

"Is my face very pink?" asked Amanda, not availing herself of this invitation.

"Charmingly pink!" he asserted.

"Then I am going to be sick," said Amanda, ever fertile of invention. "I *always* have a pink face when I am sick. Oh, dear, I feel quite *dreadfully* sick!"

Considerably alarmed, Mr. Theale sat bolt upright, and looked at her with misgiving. "Nonsense! You can't be sick here!" he said bracingly.

"I can be sick *anywhere!*" replied Amanda, pressing her handkerchief to her lips, and achieving a realistic hiccup.

"Good God! I will stop the carriage!" exclaimed Mr. Theale, groping for the check-cord.

"If only I could lie down for a little while, I should be perfectly well again!" murmured the sufferer.

"Yes, but you can't lie down by the roadside, my dear girl! Wait, I'll consult with James! Stay perfectly quiet — take another sniff at the smelling-salts!" recommended Mr. Theale, letting down the window, and leaning out to confer with the coachman, who had pulled up his horses, and was craning round enquiringly from the box-seat.

After a short and somewhat agitated colloquy with James, Mr. Theale brought his head and shoulders back into the carriage, and said: "James reminds me that there is some sort of an inn a little way farther along the road, at Bythorne — only a matter of a couple of miles! It ain't a posting-house, but a decent enough place, he says, where you could rest for a while. Now, if he were to drive us there very slowly —"

"Oh, thank you, I am so much obliged to you!" said Amanda, summoning up barely enough strength to speak audibly. "Only perhaps it would be better if he were to drive us there as fast as he can!"

Mr. Theale had the greatest dislike of being hurtled over even the smoothest road, but the horrid threat contained in these sinister words impelled him to put his head out of the window again, and to order the coachman to put 'em along.

Astonished, but willing, James obeyed him, and the carriage was soon bowling briskly on its way, the body swaying and lurching on its swan-neck springs in a manner fatal to Mr. Theale's delicate constitution. He began to feel far from well himself, and would have wrested his vinaigrette from Amanda's hand had he not feared that to deprive her of its support might precipitate a crisis that could not, he felt, be far off. He could only marvel that she had not long since succumbed. Every time she moaned he gave a nervous start, and rolled an anxious eye at her, but she bore up with great fortitude, even managing to smile, tremulously but gratefully, when he assured her that they only had a very little way to go.

It seemed a very long way to him, but just as he had decided, in desperation, that he could not for another instant endure the sway of the carriage, the pace slackened. A few cottages came into view; the horses dropped to a sober trot; and Mr. Theale said, on a gasp of relief: "Bythorne!"

Amanda greeted Bythorne with a low moan.

The carriage came to a gentle halt in front of a small but neat-looking inn, which stood on the village street, with its yard behind it. The coachman shouted: "House, there!" and the landlord and the tapster both came out in a bustle of welcome.

Amanda had to be helped down from the carriage very carefully. The landlord, informed tersely by James that the lady had been taken ill, performed this office for her, uttering words of respectful encouragement, and commanding the tapster to fetch the mistress to her straight. Mr. Theale, much shaken, managed to alight unassisted, but his usually florid countenance wore a pallid hue, and his legs, in their tight yellow pantaloons, tottered a little.

Amanda, supported between the landlord and his stout helpmate, was led tenderly into the inn; and Mr. Theale, recovering both his colour and his presence of mind, explained that his young relative had been overcome by the heat of the day and the rocking of the carriage. Mrs. Sheet said that she had frequently been taken that way herself, and begged Amanda to come and have a nice lay down in the best bedchamber. Mr. Sheet was much inclined to think that a drop of brandy would put the young lady into prime twig again; but Amanda, bearing up with great courage and nobility, said in a failing voice that she had a revivifying cordial packed in one of her boxes. "Only I cannot remember in which," she added prudently.

"Let both be fetched immediately!" ordered Mr. Theale. "Do you go upstairs with this good woman, my love, and I warrant you will soon feel quite the thing again!"

Amanda thanked him, and allowed herself to be led away; whereupon Mr. Theale, feeling that he had done all that could be expected of him, retired to the bar-parlour to sample the rejected brandy. Mrs. Sheet came surging in, some twenty minutes later, bearing comfortable tidings. In spite of the unaccountable negligence of the young lady's abigail, in having omitted to pack the special cordial in either of her bandboxes, she ventured to say that Miss was already on the high road to recovery, and, if let to lie quietly in a darkened room for half an hour or so, would presently be as right as a trivet. She had obliged Miss to drink a remedy of her own, and although Miss had been reluctant to do so, and had needed a good deal of urging, anyone could see that it had already done much to restore her.

Mr. Theale, who was himself sufficiently restored to have lighted one of his cigarillos, had no objection to whiling away half an hour in a snug bar-parlour. He went out to direct James to stable his horses for a short time; and while he was jealously watching James negotiate the difficult turn into the yard behind the inn, the coach which carried his valet and his baggage drove up. Perceiving his master, the valet shouted to the coachman to halt, and at once jumped down, agog with curiosity to know what had made Mr. Theale abandon the principles of a lifetime, and spring his horses on an indifferent road. Briefly explaining the cause, Mr. Theale directed him to proceed on the journey, and, upon arrival at the hunting-box, to see to it that all was put in readiness there for the reception of a female guest. So the coach lumbered on its way, and Mr. Theale, reflecting that the enforced delay would give his housekeeper time to prepare a very decent dinner for him, retired again to the bar-parlour, and called for another noggin of brandy.

Meanwhile, Amanda, left to recover on the smothering softness of Mrs. Sheet's best feather-bed, had nipped up, scrambled herself into that sprig-muslin gown which Povey had so kindly washed and ironed for her, and which the inexorable Mrs. Sheet had obliged her to put off, and had tied the hat of chip-straw over her curls again. For several hideous minutes, after swallowing Mrs. Sheet's infallible remedy for a queasy stomach, she had feared that she really was going to be sick, but she had managed to overcome her nausea, and now felt ready again for any adventure. Mrs. Sheet had pointed out the precipitous back-stairs to her, which reached the upper floor almost opposite to the door of the best bedchamber, and had told her that if she needed anything she had only to open her door, and call out, when she would instantly be heard in the kitchen. Amanda, having learnt from her that the kitchen was reached through the door on the right of the narrow lobby at the foot of the stairs, the other door giving only on to the yard, had thanked her, and reiterated her desire to be left quite alone for half an hour.

In seething impatience, and peeping through the drawn blinds, she watched Mr. Theale's conferences with James, and with his valet. When she judged that James had had ample time in which to stable his horses, and, like his master, seek solace in the inn, she fastened her cloak round her neck, picked up her bandboxes, and

186

emerged cautiously from the bedchamber. No one was in sight, and, hastily concocting a story moving enough to command Mrs. Sheet's sympathy and support, if, by ill-hap, she should encounter her on her perilous way to that door opening on to the yard, she began to creep circumspectly down the steep stairs. A clatter of crockery, and Mrs. Sheet's voice upraised in admonition to some unknown person, apparently engaged in washing dishes, indicated the position of the kitchen. At the foot of the stairs a shut door promised egress to the yard. Drawing a deep breath, Amanda stole down the remaining stairs, gingerly lifted the latch of the door, and whisked herself through the aperture, softly closing the door behind her. As she had expected, she found herself in the yard. It was enclosed by a rather ramshackle collection of stables and outhouses, and paved with large cobbles. Pulled into the patch of shade thrown by a large barn stood the yellow-bodied carriage; and, drawn up, not six feet from the backdoor of the inn, was a farm-tumbril, with a sturdy horse standing between its shafts, and a ruddy-face youth casting empty sacks into it.

Amanda had not bargained for this bucolic character, and for a moment she hesitated, not quite knowing whether to advance, or to draw back. The youth, catching sight of her, stood staring, allowing both his jaw, and the empty crate he was holding, to drop. If Amanda had been unprepared to see him, he was even more unprepared to see her, emerging from the Red Lion, such a vision of beauty as she presented to his astonished gaze.

"Hush!" commanded Amanda in a hissing whisper.

The youth blinked at her, but was obediently silent.

Amanda cast a wary look towards the kitchen-window. "Are you going to take that cart away?" she demanded.

His jaw dropped lower; he nodded.

"Well, will you let me ride in it, if you please?" She added, as she saw his eyes threaten to start from their sockets: "I am escaping from a Deadly Peril! Oh, pray make haste, and say I may go in your cart!"

Young Mr. Ninfield's head was in a whirl, but his mother had impressed upon him that he must always be civil to members of the Quality, so he uttered gruffly: "You're welcome, miss."

"Not so loud!" begged Amanda. "I am very much obliged to you! How shall I climb into it?"

Young Mr. Ninfield's gaze travelled slowly from her face to her gown of delicate muslin. "It ain't fitting!" he said, in a hoarse whisper. "There's been taties in it, and a dozen pullets, and a couple o'bushels o' kindling!"

"It doesn't signify! If you could lift me into it, I can cover myself with those sacks, and no one will see me. Oh, pray be quick! The case is quite *desperate! Can't* you lift me?"

The feat was well within Mr. Ninfield's power, but the thought of picking up this fragile beauty almost made him swoon. However, she seemed quite determined to ride in his cart, so he manfully obeyed her. She was feather-light, and smelled deliciously of violets. Mr. Ninfield, handling her with all the caution he would have expended on his mother's best crockery, suffered another qualm. "I don't like to!" he said, holding her like a baby in his muscular arms. "You'll get your pretty dress all of a muck!"

"Joe!" suddenly called Mrs. Sheet, from within the house. *"Joe!"*

"Quickly!" Amanda urged him.

Thus adjured, Mr. Ninfield gave a gulp, and tipped her neatly into the cart, where she instantly lay down on the floor, and became screened from his bemused gaze by the sides of the cart.

"The pickled cherries for your ma, Joe!" screeched Mrs. Sheet from the kitchen-window. "If I hadn't well-nigh forgot them! Wait, now, till I fetch the jar out to you!"

"Do not betray me!" Amanda implored him, trying to pull the empty sacks over herself.

Mr. Ninfield was astonished. Mrs. Sheet, besides being a lifelong crony of his mother's, was his godmother, and he had always looked upon her as a kindly and benevolent person. As she came out into the yard, he almost expected to find that she had undergone a transformation, and was relieved to see that her plump countenance was still as good-natured as ever. She handed a covered jar to him, bidding him take care to keep it the right way up. "And mind you give my love to your ma, and thank her for the eggs, and tell your pa Sheet would have settled for the kindling, and that, only that he's serving a gentleman," she said. "We've got Quality in the house: a very fine-seeming gentleman, and the prettiest young lady you ever did see! Likely she's his niece. Poor lamb, she was took ill in the carriage, and is laid down in my best chamber at this very moment."

Mr. Ninfield did not know what to reply to this, but as he was generally inarticulate his godmother set no particular store by his silence. She gave him a resounding kiss, repeated her injunction to take care of the pickled cherries, and went back into the house.

Mr. Ninfield picked up the empty crate, and peeped cautiously over the side of the cart. From its floor a pair of bright, dark eyes questioned him. "Has she gone?" whispered Amanda.

"Ay."

"Then pray let us go too!"

"Ay," said Mr. Ninfield again. "I'll have to put this crate in — if convenient, miss."

"Yes, pray do so! And I will hold the jar for you," said Amanda obligingly.

Matters being thus satisfactorily arranged, Mr. Ninfield went to the horse's head, and began to lead the placid animal out of the yard, on to the road. The wheels of the cart being shod with iron, Amanda was considerably jolted, but she made no complaint. The horse plodded along the road in a westerly direction, Mr. Ninfield walking beside it, pondering deeply the extraordinary adventure that had befallen him. His slow but profound cogitations caused him, at the end of several minutes, to say suddenly: "Miss!"

"Yes?" replied Amanda.

"Where would you be wishful I should take you?" enquired Mr. Ninfield.

"Well, I am not perfectly sure," said Amanda. "Is there anyone in sight?"

"No," replied Mr. Ninfield, having stared fixedly up and down the road for a moment or two.

Reassured on this point, Amanda knelt up, and looked down at her rescuer over the side of the cart. "Where are you going yourself?" she asked chattily.

"Back home," he replied. "Leastways —"

"Where is your home? Is it on this road?"

He shook his head, jerking his thumb towards the south. "Whitethorn Farm," he explained laconically.

"Oh!" Amanda looked thoughtfully at him, considering a new scheme. A slow tide of bashful crimson crept up to the roots of his hair; he smiled shyly up at her, and then looked quickly away, in case she should be affronted. But the smile decided the matter. "Do you live there with your mother?" asked Amanda.

"Ay. And me dad. It's Dad's farm, and Granfer's afore him, and me great-granfer's afore *him*," he said, becoming loquacious.

"Would your mother let me stay there for a little while, do you think?"

This brought his head round again. He had not the smallest notion of what his mother's views might be, but he said ecstatically: "Ay!"

"Good!" said Amanda. "It so happens that I never thought of it before, but I now see that the thing for me to do is to become a dairymaid. I should like it of all things! I daresay you could teach me how to milk a cow, couldn't you?"

Mr. Ninfield, dazzled by the very thought of teaching a fair princess to milk a cow, gulped, and uttered once again his favourite monosyllable: "Ay!" He then fell into a daze, from which he was recalled by the sight of an approaching vehicle. He pointed this out to Amanda, but she had seen it already, and had disappeared from view. He gave it as his opinion that she had best remain hid until they reached the lane leading, by way of the village of Keyston, to Whitethorn Farm. Fortunately, since she found it extremely uncomfortable to crouch on the floor of the cart, this was not very far distant. As soon as Mr. Ninfield told her that they had left the post-road, she bobbed up again, and desired him to lift her down, so that she could ride on the shaft, as he was now doing.

"For it smells of hens on the floor," she

193

informed him, "besides being very dirty. Do you think your mother would be vexed if we ate some of these pickled cherries? I am excessively hungry!"

"No," said Mr. Ninfield, for the second time recklessly committing his parent.

CHAPTER NINE

At the end of half an hour Mr. Theale consulted his watch. He thought that he would give Amanda a little longer, and took himself and his cigarillo out on to the road. There was nothing much to be seen there, and after strolling up and down for a few minutes he went back into the inn, where the landlord met him with the offer of a slice or two of home-cured ham, by way of a nuncheon. It was not yet noon, but Mr. Theale had partaken of breakfast at an unwontedly early hour, and the suggestion appealed strongly to him. He disposed of several slices of ham, followed these up with a generous portion of cheese, dug from the centre of a ripe Stilton, and washed down the whole with a large tankard of beer. He then felt fortified against the rigours of travel, and, as Amanda had still not re-appeared, requested Mrs. Sheet to step upstairs to see how she did.

Mrs. Sheet climbed laboriously up the stairs, but soon came back again, to report that the young lady was not in the best bedchamber.

"Not there?" repeated Mr. Theale incredulously.

"Happen she's in the coffee-room, sir," said Mrs. Sheet placidly.

"She ain't there," asserted the landlord. "Stands to reason she couldn't be, because his honour's been eating a bite of ham there this half hour past. I daresay she stepped out for a breath of fresh air while you was eating your nuncheon, sir."

Mr. Theale felt that this was unlikely, but if Amanda was not in the Red Lion there seemed to be no other solution to the mystery of her disappearance, and he again stepped out on to the road, and looked up and down it. There was no sign of Amanda, but Mr. Sheet, who had followed him out of the inn, thought that very likely she had been tempted to explore the spinney that lay just beyond the last straggling cottages of the village. Sir Gareth would not have wasted as much as five minutes in hunting for Amanda through a spinney, but Mr. Theale, as yet unacquainted with her remarkable propensity for running away, supposed that it was just possible that she had walked out for a stroll, as he himself had done earlier. No doubt, with the sun beating down upon the road, she had not been able to resist entering the spinney. It was thoughtless of her, and, indeed, decidedly vexatious, but young persons, he believed, were irresistibly drawn by woodland, and had, besides, very little regard for the clock. He walked down the road until he came abreast of the spinney, and shouted. When he had done that several times, he swore, and himself entered the spinney through a gap in the hedge. A track wound through the trees, and he went down it for some distance, shouting Amanda's name at intervals. It was not as hot under the trees as on the sun-scorched road, but quite hot enough to make a full-bodied gentleman, clad in a tightly fitting coat, and with a voluminous neckcloth swathed in intricate folds under his chin, sweat profusely. Mr. Theale mopped his face, and realized with annoyance that the high, starched points of his collar had begun to wilt. He also realized, although with some incredulity, that Amanda had given him the slip; but why she had done so, or where she could be hiding, he could not imagine. He retraced his steps, and as he plodded up the dusty road the disquieting suspicion entered his head that she was not, after all, a member of the muslin company, but in truth the innocent child she looked to be. If that were so, her desire to escape from Sir Gareth's clutches (and, indeed, his own) was very understandable. No doubt, thought Mr. Theale, virtuously indignant, Sir Gareth had encountered her after her expulsion from her amorous employer's establishment, and had taken dastardly advantage of her friendless, and possibly penniless, condition. Mr. Theale's morals were erratic, but he considered that such conduct was beyond the line of what was allowable. It was also ramshackle. Deceiving innocent damsels, as he could have told Sir Gareth from his own experience, invariably led to trouble. They might appear to be alone in the world, but you could depend upon it that as soon as the mischief was done some odiously respectable relative would come to light, which meant the devil to pay, and no pitch hot.

This reflection brought with it certain unwelcome memories, and made Mr. Theale feel that to abandon Amanda to her fate, which had at first seemed the most sensible thing to do, would perhaps be unwise. Since she knew his name, it would be prudent to recapture her, for heaven alone knew what sort of account she might spread of the day's events if he was unable to convince her that his interest in her had all the time been purely philanthropic. That could quite easily be done, given the opportunity. The thing to do then, he decided, would be to deliver her into his housekeeper's charge, and to leave it to that capable matron to discover what family she possessed. Of course, if she really had no relations living, and seemed inclined, once her alarm had been soothed, to take a fancy to him — But that was for the future. The immediate task was to find her, and that, in so small a village, ought not to be very difficult.

Mr. Theale, arrived once more at the Red Lion, proceeded to grapple with the task. It proved to be fatiguing, fruitless, and extremely embarrassing. Mrs. Sheet, on thinking the matter over, had remembered the bandboxes. It was just conceivable, though very unlikely, that Amanda had wandered out to take the air, and had contrived to lose herself; that she had burdened herself with two bandboxes for a country stroll was quite inconceivable, and indicated to Mrs. Sheet not a stroll but a flight. And why, demanded Mrs. Sheet of her lord, should the pretty dear wish to run away from her lawful uncle?

Mr. Sheet scratched his head, and admitted that it was a regular doubler.

"Mark my words, Sheet!" she said. "He's no more her uncle than what you are!"

"He never said he was her uncle," Mr. Sheet pointed out. "All he said was that she was a young relative of his."

"It don't signify. It's my belief he's no relation at all. He's a wolf in sheep's clothing."

"He don't *look* like one," said the landlord dubiously.

"He's one of those seducing London beaux," insisted his wife. "He's got a wicked look in his eye: I noticed it straight off. Them bandboxes, too! I thought it was queer, a young lady not having what I'd call respectable luggage."

"The luggage was on the other coach," argued the landlord.

"Not hers, it wasn't," replied Mrs. Sheet positively. "She had all her things packed into those two boxes, for I saw them with my own eyes. Lor' bless me, why ever didn't she tell me my fine gentleman was making off with her unlawful? I wish I knew where she was got to!"

But no efforts of hers, or of Mr. Theale's, could discover the least trace of Amanda. She had apparently been snatched up into the clouds, for no one in the village had seen her, and no one could recall that any of the vehicles which had passed through it had halted to pick up a passenger. Mr. Theale was forced, in the end, to accept the landlord's theory, which was that Amanda had slipped unperceived up the road, and had been picked up beyond the village by some carriage or stage-coach. Mrs. Sheet clicked her tongue disapprovingly and shook her head; but since it would never have occurred to her that a young lady of undoubted quality, dressed, too, in the first style of elegance, would have sought refuge in a farm-tumbril, the suspicion that Joe Ninfield might be able to throw light on the mystery never so much as entered her mind. And if it had entered it, she would have dismissed it, because she knew that Joe was a shy, honest lad, who would never dream either of deceiving his godmother, or of taking up with a strange girl who was plainly a lady born.

Mr. Theale was forced to continue his journey alone; and by the time he climbed into his carriage again, not only was he exhausted by his exertions, but he was as much ruffled as it was possible for a man of his temperament to be. His enquiries in Bythorne awoke a most unwelcome curiosity in its inhabitants' breasts; and although Mr. Sheet continued to treat him with proper deference it was otherwise with the redoubtable mistress of the house, who made no attempt to conceal her unflattering opinion of him. Lacking the inventive genius which characterized Amanda, he was quite unable to offer Mrs. Sheet an explanation which carried conviction even to his own ears; and an attempt to depress her presumption merely provoked her into favouring him with her views on so-called gentlemen who went ravening about the country, dressed up as fine as fivepence, the better to deceive the innocent maidens they sought to ruin.

It was some time before his spirits recovered their tone. The wooden countenance of his coachman did nothing to allay the irritation of his nerves. Mr. Theale cherished few illusions, and he was well aware that James had not only heard every word of Mrs. Sheet's homily, but would lose no time in regaling his fellow-servants with the tale of his master's discomfiture. James would have to be sent packing, which was as vexatious as anything that had happened during this disastrous day, since no other coachman had ever suited him half as well. Moreover, so many hours had been squandered that it was now doubtful whether he would reach Melton Mowbray that evening. The moon was at the full, but although moonlight would enable him to continue his journey far into the night, it would not save from being spoiled the excellent dinner that would certainly be prepared for his delectation, or prevent his becoming fagged to death. He was much inclined to think that if only he had not directed his valet to drive on he would have spent the night at Oakham, where, at the Crown, he was well-known, and could rely upon every attention's being paid to his comfort. But his valet and his baggage were gone past reclaim, and the only piece of luggage he carried with him was his dressing-case.

He was still trying to decide, four miles beyond Thrapston, what would be best to do, when Fate intervened, and settled the question for him: the perch of the carriage broke, and the body fell forward on to the box.

Although considerably shaken, Mr. Theale was not much hurt by this accident. Its worst feature was the necessity it put him under of trudging for nearly a mile to the nearest inn. This was at the village of Brigstock, and was a small posting-house, too unpretentious to have hitherto attracted Mr. Theale's patronage. His intention was to hire a post-chaise there, but so snug did he find its parlour, so comfortable the winged chair into which the landlord coaxed him, so excellent the brandy with which he strove to recruit his strength, and so tempting the dinner that was offered him, that he very soon abandoned all idea of proceeding any farther on his journey that day. After the cavalier treatment he had been subjected to by Mrs. Sheet, the solicitude of the host of the Brigstock Arms came as balm to his bruised spirit. Besides, his natty boots were pinching his feet, and he was anxious to have them pulled off. The landlord begged him to accept the loan of a pair of slippers, promised that a night-shirt and cap should be forthcoming, and assured him that nothing would give his good wife more pleasure than to launder his shirt and neckcloth for him while he slept. That clinched the matter: Mr. Theale graciously consented to honour the house with his custom, and stretched out a plump leg to have the boot hauled off. Once rid of Hessians which were never made for country walking, he began to revive, and was able to devote a mind undistracted by aching feet to the important question of what dishes to select for his dinner. Encouraged and assisted by the landlord, he ordered a delicate yet sustaining meal to be prepared, and settled down to enjoy the healing properties of cigarillos, a comfortable chair, and a bottle of brandy.

It was not long before a gentle sense of well-being began to creep over him; and then, just as he was wondering whether to light another cigarillo, or to take a nap before his dinner, his peace was shattered by the purposeful entry into the parlour of Sir Gareth Ludlow.

Mr. Theale was astonished. He had to blink his eyes several times before he could be sure that they had not deceived him. But the newcomer was certainly Sir Gareth, and, from the look on his face, he seemed to be in a thundering rage. Mr. Theale noticed this fleetingly, but his interest was claimed by something of greater importance. Sir Gareth's blue coat was protected from the dust by a driving coat of such exquisite cut that it held Mr. Theale entranced. None knew better than he how seldom a voluminous coat with several shoulder-capes showed a man off to advantage, or how often it made him appear to be as broad as he was long. Sir Gareth, of course, was helped by his height, but the excellence of his figure could not wholly account for the graceful set of the folds that fell almost to his ankles, or for the precision with which half a dozen or more capes were graduated over his shoulders.

"Who," demanded Mr. Theale reverently, "made that coat for you?"

Sir Gareth had endured a wearing and an exasperating day. It had not been difficult to trace Mr. Theale to Brampton, although a good deal of time had been wasted in seeking news of him in all the inns with which Huntingdon was too liberally provided. It had been after Brampton that the trail had become confused. That he had continued along the road which ran from Ely to Kettering was established by one of the ostlers at Brampton, but at Spaldwick, where, after studying his road-book, Sir Gareth expected to hear that he had stopped for a change, no one seemed to have seen him. That indicated that he had made Thrapston his first change, for there was no other posting-house to be found on that stretch of the road. At the next pike, the keeper rather thought that he had opened to three, or maybe four, yellow-bodied carriages, one of which, unless he was confusing it with a black chaise with yellow wheels, had turned northward into the lane which bisected the post-road. Sir Gareth, after a glance at his map, decided not to pursue this, for it led only to a string of tiny villages. A mile farther on, another, and rather wider, lane offered the traveller a short cut to Oundle, and here Sir Gareth halted to make enquiries, since it was possible, though unlikely, that Oundle was Mr. Theale's direction. He could not discover that any yellow-bodied carriage had turned into the lane that morning, but a sharp-eyed urchin volunteered the information that he had seen just such a turn-out, closely followed by a coach with trunks piled on the roof, driving along towards Thrapston a couple of hours back. There could be no doubt that this was Mr. Theale's cortège, and Sir Gareth, after suitably rewarding his informant, drove on, confident that he would glean certain tidings of the fugitives at one of Thrapston's two posting-houses. He swept through Bythorne, never dreaming that the carriage he was chasing was at that moment standing in the yard behind the modest little inn, with its shafts in the air.

Thrapston lay only four miles beyond Bythorne, and was soon reached, but neither at the White Hart nor at the George could Sir Gareth discover any trace of his quarry. Mr. Theale was perfectly well-known at both these inns, and landlords and ostlers alike stated positively that he had not been seen in the town for several months.

It seemed so incredible that Mr. Theale should not have changed horses in Thrapston that Sir Gareth had wondered if he could have bribed all these persons to cover his tracks. But those whom he questioned were so plainly honest that he dismissed the suspicion, inclining rather to the theory that just as he had chosen to stop in Brampton instead of Huntingdon, so too had Mr. Theale preferred to pause for the second change of horses at some house beyond a town where his was a familiar figure. On the road which ran through Corby, Uppingham, and Oakham to Melton Mowbray there appeared to be, on the outskirts of Thrapston, a suburb, or a village, called Islip. Stringent enquiry dragged from the landlord of the George the admission that a change of horses *could* be obtained there — by such gentlemen as were not overparticular.

Meanwhile, Sir Gareth's own pair, carefully though he had nursed them, were spent, and must be stabled. It was not his practice to leave his blood-cattle in strange hands, so when Trotton heard him issuing instructions at the George on the treatment the bays were to receive, and was himself ordered to see them properly bestowed, and realized that he was not to be left in charge of them, he knew that his master's must indeed be a desperate case.

Sir Gareth, driving a pair of job horses, drew a blank at Islip, and another at Lowick. He then struck eastward, reaching, by way of an abominable lane, the road that linked Thrapston to Oundle. Here he was similarly unsuccessful, and broke back to the road that led to Kettering. Nowhere had anyone seen a yellow-bodied carriage, followed by a coach laden with baggage. He drove back to Thrapston, and, convinced in spite of all discouragement that Mr. Theale was heading for the neighbourhood of Melton Mowbray, once more drove out of the town in that direction. How Mr. Theale's coachman could have contrived, on such a sweltering day, to have pushed his horses beyond Islip he knew not, but that the yellow-bodied carriage had taken the road to Melton Mowbray he was certain. And he was perfectly right, as he knew, as soon as he came upon the derelict, a mile short of Brigstock.

There was considerable cause for satisfaction in this, but Sir Gareth had been driving all day, and he had eaten nothing since his interrupted breakfast at Brancaster. By the time he arrived at the Brigstock Arms he was holding his temper on a tight rein; and when he entered the parlour to find Mr. Theale lounging at his ease, with a bottle at his elbow, and his slippered feet on a stool, an impulse surged up within him to pluck that conscienceless hedonist out of his chair with one hand for the simple purpose of sending him to grass with one scientifically placed punch from the other. Indeed, it had already formed itself into a fist when Mr. Theale spoke.

Mr. Theale's words gave Sir Gareth pause. He stood looking contemptuously down at him, his right hand unclenching as he recognized his condition. It would have been unjust to have described Mr. Theale as drunk. It was his boast that no one had seen him deep-cut since the days of his youth, and certainly his capacity for brandy was prodigious. But his potations had cast a pleasant haze over the world, as he saw it, and they had induced in him a mood of immense affability. It was clearly out of the question to deal with him as he deserved. Sir Gareth said curtly: "I see. Where is Miss Smith?"

"Schultz?" enquired Mr. Theale knowledgeably.

"Where — is — Miss — Smith?" repeated Sir Gareth.

"Never heard of her," said Mr. Theale. "Now I come to think of it, Weston makes for you, doesn't he?"

"Where is Amanda Smith?" demanded Sir Gareth, altering the wording of his question.

"Oh, her!" said Mr. Theale. "Damned if I know!"

"Doing it rather too brown!" Sir Gareth said, with a distinct rasp in his voice. "Don't try to gammon me you didn't carry her off from Brancaster this morning!"

"Was it only this morning?" said Mr. Theale, mildly surprised. "I daresay you're right, but it seems longer."

"Where is she?"

"I keep telling you I don't know. Yes, and now I come to think of it, a pretty cool hand you are, my boy! First you bring that fancy-piece to Brancaster, and next, dammed if you don't have the effrontery to come smash up to me, trying to get me to give her up to you! If I weren't a very easy-going man I should very likely call you to account. Thought you had more delicacy of principle."

"Rid your mind of two illusions at least! Amanda is neither my mistress nor a fancy-piece!"

"She isn't? As a matter of fact, I'd got to thinking she might not be. You take the advice of a man who's older than you, my boy, and has seen more of the world than you ever will! If she ain't Haymarket ware, hedge off! I don't say she ain't a tempting armful — well, I thought so myself! — but you may take it from me — !"

"I wish to take nothing from you but that child!" interrupted Sir Gareth. "Stop cutting shams, and tell me what you've done with her! I warn you, Theale, I'm in no mood to listen to any more of your lies!"

"Now, don't get in a tweak!" recommended Mr. Theale. "It's no use your asking me what I've done with that chit, because I haven't done anything with her. She gave me the bag. I don't deny I wasn't best pleased at the time, but I'm not at all sure now that it ain't a good thing. Shouldn't wonder at it if she'd have put me in the basket. You too. Forget her, my boy! After all, not the thing to offer for poor Hester one moment, and to go chasing after Amanda the next."

"When did she give you the bag and where?" demanded Sir Gareth, ignoring this piece of advice.

"I forget the name of the place, but she'd been eating a lot of raspberries."

"What?"

"I don't wonder you're surprised. You'd have been even more surprised if you'd seen the cream she kept pouring over them. I warned her how it would be, but there was no stopping her. Swore she was in high gig, and so she was, then. That didn't last, of course. She began to feel queasy — at least, that's what she said. She may have been bamboozling me, though shouldn't think anyone could have eaten all those raspberries without becoming as sick as a horse. She sat there, moaning, and saying she must lie down. Got me to stop the carriage in some village or other. I daresay I'll remember its name in a minute: it wasn't far from Thrapston. Anyway, we went into an inn there, and Amanda went off upstairs with the landlady — a devilish woman, that! I give you my word, if I'd known what a shrew she was I wouldn't have set foot inside the place!"

"Never mind the landlady!" said Sir Gareth impatiently.

"Yes, it's all very well for you to say never mind the landlady, but you didn't have to listen to her talking as though you were a regular Queer Nabs, which I'll be damned if I am!"

"The landlady rumbled you, did she? Good! What happened when Amanda went upstairs?"

"I had a glass of bingo. I needed it, I can tell you, because what with being bounced about in the carriage, and thinking every moment Amanda was going to cast up accounts, I was feeling damned queasy myself."

"For God's sake — !" exclaimed Sir Gareth. "I don't wish to know what you drank, or what you felt like! What happened to Amanda?"

"How should I know? The landlady said she was going to lie down for half an hour, and that's the last I heard of her, or anyone else, for that matter."

"Do you mean that she left the inn without anyone's seeing her?"

"That's it," nodded Mr. Theale. "Tipped me the double, the sly little cat! Queer business: she just disappeared, though the lord alone knows how she managed it! A pretty fix to have found myself in! Yes, and a pretty breeze she raised, too!"

"Are you telling me," said Sir Gareth dangerously, "that you left that child to fend for herself while you drove off at your ease?"

"There wasn't much ease about it," objected Mr. Theale. "To start with, it's no pleasure to me to jaunter along in a carriage, and to go on with, the damned perch broke, and I had to walk a good mile in tight boots."

"Did you make *no* effort to find Amanda?"

"Yes, I did, and how the devil I came to do anything so cork-brained — at my time of life, too! — has me lurched!"

"Where did you search for her?"

"All over the village," replied Mr. Theale bitterly. "You wouldn't think I could be such a gudgeon, would you? Because no sooner did those gapeseeds know that Amanda had given me the bag than they began to think there was something havey-cavey going on. Naturally, I'd told 'em at the inn, when we arrived there, that Amanda was a young relative of mine. Of course, as soon as she slipped off, *that* wouldn't fadge."

"Where, besides the village, did you search?"

"In a spinney. The landlord thought she might have gone there for a breath of air. Shouted myself hoarse, but to no purpose. That was before I guessed she'd tipped me the double." He poured some more brandy into his glass, and drank it, and suddenly ejaculated: "Bythorne! That was the name of the place! I thought it would very likely come back to me."

"Bythorne! Good God! Then — when you couldn't find her in the village, where next did you go?"

Mr. Theale lowered the glass, and looked at him in patient resignation. "Well, if ever I met such a fellow for asking muttonheaded questions! I came here, of course. Where did you think I went?"

"I thought," said Sir Gareth, in a deadly voice, "that you must have searched any road or track that may lead from the village! Was it likely, if Amanda was trying to escape from you, that she would remain in a village which, as I recall, consists of nothing more than two rows of cottages, flanking the post-road?"

"Oh, you did, did you! You must have windmills in your head! Why the devil should I make a cake of myself, scouring the countryside for a girl I can see I'm dashed well rid of?"

"It would be useless to tell you!" Sir Gareth said, an angry pulse throbbing in his cheek. "But if you were not fifteen years my senior, as fat as a hog, and castaway into the bargain, I would hand you such a supply of home-brewed as would send you to bed for a month!"

"Not if you want to have me for an uncle," said Mr. Theale, quite undismayed. "Chuffy thing to do. And let me tell you, my boy, that no one's ever seen me castaway since I was up at Oxford. Never more than a trifle up in my hat: ask anyone!" He watched Sir Gareth pick up his hat and gloves, and stride towards the door, and said: "*Now* where are you off to? Ain't you stopping to dinner?"

"I am not!" replied Sir Gareth, over his shoulder. "Surprising though it may seem to you, I am going to Bythorne!"

The door shut with a snap behind him. Mr. Theale shook his head sadly, and picked up the brandy-bottle again.

"Queer in the attic," he remarked. "Poor fellow!"

CHAPTER TEN

Mr. Sheet, summoned for the second time in one day to attend to a member of the Quality, was gratified, but a little flustered. He owned a snug property in the Red Lion, but he had never aspired to cater for carriage-people. His cellars were well stocked with beer and spirits, but he could see at a glance that if this tall exquisite in the awe-inspiring driving coat and the gleaming top-boots meant to dine in his house, he would infallibly call for a bottle of wine. Furthermore, notable cook though Mrs. Sheet was, it was doubtful if the sort of fancy dishes such an out-and-outer would demand lay within the boundaries of her skill. Then Sir Gareth disclosed his errand, and Mr. Sheet became still more flustered. He had naturally discussed with his wife the extraordinary affair of the young lady with the bandboxes, and at great length; and the more he had considered the matter the stronger had become his uneasy conviction that they had not heard the last of it. He did not think that blame could possibly attach to anything he had done, but still he had had a presentiment that there was trouble in store for him.

"Yes, sir," he said, "there *was* a young lady come here this morning, with a stout gentleman, but she up and ran away, and more than that I can't tell your honour, not if I was to be hung for it!"

He found that the visitor's gray eyes were uncomfortably penetrating, but he met them squarely enough, if a trifle nervously. Sir Gareth said: "I think I should tell you that I am that young lady's guardian. I have been looking for her all day, with what anxiety you may guess! I haven't found her, but I did find the stout gentleman, and what I learned from him made me hope with all my heart that I should find Miss Smith here."

The landlord shook his head. "No, sir. I'm sure, if we'd known — but she never said nothing, and being as the stout gentleman said as she was a relation of his —"

"What's all this?"

The voice came from behind Sir Gareth, and he turned quickly, to find himself confronting a buxom dame in a neat cap,

219

tied under her plump chin in a starched bow, and with her hands folded over her ample stomach. She had a comely, good-humoured face, which yet held much determination, but there was a martial light in her eye, and she was regarding Sir Gareth, if not with hostility, certainly with suspicion.

"The gentleman was asking for that young lady, Mary," explained Mr. Sheet. "Him being her guardian, by what he tells me."

"That's as may be," said Mrs. Sheet cryptically.

"I beg you will tell me, ma'am, did you, as I suspect, come to her rescue?" asked Sir Gareth. "Have you got her here, in safety?"

By this time, she had taken him in thoroughly, from his booted heels to his ordered brown locks. Her gaze came to rest on his face; and after a thoughtful moment her own face relaxed a little. "No, sir, I have not — which isn't to say that I don't wish I had, for dear knows there was no call for her to run off like she did, if she'd only told me the trouble she was in! And who might you be, if I might make so bold, sir?"

Sir Gareth gave her his card. "That is my name, and my direction, ma'am."

She studied the card, and then favoured him with another long stare. "And by what you was saying to Sheet, sir, you're the young lady's guardian?"

"I am," replied Sir Gareth, reflecting that this at least was true, even though he was self-appointed. A sudden and rueful smile flashed in his eyes. "For my sins! I will be perfectly frank with you, ma'am, and tell you that Miss Smith is the most wilful little monkey it has ever been my ill-fortune to have to do with. Her latest exploit is to run away from the seminary, where she was a parlour-boarder. I imagine I need not tell you that I am in considerable anxiety about her. If you can assist me to find her, I shall be very much in your debt."

Mr. Sheet, watching his wife with some misgiving, was relieved to see that she had apparently decided in the gentleman's favour. The belligerent expression had vanished, and it was with cordiality that she replied: " 'Deed, and I wish I could, sir, for such a sweet, pretty young creature I never did see! But it's true, what Sheet was saying to you: she never said a word to either of us, but slipped off unbeknownst. Run away from school, had she? But however did she come to take up with that dressed-up old fidget? Sheet got the notion into his head he was her uncle, but that I'll be bound he's not!"

"No — the dancing-master!" said Sir Gareth, with a certain vicious satisfaction.

Her jaw dropped. "What, and run off with one of the young ladies at the school? Well, I never did in all my life!"

"Miss Smith," said Sir Gareth, rivalling Amanda in inventiveness, "is a considerable heiress. By what means that fellow inserted himself into her good graces, I know not, but there can be little doubt that his object was to possess himself of her fortune. She is not yet seventeen, but had he succeeded in reaching Gretna Green with her, and making her his wife, what could I have done?"

Her eyes were as round as crown-pieces, but she nodded her head understandingly. "Ay, a pretty kettle of fish that would have been, sir! Well, I never liked him, not from the start, and what has me in a puzzle is what made her take a fancy to him! Why, he's old enough to be her grandpa, and as fat as a flawn besides!"

"I am very sure she had no fancy for him at all," said Sir Gareth. "If I know her, she encouraged his pretensions only to win his aid in escaping from the school! Once she believed herself to be beyond the reach of — er — Miss Hitchin, she wouldn't hesitate to give him the bag. For that at least I may be thankful! But where is she?"

"Ah, that's the question!" said Mr. Sheet

profoundly.

"Well, surely to goodness, sir, she wouldn't run away without she had some place to go!" exclaimed Mrs. Sheet. "Hasn't she got any relations, or maybe some friend that would be glad to have her?"

"She's an orphan. She would certainly not seek refuge with any relation, for she knows very well that they would instantly tell me where she was. Nor do I know of any of her acquaintances who would do anything so improper as to conceal her whereabouts from me. What I suspect is that she means to hire herself out as an abigail, or something equally foolish."

"Whatever for, sir?" gasped Mrs. Sheet. "A young lady like her? Good gracious, she must be fair desperate to think of such a thing! Seems to me, begging your pardon, sir, that this school you've sent her to must be a very bad sort of a place!"

"Oh, no, on the contrary!" he replied. "Pray don't imagine, ma'am, that Miss Smith has been unkindly treated there, or, in fact, anywhere! The mischief is that she has been far too much indulged. No one but myself has ever thwarted her, and, since she is extremely highspirited, she will go to any lengths to get her own way. This exploit, I have no doubt at all, is an attempt to force me to take her away from school, and to allow her to be brought out into the world before she is seventeen."

"Oh, what a naughty girl!" Mrs. Sheet said, shocked. "Why, she might run into all sorts of trouble, sir!"

"Exactly so! You know that, and so do I know it, but she has no more notion of it than a kitten. It's imperative I should find her before she discovers it."

She nodded. "Yes, indeed! Oh, dear, if I'd had only an inkling how it was — ! The idea of a lovely young thing like she is, wandering about by herself, and nothing but them two bandboxes to call her own! But where she can have got to I know no more than you, sir. She didn't hide herself in the village, that's certain, for there's not a soul has seen her, and I don't see how she could have walked down the street without *someone* must have caught sight of her. We did wonder if she got taken up in someone's carriage, but I disremember that we had so much as a gig pull up here while she was in the house. And as for the stage, Mrs. Bude, which keeps the chandler's shop, put a parcel on to it when it came through Bythorne at noon, and she's certain sure there was no young lady got into it."

Sir Gareth spread open his map, and laid

224

it on the table. "I doubt very much whether she would have tried to escape by way of the post-road. She must have known she would be pursued, and the first thing she would do would be to get as far away from it as possible. Could she have slipped out of this house by a back way?"

"She *could,*" Mrs. Sheet replied doubtfully. "There's a door leading into the yard, but there was the coachman, and a lad, that brought some chickens and potatoes, and I should have thought they'd have been bound to see her."

"The coachman came into the tap, soon as he'd stabled the horses," interposed Mr. Sheet.

"Yes, but Joe didn't!" she objected.

"Happen Joe did see her. He wouldn't think anything of it, not Joe! Likely he wouldn't hardly have noticed her."

"I daresay she may have waited until his back was turned," said Sir Gareth. "Can the lane that crosses the post-road be reached by way of the fields behind this house?"

"Well, you could get to it that way, sir, but it's rough walking, and how would the young lady have known there was a lane?"

"She might not, but if she was on the look-out for a way of escape she would have seen that lane, just before the carriage reached Bythorne. As I remember, there is a sign-post, pointing to Catworth and Kimbolton." He laid his finger on the map. "Catworth, I take it, is no more than a small village. Has it an inn? No, too near the postroad: she wouldn't try to establish herself there. Kimbolton, then. Yes, I think that must be my first goal." He folded up the map again, and straightened himself. He saw that Mrs. Sheet was regarding him wonderingly, and smiled. "I can only go by guess, you know, and this seems to me the likeliest chance."

"But it's all of seven miles to Kimbolton, sir!" expostulated Mrs. Sheet. "Surely she wouldn't trudge all that way, carrying them bandboxes?"

He thrust the map into his pocket, and picked up his hat. "Very likely not. From my knowledge of her, I should imagine that if she saw any kind of vehicle on the road she coaxed its driver into taking her up. And I hope to God she fell into honest hands!"

He moved towards the door, but before he reached it the aperture was filled by a burly figure, in gaiters and a frieze coat, at sight of whom Mrs. Sheet uttered a pleased exclamation. "Ned! The very person I was wishful to see! Do you wait a moment, sir, if you please! Come you in, Ned, and

226

answer me this! When he got home, did Joe say anything to you, or Jane, about a young lady which we've got a notion he maybe saw in our yard when he was unloading the potatoes from the cart?"

The burly individual, rather bashfully pulling his forelock to Sir Gareth, replied, in a deep, slow voice: "Ay, he did that. Leastways, in a manner of speaking, he did. Which is what brings me here, because Jane ain't by no means easy in her mind, and what she says is, if anyone knows the rights of it, it'll be Mary."

"Sir Gareth, sir, this is Ned Ninfield, which is Joe's father, Joe being the lad I told you about," said Mrs. Sheet, performing a rapid introduction. "And this gentleman, Ned, is the young lady's guardian, and he's looking for her all over, she having run away from school."

Mr. Ninfield's ruminative gaze travelled to Sir Gareth's face, and became fixed there, while he apparently revolved a thought in his mind.

"Did your son see the way she went?" asked Sir Gareth.

This question seemed to strike Mr. Ninfield as being exquisitely humorous. A grin spread over his face, and he gave a chuckle. "Ay! In a manner of speaking, he did. She never said nothing about any school, though."

"Lor', Ned!" cried Mrs. Sheet, in sharp suspicion. "You're never going to tell me you've seen her too? Where is she?"

He jerked his thumb over his shoulder, saying laconically: "Whitethorn."

"*Whitethorn?*" she gasped. "However did she come to get there?"

He began to chuckle again. "In my cart! Joe brought her. Proper moonstruck, he was."

"Ned Ninfield!" she exploded. "You mean to tell me Joe didn't know no better than to offer a young lady like she is a ride in that dirty cart of yours?"

"Seems it was her as was set on it, not him. Told him to pick her up, and pop her into the cart where no one wouldn't see her. Which he done. And I don't know as I blame him," added Mr. Ninfield thoughtfully. "Not altogether, I don't."

"I don't believe it!" Mrs. Sheet declared.

"Oh, yes!" Sir Gareth interposed, a good deal amused. "Nothing, in fact, is more likely! Not so long ago, she hid herself in a carrier's cart. I expect she enjoyed the ride."

"She did that, your honour," corroborated Mr. Ninfield. "She and my Joe ate up the better part of a jar of pickled cherries

228

between 'em, what's more. Sticky! Lor', you ought to have seen 'em!"

"The cherries I sent Jane special!" ejaculated Mrs. Sheet.

Sir Gareth laughed. "I offer you my apologies, ma'am: I told you she was a little monkey!" He turned, stretching out his hand to the farmer. "Mr. Ninfield, I'm very much in your debt — and more thankful than I can describe to you that my ward had the good fortune to fall in with your son. By the way, I do hope to God you didn't tell her you were coming here to make enquiries about her? If you did, she will certainly have fled from the house before I can reach it."

"No, sir, she don't know nothing about it," Mr. Ninfield replied, rather coyly wiping his hand on his breeches before grasping Sir Gareth's. "But the thing is — well, it's like this, sir! I'm sure I'm not wishful to give offence, but — you wouldn't be the gentleman as is father to a young lady as had Miss Amanda to wait on her, would you?"

"I would not!" said Sir Gareth, recognizing Amanda's favourite story. "I collect you mean the gentleman who made such improper advances to her that his sister — most unjustly, one feels — turned her out of the house without a moment's warning. I haven't a daughter, and I am not even married, much less a widower. Nor has Miss Amanda ever been a waiting-woman. She got the notion out of an old novel."

"Well, I'm bound to say you didn't look to me like you could be him," said Mr. Ninfield. "Downright wicked, that's what I thought, but my good lady, she wouldn't have it. She says to me private that she'd go bail Miss was telling us a lot of faradiddles, because nothing wouldn't make her credit that Miss was an abigail, nor ever had been. So it was a school she run away from, was it, sir? Well, *that* won't surprise the wife, though she did think it was p'raps her home she run away from: likely, because someone had crossed her. Powerful hot at hand, I'd say — meaning no disrespect!"

"You're very right!" Sir Gareth said. "Under what disguise does she hope to remain in your house, by the way? Has she offered herself to your wife as a chambermaid?"

"No, sir," grinned Mr. Ninfield. "When last I see her, she was making my Joe teach her how to milk the cows, and just about as happy as a grig."

"Ah, going to be a dairymaid, is she?" said Sir Gareth cheerfully. An idea that had peeped into his mind now began to take hopeful possession of it. He looked at Mr. Ninfield consideringly, and said, after a moment: "Is she a troublesome charge? Do you think Mrs. Ninfield would be prepared to keep her as a boarder for a few days?"

"*Keep* her, sir?" repeated Mr. Ninfield, staring at him.

"The case, you see, is this," said Sir Gareth. "Either I must take her back to school, or I must make some other arrangements for her. Well, I have been most earnestly requested *not* to take her back to the school, which puts me in something of a fix, for I can't hire a governess for her at a moment's notice. I must convey her to my sister's house in town, and, frankly, I am very sure she won't want to go with me there. Nor, I must add, am I anxious to saddle my sister with such a charge. It occurs to me that if she is happy in your wife's care it would perhaps be as well to leave her there until I am able to provide for her suitably. I daresay, if she did not know that I was aware of her direction, she would be glad to stay with you, and would no doubt enjoy herself very much, milking cows, and collecting eggs, and in general fancying herself to be very useful."

"I'll be bound she would, the pretty dear!"

said Mrs. Sheet approvingly. "A very good notion, I call it, and just what will put dancing-masters and such out of her head."

But Mr. Ninfield dashed Sir Gareth's hopes. "Well, sir," he said apologetically, "I'm sure I'd be pleased to have her, and it goes against the shins with me to act disobliging, but it's Joe, you see. She's got him so as he don't know whether he's on his head or his heels. He don't take his eyes off her, and when he told his ma that Miss was like a princess out of one of them fairy stories, Mrs. Ninfield she said to me, private, that we must find out quick where she comes from before Joe gets ideas into his head which is above his station. Because it wouldn't do, sir."

"No, it wouldn't do," agreed Sir Gareth, relinquishing his scheme with a pang. "If that is how the land lies, of course I must take her away immediately. Where is your farm?"

"It's a matter of three miles from here, sir, but it ain't a very good road. You go up the post-road, about half a mile, and there's a lane turns off to your left. You follow that past Keyston, until you see a rough track, left again. You go down that for a mile and a half, maybe a bit more, like as if you was heading for Catworth, and just afore you come to a sharp bend you'll see Whitethorn. You can't miss it."

"Good gracious, Ned, where have your wits gone begging?" interrupted Mrs. Sheet impatiently. "Just you get back into your gig, and lead the gentleman!"

"Thank you, I wish you will!" Sir Gareth said. "In the direction of Catworth, is it? Tell me, can I, without too much difficulty, reach Kimbolton from Whitethorn?"

"Yes, sir, easy, you can. All you've to do is to go on down the lane till you come to the post-road — the one as runs south of this one, between Wellingborough and Cambridge. Then you swing left-handed into it, and Kimbolton's about five miles on."

"Excellent! I'll rack up there for the night, and carry the child off to London by post-chaise tomorrow — if she doesn't contrive to give me the slip from the posting-house there! But before we set out you must join me in a glass. Ma'am, what may I have the pleasure of desiring your husband to serve you with?"

"Well, I'm sure, sir!" said Mrs. Sheet, slightly overcome. "Well, I don't hardly like to!"

However, succumbing to persuasion, she consented to drink a small glass of port. The landlord then drew three pots of his own home-brewed; and Sir Gareth, basely plotting Amanda's undoing, said thoughtfully: "Now, I wonder what trick that abominable child will play on me next? She'll put up a spirited fight, that's certain! The last time she was in mischief she told a complete stranger that I was abducting her. I only wish I may not be in her black books for months for having disclosed that she's still a schoolgirl. Nothing enrages her more!"

Mrs. Sheet said wisely that girls of her age were always wishing to be thought quite grown-up; and Mr. Ninfield, hugely tickled by the thought of Sir Gareth's figuring as an abductor, confessed that he and his good lady had suspected from the start that Miss was cutting a sham.

"Ah, well, of course she didn't ought to tell such faradiddles," said Mrs. Sheet, "but it's only playacting, like children do, when they start in to be Dick Turpin, or Robin Hood."

"Exactly so," nodded Sir Gareth. "But it is really time she grew out of it. Unfortunately, she is still at the stage when she pines for adventure. As far as I can discover, she thinks it a dead bore to be a schoolgirl, and so is for ever pretending that she is someone else. I could wish that some of her stories were less outrageous."

Everyone agreed that it was very embarrassing for him, and the symposium presently ended on a note of great cordiality. Sir Gareth had acquired three firm friends and supporters who were as one in thinking him the finest gentleman of their acquaintance, not high in the instep, but, as Mr. Sheet later expressed it, a real top-of-the-trees, slap up to the echo.

Trotton, upon hearing that the end of the hunt was in sight, was extremely thankful. It had appeared to him that his besotted master was prepared to continue driving throughout the night, and he, for one, had had enough of it. Moreover, he had been even more reluctant than Sir Gareth to leave the bays in a strange stable, having taken a dislike to the head ostler, an unfortunate circumstance which led to his becoming more and more convinced that those peerless horses would be subjected to the worst of bad treatment. He now learned that it would be his task to drive them back to London by easy stages, and grew instantly more cheerful.

"You will have to come with me to Kimbolton," Sir Gareth said, drawing on his gloves. "I shall be escorting the young lady to my sister's house tomorrow, and shall hire a chaise for the purpose. You may then drive the curricle back to Thrapston, settle my account there for the hire of these tits, and bring the bays up to London after me. I shan't look for you to arrive for at least two days, so take care you don't press 'em!"

"No, sir," said Trotton, in a carefully expressionless voice. "I wouldn't be wishful to do so — not in this hot weather!"

"Because," said Sir Gareth, as though he had not heard, but with the glimmer of an appreciative smile in his eyes, "I have already worked 'em far harder than I ought."

"Just so, sir!" said his henchman, grinning at him.

It did not take long to accomplish the journey to Whitethorn Farm. Leaving Trotton with the curricle, Sir Gareth was ushered by Mr. Ninfield into the rambling old house. Dusk was beginning by this time to shadow the landscape, and in the large, flagged kitchen the lamp had been kindled. Its mellow light fell on Amanda, on the floor, and playing with a litter of kittens. Seated in a windsor chair, with his hands clasped between his knees, was a stalwart youth, watching her with a rapt and slightly idiotic expression on his sunburnt countenance; and keeping a wary eye on both, while she vigorously ironed one of her husband's shirts, was a matron of formidable aspect.

Amanda glanced up casually as the door opened, but when she saw who had entered the kitchen she stiffened, and exclaimed: *"You!* No! *No!"*

Young Mr. Ninfield, although not quick-witted, took only a very few seconds to realize that here, in the person of this bang-up nonesuch, was Amanda's persecutor. He got up, clenching his fists, and glaring at Sir Gareth.

He was perfectly ready, and even anxious, to do battle, but Sir Gareth took the wind out of his sails, by first nodding at Amanda, and saying amiably: "Good-evening, Amanda!" and then coming towards him, with his hand held out. "You must be Joe Ninfield," he said. "I have to thank you for taking such excellent care of my ward. You are a very good fellow!"

"It's the young lady's guardian, Jane," Mr. Ninfield informed his wife in a penetrating aside.

"It is *not!"* Amanda declared passionately. "He is trying to abduct me!"

Joe, who had numbly allowed Sir Gareth to grasp his hand, turned his bemused gaze upon her, seeking guidance. "Throw him out!" ordered Amanda, a sandy kitten clasped to her breast in a very touching way.

"You'll do no such thing, Joe!" said his mother sharply. "Now, sir! P'raps you'll be so good as to explain what this means!"

"All's right, Jane," Mr. Ninfield said, chuckling. "It's like you thought, only that it was school Miss ran off from."

"I didn't!" cried Amanda, her face scarlet with rage. "And he's not my guardian! I don't even *know* him! He is an abominable person!"

"Of course I am!" said Sir Gareth soothingly. "Though how you know that, when you are not even acquainted with me, I can't imagine!" He smiled at Mrs. Ninfield, and said in his charming way: "I do hope, ma'am, that she has not been troublesome to you? I can't thank you enough for your kindness to her!"

Under Amanda's baffled and infuriated gaze, Mrs. Ninfield dropped a curtsy, stammering: "No, no! Oh, no, indeed sir!"

Sir Gareth glanced down at Amanda. "Come, my child, get up from the floor!" he said, in a voice of kindly authority. "Where is your hat? I never abduct ladies without their hats, so put it on, and your cloak too!"

Amanda obeyed the first of these commands, largely because she found herself at a disadvantage when sitting at his feet. She could see that the tone he had chosen to adopt had had its inevitable effect, even upon her moonstruck admirer, but she made a desperate bid for freedom. Staring up into his amused eyes, she said: "Very well! If you are my guardian, *who am I?*"

"An orphan, cast upon the world without a penny," he replied promptly. "You have lately been employed by a young lady, whose widowed father — a most reprehensible person, I fear — made such improper advances to you, that —"

"Oh, how I much hate you!" she cried, flushing with mortification, and stamping her foot. "How dare you stand there telling such lies?"

"Well, but, missie, it's what you told us yourself!" said Mr. Ninfield, hugely entertained.

"Yes, but that was because — well, that was just make-believe! *He* knows it isn't true! And it isn't true that he is my guardian, or that I ran away from school, or *anything!*"

Mrs. Ninfield drew a long breath. "Sir, *are* you her guardian, or are you not?" she demanded.

"No," he replied, his voice grave, but his eyes dancing. "I am an abductor. I met her only yesterday, and that by chance, snatched her up into my curricle, and bore her off in spite of all her protests to a gloomy mansion in the heart of the country. I need scarcely tell you that she contrived to make her escape from the mansion while I slept. However, it takes a good deal to daunt a thorough-going villain, so you won't be surprised that here I am, having hunted her down remorselessly. I am now about to carry her off to my castle. This, by the way, is perched on a precipitous rock, and, besides being in an uncomfortable state of neglect and decay, is inhabited only by ghosts and sinister retainers of mine. From this fortress, after undergoing a number of extremely alarming adventures, she will, I have little doubt, be rescued by a noble youth of handsome though poverty-stricken aspect. I expect he will kill me, after which it will be found that he is the wronged heir to a vast property — probably mine — and all will end happily."

"Now, sir — !" protested Mrs. Ninfield, trying not to laugh. "Give over your nonsense, do!"

Joe, having listened with painstaking concentration to the programme laid down for Amanda's future entertainment, once more clenched his large fists, and uttered, slowly, but with determination: "I won't have her put in no castle."

240

"Don't be a gaby!" said his mother. "Can't you see the gentleman's only making game of her?"

"I won't have him make game of her neither," said Joe stubbornly.

"Please to pay no heed, sir!" begged Mrs. Ninfield. "Now, that's enough, Joseph! Do you want the gentleman to think you're no better than a knock-in-the-cradle, which I'll be bound he does?"

"Not at all! I think he's a splendid fellow," said Sir Gareth. "Don't worry, Joe! I was only funning."

"I don't want you to take her anywhere," Joe muttered. "I'd like her to stay here, fine I would!"

"Yes, and so would I have liked to stay here!" said Amanda warmly. "I never enjoyed anything half as much, particularly feeding all those droll little pigs, and these lovely kittens, but everything is spoilt now that Sir Gareth knows where I am, and it would be of no use staying here any more." Her voice trembled, and a tear sparkled on the end of her long lashes. She kissed the sandy kitten, and reluctantly set it down on the floor, giving such a pathetic sniff that Mr. Ninfield, a tenderhearted man, said uncomfortably: "Don't you take on, missie! P'raps, if my missis is agreeable —" He stopped, as he caught his wife's eye, and coughed in some embarrassment.

"Cheer up, my child!" Sir Gareth said. "This is no time for tears! You must instantly set about the task of thinking how best to revenge yourself on me."

She cast him a darkling look, but said nothing. Inspiration came to Joe, his withers unbearably wrung by her distress. Swooping upon the sandy kitten, he picked it up by the scruff of its neck, and held it out to Amanda. "You take him!" he said gruffly.

Nothing could have succeeded better in diverting her mind at that moment. Her face brightened; she clasped the kitten again, exclaiming: "*Oh!* How excessively kind of you! I am *very* much obliged to you! Only —" Her eyes turned apprehensively towards her hostess, and she said prettily: "Perhaps it is your kitten, and you would not wish me to take it away?"

"I'm sure you've very welcome to it, miss, but I'll be bound the gentleman won't want to be worried by a kitten on the journey," Mrs. Ninfield responded.

"I am going to take this dear little kitten with me," said Amanda, addressing herself to Sir Gareth, with immense dignity, and a challenge in her eye.

"Do!" he said cordially, tickling the kitten's ear. "What shall you call it?"

She considered the matter. "Well, perhaps Honey, because of his colour, or —" She broke off as her gaze alighted on the kitten's donor. "No, I shan't!" she said, bestowing a brilliant smile upon him. "I shall call him Joseph, after *you,* and that will remind me of feeding the pigs, and learning to milk the cow!"

At these very beautiful words, Joe was so overcome that he grew beetroot-red, and lost all power of speech, merely swallowing convulsively, and grinning in a way that made his fond mother itch to box his ears. Mr. Ninfield went off in a practical spirit, to find a covered basket; and in a very short time Sir Gareth, silently invoking a powerful blessing on the head of one who had, however unwittingly, averted the threat of a disagreeable scene, was handing his charge up into the curricle, and delivering into her hands a basket in which one small kitten indignantly vociferated his disapproval of the change in his circumstances.

CHAPTER ELEVEN

It was not to be expected that Amanda's pleasure in having acquired a new pet would for long save Sir Gareth from recrimination. She had never been wholly diverted, but had ceased from further argument because she had perceived how deftly he was cutting the ground from beneath her inexperienced feet. It made her very angry, but she could not help admiring, secretly, a strategy which she recognized to be masterly; nor, in spite of a strengthened determination to put him utterly to rout, did she think the worse of him for having got the better of her. But that she was certainly not going to tell him, far preferring to relieve her feelings by delivering herself of a comprehensive indictment of his character. To this, Trotton, perched up behind her, listened in shocked and wondering silence. What Sir Gareth could see in such a young termagant to make him fall madly in love Trotton could not imagine, but he did not for an instant doubt that his master was clean besotted.

"You are meddlesome, and tyrannical, and untruthful, and, which is worse than all, *treacherous!*" scolded Amanda.

"Not treacherous!" protested Sir Gareth. "I promise you, I told none of those people the true story."

"I am quite astonished that you didn't, for I dare-say you don't care a button about breaking your solemn word to people!"

"I didn't think they would believe me," explained Sir Gareth.

"And above everything you are shameless!" said Amanda indignantly.

"No, not quite, because, I assure you, I am shocked at my own mendacity."

"You are?" she exclaimed, turning her head to study his profile.

"Profoundly! I never knew I had it in me to tell so many bouncers."

"Well, you *did* — brazenly, too!"

"Yes, and you don't know the half of it. When I think of the Banbury story I told at the Red Lion, I know that I am sunk beyond reproach."

This ruse succeeded. "What was it?" Amanda demanded, much interested.

"Why, I said that you were a great heiress, and had eloped with the dancing-master, who wanted to marry you for the sake of your fortune."

"Did you *indeed* say that?" Amanda asked, awed.

"Yes — brazenly!"

"Well, it doesn't make your conduct any better, and I am *very* angry with you, but I must say I do think it was a splendid story!" Amanda said, rather enviously. "Particularly the bit about the dancing-master!"

"Yes, I liked that bit, too," owned Sir Gareth. "Did you really eat enough raspberries to make you sick?"

"Well, I ate a great many raspberries, but I wasn't sick. That was only pretending, because I couldn't think of any other way to be rid of that horrid old man. I wonder what became of him?"

"An evil fate. After searching for you in a wood until he was exhausted, he got a tremendous scold from Mrs. Sheet, and then, to crown his day, the perch of his carriage broke, and he was obliged to walk a mile in tight boots to the nearest inn."

She gave a giggle, but said: "Have you seen him, then?"

"I have."

"What happened!" she asked, filled with pleasurable anticipation.

"He told me where he had lost you, and I

drove back to Bythorne immediately."

"Is *that* all?" she said, disappointed. "I quite thought that you would have challenged him to a duel!"

"Yes, I know it was very poor-spirited of me," he agreed, "but really I think he has perhaps been punished enough. I fancy he can't have enjoyed the drive in your company."

"No, and I didn't enjoy it either!" said Amanda. "He tried to make love to me!"

"I should forget about him, if I were you, for he is certainly not worth remembering. But it is not wise, my child, to let strangers make off with you, however old and respectable they may seem to you."

"Well!" she cried. "When you have been *forcing* me to go with you ever since I met you, which I wish I never had, because although you are quite old, it is very plain to me that you are not in the least respectable, but, on the contrary, a deceiving person, and quite as odious as Mr. Theale!"

He laughed. "A home thrust, Amanda!" he acknowledged. "But at least I am not as fat as Mr. Theale, however odious!"

"No," she conceded, "but you took much worse advantage of me!"

"Did I indeed?"

"Yes, you did! For when you told Mrs.

Ninfield those lies about me, you made it seem as though they were true, and then, when you did tell the truth, you made it sound like a lie! It was — it was the shabbiest trick to play on me!"

He was amused, but he said: "I know it was. Indeed, most unhandsome of me, and I do most sincerely feel for you. It must be very disagreeable to be paid back in your own coin. And the dreadful thing is that I believe it is rapidly becoming a habit with me. I have already thought of another very truthful-sounding lie to tell about you, if you insist on denying that you are my ward."

"I think you are abominable!" she said hotly. "And if you do not instantly tell me where we are going I shall jump out of your horrid carriage, and very likely break my leg! *Then* you will be sorry!"

"Well, of course, it might be a little tiresome to be obliged to convey you to London with your leg in a splint, but on the other hand you wouldn't be able to run away from me again, would you?"

"London?" she ejaculated, ignoring the rest.

"Yes, London. We are going to spend the night at Kimbolton, however."

"No! No! I won't go with you!"

He caught the note of panic, and said at

once: "I am taking you to my sister's house, so don't be a goose, Amanda!"

The panic subsided, but she reiterated her determination not to go with him, and was not in the least reconciled to her fate when he told her that she would meet his nephews and nieces there. She had a tolerably clear picture of all that would happen. Mrs. Wetherby would treat her as though she were a naughty child; she would be relegated to the schoolroom, where the governess would have orders never to let her out of her sight; Sir Gareth would discover her name from Neil; and she would be taken ignominiously home, having failed either to achieve her object, or to prove to her grandfather that she was an eminently grown-up and capable woman.

The blackest depression descended upon her spirits. Sir Gareth was not going to give her the smallest opportunity to escape from him a second time; and even if he did, her experiences had taught her that it was of very little avail to escape if one had no certain goal to make for. She felt defeated, tired, and very resentful; and for the remainder of the way refused even to open her lips.

There was only one posting-house in Kimbolton, and that a small and old-fashioned building. It did not hold out much promise of any extraordinary degree of comfort, but it possessed one feature which instantly recommended it to Sir Gareth. As he drew up before it, and ran a critical eye over it, he saw that its windows were all small casements. This circumstance solved for him a problem which had been exercising his mind for several miles. Sir Gareth had not forgotten the story of the elm tree.

The landlord, recognizing at a glance the quality of his unexpected guests, was all compliance and civility; and if at first he thought that it was odd conduct on the part of so grand a gentleman as Sir Gareth to carry his ward on a journey in an open carriage, and without her maid, he very soon banished any unworthy suspicions from his mind. There was little of the lover to be detected in Sir Gareth's demeanour, and as for the young lady, she seemed to be in a fit of the sullens.

Amanda made no attempt to deny that she was Sir Gareth's ward. However innocent she might be of the world's ways, she was well aware of the impropriety of her situation, having been carefully instructed in the rules governing the social conduct of young ladies. It had been permissible, though a trifle dashing, to drive with Sir

Gareth in an open curricle; driving with Mr. Theale in a closed carriage Aunt Adelaide would have stigmatized as fast; while putting up at an inn in the company of a gentleman totally unrelated to her was conduct reprehensible enough to put her beyond the pale. Amanda accepted this without question, but was quite unembarrassed by her predicament. None of the vague feelings of alarm which had attacked her in Mr. Theale's carriage assailed her; and it did not for an instant occur to her that Sir Gareth, odious though he might be, was not entirely to be trusted. On first encountering him, she had been astonished to learn that so charming and personable a man could be an uncle; she would scarcely have been surprised now to have discovered that he was a great-uncle; and felt no more *gêne* in his company than if he had been her grandfather. However, she knew that her private belief that, so far from damaging her reputation, his presence was investing her adventure with a depressing respectability, would not be shared by the vulgar, so she not only held her peace when he spoke to the landlord of his ward, but seized the first opportunity that offered of pointing out to him the gross impropriety of his behaviour. Looking the picture of outraged virtue, she announced, with relish, that she was now ruined. Sir Gareth replied that she was forgetting Joseph, and recommended her, instead of talking nonsense, to restrain her chaperon from sharpening his tiny claws on the polished leg of a chair.

After such a callous piece of flippancy as this, it was only to be expected that when Amanda accompanied her protector downstairs to the coffee-room she should do so with all the air of a Christian martyr.

The landlord had been profuse in apologies for his inability to offer Sir Gareth a private parlour. The only one the White Lion possessed was occupied already by an elderly gentleman afflicted with gout, and although the landlord plainly considered Sir Gareth more worthy of it, he doubted whether the gouty gentleman would share this view.

But Sir Gareth, in spite of having thrown a judicious damper over Amanda's sudden access of maidenly modesty, was a great deal more aware of the perils of her situation than she, and he had no desire to add to the irregularity of this journey by dining with her in a private parlour. The landlord, relieved to find him so accommodating, assured him that every attention would be paid to his comfort, and added that since the only other visitor to the inn was one very quiet young gentleman he need not fear that his ward would be exposed to noisy company.

The coffee-room was a pleasant, low-pitched apartment, furnished with one long table, a quantity of chairs, and a massive sideboard. The window-embrasure was filled by a cushioned seat, and this, when Sir Gareth and Amanda entered the room, was occupied by the quiet young gentleman, who was reading a book in the fading daylight. He did not raise his eyes from this immediately, but upon Sir Gareth's desiring the waiter to bring him a glass of sherry, he looked up, and, his gaze falling upon Amanda, became apparently transfixed.

"And some lemonade for the lady," added Sir Gareth unthinkingly.

He was speedily brought to realize that he had been guilty of gross folly. Amanda might be forced to acknowledge him as her guardian, but she was not going to submit to such arbitrary treatment as this. "Thank you, I don't care for lemonade," she said. "I will take a glass of sherry."

Sir Gareth's lips twitched. He met the waiter's understanding eye, and said briefly: "Ratafia."

Amanda, having by this time discovered

the presence of the quiet young gentleman, thought it prudent to refrain from further argument, and relapsed into dejection. The quiet young gentleman, his book forgotten, continued to gaze at her exquisite profile, in his own face an expression of awed admiration.

Sir Gareth, already aware of his presence, was thus afforded the opportunity to study him at leisure. He would not ordinarily have felt it necessary to pay much heed to a chance-met traveller, but his short acquaintance with Amanda had taught him that that disastrously confiding damsel would not hesitate to turn any promising stranger to good account.

But what he saw satisfied him. The quiet young gentleman, whom he judged to be perhaps eighteen or nineteen years of age, was a slender youth, with a damask cheek, a sensitive mouth, and a pair of rather dreamy gray eyes. He was attired in a riding-dress whose cut, without aspiring to the heights achieved by Weston, or Schultz, or Schweitzer and Davidson, advertised the skill of a reliable provincial tailor. Tentative ambition was betrayed by a waistcoat of such bold design as might be relied upon to appeal to the taste of Oxford or Cambridge collegiates; and the intricate, if not entirely felicitous, arrangement of his neckcloth exactly resembled the efforts of Mr. Leigh Wetherby to copy the various styles affected by his Corinthian uncle.

As though conscious of Sir Gareth's scrutiny, he withdrew his rapt gaze from Amanda, and glanced towards him, blushing slightly as he realized that he had been under observation. Sir Gareth smiled at him, and addressed some commonplace to him. He replied with a little stammer of shyness, but in a cultured voice which confirmed Sir Gareth's estimate of his condition. An agreeable, well-mannered boy, of good-breeding but little worldly experience, decided Sir Gareth. Too young to appear to Amanda in the light of a potential rescuer, but he might serve to make her forget her injuries, he thought. In any event, since he would shortly be sitting down to table with them, he could not be ignored.

Within a very few minutes, the young gentleman, his reading abandoned, had joined his fellow-guests beside the empty fireplace in the middle of the room, and was chatting easily with his new acquaintance. Sir Gareth had seemed to him at first rather awe-inspiring, clearly a man of fashion, possibly (if his highly polished top-boots were anything to go by) a top-sawyer, but he soon found that he was not at all proud, but, on the contrary, very affable and encouraging. Long before the covers were set on the table, the young gentleman had disclosed that his name was Hildebrand Ross, and that his home was in Suffolk, where, Sir Gareth gathered, his father was the squire of a village not far from Stowmarket. He had got his schooling at Winchester, and was at present up at Cambridge. He had several sisters, all older than himself, but no brothers; and it was not difficult to guess that he was at once the hope and the darling of his house. He told Sir Gareth that he was on his way to Ludlow, where he expected to join a party of college friends on a walking tour of Wales. His intention had been to have spent the night at Wellingborough, but he had been attracted to the White Lion by its air of antiquity: did not Sir Gareth think that in all likelihood the inn had been standing here, just as it did today, when Queen Katherine had been imprisoned at Kimbolton?

This question could not fail to catch Amanda's attention, and she temporarily abandoned her role of martyred innocence to demand further information. Delighted as much to expound what appeared to be a favourite subject as to converse with the most stunningly beautiful creature he had ever beheld, Mr. Ross turned eagerly towards her. Sir Gareth, thankful, at the end of a wearing day, to be relieved of the necessity of entertaining his charge, retired from the conversation, enjoying his sherry in peace, and listening, in a little amusement, to Mr. Ross's earnest discourse.

Mr. Ross seemed to be a romantically minded youth, with a strong liking for historic subjects. He thought that there was promising matter for a dramatic tragedy, in blank verse, in the Divorce and Death of Queen Katherine of Aragon. Only, did Amanda feel that it would be presumptuous for a lesser poet to tread in the steps of Shakespeare? Yes (blushing), his ambition was to enter the field of literature. As a matter of fact, he had written a quantity of verse already. Oh, no! not published! Just fugitive fragments written when he was quite young, which he would be ashamed to see in print. He rather thought that his talent was for Drama: at least (blushing more fierily), so one or two knowledgeable persons had been kind enough to say. To own the truth, he had already written a short play, while still at Winchester, which had been performed by certain members of the Sixth. Mere schoolboy stuff, of course, but one of the situations had been considered powerful, and he fancied that there were several passages that were not wholly contemptible. But he must sound like a coxcomb!

Reassured on this point, he confided that he had for long nursed an ambition to write a Tragic Drama about Queen Katherine, but had hitherto put the project from him, fearing that until he had gained experience and knowledge of the world he might not do justice to his subject. The moment now seemed ripe; and the sight of Kimbolton, where, as Amanda was of course aware, the unfortunate queen had died, had put one or two very good notions in his head.

Amanda, who had never before met an author, much less a dramatic poet, was impressed. She begged Mr. Ross to tell her more; and Mr. Ross, stammering with mingled shyness and gratification, said that if she was sure she would not think him the greatest bore in nature, he would very much value her opinion of his play, as he at present conceived it.

Sir Gareth, lounging in a deep chair at his ease, with his shapely and superbly booted legs crossed at the ankles, watched them with a smile lurking at the back of his eyes. An attractive pair of children: the boy a little shy, and obviously dazzled, the girl quite free from any sort of self-consciousness, and pretty enough to turn far more seasoned heads than young Ross's. She was having much the same effect upon him as she had had upon Joe Ninfield, but she couldn't do much damage to his heart in one evening. As for the budding dramatist's play, it seemed uncertain whether it would turn out to be a chronicle, starting with Katherine's marriage to Prince Arthur (because that would make a splendid scene), and taking, according to Sir Gareth's silent estimate, at last three nights to perform, or a shorter but much gloomier production, starting with a divorce, and ending with an autopsy. The young couple, rapidly arriving at a comfortable state of intimacy, were hotly embroiled in argument by the time the covers were set on the table. Mr. Ross, in thrilling accents, had told Amanda the story of Katherine's exposed heart, so indelibly blackened that not all the efforts of the chandler sufficed to wash it clean. And then the chandler had cut it in twain, and behold! It was black right to the core, with a nameless Thing clutching it so tightly that it could not be wrenched away. Amanda listened to this horrid tale with her eyes growing rounder and rounder, and was enthusiastic in her appreciation of it. Mr. Ross said that it had taken strong possession of his mind also, but he doubted whether the scene would prove suitable for dramatic production. Amanda could see no difficulty. The autopsy would be performed, naturally, on a dummy, and a sponge, well soaked in pitch, would make an excellent heart. She was persuaded that no other dramatist had ever hit upon so splendid and original a final scene. But Mr. Ross, while conceding the splendour and the originality, was inclined to doubt whether it would take the public's fancy.

At this point, Sir Gareth, who had been controlling himself admirably, caught the waiter's astonished eye, and burst out laughing. As two startled faces turned towards him, he got up, saying: "Come to dinner, you young ghouls! And I give you fair warning that anyone offering me blackened hearts as an accompaniment to roast chicken will be instantly banished from the table!"

Mr. Ross, taking this in good part, grinned, but even as he rose to his feet he noticed that a distressing change had come over Amanda. A moment earlier she had been all animation and interest, her expressive eyes full of sparkle and the enchanting smile, with its hint of mischief, never far from her lips; now, as though at the waving of a wand, all the liveliness had vanished from her face, her eyes had clouded, and she looked as though she had awakened suddenly from a pleasant dream to very disagreeable reality. For an anxious moment Mr. Ross wondered whether he could possibly have said anything to offend her. Then Sir Gareth, waiting behind the chair which he had pulled out for her at the table, said, not exactly imperatively, but in a voice of authority: "Come along, my child!"

She rose with obvious reluctance, and, as she took her place at the table, cast a look up at her guardian which considerably surprised Mr. Ross, so resentful was it. He could only suppose that there had been some disagreement between them. Sir Gareth seemed to be very pleasant and good-humoured, but perhaps, under his charm of manner, he was a stricter guardian than one would guess. This conclusion was almost immediately borne out by his refusal to permit Amanda to fetch her kitten down to the coffee-room. Hardly had she seated herself than she started up again, saying that Joseph must be allowed to share the repast. She would have left the table on the words, but Sir Gareth's hand shot out, and caught her wrist. "Oh, no!" he said.

He sounded amused, but the colour rushed up into Amanda's face, and she tried to wrench free, exclaiming in a low, shaking voice: "I wasn't! I didn't even *think* of — Let me go!"

He released her wrist, but he too had risen, and he obliged her to sit down again, his hands on her shoulders. He kept them there for a minute. "Joseph shall join us after dinner," he said. "I don't think we want him at table."

He went back to his place, and, as though nothing had happened, began to talk to Hildebrand.

Had he been asked to consider the question dispassionately, Hildebrand would have given his vote against the inclusion of a kitten at the board, but confronted by Amanda's mortified face it was impossible to be dispassionate. She was biting her pretty lip, her eyes downcast, and her cheeks still flushed, and these signs of discomfiture made Sir Gareth's conduct seem a little tyrannical. However, he had seen his sisters behave in very much the same way when thwarted, and he thought that probably she would recover from her pet if no heed were paid to her, and he resolutely turned his eyes away from her, and listened to what Sir Gareth was saying to him.

Meanwhile, Amanda, rejecting the soup, was struggling with her emotions. Mr. Ross had been quite right in thinking that she had been jerked back to disagreeable reality. While she had been listening to his delightful anecdotes of Queen Katherine, she had forgotten what the future held in store for her. Sir Gareth's voice had recalled her, and all the evils of her situation came rushing in on her with such force that she almost burst into tears. A bitter sense of frustration possessed her, and the fact that Sir Gareth, who was its author, was as good-humoured as ever did nothing to soothe her. It made her very angry to be treated as though she were a child whose troubles were trivial, and would soon be forgotten; and the look Hildebrand had seen her cast at him had indeed been resentful. She had toyed with the notion of refusing to sit down to dinner, but had found herself, to her further annoyance, obeying that pleasantly spoken yet determined summons. She didn't quite know why, but it hadn't seemed possible to do anything else. Then he had refused to let her fetch her dear little kitten, because he had suspected that she was going to run away again. Since she really hadn't any such intention, this seemed to her the height of injustice, and made the cup of her wrongs flow over. And now, instead of trying to atone for the insult by coaxing her to drink her soup, and wooing her with soft words, as Grandpapa would certainly have done, he was paying no heed to her at all, but talking to Mr. Ross instead. This was treatment to which she was quite unaccustomed, for although Neil had never tried to coax her out of a tantrum his methods of dealing with her had not so far included ostracism.

The sense of ill-usage grew. Not even the budding playwright, who had seemed to have a great deal of sensibility, cared a button whether she ate what was set before her, or starved. He was telling Sir Gareth all about his horse, which had been given him as a birthday present by his father. The noble animal was even now in the stable attached to the White Lion, for he was riding to Ludlow, which was far preferable to going by a stuffy coach: did not Sir Gareth agree? His mama had not liked his going off quite by himself, but Father perfectly understood that one wanted to be free to go where one chose when one was enjoying the Long Vacation. He was a great gun: not at all like some fathers one had met, who were always finding fault, or getting into a grand fuss, merely because their sons had forgotten to write home for a week or two.

How odious Sir Gareth was, thought Amanda, to encourage young Mr. Ross to forget all about her! It was all of a piece: no doubt he was making himself agreeable just to spike her guns, in case she should try to enlist Mr. Ross as an ally. That was what he had done at Whitethorn Farm, turning even kind Mr. Ninfield against her, and inducing him to believe all the shocking lies he had uttered.

But Mr. Ross had not forgotten her. He had been covertly watching her, and he now ventured to turn his face fully towards her, and to smile at her. She smiled back at him, but so pathetically that he became convinced that something must be very much amiss.

She grew rather more cheerful after dinner, for her stern guardian permitted her to bring Joseph down to the coffee-room, and after Joseph had been regaled with a portion of minced chicken he very obligingly diverted the company by engaging in a protracted form of guerrilla warfare with a ball of screwed-up paper.

In the middle of this entertainment, Trotton came in for any final orders his master might wish to give him, and while Sir Gareth was talking to him Mr. Ross seized the opportunity to whisper: "I beg pardon, but — is anything amiss?"

His fears were then confirmed. Amanda's eyes flew towards Sir Gareth in a way that clearly showed her dread of him, and she whispered in reply: "*Everything!* Hush!"

He was obediently silent, but he resolved to pursue his enquiries as soon as Sir Gareth gave him the chance to speak to her alone. Unfortunately, Sir Gareth gave him no chance, but very soon dashed all his hopes by breaking up the party at an early hour. He said that since she had had a long and a tiring day, and would have another tomorrow, Amanda must go to bed in good time.

"But I don't wish to go to bed, for I am not in the *least* sleepy!" objected Amanda.

"I'm sure you're not, but I am, and you can see that Joseph is too," returned Sir Gareth.

The very speaking look she exchanged with Mr. Ross, as she reluctantly rose from her chair, was intended to convey to him her opinion of persons who ordered her to bed as though she was a baby, but he interpreted it as an appeal for aid, and his chivalry was fired.

Sir Gareth, an amused observer of this by-play, thought it time to call a halt. If this romantic and impressionable youth saw much more of Amanda, it seemed likely that his walking tour would be ruined by a severe attack of frustrated calf-love, which would be rather too bad, for he looked just the kind of oversensitive boy to be seriously upset by it. So he bade him a kind but firm goodnight, shaking hands with him, and saying that perhaps they had better call it goodbye, since he and Amanda would be leaving Kimbolton very early in the morning.

He then swept Amanda inexorably away. Mr. Ross, bent on making an assignation with this distressed damsel, conceived the happy notion of slipping a note under her bedroom door, and suddenly realized that he had no idea which room had been allotted to her. The only way of discovering this seemed to be to go upstairs himself, as though on his way to bed, and listen carefully at all the possible doors for some sound that would disclose her exact whereabouts. He was pretty sure that she would talk to Joseph while she made herself ready for bed, and in this hope he too mounted the stairs.

CHAPTER TWELVE

He found, when he reached the square landing at the head of the stairs, that it was going to be a simpler matter than he had feared to locate Amanda's room. The sound of her voice came to him, from the corridor that led from the landing to the end of the house, and it was evident that instead of retiring immediately to bed she had detained Sir Gareth to engage him in hot argument.

"You have no *right* to force me to go with you!"

"Very well: I have no right, but nevertheless you will go with me," Sir Gareth replied, rather wearily. "For heaven's sake, stop arguing, and go to bed, Amanda!"

Hildebrand hesitated. By all the canons of his upbringing he ought either to advertise his presence, or to go away. He had almost started to tiptoe down the stairs again when it occurred to him that too scrupulous a regard for his own honour in this instance might militate against his being able to rescue Amanda. He remained where he was, not, indeed, quite comfortable, but fairly well persuaded that Amanda at least would raise no objection to his eavesdropping. Her next words almost brought tears of sympathy to his eyes.

"Oh, if you had a *heart* you would let me go!" she said tragically.

From the chuckle that followed this impassioned outburst, it was to be inferred that Sir Gareth was not at all moved by it. "That is a splendid line, and very creditably delivered," he approved. "Now you must ring down the curtain, for fear of falling into anticlimax! Have you everything you need for the night?"

She paid no heed to this, but said, in a voice trembling with indignation: "I was never so deceived in anyone! No, or those others!"

"What others?"

"All of them! — that fat landlady, and the Ninfields, and now Mr. Ross! You made them all l-like you, because you have ch-charming manners, and address, and they believed you when you told the w-wickedest untruths, and you make it so that it is no *use* for me to tell them that you are not a gentleman at all, but a *snake!*"

"Poor Amanda! Now, listen, you foolish child! I know I seem to you to be heartless, and detestably tyrannical, but, believe me, you'll thank me for it one day. Come, now, dry your eyes! Anyone would suppose that I really was going to carry you off to that mouldering castle of mine! Instead of that I am taking you to London. Is that so dreadful? I daresay you will enjoy it. How would it be if I took you to the play?"

"No!" she said passionately. "I am not a child, and I won't be bribed like that! How dare you talk to me of going to a stupid play, when you are determined to ruin my life? You *are* detestable, and I see that it is useless to appeal to your better nature, because you haven't got a better nature!"

"Black to the core — like Queen Katherine's heart," agreed Sir Gareth gravely. "Go to bed, my child: the future won't look so ill in the morning. There is, however, just one thing I must tell you before I bid you goodnight. Much as I regret the necessity, I am going to lock your door."

"No!" cried Amanda pantingly. "You shan't, you shan't! Give me back that key! Give it back to me *instantly!*"

"No, Amanda. I warned you that you were

not dealing with a flat. If I gave it to you, you would run away as soon as you thought I was asleep. You are not going to escape again."

"You can't be so inhuman as to lock me up! I might be *ill!*"

"Oh, I don't think you will be!"

"I might *die!*" she urged.

"Well, if you did that, it wouldn't signify whether you were locked in, or not, would it?"

"Oh, how hateful you are! I might be burnt in my bed!"

"If the house should happen to catch fire, I will engage not only to rescue you, but Joseph as well. Goodnight — and dream of a revenge on me!"

Mr. Ross heard the click of a closing door, and the grating of the key in the lock. He moved softly forward to peep round the angle of the wall, and was in time to see Sir Gareth withdraw the key from the lock of a door, and cross the corridor to a room directly opposite.

For several minutes Mr. Ross remained on the landing, not knowing just what he ought to do. When he had heard Amanda beg Sir Gareth not to lock her door, his impulse had been to dash to her support. But before he could do so, all the awkward-

271

ness of his situation had been realized, and he had hesitated. Profoundly shocked though he was, and burning to perform some heroic deed for Amanda's sake, he yet could not feel that he would be justified in intervening, or ever, perhaps, successful. It was cruel of Sir Gareth to lock the door on Amanda, but if he was her guardian no one could gainsay his right to do so. The things Amanda had said to him certainly indicated that he had behaved very badly to her, but what he had done, or why she was so reluctant to accompany him to London, could at present be matters only for conjecture.

He decided that his first step must be to find a way of approaching Amanda, and he did not immediately perceive how this was to be accomplished. A whispered conversation through the keyhole would be a very indifferent way of communicating with her, and might well bring Sir Gareth out upon him. A little further consideration, however, put him in mind of the fact that her bedroom must, from its position, look out on to the small, walled garden at the back of the inn, and he conceived the happy idea of walking out into this, and of attracting Amanda's attention by throwing stones at her window.

Fortunately, since he might have been hard put to it to distinguish her window amongst several others which looked on to the garden, this expedient was found to be unnecessary. Amanda's window stood open, and Amanda was kneeling at it, clearly silhouetted by the candle behind her, her elbows on the ledge, and her face propped between her hands.

Thrust firmly into her room, and the door closed on her, the agitation from which she was suffering had found relief in a burst of tears. Without having precisely decided on a course of action, she had been turning over in her mind a plan of escaping from the White Loin as soon as it was light; and the discovery that Sir Gareth had been aware of this provoked her to quite irrational fury. Though she meant to outwit him if she could, it was insulting of him to suspect her; and his calm air of mastery made her want to hit him. Well, she would show him!

The first step towards showing him had been to run to the window, to ascertain whether it were possible to climb down from it, or even, since the upper storey of the house was at no great height from the ground, to drop down from it. She had not previously thought of this way of escape, and so had not inspected the window. It needed only the most cursory inspection now to inform her that to squeeze herself through it would be impossible. She began to cry again, and was still convulsively sobbing when Mr. Ross came cautiously into the garden through a wicket-gate opening into the stable-yard, and saw her.

The moon was up, brightly illuminating the scene, so there was really no need for Mr. Ross, softly treading along the flagged path until he stood immediately beneath Amanda's window, to attract her attention by saying, thrillingly, "Hist!" Amanda had seen him as soon as he entered the garden, and had moodily watched his approach. She could think of no way in which he could be of assistance to her.

"Miss Smith! I must have speech with you!" piercingly whispered Mr. Ross. "I heard all!"

"All what?" said Amanda crossly.

"All that you said to Sir Gareth! Only tell me what I can do to help you!"

"No one can help me," replied Amanda, sunk in gloom.

"*I* can, and will," promised Mr. Ross recklessly.

A faint interest gleamed in her eyes. She abandoned her despairing pose, and looked down at his upturned face. "How? He locked me in, and the window is too small for me to get out of."

"I will think of a way. Only we cannot continue talking like this. Someone may hear us! Wait! There is bound to be a ladder in the stables! If I can contrive to do so unobserved, I'll fetch it, and climb up to you!"

Amanda began to feel more hopeful. Up till now she had not considered him in the light of a possible rescuer, for he seemed to her very young, and no match for a man of Sir Gareth's fiendish ingenuity. He now appeared to be a man of action and resource. She waited.

Time passed, and the slight hope she was cherishing dwindled. Then, just as she was thinking that there was nothing to do but to go to bed, Mr. Ross came back, bearing a short ladder, which was used for climbing into the hay-loft. He set this up against the wall of the house, and mounted it. He had to climb to the topmost rung before his head rose above the window-sill, and his hands could grasp it, and the last part of the ascent was somewhat precariously accomplished.

"Oh, pray be careful!" begged Amanda, alarmed but admiring.

"It's quite safe," he assured her. "I beg

pardon for having been such an age: I had to wait, you see, because that man — your guardian's groom — was giving the head ostler all manner of directions. Why are you locked in?"

"Because Sir Gareth is determined not to let me escape," she replied bitterly.

"Yes, but — you see, I did not perfectly understand from what you was saying to him why you wish to escape, or what he means to do with you. Of course, I saw how much you feared him long before!"

"Saw how much I — oh! Oh, yes!" said Amanda, swallowing with an effort her very natural indignation. "I am wholly in his power!"

"Yes, well, I suppose — I mean, if he's your guardian, you must be. But what has he done to frighten you! Why did you say he was a snake?"

Amanda did not answer for a moment. She was feeling tired, quite unequal to the task of rapidly composing a suitable explanation. A sigh broke from her. The sadness of this sound wrought powerfully upon Mr. Ross. He ventured to remove one hand from the sill, and to lay it tenderly on hers. "Tell me!" he said.

"He is abducting me," said Amanda.

Mr. Ross was so much astonished that he

nearly fell off the ladder. *"Abducting* you?" he gasped. "You cannot be serious!"

"Yes, I am! And, what is more, it's true!" said Amanda.

"Good God! I would not have believed it to have been possible! My dear Miss Smith, you may be easy! I will instantly have you set free! There will be no difficulty. I have but to inform the parish constable, or perhaps a magistrate — I am not perfectly sure, but I shall speedily discover —"

"No, no!" she interrupted hastily. "It would be useless! *Pray* do not do so!"

"But I am persuaded it is what I should do!" he expostulated. "How should it be useless?"

She sought wildly for some explanation which would satisfy him. None occurred to her, until, just as she was wondering whether she dared tell him the truth, or whether (which she suspected) he would disapprove as heartily as Sir Gareth of her plan of campaign, there flashed into her brain a notion of transcendent splendour. It almost took her breath away, for not only was it an excellent story in itself: it would, properly handled, afford her the means of being exquisitely revenged on Sir Gareth. It was Sir Gareth's own story, now to prove his undoing. "You see," said Amanda, drawing a deep, ecstatic breath. "I am an heiress."

"Oh!" said Mr. Ross, rather at a loss.

"I was left an orphan at an early age," she continued embellishing Sir Gareth's crude handiwork. "Alas! I am quite alone in the world, without kith or kin."

Mr. Ross, himself a great reader of romances, found nothing to object to in the style of this narrative, but cavilled a little at the matter. "What, have you no relations at all?" he asked incredulously. "No cousins, even?"

Amanda thought him unnecessarily captious, but obligingly presented him with a relative. "Yes, I have an uncle," she conceded. "But he cannot help me, so —"

"But why not? *Surely* —"

Amanda, regretting the creation of an uncle who seemed likely to prove an embarrassment, with great presence of mind placed him beyond Mr. Ross's reach. "He is in Bedlam," she said. "So we need not think any more about *him.* The thing is that —"

"Mad?" interrupted Mr. Ross, in horrified accents.

"*Raving* mad," said Amanda firmly.

"How very dreadful!"

"Yes, isn't it? Because I have no one to turn to but Sir Gareth."

"Is he a dangerous madman?" asked Mr.

Ross, apparently fascinated by the uncle.

"I do wish you would stop asking questions about my uncle, and attend to what I am saying!" said Amanda, exasperated.

"I beg pardon! It must be excessively painful for you!"

"Yes, and it is quite beside the point, too. Sir Gareth, wishing to possess himself of my fortune, is determined to force me into marriage with himself, and for this purpose is carrying me to London."

"To London? I should have thought —"

"To London," repeated Amanda emphatically. "Because that is where he lives, and he means to incarcerate me in his house until I submit. And it's no use saying the parish constable would stop him, because Sir Gareth would deny every word, and say that he was taking me to live with his sister, who is a very disagreeable woman, and would do anything to oblige him. And everyone would believe him, because they always do. So you would only make a great noise, which I should very much dislike, and all to no purpose."

Mr. Ross could see that this was very likely, but he was still puzzled. "Where have you been living?" he demanded. "I don't perfectly understand. You said he abducted you: haven't you been residing under his roof?"

"No, no, I have hitherto resided with a very respectable woman, who —" She stopped, and decided to eliminate a possible danger. "Who is dead. I mean, she died two years ago, and Sir Gareth then placed me in a seminary, which is exactly the sort of thing he *would* do! Only now that I am old enough to be married, he came and removed me, and naturally I was pleased, because *then* I believed him to be everything that was amiable. But when he told me that I must marry him —"

"Good God, I should have thought he would have had more address!" exclaimed Mr. Ross. "Told you that you must marry him when he had only that instant removed you from the seminary?"

"Oh, no! The thing was that he supposed I should like the notion, because previously I had been excessively attached to him, on account of his being so handsome, and agreeable. Only, of course, I never thought of marrying him. Why, he's quite old! So then I was in a great fright, and I ran away from the place where we were staying last night, and he chased me all day, and found me at last, and brought me here. And I cannot think how to escape again, and oh, I am so very unhappy!"

The passionate sincerity with which these final words were uttered pierced Mr. Ross to the heart. He was ashamed to think that he had for a moment doubted the story, and in some agitation implored Amanda not to cry. Amanda, between sobs, told him of her earlier adventures. These had been wholly enjoyable at the time, but regarded in retrospect, now that she was tired and defeated, the day seemed to her to have been one of unrelieved misery and discomfort.

Mr. Ross had no difficulty in believing this at least. He would, indeed, have found it impossible to have believed that anything less than the direst necessity could have induced a gently-born young female to have taken so unprecedented and perilous a step as to cast herself upon the world as she had done. From the moment of her escape, the poor little thing had been mercilessly hounded. It did not surprise him to learn that the fat old gentleman who had with such false kindness offered to carry her to Oundle had tried to take advantage of her innocence. His sensitive nature made it easy for him to imagine the desperation of terror which must have had her in its grip; and the thought of so fragile and lovely a creature cowering on the floor of a farm-cart made him shudder, not the smallest suspicion entering his head that she had thoroughly enjoyed this part of her adventure. The description of the devilish cunning employed by Sir Gareth to regain possession of her lost nothing in the telling. Sir Gareth began, in Mr. Ross's mind, to assume an aspect of smiling villainy. He wondered how he should have been taken-in by his pleasant manners, until he remembered certain warnings given him by his father against too readily trusting smooth-tongued and apparently creditable gentlemen of fashionable appearance. The world, said the Squire, was full of plausible banditti on the lookout for green young men of fortune. Their stock-in-trade was winning charm, and they frequently bestowed titles upon themselves, generally military. No doubt they were also on the look-out for rich wives, but naturally the Squire had not thought it necessary to tell his son this.

Had some chance brought Mr. Ross face to face with Sir Gareth again, it was possible that his leaping imagination would have suffered a check. But Sir Gareth had gone to bed, and Mr. Ross's last sight of him had been of him in the corridor, locking Amanda into her room. Every word he had said to Amanda bore out the truth of her story, and of his cynical heartlessness there could be no doubt. Only a hardened scoundrel, in Mr. Ross's opinion, could have laughed at Amanda's anguish. Sir Gareth, not content with laughing, had mocked at her distress. He had also (now one came to think of it) tried to deceive her with promises of generous entertainment in London.

No chance brought Sir Gareth on to the scene to counteract the combined influences on an impressionable youth of Amanda and a full moon. Perched on the stable-ladder, a modern Romeo and his Juliet discussed ways and means.

It did not take them long to discard the trappings of convention. "Oh, I wish you will not call me Miss Smith!" said Juliet. "Amanda!" breathed Mr. Ross reverently. "And my name is Hildebrand."

"Isn't it odd that we should both of us have the most ridiculous names?" said Amanda. "Do you find yours a sad trial?"

Struck by her rare understanding, Mr. Ross told her just how sad a trial his name had been to him, and explained to her the precise circumstances which had led to his being given a name calculated to blight his scholastic career. He had never dreamed it could sound well until he heard it on her lips.

After this digression, they became more practical, and very much more argumentative. A number of schemes for Amanda's deliverance, all of which depended upon some extremely improbable stroke of good fortune, were considered, and dismissed regretfully; and a promising new alliance was nearly ruptured by Hildebrand's rejection of a daring suggestion that he should creep into Sir Gareth's room, and steal from under his pillow (where there could be no doubt it was hidden) the key to Amanda's room. In Hildebrand, an inculcated respect for convention warred with a craving for romance. The thought of the construction Sir Gareth would inevitably place on the attempted theft of the key, should he wake (as Hildebrand rather thought he would) before the accomplishment of the design, made that young gentleman blush all over his slim body. He was naturally unable to disclose to Amanda the cause of his reluctance, and so was obliged to endure the mortification of being thought a wretchedly cowardly creature.

"Oh, well, if you are *afraid* — !" said Amanda, with a disdainful shrug of her shoulders.

Her scorn sharpened his wits. The glimmerings of a plan, more daring than any that had occurred to her, flickered in his brain. "Wait!" he commanded, his brows knit portentously. "I have a better notion!"

She waited. After a prolonged silence, pregnant with suspense, Mr. Ross said suddenly: "Are you willing to place your honour in my hands?"

"Yes, yes, of course I am!" responded Amanda, agog with expectation.

"And do you think," he asked anxiously, descending with disconcerting rapidity from these heights, "that, if I were mounted on my horse, Prince, you could contrive to leap up before me?"

"I could, if you reached down your hand to me," replied Amanda optimistically.

He considered this for a daunted moment. "Well, I shall be holding a pistol in my right hand, and I shouldn't *think* I could contrive to hold the bridle in it as well," he said dubiously. "I could try, of course, but — no, I think it would be best if I tucked the reins under my knee. And even if Prince does become restive it won't signify, once I have you firmly gripped. All you have to do is to set your foot on mine in the stirrup, and spring the moment I tell you to. Do you think you can do that?"

"Are you going to ride off with me across your saddlebow?" demanded Amanda eagerly.

"Yes — well, no, not precisely! I mean, I thought, if you put your arms round me, you could sit before me — just until we were beyond the reach of pursuit!" he added quickly.

"Yes, that would be much more comfortable," she agreed. "Of course I could do it!"

"Well, when the notion first came to me, I thought you could, too, but now I come to think of it more particularly, I can see that it is a thing we ought to practise."

"No, no, I am persuaded there can be not the least difficulty!" she urged. "Only think how knights in olden times were for ever riding off with distressed ladies!"

"Yes, and in armour, too!" he said, forcibly struck. "Still, we don't know but what they may have bungled it before they acquired the habit, and it won't do for us to bungle it. I think I had better dismount, and hold Prince while you get upon his back. Are you able to mount without assistance?"

"Certainly I am! But what are you going to do?"

"Hold you up on the road to Bedford!" disclosed Hildebrand.

Amanda uttered a squeak, which he correctly interpreted as an expression of admiration and approval, and gave a little jump of excitement. "Like a highwayman? Oh, what a *splendid* scheme! *Pray* forgive me for not having thought you had any courage!"

"It's a pretty desperate thing to do, of course," said Hildebrand, "but I can see that only desperate measures will answer in this case and I would do *anything* to save you from your guardian! I cannot conceive why your father left you in the care of such an infamous person! It seems the oddest thing!"

"He was deceived in him, but never mind that!" said Amanda hastily. "How do you know he means to go to Bedford?"

"I discovered it when I was waiting for an opportunity to seize this ladder! Only to think that I was wishing that groom at Jericho, when all the time I had been guided to the stables by Providence! Because the groom was arranging for the hire of a chaise for his master, and enquiring about the state of the road that runs to Bedford. It's not a pike-road, you know, but Sir Gareth means to go by it, just to Bedford, which is only one stage. And there you are to change from this chaise, which is a shabby, old-fashioned one, and go on to London in a better one, which, of course, may readily be hired in a place like Bedford. Four horses, too! By Jove, it is *another* instance of Providence! For, you know, if this weren't such a quiet place, with precious little custom, I daresay they would keep any number of fast vehicles for hire, and bang-up cattle as well, and I might have been at a stand. For I daresay I should have found it pretty hard to cover *two* postilions, as well as Sir Gareth. But only a pair of horses are hired for the first stage, which makes my task much easier. And I will own myself astonished if we do not find the road deserted, so early in the day! I mean, it can't be like the pike-roads, with mails and stages going up and down at all hours."

Amanda agreed to this, but was shaken by doubt. "Yes, but how will you procure a pistol?" she objected.

"Procure one! I have a pair of my own, in my saddle holsters," said Hildebrand, unable to keep a note of pride out of his voice. "Loaded, too."

"Oh!" said Amanda, rather thoughtfully.

"You need not be afraid that I don't know how to handle them. My father holds that one should be accustomed to guns as soon as possible. I don't wish to boast, but I am accounted a tolerably good shot."

"Yes, but I don't wish you to shoot Sir Gareth, or even the post-boy," said Amanda uneasily.

"Good God, no! Of course I shall do nothing of the sort! Lord, a pretty kick-up *that* would mean! I might be obliged to fire one of the pistols over the post-boy's head, to frighten him, you know, but I promise you I shan't do more. There won't be the least need. I shall hold Sir Gareth covered, and you may depend upon it he won't dare to move, with my pistol pointing at his head. He is bound to be taken quite by surprise, but *you* will not be, and you must lose not an instant in jumping down from the chaise, and mounting Prince. Then I shall get up behind you, and we shall be off in a trice." He paused, but Amanda said nothing. After a moment, he said, rather hurt: "You don't care for the scheme?"

"Yes, I do!" she replied warmly. "I like it excessively, for I have always wished to have adventures, and I can see that this would be a truly splendid adventure. Except for the pistols."

"Oh, if that is all — ! I promise you, you need not be afraid: I won't even fire in the air!"

"Oh, well, then — no, it won't do. Nothing is of any use, because I have nowhere to go to," said Amanda, plunging back into dejection.

But Hildebrand was not daunted. "Don't be unhappy!" he begged. "I had been thinking of where I should take you, and, if you should not dislike it, I fancy I have hit upon the very thing. Of course, if this had not chanced to fall at an awkward time, I should have taken you home, so that Mama could have looked after you, which, I assure you, she would have been delighted to do. But it so happens that my eldest sister is about to be confined, and Mama has gone away to be with her, while Father is at this very moment taking Blanche and Amabel to Scarborough, for a month. It is very vexatious, but never mind! I will take you to Hannah instead. She is the dearest creature, and I *know* you would be happy with her, for she used to be our nurse, and she will do anything in the world for me. And her husband is a very good sort of a man. He is a farmer, and they have the jolliest farm, not far from Newmarket. What I thought was that I should ride with you 'cross country, to St. Neots, and there hire a chaise. I suppose I shall be obliged to stable Prince there, or perhaps I could ride him as far as to Cambridge. Yes, that would be best, for I am accustomed to keep a horse when I am up, and I shall know he will be well cared-for at the livery-stables there."

"A farm?" said Amanda, reviving as though by magic. "With cows, and hens, and pigs? Oh, I should like that of all things! Yes, yes, *do* hold us up tomorrow!"

"Well, I will," he said, gratified. "Then, when I have escorted you to Nurse, I think I should post off to Scarborough, to ask Father just what ought to be done in such a case. Depend upon it, he will know exactly."

This part of the scheme held out no appeal to Amanda, but she did not say so. There would be time enough at her disposal to dissuade Hildebrand; the immediate need was to escape from Sir Gareth. It seemed to her very unlikely that he would run her to earth at Newmarket; while a farm, as she had already decided, would be an ideal refuge in which to await the capitulation of her grandfather. Her weariness forgotten with the revival of her hopes, she discussed with Hildebrand the various ramifications of his plot; and parted from him finally with only one flaw spoiling her satisfaction. Hildebrand, although willing to engage in any dangerous enterprise for her sake, drew the line at Joseph. A kitten, he said, would place the whole enterprise in jeopardy. Moreover, he doubted very much whether

Joseph would enjoy riding on a horse. He rather thought he would not. Amanda was obliged to give way on this point, and could only hope that Sir Gareth would be kind to Joseph when he found himself his sole support.

CHAPTER THIRTEEN

Mr. Ross, by his own overnight request, was roused by the boots, though not without difficulty, at an unseasonably early hour on the following morning. Having consulted his watch, he was just about to turn over in bed, and sink back into slumber, when the events of the previous evening came rushing back to him. He gave a gasp, and sat up, all desire to sleep being effectually banished by a recollection which, it had to be admitted, was extremely unwelcome.

It was extraordinary what a difference daylight made. A plan which had seemed, in the moonlight, to have everything to recommend it, was no sooner inspected in the clear light of the morning than it was found to bear the hall-marks, if not of madness, at least of alarming foolhardiness. Mr. Ross, thinking it over, was inclined to think he had been bewitched. It was not that he disliked the plan: given the right setting, there was nothing he had rather do than ride off with Amanda on his saddle-bow. The mischief was that the right setting was lacking. The adventure demanded an odd dragon or two in the background, and a few false knights in full armour. One could make do, at a pinch, with love-locks and a leather coat, exchanging the dragons and the knights for a contingent of Roundheads; but a nineteenth-century scene was hopelessly anachronous. It was not an encounter with a dragon which one would have to avoid, but one with a stage-coach, or a carrier's van; and instead of winning great worship by the deed one was much more likely to be sent to prison, or, at the very least, severely reprimanded for having done something that one's elders would say was not the thing.

Sitting up in bed, hugging his knees, and staring out of the window at the promise of another hot day, Mr. Ross seriously considered crying off from the engagement. But the more he thought about it, the more impossible did it appear that he could do so. For one thing, he could scarcely climb a ladder to Amanda's window in broad daylight; for another, his last words to her had been an assurance that she might trust him, and to fail her at the eleventh hour would be conduct of unforgivable baseness. She had already doubted his mettle, too. There was nothing for it but to do his best to carry the adventure through to a triumphant conclusion. Instead of wishing that he had not been quite so impulsive, he forced his mind to dwell on the wrongs Amanda had suffered at the perfidious Sir Gareth's hands; and in this way he managed to keep up his resolution. By sacrificing one of a pair of black silk evening stockings, he contrived to fashion a very tolerable mask, and when he tried it on in front of the mirror, with his frieze riding-cloak wrapped round him, and his hat pulled low on his brow, the effect was so awe-inspiring that his spirits rose considerably. But he had little appetite for his breakfast. However, he drank some coffee, and ate a slice of ham, taking care, in case Sir Gareth should later enquire for him, to talk at great length to a bored and sleepy waiter about his plans for his supposed journey into Wales. He asked searching questions about the road, and the towns he would reach, and rose at last from the table with the comfortable conviction that if Sir Gareth asked any questions he would certainly be told that Mr. Ross, desirous of covering as much ground as possible before the heat of the day made travel disagreeable, had set forward on his way to Wales an hour earlier.

But Sir Gareth made no enquiries. In his experience, very young gentlemen found it much harder to wake up in the morning than did their seniors. He was frequently obliged, when he invited Mr. Leigh Wetherby to visit him in the country, to employ the most ruthless methods of getting his nephew out of bed; and he had not expected to see Hildebrand at the breakfast-table.

He was glad to find that his captive was apparently resigned to her fate. She attempted no further argument, and if her expression was discontented, and the glances she cast at him repulsive, at least she was able to enjoy a pretty substantial breakfast. He refrained tactfully from addressing anything but commonplace remarks to her; and to these he received cold and generally monosyllabic answers.

The start to the journey was slightly delayed by the tardiness of the post-boy in presenting himself at the White Lion for duty. He had been granted a holiday on the previous day, and pleaded that he had not known that his services had been commanded for such an early hour. There was no post-master at the inn, since only two boys were employed there, and the landlord told Sir Gareth that all postilions were the same: dratted nuisances, always taking twice as long as they ought to lead their horses home lear, quarrelling amongst themselves, and for ever sneaking off into the village when they should have been at hand, ready to put off their white overalls, and jump into the saddle. He was incensed with this one for having stayed away all night; but there was one person who would been a good deal relieved, had he known of the defection. Mr. Ross, trotting along the Bedford road, on the look-out for a suitable ambush, had suddenly realized that a post-boy from the White Lion could scarcely fail to recognize the handsome chestnut which had been stabled in one of the loose boxes there.

The chaise which Sir Gareth had been forced to hire was not one of the light, modern vehicles, nor was it very well-hung. Sir Gareth, observing the scornful and slightly affronted glance which Amanda pointedly cast at its worn squabs, gravely apologized for conveying her to Bedford in a carriage wholly unworthy of her dignity, and promised to transfer her there into the smartest and fastest chaise the best posting-house could produce. She sniffed.

She was plainly determined not to un-bend; and since Sir Gareth had not the smallest wish to make civil conversation at so early an hour, he did not attempt to charm her out of her sulks, but leaned back in his own corner of the chaise, idly looking out of the window at as much of the countryside as he could see. This was not very much, for the lane, which was narrow, and appeared to be little used, was bordered by uneven and straggling hedges. It passed through no towns, and the few villages it served were none of them more than hamlets. Here and there a cluster of farm-buildings were to be seen, and several narrow lanes, no better than cart-tracks, debouched on to it. After a time, wearying of a singularly uninteresting prospect, Sir Gareth turned his head, and surveyed Amanda. It struck him immediately that her expression of sullen resignation had vanished, and, an instant later, that there was an air of suppressed excitement about her. There was a pretty colour in her cheeks, her eyes were very bright, and she was sitting bolt upright, her hands clasped tightly in her lap.

"Amanda," said Sir Gareth, with mock severity, "what mischief are you brewing?"

She jumped guiltily. "I shan't tell you! But I said I should make you sorry, and I *shall!*"

He laughed, but forbore to tease her. He

wondered what fantastic plot she was hatching, but not with any feeling of uneasiness. He would certainly have to keep an eye on her when they broke the journey for rest and refreshment, but he rather suspected that she would not attempt to escape again until they reached London. Well, between them, Beatrix and Miss Felbridge ought to be able to keep her under guard until he could hand her over to her grandfather.

He was lying back, with his eyes half closed, hoping that he would not find, upon enquiry at the Horse Guards, that the Brigade-Major had left town, when a loud shout smote his ears, and the chaise drew up with a jarring lurch. "What the devil — ?" he exclaimed, and sat up, looking out of the window to see what had caused the abrupt halt.

The chaise had stopped just short of a small crossroad, and the cause was instantly apparent. A sinister figure, with a mask over his face, and a voluminous cloak enveloping his frame, was covering the astonished post-boy with a silver-mounted pistol, and threatening, in alarmingly gruff accents, to blow his head off if he moved an eyelid. The apparition was bestriding a good-looking hack, and finding it a little difficult at one and the same time to keep this animal still and the pistol correctly levelled.

One comprehensive glance told Sir Gareth all he wished to know. His lips twitched, he looked round at Amanda, saying: "You little fiend!" and then opened the door of the chaise, and sprang lightly down on to the road.

Mr. Ross became flustered. Events were not turning out quite as he had expected. He had certainly found an excellent ambush in the little cross-road, and the post-boy had not hesitated to obey at least the first part of his command to stand and deliver. Unfortunately, Prince, also bidden savagely to stand, was not as docile. For one thing, he was unaccustomed to shouts being uttered just above his head, and, for another, he could tell that his master was strangely nervous. He began to fidget, backing, sidling, trying to get his head. The harassed Mr. Ross knew that Amanda would find it very hard to mount him, and became more flustered. A quick look showed him that Amanda, instead of nipping out of the chaise by the off-side door, was having difficulty in opening it. And he had not bargained for Sir Gareth's jumping down in such a reckless fashion. Everything, in fact, was going wrong. He dismounted swiftly, and ordered Sir Gareth to stand where he was, but as he dared not release Prince's bridle, and had not had the forethought to dismount on the right instead of the left, he found himself in a most awkward fix, trying to keep Sir Gareth covered by the pistol gripped in his right hand while his left was being dragged across his chest by Prince's efforts to back away.

"Don't brandish that pistol about, you young fool!" Sir Gareth said.

"Put up your hands!" retorted Hildebrand. "If you move another step I shall fire!"

"Nonsense! Come, now, enough of this folly! Give me the pistol at once!"

Hildebrand, seeing Sir Gareth advancing in the coolest fashion, took an involuntary step backwards. Out of the corner of his eye, he saw that the post-boy had slid out of his saddle, and was preparing to attack him from the rear; he tried to shift his position so that he could keep both men covered; Prince, now thoroughly alarmed, cannoned into him; and the unexpected jolt caused his finger to tighten round the trigger of his pistol. There was a loud report; Amanda screamed; the post-boy made a dive for his startled horses' heads; Prince reared up, snorting with fright; and Sir Gareth reeled back against the wheel of the chaise, a hand clapped to his left shoulder.

"How could you? Oh, how *could* you?" Amanda cried, almost tumbling out of the chaise. "You *promised* me you would not! Now see what you've done! Are you badly hurt, sir? Oh, I am so very sorry!"

Sir Gareth could not see her very clearly. The world was spinning before his eyes, and his limbs were turning to water. His senses were slipping away too, but he knew what had happened, and he managed, before he lost consciousness, to speak one word: *"Accident . . . !"*

Amanda was on her knees beside him. He had fallen on his left side, and she had seen that his hand had been pressed to that shoulder, and, exerting all her strength, she managed to pull him over on to his back. She then saw the charred rent in his coat, and, far more terrifying, the ominous stain that was rapidly spreading. She tried to pull the coat away from that shoulder, but Sir Gareth's coats were all too well cut. She cried out: "Help me, one of you! *Help* me!" and began with feverish haste to rip off Sir Gareth's neckcloth. The post-boy hesitated. His horses, no fiery steeds, had quietened, but his eyes were fixed wrathfully on the supposed highwayman, and he seemed more than half inclined to go to him rather than to Amanda. She looked round, while her hands folded and refolded Sir Gareth's neckcloth into a pad, and said furiously: "*Help* me, I said!"

"Yes, miss, but — is he to be let make off?" the post-boy said, taking a reluctant step towards her, but keeping his glowering eyes on Hildebrand.

"No, no!" Hildebrand uttered hoarsely. "I won't — I wouldn't — !"

"Never mind, never mind, come here!" Amanda commanded, thrusting her hand, with the pad held in it, inside Sir Gareth's coat.

The post-boy went to her, but when he saw Sir Gareth's pallor, and the blood-soaked coat, he thought he was dead, and muttered involuntarily: "Gawd, he's snuffed it!"

"Lift him!" Amanda said, her teeth clenched to control their chattering. "Lift him, and get his coat off! I'll help you as much as I am able, but I must keep my hand pressed to the wound!"

"It ain't no manner of use, miss!"

"Do as I bid you!" she said angrily. "He's not dead! He is bleeding *dreadfully,* and I *know* he would not if he were dead! Oh, hurry!"

He cast her a look of compassion, but he

obeyed her, raising Sir Gareth in his arms, and contriving, with a little assistance from her, to strip the coat off. She did her best to keep her determined little hand pressed hard over the wound, but the bright red blood welled up, dyeing her fingers scarlet, and dripping on to her light muslin skirt. Mr. Ross, his horse at last under his control, turned to see what aid he could render, and beheld this horrid sight. With a shaking hand, he stripped off his improvised mask, and flung it down. Had either Amanda or the post-boy had leisure to look at him, they would have seen that his face was almost as white as his victim's. His lips parted stickily, he swallowed convulsively, took one wavering step forward, and sank without a sound on to the dusty road.

The post-boy glanced up quickly, and his jaw dropped. "Well, I'll be gormed!" he ejaculated. "Lord love me, if he ain't gone off in a swound! A fine rank-rider *he* is!"

"Take his neckcloth off!" Amanda said. "Quick!"

The post-boy snorted. "Let him lay!"

"Yes, yes, but bring me his neckcloth! This is not enough! Oh, hurry, hurry!"

He still thought that all her labour would be in vain, but he did as she bade him, only pausing beside Hildebrand's inanimate form long enough to wrench the second pistol out of the saddle-holster, and to thrust it into the bosom of his own tightly-fitting jacket. Prince started uneasily, and flung up his head, but the placidity of the post-horses seemed to reassure him, and he remained standing by his master's body.

Amanda had succeeded in reducing the flow of blood, but it was still welling up under the soaked pad. Panic gripped her. The post-boy was obedient, but slow to understand her orders, and he appeared to be incapable of acting on his own initiative; Hildebrand, who should have rushed to her aid, had fainted instead, and was only just beginning to show signs of recovery. Furious with them both, frightened out of her wits, she wanted more than anything to scream. Pride and obstinacy came to her rescue: she was the daughter of a soldier, and she meant to become the wife of a soldier; and own herself beaten she would not. She overcame her rising hysteria after a struggle that made her feel weak and rather sick, and forced her shocked mind to concentrate. Sir Gareth had been hit in the hollow of his shoulder, and a much larger pad than one made by folding a neckcloth must be bound tightly in place before she dared relax the pressure of her desperate little hands. She looked round helplessly, unable for a moment to think of anything; then she remembered that Sir Gareth's portmanteaux were strapped on the back of the chaise, and she ordered the post-boy to unstrap them. "Shirts! Yes, shirts! There must be shirts! And more neckcloths to tie it in place — get them!"

The post-boy unstrapped the portmanteaux, but hesitated, saying: "They'll be locked, surely!"

"Break the locks, then!" she said impatiently. "Oh, if there were only *someone* who could help me!"

By this time, Hildebrand had struggled up. He was sick, and dizzy, and his legs shook under him, but Amanda's anguished cry pulled him together. The blood rushed up into his face; he said thickly, engulfed in shame: "I'll do it!" and went unsteadily to where the post-boy had set one of the portmanteaux down on the road.

"Ho, yes?" said the individual, bristling. "You will, will you? *And* make off with the gentleman's goods, I daresay!"

"Idiot!" The word burst from Amanda. "Can't you see he's not a highwayman? Let him get at that case! I — I *command* you!"

She sounded so fierce that the post-boy gave way instinctively. The portmanteaux was not locked, and with trembling hands Hildebrand flung back the lid, and began to toss over Sir Gareth's effects. He found shirts, and many neckcloths, and a large sponge, at sight of which Amanda exclaimed: "Oh, yes, yes! Tie that up in a shirt, tight, *tight,* and bring it to me! Oh, no, give it to the post-boy, and whatever you do, Hildebrand, don't look this way, or you will go off again in a faint, and there is no *time* to waste in fainting!"

He was too much overcome to answer her, but although he dared not let his eyes stray towards her he could do what she asked, and could even knot several of the neckcloths together. Between them, Amanda and the post-boy contrived to bind the improvised swab tightly in place; and while they worked, Amanda demanded to be told where the nearest inn, or house could be found. The post-boy at first could think of nothing nearer than Bedford, which was some eight miles distant, but upon being adjured pretty sharply to find his wits he said that there was an inn at Little Staughton, a mile down the cross-road. He added that it wasn't fit for the likes of Sir Gareth, upon which, Amanda, wrought up to a dangerous pitch of exasperation, told him he was a cloth-headed gapeseed, an unladylike utterance which was culled from her grandfather's vocabulary, and which considerably startled the post-boy. She directed him to strap up the portmanteaux again; and while he was doing it, she turned her attention to Hildebrand, informing him that he must help to lift Sir Gareth into the chaise. "It is of no avail to tell me you can't, because you *must!*" she said severely. "And I forbid you to faint until Sir Gareth is safely bestowed! You may then do so, if you wish, but I can't stay for you, so you must take care of yourself. And I shan't have the least compunction in leaving you, for this is all your fault, and now, when we are in this fix, you become squeamish, which puts me out of all patience with you!"

The unhappy Hildebrand stammered: "Of course I will help to lift him! I don't *wish* to faint: I can't help but do so!"

"You can do anything if only you will have a little resolution!" she told him.

This bracing treatment had its effect upon him. He could not but shudder when his eyes fell on her bloodstained gown, but he quickly averted them, choked down his nausea, and silently prayed that he might not again disgrace himself. The prayer was answered. Sir Gareth was lifted as tenderly as was possible into the chaise, where

Amanda received him, and Hildebrand was still on his feet. This unlooked-for triumph put a little heart into him, and he suddenly looked very much less hang-dog, and said that he would ride on ahead to warn them at the inn to prepare to house a badly wounded man.

Amanda warmly approved this suggestion, but the post-boy, who still felt that Hildebrand was a dangerous rogue, opposed it, even going to the length of pulling out the pistol from his jacket. Hildebrand, he said, would ride immediately in front of him, so that he could put a bullet through him if he tried to gallop away.

"What a detestably stupid creature you are!" exclaimed Amanda. "It was all a jest — a wager! Oh, I can't explain it to you now, but Sir Gareth knew it was an accident! You heard him say so! Yes, and you don't suppose he would call a real highwayman a young fool, do you? Doesn't that *show* you that he knew him? And he won't try to escape, because I assure you he is excessively fond of Sir Gareth. Go *at once,* Hildebrand! And get on your horse, and follow him, and oh, pray, *pray* drive carefully!"

"Shoot me if you wish!" Hildebrand said, seizing his horse's bridle. "I don't care! I'd rather that than be hanged, or transported!"

With these reckless words he mounted Prince, clapped his heels to the horse's flanks, and shot off down the lane.

The chaise followed at a very much more sober pace, but the lane was so narrow that the post-boy found it impossible to avoid the many pot-holes. The best he could do, whenever he saw a particular large one ahead, was to rein the horses in to a walk, lessening the jolt as much as he could. But nothing could avail to make the short journey anything but a very rough one. Amanda kept an anxious eye on her bandages, terrified that the pad might shift, and the bleeding start again. So tall a man could not be laid flat in a chaise, but Amanda had clasped her arms round Sir Gareth, supporting his head on her shoulder, and trying as best she might to ease the frequent bumps for him. Under her hand she fancied that she could feel his heart faintly beating, which brought such relief to her overcharged nerves that thankful tears sprang to her eyes, and rolled unheeded down her cheeks.

Finding that the bandages were holding, her most pressing anxiety abated, and she was able to consider all the other anxieties attached to her predicament. Chief amongst these was the stringent need to rescue Hildebrand from the consequences of his folly. She was not much given to self-blame, but there could be no doubt that she had been to some extent responsible for the accident. To be sure, she had extracted from Hildebrand a promise that he would not fire his pistols, but she now saw that she should have known better than to have placed the slightest reliance on his keeping his head in emergency. And although no one (or, at any rate, no one with the smallest sense of justice) could blame her for having accepted his proffered services, she did feel that she was very much to blame in having consented to any plan that could possibly put poor Sir Gareth in danger. If she had not blackened Sir Gareth's character, Hildebrand would never have dreamt of holding up the chaise; and that she had blackened his character now filled her with unaccustomed remorse. It really seemed more dreadful than all the rest, for as soon as he had sunk lifeless to the ground, her resentment had vanished, and she had seen him, not as a cruel marplot, but as her kind and endlessly patient protector. But this, she owned, Hildebrand could not have guessed, from anything she had told him; and however stupid it was of him not to have known, only by looking at Sir Gareth, that he was in every respect an admirable person, it was not just that he should suffer a hideous penalty for his folly. Sir Gareth had not wished him to suffer. With what might prove to have been his last word on earth he had exonerated Hildebrand. The thought of this noble magnanimity affected her so much, that she exclaimed aloud: "Oh, I *wish* I had not told those lies about you! It was all my fault!"

But Sir Gareth could not hear her, so it was useless to tell him how sorry she was. And even if he had not been unconscious, she thought, her practical side reasserting itself, repentance would not mend matters. She dared not relax her arms from about him, so she could not wipe away her tears, but she stopped crying, and forced herself to think what she ought next to do. Her arms were aching almost unbearably, but that was unimportant. The important thing was to save Hildebrand from the clutches of the law. He was stupid, he lacked resolution, but she was going to need his services.

By the time the chaise reached the little village, she had herself well in hand, and knew just what must be done. Her face might be tearstained, but the landlord of the Bull Inn, horrified by the disjointed tale jerked out by a pallid young gentleman on the verge of nervous collapse, and expecting to receive a damsel in hysterics, very speedily learned that Amanda was made of sterner stuff than Hildebrand. She might look a child, but there was nothing childlike in the way in which she assumed command over the direction of affairs. Under her jealous supervision, the landlord and the post-boy bore Sir Gareth up the narrow stairs to a bedchamber under the eaves, and laid him upon the bed there; and while they were doing it she told Hildebrand, in a fierce whisper, not to say a word, but to leave all to her; and demanded from the landlord's wife the direction of the nearest doctor, and upon learning that that shocked dame knew of no doctor other than Dr. Chantry, who attended the Squire, and lived at Eaton Socon, instantly ordered Hildebrand to jump on his horse again, and ride like the wind to summon this practitioner to Sir Gareth's side.

"Yes, of course!" Hildebrand said eagerly. "But I don't know how to get there, or — or where to find the doctor, or what to do if he should not be at home!"

"Oh, do *try* not to be so helpless!" cried Amanda. "This woman will tell you where he lives, and if he is gone out you will follow him — and do not *dare* to come back without him!" She then turned on Mrs.

Chicklade, and said: "Tell him *exactly* where to go, for you can see how stupid he is!"

"I am not stupid!" retorted Hildebrand, stung to anger. "But I was never in this part of the country before, and I don't even know in which direction I should ride!"

"No!" retorted Amanda, already halfway up the steep stairs. "I don't know either, but I wouldn't stand there looking like a gaby, and saying *how — how — how!*"

With that, she sped on her way, leaving him seething with indignation, but considerably stiffened by a determination to prove to her his worth.

Amanda found the landlord tightening the bandages round Sir Gareth's torso, and directing the postboy to fetch up some brandy from the tap. She was thankful to perceive that in this large, stolid man she had acquired a helper who could apparently act on his own initiative, and asked him anxiously if he thought Sir Gareth would live.

"There's no saying, miss," he replied unencouragingly. "He ain't slipped his wind yet, but I'd say he's lost a deal of claret. We'll see if we can get a drop of brandy down his throat."

But when the post-boy came back with this restorative, closely followed by Mrs.

Chicklade, it was found to be of no avail, for it ran out of the corners of Sir Gareth's mouth. The landlord thought this a shocking waste of good liquor, and set the glass down, saying that there was nothing for it but to send for the doctor. When Amanda disclosed that Hildebrand had already sped forth on this errand, the postboy was loud in his disapproval. He said that the young varmint would never be seen again, and at once launched into a graphic description of the hold-up.

Until that moment, the Chicklades knew no more than they had learnt from Hildebrand, which was very little. So strange a story as was now recounted immediately convinced Mrs. Chicklade that she had been only too right when she had strongly counselled her husband not to have anything to do with a desperately wounded man. She had known from the moment of clapping eyes on Hildebrand that there was something havey-cavey about him; and as for Amanda, she would like to know, she said, how she came to be hand-in-glove with such a murdering young rascal.

"I wish you will stop thinking he is a highwayman!" said Amanda. "It was all make-believe — just funning!"

"Funning?" gasped Mrs. Chicklade.

"Yes, I tell you! He never meant to fire his pistol: indeed, he promised me he would not!"

"What did he want to take and cock it for, if he wasn't meaning to fire it, miss?" demanded the postboy shrewdly.

"Oh, that was in case you would not pull up!" explained Amanda. "To fire over your head, and put you in a fright. And although I didn't wish him to do so at first, I must say I am excessively sorry now that he didn't, because if only he had there would have been no harm done."

"I never did!" exclaimed Mrs. Chicklade. "Why, you're as bad as he is! I believe the pair of you was in a plot to rob the poor gentleman, and what I want to know is how you came to wheedle yourself into his company, which it's as plain as a pikestaff you must ha' done, and very likely too, for a bolder piece I never did see, not in all my days!"

"Easy, now!" interposed the landlord, in his deep voice. "I'll allow it's a queer-sounding business, but you've no call to speak so rough to the young lady, my dear. Who is the gentleman, missie?"

"*I* can tell you that!" said the post-boy officiously. "He's Sir Gareth Ludlow, and a bang-up tulip, and him and her was putting-up in Kimbolton last night. He hired me for to carry them to Bedford."

The landlord looked Amanda over thoughtfully. "Well, now, miss, you ain't his wife, because you've got no ring on your finger, and he don't look to me old enough to be your pa, nor yet young enough to be your brother, so what's the game?"

"Ah, answer *that* if you can!" said Mrs. Chicklade.

"He is my uncle," replied Amanda calmly. "And also he is Mr. Ross's uncle. Mr. Ross is the man who shot him, but quite by accident. In fact, Mr. Ross and I are cousins, and it is true that we were hand-in-glove, but only to play a trick on Sir Gareth. But Sir Gareth recognized him, and I daresay he knew that he was not at all to be trusted with a pistol, because he told him not to brandish it about, and said he was a young fool. *Didn't* he?"

"Ay," responded the post-boy reluctantly. "But —"

"And then *you* got off your horse, and of course my cousin thought you meant to attack him, which was the cause of the accident. Because that put him in a fluster. And then his horse began to be very restive, and in the middle of it all the gun went off. He never, never meant to fire it at Sir Gareth! He wasn't even looking at him!"

"He said to the gentleman, *If you come a step nearer, I'll fire!* he said. Yes, and he threatened to blow the head off my shoulders, what's more!"

"It seems to me a great pity that he didn't do so!" said Amanda. "I am quite *tired* of talking to anyone so stupid! If you had a particle of commonsense you would know that if he had wished to escape he might have done so when you were helping me to bind the neckcloths round Sir Gareth! And if he had meant to shoot Sir Gareth, he wouldn't have fallen down in a swoon, in that silly way, which you know very well he did!"

"Swooned off, did he?" said the landlord. "It don't surprise me. He was looking just about as sick as a cushion when he came bursting in here. Seems to me it's likely as not it happened the way you say it did, miss, but there's no sense in argufying, whatever the rights of it may be. Martha, my dear, you take the young lady to the other bedchamber, where she can wash the blood off her hands, and put on a clean gown. When you've done that, you can pop a brick in the oven, because the gentleman's powerful cold. And as for you, young fellow, you can fetch up his baggage, and help me get the clothes off him, so as he can be laid between sheets, comfortable."

Amanda cast a doubtful glance at Sir Gareth, but as she could think of nothing she could do to revive him, and the landlord seemed dependable, she allowed herself to be led by her disapproving hostess into the room beside the one to which Sir Gareth had been carried.

By the time Hildebrand returned to the inn, announcing that the doctor was following as fast as he could in his gig, not only had Amanda changed her gown, but she had further alienated Mrs. Chicklade by demanding milk for Joseph. Mrs. Chicklade said that she couldn't abide cats, and wouldn't have a pesky kitten in her kitchen, getting under her feet, but as her lord happened to come in just then, wanting to know whether the brick wasn't hot enough yet, and told her not to be disobliging, Joseph got his milk.

Chicklade reported that Sir Gareth had come out of his swoon for a brief period, when his boots were being pulled off. He had muttered something unintelligible, and had sunk back into unconsciousness before he could be got to swallow any brandy, but Chicklade considered it hopeful that he had even for no more than a minute shown a

319

sign of life. Hildebrand came hurrying in, to be met by these joyful tidings; and so great had been his dread that he would reach the inn only to find that Sir Gareth was dead that he burst into tears. This excess of sensibility did nothing to recommend him to Amanda, but considerably relieved the unbearable tension of his nerves. He was able, in a few moments, to listen with tolerable composure to the news that, during his absence, he had acquired two new relations.

"Do you perfectly understand?" Amanda asked anxiously. "Sir Gareth is our uncle, and you held him up because we had made a plan to play a trick on him."

He was far from understanding, but he nodded, adding, in a hopeless tone, that when Sir Gareth came to himself he would promptly disown him.

"Of course he will not!" said Amanda. "He wouldn't dream of doing such an unhandsome thing!"

This remark was quite incomprehensible to him, but before he could demand enlightenment the doctor had arrived, and he was left to puzzle over it in solitude.

The doctor was surprised to be received by so youthful a lady, and although he accepted without question that she was his patient's niece he was much inclined to think that Mrs. Chicklade would be a more competent assistant to him in any surgery that he might have to perform. But when he saw what she had already done for Sir Gareth he changed his mind. While he unpacked his bag, and Chicklade went off to bring up a bowl of hot water, he asked her a good many questions about the affair, shooting a curious look at her every now and then from under his bushy eyebrows. He said finally that she was a very remarkable young lady, and begged pardon for having doubted her fortitude.

In the event, the operation of extracting the bullet was a sight which tried her fortitude severely, and it was only by a supreme exercise of will-power that she managed to remain at the bedside, handing Dr. Chantry the various instruments, and swabs of lint which he from time to time called for.

Sir Gareth came round under the doctor's hands, and uttered a groan that made Amanda wince in sympathy. The doctor spoke to him in heartening accents, and he opened his eyes. After a bewildered moment, he seemed to realize what had happened to him, for he said, faintly, but perfectly clearly: "I remember. Not the boy's fault!"

The doctor directed Chicklade, under his breath, to hold him, but after a very few minutes of endurance he lost consciousness again.

"Ay, and just as well," grunted Dr. Chantry, when Chicklade, rather alarmed, drew his attention to this circumstance. "It's in devilish deep, I can tell you. No sense in bringing him round, poor fellow, till I have him tied up comfortably."

It seemed to Amanda a very long time before this last operation was performed, and she could not believe that Sir Gareth would find it comfortable. But the doctor said that by God's mercy the bullet had not touched a vital spot, which made her feel very much more cheerful, until he added that no one could say yet how it would turn out, though he hoped that with perfect quiet and good nursing all might be well.

"But he won't die, will he?" Amanda asked imploringly.

"I trust not, young lady, but it's a nasty wound, and he has lost a great deal of blood. I can tell you this: if you hadn't behaved with such presence of mind he wouldn't be alive now."

But Amanda, who had always longed to play a heroine's part, could only see herself as little better than a murderess, and impatiently brushed this aside, saying: "Tell me exactly what I must do to make him better! *Everything* I must do!"

He patted her shoulder. "No, no, you're too young, my dear! Now, don't fret! I don't anticipate that there will be any complications, but what we want is an experienced woman to look after him."

"I'll send round to Mrs. Bardfield, sir," Chicklade said.

"Oh, the midwife! Ay, an excellent notion! There's little to be done for him at present but to keep him quiet, but I shall send my boy over with a cordial, and some laudanum, in case he should grow restless. I've given him something to make him sleep, but if the wound should become inflamed he may develop a little fever presently. No need to be unduly anxious, however. I shall be over to take a look at him this evening, never fear!"

Chapter Fourteen

For a long time after the doctor's departure, Amanda remained seated beside Sir Gareth's bed. To her eye, Dr. Chantry did not compare favourably with such members of the faculty as had previously come in her way, but she could see that whatever it was that he had obliged his patient to swallow had certainly been of benefit to him. He was still dreadfully pale, but he no longer lay in a death-like swoon. He seemed to be heavily asleep, but from time to time his hand, which was lying outside the blankets, twitched, or he moved his head restlessly on the pillow.

At noon, Chicklade came softly into the room, and whispered to her that Mrs. Bardfield was below-stairs, having come up from her cottage at the other end of the village to take a look at her patient.

"She'll sit up with him tonight, miss. Doctor says he won't want anything for a while yet, so I don't doubt we can manage well enough till dinner-time. Will I bring her up, so as she can see how the gentleman is?"

Amanda gave ready permission. In emergency, she could act not only with courage, but with an inborn sense of what was needed; but confronted with a sickbed she was conscious of ignorance. It was with a thankful countenance that she rose to greet a woman of experience of sick-nursing.

She suffered a severe revulsion of feeling. The lady who presently wheezed her way up the stairs, and entered the room with no light tread, was not one whose appearance invited confidence. She was extremely stout, and although she seemed from her ingratiating smile to be good-humoured Amanda thought her countenance very unprepossessing. She liked neither the expression of her curiously hazy eyes, nor their inability to remain fixed for more than a moment on any one object. The cap which she wore under a large bonnet was by no means clean, and there emanated from her person an unpleasant aroma of which the predominant elements were onions, stale sweat, and spirituous liquor. The floor shook under her heavy tread, and when she bent over Sir Gareth, she said: "Ah, poor dear!" in an unctuous voice which filled Amanda with loathing. She then laid her hand on his brow, and said: "Well, he ain't feverish, which is one good thing, but he looks mortal bad." After that, she adjusted his pillows with hearty goodwill, and ruthlessly straightened the blankets that covered him. He was too heavily drugged to wake, but Amanda could bear no longer to see Mrs. Bardfield's rough and not over-clean hands touching him, and she said sharply: "Don't! Leave him alone!"

Mrs. Bardfield was accustomed to the nervous qualms of sick persons' relatives, and she smiled indulgently, saying: "Lor' bless you, dearie, you don't want to worrit your head now I'm here! Many's the gentleman I've nursed, ay, and laid out too! Now, I'll stay beside him for a while, because Mr. Chicklade's got a nice bit of cold meat and pickles laid out for a nuncheon for you and the young gentleman, and a pot of tea besides. That'll do you good, and you'll know your poor uncle's in safe hands."

Amanda managed to thank her, though in a choked voice, and fled down the stairs to find Hildebrand. He was awaiting her in the small parlour, and when he saw her face he started forward, exclaiming in horror: "Good God, what is it? Oh, is he *worse?*"

"No, no! I wouldn't have left him if he

hadn't been better! It is that detestable old woman! Hildebrand, she shan't touch him! I won't permit it! She is dirty, and rough, and she says she lays people out!"

"Yes, I know — I saw her, and I must own — But what are we to do, if you turn her off? *You* cannot nurse Sir Gareth, and Mrs. Chicklade seems very unamiable, so that I shouldn't think —"

"Oh, no! I know just what I ought to do, only I cannot! I don't even know her name! His sister, I mean. So I have made up my mind that Lady Hester must come, and I think she would be willing to, because she is very kind, and she said she would like to help me if she could. And besides that, Mr. Theale told me that Sir Gareth was going to offer for her, and although I don't know if it was true, perhaps it was, and she would *wish* me to send for her! So —"

"Going to offer for her?" broke in Hildebrand. "But you said he was determined to marry you!"

"Yes, I know I did, but it wasn't true! I can't think how you came to imagine it was, for of all the *absurd* things — ! I suppose I shall have to explain it all to you, but first I must know if that stupid post-boy is still here."

"I think he's in the tap, but I've paid him

off. I — I thought that would be the right thing to do."

"Oh, yes, but I find we shall need him, *and* the chaise! Hildebrand, I do hope to goodness he doesn't still wish to inform against you?"

"No," he replied, flushing. "I — I told Dr. Chantry, and he made all right. And I must tell you, Amanda, that even if Sir Gareth hasn't behaved well towards you, he has behaved towards me with a generosity I can *never* repay. When the doctor told me what he said when he came to himself —" He broke off, his lip quivering.

"Yes, he is the kindest creature!" she agreed. "And though he made me very angry — and I *still* cannot feel that he had any business to interfere, and ruin my plan! — he didn't do any of the things I said he did. Never mind that now! You must go and tell the post-boy that you will be requiring him to drive you to Brancaster Park, to bring back Lady Hester. I am not perfectly sure how many miles it is to Chatteris, but I shouldn't think we can be very far from it."

"Chatteris?" he interrupted. "It must be five-and-twenty miles away, and very likely more!"

"Well, and if it is, *surely* you don't mean to say you won't go?" she demanded. "Of all the *paltry* things!"

"Of course I don't!" he retorted, glaring at her. "But I am not going to hire a chaise for a drive of fifty miles and more! Besides, the post-boy Sir Gareth hired wouldn't agree to it, because he was hired to go to Bedford, and nowhere else. And even if he did consent, I wouldn't have him!"

"But —"

"I'll tell you what it is, Amanda!" said Mr. Ross, in a most unadmiring tone. "You fancy no one can think of anything but yourself!"

"Well, no one has!" she said, firing up. "And certainly not you, for you only —"

"Who thought of riding on ahead to prepare the Chicklades?"

"Oh, that!" said Amanda, hunching up one shoulder.

"Yes, that!" he said furiously. "And, what's more, it was I who thought of holding up the chaise, not you!"

"Well, if you mean to boast of that, I suppose you will say next that you thought of shooting Sir Gareth!" cried Amanda.

Battle was now fairly joined, and for the next few minutes two overwrought young persons found relief for their shocked nerves in a right royal quarrel. Sir Gareth on his sick-bed, and the nuncheon on the table were alike forgotten in a wholesale exchange of recriminations. Chicklade, coming into the parlour with a dish of fruit, stopped on the threshold, and for several moments listened, unperceived, to a quarrel which was rapidly sinking to nursery-level. Indeed, when he presently rejoined his wife, he told her, with a chuckle, that there could be no doubt that the young lady and gentleman were related: to hear them, you'd have thought them brother and sister.

As soon as they became aware of his presence, their quarrel ceased abruptly. In cold and haughty silence, they took their places at the table. Neither had any appetite, but each drank a cup of tea, and felt better. Amanda stole a surreptitious look at Hildebrand, found that he was stealing one at her, and giggled. This broke the ice; they both fell into laughter; after which Hildebrand begged pardon, if he had been uncivil; and Amanda said that she hadn't really meant to say that she was sure he couldn't write a play.

Friendly relations were thus re-established, but Hildebrand's brief period of enchantment was over. It had not, in fact, survived the impatience she had shown when he had recovered from his swoon. She was still a very pretty girl, though not (when one studied her dispassionately) as beautiful as he had at first thought her; and she certainly had a great deal of spirit, but he preferred girls with gentler manners. He was inclined to think that, in addition to being much too masterful, she was unbecomingly bold. By the time she had confided to him, under the seal of secrecy, the exact circumstances which had led up to her encounter with Sir Gareth, he was sure of this. His shocked face, and unhesitating condemnation of her plan of campaign, very nearly resulted in the resumption of hostilities. To disapproval of her outrageous scheme was added indignation that she should have enlisted his support by painting Sir Gareth in false colours. He exclaimed that it was the shabbiest thing; and as she secretly agreed with him her defence lacked conviction.

"But it *is* true that he abducted me," she argued.

"I consider that his behaviour has throughout been chivalrous and gentlemanly," replied Hildebrand.

"I thought you looked to be stuffy as soon as I saw you," said Amanda. "That is why I didn't tell you how it really was. And I was quite right."

"It is not a question of being stuffy," said

Hildebrand loftily, "but of having worldly sense, and proper notions of conduct. And now that I know the truth I can't suppose that this Lady Hester would dream of coming here. How very much shocked she must have been!"

"Well, she was not!" said Amanda. "She was most truly sympathetic, so you know nothing of the matter! And also she told me that she has had a very dull life, besides being obliged to live with the most disagreeable set of people I ever saw, so I daresay she will be very glad to come here." She paused, eyeing him. He still looked dubious, so she said in another, and much more earnest voice: "*Pray*, Hildebrand, go and fetch her! That dreadful old woman upstairs will very likely kill poor Sir Gareth, because she is rough, and dirty, and I can see she means to lay him out! I won't permit her to nurse him! I will nurse him myself, only — only that doctor said that he might grow feverish, and if, perhaps, I didn't do the things I should for him, and he didn't get better, but *worse*, and there was only you and me to take care of him — Hildebrand, I *can't!*"

She ended on a note of suppressed panic, but Hildebrand was already convinced. The picture her words had conjured up made him blench. In his relief at finding that he had not killed Sir Gareth outright, optimism, which he now saw to have been unjustified, had sprung up in his breast. The thought that Sir Gareth might still die, here, in this tiny inn, far from his own kith and kin, attended only by a schoolroom miss and his murderer, made him shudder. Before his mind's eye flitted a horrifying vision of himself seeking out Sir Gareth's sister, and breaking to her the news that her brother was dead, and by his hand. He set his teacup down with a jar, exclaiming: "Good God, no! I hadn't considered — of course I will go to Chatteris! I never meant that I would not — and even if this Lady Hester should refuse to come back with me she will be at least able to tell me where I may find Sir Gareth's sister!"

"She *will* come!" Amanda averred. "So will you go at once to tell the post-boy he must drive you to Brancaster Park?"

"No," replied Hildebrand, setting his jaw. "I'll have nothing to do with the fellow! Besides, what a shocking waste of money it would be to be hiring a chaise to carry me to Brancaster Park, when I shall reach it very much more quickly if I ride there — or, at any rate, to Huntingdon, where I may hire a chaise for Lady Hester's conveyance

— that is, if you think she won't prefer to travel in her own carriage?"

Amanda, thankful to find him suddenly so amenable, said approvingly: "That is an excellent notion, and *much* better than mine! I see you have learnt habits of economy, which is something I must do too, for an expensive wife would not suit Neil at all, I daresay. But I have a strong feeling that that odious Lady Widmore would cast a rub in the way of Lady Hester's coming to my aid, if she could, and she would be bound to discover what she meant to do, if Lady Hester ordered her carriage. In fact, the more I think of it, the more I am persuaded that Lady Hester must slip away secretly. So, when you reach Brancaster Park, you must insist on seeing her *alone,* and on no account must you disclose your errand to anyone else."

Hildebrand was in full agreement with her on this point, having the greatest reluctance to spread further than was strictly necessary the story of the day's dreadful events, but an unwelcome consideration had occurred to him, and he said uneasily: "Will it not make Mrs. Chicklade even more unamiable, if we bring Lady Hester here to stay? You know, I don't like to mention it to you but she has been saying *such* things! I don't think Chicklade will attend to her, because he seems to be a good sort of a fellow, but she wants him to tell Dr. Chantry he won't have Sir Gareth here, or any of us, because nothing will persuade her we are respectable persons — which, when one comes to think of it, we are not," he added gloomily. "Depend upon it, she doesn't believe the hum you told her, about Sir Gareth's being our uncle."

"We must remember always to say 'my uncle' when we have occasion to mention him," nodded Amanda. "In fact, we had better call him Uncle Gareth even between ourselves, so that we get into the habit of it."

"Yes, but she is so horridly suspicious that I daresay that won't answer. And, in any event, it wouldn't explain Lady Hester. I don't think we ought to say that she is betrothed to Sir — to Uncle Gareth — if you are not perfectly sure of it. Ten to one, it would make her feel very awkward, if it turned out to be no such thing."

"Yes, very true," she replied, frowning over this difficulty. "I don't at all wish to put her in an uncomfortable situation, so we must think of some tale which that disagreeable woman *will* believe."

He watched her doubtfully, but after a

moment her brow cleared, and she said: "Of course I know the very thing to make all right! Lady Hester must be my aunt! Because it is the circumstance of my having no chaperon that makes Mrs. Chicklade so disobliging. While I was putting off my stained gown, she kept on asking me the most impertinent questions, and saying that she wondered that my mother should let me travel in such a way, just as if she was sure I had no mother, which, indeed, I haven't, as I told her. And also I told her that I had an aunt instead, and I could see that she didn't believe me, though it is quite true. So, I think, Hildebrand, that the thing for you to do is to inform Chicklade that you feel it to be your duty to fetch your aunt, and that will convince Mrs. Chicklade that I *was* speaking the truth!"

Thus it was arranged, Chicklade greeting the suggestion with instant approval, and a good deal of relief. Hildebrand saddled Prince, and rode off, leaving Amanda preparing to banish Mrs. Bardfield irrevocably from the sick-room. It seemed likely that she would enjoy this task very much more than he expected to enjoy his.

He managed to reach Huntingdon in good time, by riding wherever possible across country. He learned there that his goal was situated very much nearer to St. Ives, and so rode on to that town. At the Crown, he was able to hire a post-chaise and pair, and to stable Prince; and midway through the afternoon he arrived at Brancaster Park.

Amanda, having strictly enjoined him to disclose his errand to none but Lady Hester, had seemed to think there could be no difficulty about doing this, but when he was admitted into the house by a servant, who civilly enquired what his name was, he saw that it was only too probable that Lady Hester would refuse to receive a gentleman quite unknown to her. He explained, stammering a little, that his name would not be familiar to her ladyship; and then, as he thought the servant was looking suspiciously at him, he added that he was the bearer of an urgent message. The man bowed, and went away, leaving him in a large saloon, where he instantly fell a prey to all sorts of forebodings. Perhaps the Earl would come in, and demand to know his business; perhaps Lady Widmore would intercept the message to her sister-in-law; or, worse than all, perhaps Lady Hester was not at home.

The minutes ticked by, and he became more and more apprehensive. He hoped that his neckcloth was straight, and his hair tidy, and, seeing that a mirror hung at one end of the room, he went to it, to reassure himself on these points. He was engaged in smoothing his rather creased coat when he heard the door open behind him, and turned quickly to find that he was being regarded by a lady in a pomona green half-dress and a lace cap tied over her softly waving brown hair. Much discomposed to have been surprised preening himself in front of a mirror, he blushed scarlet, and became tongue-tied.

After thoughtfully observing these signs of embarrassment, the lady smiled, and stepped forward, saying: "Pray do not mind! I know *exactly* how one is always quite positive that one's hat is crooked, or that there is a smut on one's face. How do you do? I am Hester Theale, you know."

"How do you do?" he returned, still much flushed. "My name is Ross — Hildebrand Ross, but — but you don't know me, ma'am!"

"No," she agreed, sitting down on the sofa. "But Cliffe said that you have a message for me. Won't you be seated?"

He thanked her, and sat down on the edge of a chair, and swallowed once or twice, trying to think how best to explain himself to her. She waited patiently, her hands folded in her lap, and smiled encouragingly at him.

"It is Amanda!" he blurted out. "I mean, it was she who made me come, because she said she knew you would help her, but I didn't above half like to do it, ma'am, only — only the case is so desperate, you see!"

She looked startled, and exclaimed: "Oh, *dear!* Didn't Sir Gareth find her, then? Of course I will do anything I can to help her, and if my uncle is the cause of her sending you to me, it is quite too dreadfully mortifying — though only to be expected, I am ashamed to say."

"No, no! I mean, Sir Gareth did find her, but — well, it isn't for herself that Amanda wishes you to go to her, but for him!"

She blinked at him. "I beg your pardon?" she said, bewildered.

He got up jerkily, squaring his shoulders. "The thing is — I don't know how to tell you — but I — but he is very ill, ma'am!"

"Sir Gareth very ill?" she repeated, still looking bewildered. "Surely you must be mistaken? He was perfectly stout when I saw him yesterday!"

"Yes, but the thing is that I have shot him!" said Hildebrand, rushing his fence.

He hoped very much that she would not swoon away, or fall into hysterics, and was at first relieved that she neither moved nor spoke. Then he saw that not only was she alarmingly pale, but her eyes were staring at him blindly, and he had a horrid fear that perhaps she was about to have a spasm. But when she spoke, it was in a strangely calm voice that seemed to come from a long way away. "You said — very ill. Did you mean — dead?"

"No, upon my honour!" he answered eagerly. "And the doctor assured us that the bullet didn't touch a vital spot, but he lost so much blood, in spite of Amanda's doing all she could to stanch it — which, I must say, she did — and it was in so deep, that he may become feverish, and there is only Amanda to nurse him — though I am ready to do *anything* in my power — because she won't let the midwife touch him. She says she is dirty and rough, and for my part I think she's an elbow-crooker, because she reeks of spirits."

She listened to this not very lucid speech intently, but it was apparently beyond her comprehension, for when he stopped she got up, and went to him, laying her hand on his sleeve, and saying: "I beg your pardon, but I don't understand what you are trying to tell me. I think there has been an accident, has there not? And Sir Gareth was hurt, but not fatally?"

"Yes — that is, I never meant to shoot

him, I swear!"

"Oh, no, I am sure you could not have meant to!"

These soothing words, and the smile that went with them, made him say impulsively: "I was afraid you would be very angry. But Amanda said you would not, ma'am — though when you learn the whole —"

"I don't think I shall be *angry*. But I should be very much obliged to you if you would sit down beside me here, on the sofa, and tell me just how it happened, because at present it does seem very odd to me that Sir Gareth should have been shot. Unless, of course, you had taken your gun out after wood-pigeons, and shot him by accident?"

"Worse!" uttered Hildebrand, with a groan. "I held up his chaise!"

"But he wasn't travelling in a chaise," said Lady Hester.

"Yes, he was, ma'am. A hired chaise, to carry him and Amanda to Bedford."

"Is that where she lives?" Lady Hester asked hopefully.

"Oh, no! At least, I don't know, but I shouldn't think so. He was meaning to hire a better chaise there, for they only had one at Kimbolton, and the shabbiest old thing! That is where I fell in with them. I am on my way to Wales."

"Now I begin to understand!" she said, pleased to find that he was not, as she had begun to fear, suffering from sun-stroke. "I daresay you fell into conversation with Amanda, and that is how it all came about. What a resourceful girl she is, to be sure!"

"Yes, I suppose she is," he said reluctantly. "Though it wasn't she who thought of holding up the chaise. *I* thought of it!"

"I expect you are very resourceful too," she said kindly.

"Well, I did think of that — not that I wish to boast, and of course I see *now* that it was very wrong — but from the way Amanda talks, you would imagine — You see, ma'am, this is how it was!"

He then poured into her ears an account of the whole affair. He discovered her to be a good listener, and since she did not put him out by uttering exclamations of horror or condemnation, he was encouraged to confide everything to her, even his own unfortunate weakness, which he could not mention without severe mortification. Indeed, he found it difficult to describe the scene in the lane without turning squeamish, and he was not at all surprised that his words drove the colour out of Lady Hester's cheeks again. "It was horrible!" he muttered, covering his face with his hands, and shuddering. *"Horrible!"*

"Yes," she agreed faintly. "But you said — surely you said! — not fatal?"

"Dr. Chantry told us that he did not anticipate that it would be so, but he says he must be most carefully nursed, and that is why Amanda made me come to fetch you, because she doesn't know where his sister lives, or even what her name is."

"To fetch me?" she said, startled. "But —" She stopped, looking at him blankly.

"Oh, if you please, *won't* you come?" Hildebrand begged. "I told Amanda I was sure you would not, but the case is desperate, and even if you tell me where to find Sir Gareth's sister it must be at least two days before she could reach him, and it might be too late! And, what is more," he added, bethinking himself of a fresh difficulty, "I don't think I have enough money left to pay for such an expensive journey."

"Oh, if only I *could* come!" she said, in an anguished tone. She got up quickly, and began to walk about the room. "You see, it isn't possible! My father has gone to Brighton, but there is still my brother, and his wife, and the servants —" Again she stopped, but this time it was as though an idea had occurred to her. Hildebrand watched her anxiously. Suddenly her myopic gaze focused on his face, and she smiled. "Dear me, what a very poor creature I must seem to you! You see, I have never been in the habit of doing anything at all out of the way, so you must forgive me for not immediately thinking that I could. I daresay nothing could be easier. After all, Amanda contrived to escape from her home without the least difficulty, and I expect she was much more closely watched than I am. Let me consider a little!"

He waited in pent-up silence, venturing after a few moments to say: "I have a chaise waiting outside, if — if you feel that you could come with me, ma'am."

"Have you? Oh, well, that makes everything perfectly simple!" she said, her worried frown lightening. "I shall tell the servants that you have come to me from my sister, Lady Ennerdale. I wonder what can have happened at Ancaster? The children, of course — they must be ill! Now, was it the Ennerdale children who had measles two years ago, or was it my sister Milford's children? No, the Ennerdales have *not* had the measles: it was whooping-cough, now I come to think of it. Very well, they shall have the measles — all five of them, which would quite account for my sister's desiring me to go to her." She smiled vaguely upon Hildebrand, and said, gathering her half-train up: "Will you wait while I direct my woman to pack for me? My sister-in-law has driven to Ely, and I do not expect her to return until dinnertime. My brother is somewhere on the estate, but even if he were to come in, I daresay we may fob him off very easily. Do you think, in case you found yourself obliged to answer any awkward questions, you could decide how it comes about that my sister sent you to fetch me rather than one of her servants? It seems an odd thing for her to have done, but I am sure you will think of a very good reason. Sir Matthew Ennerdale-Ancaster — three boys and two girls, and poor little Giles is very sickly, and my sister sadly nervous!"

With these cryptic words, she went away, leaving Hildebrand quite as nervous as Lady Ennerdale. He hoped devoutly that Lord Widmore would not come in: the information conveyed to him by Lady Hester seemed to him meagre.

Upstairs, Lady Hester overcame the difficulty of answering Povey's surprised questions by ignoring them. This, since she knew herself to be in disgrace, did not astonish Povey, but when she learned that she was not to accompany her mistress to the stricken household she was moved to the heart, and burst into tears. Lady Hester was sorry for her distress, but since some explanation would have to be forthcoming for her unprecedented conduct in going away unattended by her maid, she thought the best thing to do would be to pretend that she was still too angry with Povey to wish for her company. So she said, with gentle coldness; "No, Povey, I do not want you. Lady Ennerdale's woman will do all I require. Do not pack any evening gowns, if you please: they will not be needed."

At any other time, Povey would have expostulated, for however ill Lady Ennerdale's offspring might be it was in the highest degree unlikely that her ladyship would collapse into a state of what she, as well as Povey, would certainly consider to be squalor. But the awful punishment that had been meted out to her possessed her mind so wholly that it was not until much later that the strange nature of the packing she had mechanically performed occurred to her. It was conceivable that Lady Hester might discover a need for hartshorn, but what she wanted with a roll of flannel, or why she insisted on taking her own pillow to her sister's well-appointed house, were matters that presently puzzled Povey very much indeed.

When she came downstairs again, a plain pelisse worn over a sad-coloured morning-dress which she commonly wore when engaged in gardening, or attending to her dogs, Hester found the butler awaiting her in the hall, and she knew at once, from the look on his face, that he was not going to be as easy to deceive as the lachrymose Povey.

She paused at the foot of the stairs, drawing on her gloves, and looking at Cliffe with a little challenge in her eyes.

"My lady, where are you going to?" he asked her bluntly. "That chaise never came from Ancaster! It's from the Crown at St. Ives, and the post-boy with it!"

"Oh, dear, how vexatious of you to recognize it!" sighed Hester. "And now I suppose you have told all the other servants!"

"No, my lady, I have not, and well you know I would not!"

She smiled at him, a gleam of mischief in her face. "Don't! I *rely* on you to tell my brother, and her ladyship, that I have gone to Lady Ennerdale — because the children *all* have the measles."

"But where *are* you going, my lady?" Cliffe asked, perturbed.

"Well, I don't precisely know, but it really doesn't signify! I shall be quite safe, and not very far from here, and I shall return — oh, very soon, alas! Don't try to detain me, *pray!* I have written a very untruthful letter to her ladyship: will you give it to her, if you please?"

He took it from her, and after staring very hard at her for a moment, bowed, and said: "Yes, my lady."

"You have always been such a kind friend to me: thank you!"

"There is no one in this house, my lady, barring those it wouldn't be seemly for me to name, who wouldn't be happy to serve you — but I wish I could be sure I was doing right!"

"Oh, yes! For I am going upon an errand of mercy, you might say. Now I must not waste any more time: will you tell Mr. Ross I am quite ready to start?"

"Yes, my lady. I should perhaps mention that Mr. Whyteleafe has been with him for the past twenty minutes, however."

"Dear me, how very unfortunate! I wish I knew what Mr. Ross may have told him!" she murmured. "Perhaps I had better go to the Red Saloon myself."

She entered this apartment in time to hear Mr. Ross's firm assertion that *all* the children had the measles, though none was so alarmingly full of them as little Giles. Lady

Ennerdale, he added, was prostrate with anxiety.

"You astonish me!" exclaimed the chaplain, rather narrowly observing him. "I had not thought her ladyship —"

"Because," said Mr. Ross hurriedly, "the nurse had the misfortune to fall down the stairs, and break her leg, and so everything falls upon her shoulders!"

"Yes, is it not dreadful?" interposed Lady Hester. "Poor Susan! No wonder she should be distracted! I am quite ready to set forward, Mr. Ross, and indeed I feel that we should lose no time!"

"All the way to Ancaster!" Mr. Whyteleafe said, looking thunderstruck. "You will never reach it tonight, Lady Hester! Surely it would be wiser to wait until tomorrow?"

"No, no, for that would mean that I should not arrive until quite late, and knocked up by the journey, I daresay. We shall spend the night somewhere on the road. And then I shan't be extraordinarily fatigued, and shall be able to render my sister all the assistance possible."

"If you *must* go, Lady Hester, I wonder at it that Sir Matthew should not have had the courtesy to fetch you himself! I make no apology for speaking plainly on this head! There is a lack of consideration in such behaviour, a —"

"Sir Matthew," said Mr. Ross, "is away from home, sir. That is why I offered to be his deputy."

"Yes, and how very much obliged to you I am!" said Hester. "But do not let us be dawdling any longer, I beg!"

Mr. Whyteleafe said no more, but he was evidently very much shocked by this renewed instance of the shameless demands made upon Hester by her sisters, and it was with tightly folded lips that he accompanied her to where the chaise waited. She was afraid that he too would recognize the postboy, but he did not bestow more than a cursory glance on him, the circumstance of Lady Ennerdale's having been shabby enough to have sent a hired vehicle, with only two horses, for the conveyance of her sister, ousting all else from his head. Lady Hester was handed up into the chaise, Mr. Ross jumped in after her, the steps were let up, and in another minute they were drawing away from the house.

"Phew!" Hildebrand said involuntarily, pulling out his handkerchief, and mopping his brow. "I can't tell you how thankful I was that you came in just then, ma'am, for he was asking me all manner of questions! He would know who I was, and I was obliged to tell him that I was employed by Sir Matthew as a secretary."

"How very clever of you! I daresay he was very much surprised, for Sir Matthew is interested in nothing but sport."

"Yes, he was — in fact, he said he could not imagine what I should find to do for Sir Matthew. So I said Sir Matthew had formed the intention of going into politics."

This made her laugh so much that he lost any lingering shyness, and ventured to break to her the news that she had become, without her knowledge, Amanda's aunt. He was a little afraid that she might be affronted, for she was much younger than Amanda had led him to suppose; but she accepted the relationship with approval, and said that perhaps she had better become his aunt too.

By the time the chaise arrived at Little Staughton, they were fast friends. Dusk was falling when it drew up before the Bull Inn, and lamplight shone through several of the windows. As Hildebrand jumped down, and turned to help Lady Hester, Amanda leaned out of one of the casements set under the eaves, and called, in a voice sharpened by anxiety: "Hildebrand? Oh, Hildebrand, have you brought her?"

He looked up. "Yes, here she is! Take care

you don't fall out of the window!"

She disappeared abruptly. The hand in Hildebrand's trembled convulsively, but Lady Hester's voice, when she spoke, was quite quiet. "I must leave you to settle with the post-boy, Hildebrand. I am afraid —"

She did not say what she was afraid of, but went swiftly into the inn. As she crossed the threshold, Amanda reached the foot of the steep stairs, and fairly pounced on her, dryly sobbing from mingled fright and relief. "Oh, thank God you are come at last! He is very, very ill, and I cannot make him lie still, or even hear me! Oh, La — Aunt Hester, *come!*"

"Ah, I thought Miss would be sorry she turned off Mrs. Bardfield so hasty!" remarked Mrs. Chicklade, in the background, and speaking with a morbid satisfaction which made Amanda round on her like a young tigress.

"Go away, you odious, impertinent creature! You said you washed your hands of it, and so you may, for I don't want help from such a *heathen* as you are!"

Mrs. Chicklade's colour rose alarmingly. "Oh, so I'm a heathen, am I! Me as has been a churchgoer all my life, and kept my house respectable — till this day!"

"Good-evening."

The gentle, aloof voice acted on the incensed landlady like a charm. Cut short in mid-career, she stared at Lady Hester, her rich colour slowly fading.

"I am afraid," said Hester, with cool courtesy, "that you are being put to a great deal of trouble. It is perhaps a pity I did not, after all, bring my maid with me. My nephew thought, however, that there would be no room for her in so small a house."

Mrs. Chicklade felt herself impelled to abandon her martial attitude, and to drop an unwilling curtsy. 'I'm sure, ma'am, I'm not one to grudge a bit of trouble. All I say is —"

"Thank you," Hester said, turning away from her. "Take me up to your uncle's room, Amanda!"

Amanda was only too glad to do so. Chicklade, an expression of considerable concern on his face, was bending over the bed on which Sir Gareth tossed and muttered. He looked round as the ladies entered the room, and said: "I don't like the looks of him — not at all, I don't! Mortal bad, he is, ma'am, but I don't doubt he'll be better now he has his good lady to tend him."

Hester, casting off her bonnet and pelisse, hardly heard this speech, her attention being fixed on Sir Gareth. She went to the bed, and laid her hand fleetingly on his brow. It was burningly hot, and the eyes that glanced unrecognizingly at her were blurred with fever. She said: "Has the doctor seen him since this morning?"

"No!" answered Amanda in a choked voice. "I have been waiting and waiting for him, for he promised he would come again!"

"Then I think someone should ride over to desire him to come as soon as he may. Meanwhile, if Hildebrand will bring up the smaller of my two valises, and you, landlord, will desire your wife to set a kettle on to boil, I hope we may make him more comfortable."

"Is he going to die?" whispered Amanda, her eyes dark with dread.

"No!" Hester replied calmly. "He is not going to die, but he has a great deal of fever, and I fancy his wound is much inflamed. The arm is swollen, and these tight bandages are making it worse. Pray go down, my dear, and send Hildebrand up to me!"

Amanda sped away on this errand, and returned very speedily, followed by Hildebrand, bearing a valise. He was looking scared, and cast one shrinking glance at Sir Gareth, and then quickly averted his eyes. Lady Hester had stripped the blankets off the bed, so that Sir Gareth was now covered only by the sheet. Without seeming to notice Hildebrand's sickly pallor, she directed him, in her quiet way, to open the valise. "You will find a roll of flannel in it, and some scissors. I am going to apply fomentations to the wound. Will you help me, if you please!"

"*I* will!" Amanda said. "Hildebrand faints if he sees blood."

"He won't see any blood, and I am quite sure he will not faint."

"No, I — I swear I won't!" Hildebrand said, through his clenched teeth.

"Of course not. You could not, when we depend so entirely upon you, could you? For, you know, I am not strong enough to lift Sir Gareth. It is a great comfort to know that you are here to share the nursing with me. Amanda, while I am busy with the fomentation, do you go down and try whether there is any wine to be obtained. A little hot wine will often relieve a fever."

Amanda seemed for a moment as though she would have rebelled against what she suspected to be an attempt to exclude her from the sickroom, but after throwing a rather jealous glance at Hildebrand, she went away.

By the time she came back, carefully carrying, wrapped in a cloth, a glass of hot claret, Lady Hester had tied the last bandage, and was exchanging the very lumpy pillow on the bed for her own one of down. Hildebrand, who was supporting Sir Gareth in his arms, had not only recovered his colour, but looked to be in much better spirits. He had been able to look upon his handiwork without fainting; and Lady Hester, so far from reviling or despising him, had said that she did not know how she would go on without him.

Amanda reported that Chicklade had sent off the boy who helped him in the tap, and the small stable, to hasten the doctor, so Lady Hester said that since Sir Gareth seemed a little easier they would not try to get any of the mulled claret down his throat just at present. Hildebrand lowered him on to the pillow again, and although he was still very restless it was plain that the fomentation was already bringing him a certain measure of relief. Lady Hester sat down at the head of the bed, and began to bathe his face with lavender-water, softly directing her youthful helpers to go downstairs to wait the doctor's arrival. They tiptoed away. Left alone with Sir Gareth, Lady Hester smoothed back the tumbled curls from his brow with a loving hand. He stared up at her, and said in a hurried, fretting tone: "I must find her. I must find her."

"Yes, Gareth, you shall," she answered soothingly. "Only be still, my dearest!"

For a moment she thought that there was a gleam of recognition in his eyes; then he turned his head away, and resumed his incoherent muttering. His hand, aimlessly brushing the sheet, found her wrist, and grasped it strongly; he said, quite audibly: "You won't escape me again!"

When, presently, the doctor was brought into the room by Amanda, he thought that the lady who rose to meet him had been crying a little. He was not surprised; and he said, with rough kindness: "Well, now, what is all this I am hearing about my patient? Some fever was to be expected, you know, but you may depend upon it that a man with a good constitution will recover from worse hurts than a mere hole in his shoulder. You need not tell me that he has *that,* ma'am! I have seldom attended a more splendid specimen than your husband, and I don't doubt that between us we shall have him going on prosperously in a very short time."

"But he is not my husband!" said Hester involuntarily.

"Not your husband?" he said, looking at her very hard. "I beg your pardon, but I understood from Chicklade that Mr. Ross had fetched Sir Gareth's wife to him!"

"No," said Hester helplessly. "Oh, no!"

"Then who may you be, ma'am?" he demanded bluntly.

"She is his sister, of course!" said Amanda, with great promptness. "I suppose that when my cousin said he would fetch our aunt, Chicklade thought she must be Uncle Gareth's *wife,* but she isn't."

"Oh!" said the doctor. "So *that's* how it is!"

"Yes, that's how it is," agreed Hester, accepting the situation.

CHAPTER FIFTEEN

Sir Gareth, opening his eyes on unfamiliar surroundings, wondered where he was. He appeared to be lying in an attic, which seemed very odd, though not of any great importance. He considered the matter idly, and next discovered that something was wrong with his left shoulder. He tried to bring his other hand to feel it, but found that the effort was too much for his strength. Also, which was strange, he was very tired. Decidedly something must be wrong, he thought, unperturbed, but puzzled. He turned his head on the pillow, and his eyes fell upon a slim youth, who was watching him intently from a chair by the window. The wreaths of sleep which were clinging to his brain began to drift away. He frowned. A boy in a coffee-room, talking some non-sense about a blackened heart, and Amanda — *Amanda?* "Good God!" said Sir Gareth faintly, as memory came rushing back.

Hildebrand, uncertain whether he was himself, or still lightheaded, said tentatively: "Are you better, sir?"

"Hildebrand Ross," stated Sir Gareth. "Where the devil am I?"

"Well, I don't suppose you would know the place, sir, but pray do not be uneasy! You are quite safe."

"Did you put a bullet into me?" enquired Sir Gareth, dreamily interested.

"Yes, I did sir, but *indeed* I never meant to! Pray do not let yourself be angry with me! I mean, not *yet,* while you are so weak!"

"I remember telling you not to wave that pistol about," remarked Sir Gareth, in a reminiscent voice. "What happened after that?"

"Well, I — I shot you, sir, but don't talk about it now! The doctor says you must be perfectly quiet."

"How long have I been here?"

"Four days, sir — and I think I had better fetch Aunt Hester!" said Hildebrand nervously.

Sir Gareth, left to make what he could of this, found it beyond his comprehension, and closed his eyes again.

When he awoke for the second time, he remembered that he had been talking to Hildebrand, and looked towards the window. But Hildebrand was no longer there. Lady Hester was seated in the windsor chair, reading a book. Sir Gareth had thought that he was better, but he now suspected that he was delirious. There was a sandy kitten curled up in her lap, too, and he knew that kitten. Hester had nothing to do with Joseph, so probably he was still floating in a muddled dream. "Besides," he said aloud, "she doesn't wear a cap. How absurd!"

She looked up quickly, and rose, setting Joseph down. "Hildebrand came running to tell me that you had waked up, quite yourself again, but when I reached you, you were so soundly asleep that I almost doubted him," she said, taking his hand, and feeling his pulse. "Oh, that is so much better! Do you feel more the thing?"

His fingers closed weakly round her hand. "But this is fantastic!" he said. "Are you sure I am not dreaming?"

"Quite sure," she replied, smiling mistily down at him. "I daresay you may be wondering how I come to be here, but it is not at all important, and there is no need for you to tease yourself about it just now."

He studied the offending cap frowningly. "Why do you wear that thing?"

"Well, I think I have reached the age when

361

perhaps I should."

"Nonsense! I wish you will take it off."

"Should you mind very much if I don't?" she said apologetically. "There is something so very respectable about a cap, you know."

That made him smile. "Must you look respectable?"

"Yes, indeed I must. Now, my dear friend, I am going to call Chicklade that he may bring up the broth Mrs. Chicklade has been keeping hot for you, the instant you should wake up."

"Who is Chicklade?"

"How stupid of me! He is the landlord, an excellent man, *quite* unlike his wife, who is really the most tiresome creature. I shall let him come into the room, because he has been so very obliging, and besides that, I want him to raise you while I slip another pillow behind you. I shall warn him he must not encourage you to talk, but in case you should say something to undo us all, will you remember that Hildebrand is your nephew?"

"Either I *am* dreaming, or you must have run mad suddenly," said Sir Gareth. "Hildebrand was the name of the young idiot who shot me. That I *do* remember!"

"Yes, so *careless* of him! I daresay you will feel that you ought to give him a scold, and perhaps I should have done so, when he told me about it. But he was in such distress, and so truly repentant, that I could see it was not at all necessary. I don't mean to dictate to you, but if you should be meaning to give him up to justice, which he quite expects, poor boy, I wish you won't! He has been helping me to nurse you, and running all the errands with such readiness that it would be quite dreadfully ungrateful to send him to prison. Besides, it would appear very odd if you were to do so, when everyone thinks he is your nephew."

"Is that why he became my nephew?" he asked, looking amused.

"Yes, and I need scarcely tell you that it was Amanda's notion. She said that Hildebrand held you up for a jest, and had never meant to shoot you, which, indeed, was perfectly true. I own, Amanda is very naughty, but one cannot help admiring her! She is never at a loss!"

"Where is Amanda?" he interrupted.

"She has walked over to Great Staughton with Hildebrand, to purchase some things for me there."

"Do you mean to tell me she hasn't run away?" he said incredulously.

"Oh, no!"

"How in the world did you contrive to

keep her here?"

"Oh, I didn't! I am sure I could not. She would not think of running away *now*. Besides, she is very well-satisfied to be here, for it is the tiniest village, where I shouldn't think her grandfather would ever find her. You shall see her when you are a little stronger. Oh, I forgot to mention that she is your niece! She and Hildebrand are cousins."

"I seem to have been acquiring an alarming number of new relatives," he remarked.

"Yes," she agreed. She hesitated, colouring faintly. "Which puts me in mind that I should warn you that I shall be obliged to call you Gareth while we remain in this inn. I am afraid you may not quite like it, but —"

"On the contrary!" he said, smiling. "Are you also related to me?"

"Well, yes!" she confessed. "We — we thought it best that I should be your sister. You see, I didn't feel I *could* be your wife!"

"That also I remember," he said.

Her colour deepened; she looked away, and said in a little confusion: "The thing was that when Amanda sent Hildebrand to fetch me, she told the Chicklades that I was her aunt, which, I must say, was most sensible of her. But they supposed from that

that I must be your wife, and they told the doctor so. Which nearly led to our undoing, because you know how foolish I am! I blurted out that I was no such thing, and the doctor stared at me in such a way! However, Amanda instantly said that I was not your wife, but your sister, which perfectly satisfied him. I hope you are not vexed! Now I must go and call to Chicklade."

She went away, and when she returned a few minutes later, she was accompanied by Chicklade, who bore a small tray into the room, which he set down on the table by the bed. He then said that he was glad to see Sir Gareth looking more stout, speaking in a painstakingly lowered voice.

Sir Gareth roused himself to play the part expected of him. He said: "Thank you, I'm as weak as a cat, but you will see how quickly I shall be on my feet again. I am afraid I have been a shocking charge upon you. My sister has been telling me how you have helped to nurse me." He held out his hand. "Thank you: I am very much obliged to you! You must be heartily sick of such a troublesome guest, but really I am not to be blamed! My young fool of a nephew is the culprit."

"Ay, sir, he is that!" Chicklade said, cautiously taking the hand in his. "Properly speaking, he ought to be given a rare dressing, but I don't doubt it was Miss who set him on, and I'm bound to say he's had the fright of his life. Nor I don't grudge the trouble. If there's aught I can do, your honour has only to mention it."

"Then I beg you will shave me!" said Sir Gareth: passing his hand ruefully over his chin.

"Tomorrow, perhaps," said Hester, waiting to place another pillow behind his head. "Will you lift him now, if you please! Don't try to help yourself, Gareth; Chicklade is very strong, you will find."

"What was your fighting weight?" asked Sir Gareth, as the landlord lowered him tenderly on to the pillows.

A slow smile spread over the broad face. "Ah, I was never reduced beyond thirteen stone eight, sir, and, of course, nowadays — well! If I might make so bold, I'd say your honour displays to advantage."

"You will be able to enjoy many delightful talks about prize-fighting with Sir Gareth when he is a little stronger," said Lady Hester gently.

The landlord, thus recalled to a sense of Sir Gareth's weakness, cast an apologetic glance at her, and beat a retreat. She sat down by the bed, and offered her patient a spoonful of broth. "I hope it is good," she said, smiling at him. "As soon as your fever began to abate, Chicklade killed one of his cockerels, so that we might have a sustaining broth ready for you. Hildebrand was disgusted, because Amanda saw its neck wrung, but I daresay she was quite right to do so. She seems to think that if she goes to the Peninsula she might be obliged to kill chickens, though I myself should rather suppose that the batman would do it for her. Poor Hildebrand is very squeamish, so naturally he was much shocked at Amanda's wishing to learn how to wring a chicken's neck. Do you think you could eat a morsel of toast, if I dipped it in the broth?"

"Thank you, I had liefer eat it undipped. I detest sops! Hester, I wish you will explain to me how you come to be here! Amanda had no business to ask it of you, and how you can have prevailed upon your family to consent to such a thing I can't conceive."

"Oh, I didn't! They think I have gone to be with my sister Susan, because her children have the measles. Don't look so dismayed! I never enjoyed anything half as much, I assure you. You cannot think what a relief it is to have shaken off every one of my relations! I don't feel like myself at all, and that is a relief, too."

"But, my dear, it is the craziest thing to have done!" he expostulated, half-laughing.

"Yes, isn't it?" she agreed cordially. "That is what makes it so delightful, for I have never done anything crazy before. Just a little more of this broth! How pleased Amanda and Hildebrand will be when they learn that you have drunk it all up! I wonder whether they have been able to purchase any playing-cards in Great Staughton?"

Her inconsequence made him smile. "Do you wish for some?"

"Oh, no! Only that it is very dull for those children, and I thought if only they had some cards they could play games together in the evening, instead of quarrelling. Hildebrand was much inclined to think that it would be very wrong to buy cards, but I assured him you would have not the least objection."

"I?" he said. "What made the boy think me so strait-laced?"

"Oh, he didn't! The thing is that although he owns that we may purchase what *you* need with perfect propriety, he says that anything else is most improper: in fact, quite dishonest. We were obliged to steal your money, you see."

"How very dreadful!" he murmured. "Am

I left destitute?"

"No, indeed! And Hildebrand is keeping strict account of every penny we spend. What a huge sum of money you carry on your person, Gareth! When we found that roll of bills in your pocket I thought we need have no scruples. You see, we were at a stand, because what with paying for the post-chaises, and stabling his horse, and buying the drugs we needed for you, Hildebrand was soon ruined. Amanda had a little money, but not nearly enough to pay our shot here, or the doctor; and I had nothing but what was in my purse. I do wish I were not so shatterbrained! I ought to have broken open Widmore's strong-box, of course, but in the agitation of the moment I never thought of it."

The tone of self-censure which she used proved too much for Sir Gareth's gravity. He began to laugh, which caused him to feel a twinge in his shoulder sharp enough to make him wince. Lady Hester apologized, but said that she thought it did people no harm to laugh, even if it did hurt them a trifle.

It certainly seemed to do Sir Gareth no harm. The doctor, visiting him that evening, called upon Lady Hester to observe how famously he had responded to his treatment, and said that in less than no time he would be as right as a trivet; and although it was evident that it would, in fact, be some considerable while before he regained his strength, he began to improve so rapidly that on the following day Lady Hester permitted Amanda to visit him. She could only hope that he would not find her, in his present state, rather overpowering: perhaps, even, a little agitating. How great his interest in this turbulent beauty might be, she could not decide. Such intelligible utterances as he had made during his delirium had all concerned Amanda; she had been vaguely surprised that never once had she caught Clarissa's name in his incoherent mutterings. That seemed to indicate that his mind, if not his heart, was obsessed by Amanda. The fever past, the only sign he had given of any extraordinary interest in her had been his immediate anxiety to know where she was. But Lady Hester knew that he was not the man to betray himself; and she feared that he was going to be hurt. Amazing though it might be (and to Hester it appeared incomprehensible), he had not made the smallest impression on Amanda's heart. She liked him very well; she said he resembled all her favourite heroes of romance; and she remained unshaken in her devotion to her Brigade-Major. If Sir Gareth cherished hopes of winning her, he was doomed to disappointment; and although this would not be the tragedy that Clarissa's death had been, it would be a hurt, and Hester would have happily immolated herself to have averted it. But there was nothing she could do. She allowed Amanda twenty minutes, and then, since Amanda had not emerged, she went up to the sickroom to bring the session to an end.

The sight which met her eyes held her frozen on the threshold, and the thought flashed across her mind that she knew now how it felt to die. If it had lain within her power to have given Sir Gareth his heart's desire, she would have done it; but she had not known how sharp a pain she would suffer when she saw Amanda's face buried in his sound shoulder, and his arm about her.

He looked up, and the short agony was at an end. Never did a man more clearly signal an appeal for help than Sir Gareth at that moment. He did not look at all like a man in love; he looked extremely harassed. Then Hester perceived that Amanda was indulging in a hearty burst of tears, and the smile which held so much unexpected mischief suddenly danced in her eyes. "Good heavens, what is the matter?" she said, advancing into the room, and gently removing Amanda's hand from about Sir Gareth's neck. "Dear child, this is not at all the way to behave! Do, pray, stop crying!"

She raised her brows at Sir Gareth, in mute enquiry, and he said ruefully: "She is enjoying an orgy of remorse. I never dreamed that there could be anything more exhausting than Amanda in high gig, but I have discovered my error. Now, do cheer up, you little goose! It served me right for not heeding your warning that you would make me sorry."

"Besides, she saved your life," said Hester. "We have not liked to talk very much about the accident, but I do think you should know that if Amanda hadn't acted with the greatest presence of mind, you would have bled to death, Gareth. And she had no one to turn to, either, because poor Hildebrand swooned from the shock, and the sight of the blood. Indeed, you are very much obliged to her."

He was surprised, and a good deal touched, but Amanda would have none of his gratitude. She stopped crying, however, and raised her head from his shoulder. "Well, I *had* to do something, and, besides, it was very good practice, in case Neil should be wounded again. I didn't mean to cry, and if only you had looked vexed when I came into the room, instead of smiling at me, and holding out your hand, I shouldn't have."

"It was most inconsiderate of me, and I can only beg your pardon," he responded gravely. He watched her dry her cheeks, and then said: "Will you do something to oblige me?"

"Yes, to be sure I — at least, I *might!*" she said suspiciously. "What is it?"

"Write immediately to your grandfather, telling him that you are here, and in Lady Hester's care!"

"I thought you were trying to trick me!" she exclaimed.

"My child, it must be a week since you ran away, and all that time he has been in the greatest anxiety about you! Think! You cannot wish him —"

"You are perfectly right!" she interrupted. "What a fortunate thing it is that you should have put me in mind of it, for so many things have happened that it went out of my head! Good gracious, he may have put the advertisement in the *Morning Post* days ago! I must find Hildebrand!"

She jumped up from her knees, and sped forth, leaving the door open. Lady Hester went to shut it, saying, with mild curiosity:

"I wonder what she wants Hildebrand to do?"

"Of all the heartless little wretches!" Sir Gareth said.

She looked rather surprised. "Oh, no, not heartless! Only she is so passionately devoted to Neil, you see, that she doesn't care a button for anyone else."

"Ruthless, then. Hester, can't you prevail upon her to put that unfortunate old man out of his suspense?"

"I am afraid I can't," she said. "Of course, one can't help feeling very sorry for him, but I do think she should be allowed to marry Neil. Don't tease yourself about her, Gareth! After all, she is quite safe while she remains with us."

"You are as bad as she is," said Sir Gareth severely.

"Yes, but not so resourceful," she agreed. "And you are very tired, so you will have a sleep now, and no more visitors."

There did not seem to be any more to be said. Until he was on his feet again, Sir Gareth knew that he was powerless to restore Amanda to her family; and since he was too weak to exert himself even in argument, he abandoned the struggle, and gave himself up to lazy convalescence, accepting the fantastic situation in which he found himself, and deriving a good deal of amusement from it. His adopted family cosseted him jealously, appealed to him to settle disputes, or decide knotting problems, and made his room, as he grew stronger, their headquarters. Amanda had from the outset regarded him much in the light of an uncle. Hildebrand had thought that, so far from doing the same, he would never be able to confront him without being crushed by a sense of guilt. Once Sir Gareth was himself again, it had taken much courage to enter his room. But as Hildebrand was his chief attendant, the awful moment had to be faced. He had gone in, braced to endure whatever might be in store for him. "Well, nephew?" had said Sir Gareth. "And what have you to say for yourself?" He had had an abject apology all prepared, but it had been cut short. "Only wait until I am on my feet again!" had said Sir Gareth. "*I'll* teach you to brandish loaded pistols!"

After that, there had been no difficulty at all in looking upon Sir Gareth as an uncle. Indeed, it very soon seemed to Sir Gareth that neither Amanda nor Hildebrand remembered that he was not their uncle.

Hildebrand's chief preoccupation was how to regain possession of his horse, but since he could not bring himself to let some heavy-handed post-boy or ostler ride Prince, and spurned indignantly a suggestion that he should hire a chaise to carry him to St. Ives, so that he could himself bring Prince to Little Staughton, there seemed to be no solution to the problem. "As though I should think of leaving you for all those hours!" he said. "Besides, only consider what it would cost, sir!"

"What, is it low tide with us?"

"Good God, no! But you *can't* think I would first shoot you, Uncle Gary, and then make you pay for me to get my horse back! And in any event, I don't think I should go, because if I don't keep an eye on Amanda, the lord only knows what she'll do next!"

"Then for God's sake do keep your eye on her!" said Sir Gareth. "What fiendish plot is she hatching now?"

"Well, you know how she disappeared yesterday, and was gone for hours? — Oh, no, Aunt Hester thought we shouldn't tell you! I beg your pardon, Aunt Hester, but it don't signify, because she hadn't run away after all! Well, do you know what she did? She went to Eaton Socon in Farmer Up-wood's gig, just to discover where she could get her hands on the *Morning Post*!"

"But I think that was such a sensible thing to do!" said Lady Hester. "And she did discover it, too, which I'm sure I should never have done."

"Yes, you would, ma'am! She discovered it at the receiving-office, and anyone would have known that was the place to go to!"

"Not Aunt Hester," said Sir Gareth, his eyes quizzing her. "Who does take the *Morning Post* in these rural parts?"

"Oh, some old fellow, who lives near Colmworth, which is about four miles from here! He is an invalid, and never stirs out of his house, so Chicklade says. The thing is that if I don't go for her, Amanda swears she will go herself, to ask the old man to let her look at every *Morning Post* he has received this week!"

"You know, I have suddenly thought of something very discouraging!" said Hester. "I shouldn't wonder at it if they had been used for lighting the kitchen-fire! Now, that would be too bad, but exactly the sort of thing that is bound to happen!"

"If you think there is any chance that Amanda's grandfather may have yielded, we had better send to the office of the *Morning Post* immediately," said Sir Gareth. "In his place, I had rather have gone to Bow Street, but one never knows."

"Well, do you think I should try first at

this old fellow's house, sir?" Hildebrand asked.

"By all means — if you can think of a sufficiently plausible excuse for wishing to see so many copies of his newspaper. I daresay you will be thought insane, but if you don't regard that, why should I?"

"No, why? I shall say that I want them for you, because you are laid by the heels here, and have nothing to read."

"I wonder why I shouldn't have guessed that you would drag me into it?" observed Sir Gareth, in a musing tone.

Hildebrand grinned, but assured him that he need have no fear.

"I must own, Gareth," said Hester thoughtfully, after Hildebrand had departed, "that I can't help hoping you may be wrong about Bow Street. What shall we do, if we have Runners after us?"

"Emigrate!" he replied promptly.

She smiled, but said: "You know, it would be very exciting, but not, I think, quite comfortable, because, although we have done nothing wrong, the Runners might not perfectly understand just how it all came about. Unless, of course, Amanda is able to think of another splendid story."

"Any story of Amanda's will infallibly land us all in Newgate. I see nothing for it but emigration."

"Not *all* of us, Gareth: only you!" she said, with a gleam of humour. "She will certainly tell them that you abducted her, because nothing will persuade her that an abduction is something quite different. Oh, well, we must just hope that there may be a notice in one of the papers! And I should think that there would be, for the grandfather must wish to get Amanda back as soon as ever he may."

But when Hildebrand returned, later in the day, from his errand, she was found to have been wrong. Hildebrand came into Sir Gareth's room, laden with periodicals, which he dumped on the floor, saying breathlessly: "All for you, Uncle Gary! He *would* have me bring them, because he says he *knows* you! Lord, I thought we were in a fix then, but I don't fancy any harm will come of it."

"Oh, my God!" exclaimed Sir Gareth. "I suppose you *had* to tell him my name? Who is he?"

"Well, I never thought it would signify. And, in any event, everyone knows who you are, because the post-boy told Chicklade what your name was, when you were carried in, that day."

Amanda, who was seated on the floor,

scanning, and discarding, copy after copy of the *Morning Post,* looked up to say: "I *told* you you would only make a muff of it! If I had gone myself, I should have made up a very good name for Uncle Gary, only you have no ingenuity, and can think of nothing!"

"Yes!" retorted Hildebrand. "You would have said he was Lancelot du Lake, or something so silly that no one would have believed it!"

"Don't imagine you are going to quarrel over me!" interposed Sir Gareth. "What I want to know is not what name of unequalled splendour Amanda would have bestowed on me, but what is the name of this recluse, who says he knows me?"

Amanda, uninterested, retired again into the advertisement columns of the *Morning Post.* Hildebrand said: "Vinehall, sir: Barnabas Vinehall."

"Well, I should never have made up as silly a name as that!" interpolated Amanda scornfully.

"Good God!" ejaculated Sir Gareth. "I thought he was dead! You don't mean to say he lives *here?*"

"Yes, but there's no need for any of us to be in a quake, because he never goes out now: he told me so!" said Hildebrand reassuringly. "He is the fattest man I ever laid eyes on!"

"I fail to see —"

"No, but only listen, Uncle Gary! It's dropsy!"

"Poor man!" said Hester sympathetically. "Who is he, Gareth?"

"He was a crony of my father's. I haven't seen him for years. Dropsy, eh! Poor old Vinehall! What did you tell him, Hildebrand?"

"Well, only that you had had an accident, and were laid up here. The mischief was that I had previously said I was your nephew, because as soon as he knew your name he said I must be Trixie's eldest son. I didn't know who Trixie was —"

"— so, *of course,* you said you were not!" put in Amanda.

"No, I did not! You are not the only person who can tell untruths!" retorted Hildebrand. "I said I was!"

"Who did you say I was?" demanded Amanda.

"Nobody. You were not mentioned," replied Hildebrand, depressing pretension. "The only thing that put me in a fright, sir, was Mr. Vinehall's supposing that Aunt Hester must be this Trixie. Because I had said that your sister was nursing you, and I collect that Trixie *is* your sister."

"My only sister!" said Sir Gareth, covering his eyes with his hand. "What I have ever done to deserve being saddled with such a nephew as you — ! Go on! Let me know the worst!"

"There *is* no worst! He did say that he hoped Trixie — your sister, I mean, sir — would visit him, but I made that right immediately, by saying that she might not leave you while you were ill, and that as soon as you were better she would be obliged to hurry back to her own home. Then I said that I was sure you would wait on him, as soon as you were able, which seemed to please him very much. Then he talked about your father, and at last he made his butler tie up a great bundle of papers and periodicals for you to read, and so I made my escape. *Now* tell me if I did wrong, sir?"

"Well!" The word burst from Amanda, sitting back on her heels in a welter of newspapers, her eyes flashing. "Would you have *believed* it? He has not done it! Why — why — one would almost think he did not wish to have me back!"

"Impossible!" murmured Sir Gareth.

"Of course it is impossible!" said Hester, casting a reproving glance at him. "I daresay there has not been yet time for the advertisement to be inserted. Wait a few days longer!"

"Is Hildebrand to visit Vinehall every day?" enquired Sir Gareth. "Courting disaster — but far be it from me to complain!"

"No, for he said he would send his groom over with the newspaper," said Hildebrand. "No harm can come of that, surely, sir?"

"None at all — provided he doesn't take it into his head to come himself."

"Oh, no fear of that!" Hildebrand said cheerfully. "He told me that he finds it hard to get about, and was only sorry that he was unable to drive over to see you."

He had underrated Mr. Vinehall's spirit. On the following afternoon, when both the ladies of the party were in the parlour, Amanda standing in the middle of the room, and Lady Hester kneeling at her feet to stitch up a torn flounce on her dress, a vehicle was heard to drive up. Neither paid much heed, since this was no unusual circumstance; but after a minute, Amanda, craning her neck, managed to catch a glimpse of it, and exclaimed: "Good gracious, it's a carriage! The most old-fashioned thing! Whoever can it be?"

They were not left above a couple of minutes in suspense. Whoever it was had already entered the inn, and the arrival seemed to have thrown the Chicklades into strange confusion. A babel of voices sounded, Chicklade's deep one sharpened by surprise, and a still deeper one wheezing an answer.

"Good God!" uttered Hester, in a panic. "Could it be Mr. Vinehall? Amanda, what are we to do? If he sees me —"

The words died on her lips, for the door had been flung open, and she heard Chicklade say: "If your honour will be pleased to step into the parlour! You'll find Sir Gareth's sister and niece, and very glad to see you, sir, I'll be bound."

Gladness was not the predominant expression in either lady's face. Hester, hurriedly breaking off her thread, and getting up, was looking perfectly distracted; and Amanda's eyes fixed on the doorway, were growing rounder and rounder in astonishment.

Hildebrand had not exaggerated in his description of Mr. Vinehall. His bulk filled the aperture. He was a man in the late sixties, dressed in clothes as old-fashioned as his carriage. A stalwart footman hovered watchfully behind him, and, as soon as he was clear of the doorway, hastened to lend him the support of his arm, and to lower him on to a chair, where he sat, breathing heavily, and staring at Amanda. An appreciative smile gradually spread over his very red face, and he said: "So you are little Trixie's girl, my dear? Well, well, you don't resemble her greatly, but *I've* no complaint to make! I'll wager you'll break as many hearts as she did!" His mountainous form shook alarmingly, and a rumbling laugh appeared to convulse him. The footman patted him on the back, and after wheezing a good deal, he gasped: "You don't know who the devil I am, eh? Well, my name's Vinehall, and I knew your mama when she was in a cradle. Gary, too. To think of his being within five miles of my place, and me having not a suspicion of it! If it hadn't been for your brother's coming to call on me yesterday, I daresay I should never have been a penny the wiser, for the only news I get is from the doctor, and he hasn't been next or nigh me for ten days. Damme, I thought, when the lad was gone off, why don't I heave myself into my carriage, and go to see Gary, since he can't come to see me? So here I am, and not a penny the worse for it. Now, where's your mama, my dear? I'll warrant she'll bless herself when she hears who's come to wait on her!"

"She — she isn't here, sir," said Amanda.

"Not here? Where's she gone off to, then? The boy told me she couldn't leave Gary!"

"I don't know. I mean, she never was here! It is my Aunt Hester who is nursing Uncle Gary!"

"But your brother said —"

"Oh, I expect he did not hear just what you were asking him!" said Amanda glibly. "He is very deaf, you know!"

"God bless my soul! Didn't seem to be deaf to me!"

"No, because he very much dislikes to have it known, and so he pretends that he can hear quite well."

"You don't mean it! I should never have suspected it. So Trixie ain't here after all! Who is this Aunt Hester you spoke of? One of your papa's sisters?" He seemed to become aware of Hester, standing frozen behind Amanda, and bowed. "How de do, ma'am? You'll excuse my getting up!"

"Yes, indeed!" Hester said faintly. "How do you do?"

He frowned suddenly. "Ay, but you can't be Gary's sister, if you're a Wetherby!"

"No, no! I mean, I'm not a Wetherby! That is —"

Amanda, observing her flounderings, rose nobly, but disastrously, to the rescue. "She is Uncle Gary's *other* sister," she explained.

"Other sister? He ain't got another!" said Mr. Vinehall. "Never more than three of

386

them: Gary, poor Arthur, and Trixie! What's the game, you little puss? Trying to humbug an old man? No, no, you'll catch cold at that!"

"Excuse me!" Hester said, unable to bear another moment of what was fast developing into an inquisition. "I will see if Sir Gareth can receive you, sir!"

With these hastily uttered words, she slipped from the room, and fled upstairs, tripping on her dress, and arriving in Sir Gareth's room out of breath, and with her cap crooked. "Gareth!" she gasped. "The most dreadful thing! We are quite undone!"

He lowered the copy of the *Quarterly,* which he had been reading. "Good God, what is it?"

"Mr. Vinehall!" she said, sinking limply into a chair.

"What, here?" he demanded.

"In the parlour, talking to Amanda. He has come to see you!"

"Now we *are* in the basket!" said Sir Gareth, accepting the situation with maddening calm. "Has he seen you?"

"Yes, of course he has, and of course he knew I wasn't Mrs. Wetherby! I was ready to sink, for I could think of nothing to say, and Amanda made a fatal mistake! Gareth, how *can* you lie there laughing?"

"My dear, I can't help but laugh when you burst in upon me looking perfectly demented, and with that ridiculous cap over one eye! I do wish you will throw it away!"

"This is *no* moment to be discussing my cap!" she scolded. "Amanda told him I was your *other* sister!"

"Now, that is not worthy of Amanda," he said, shaking his head. "He won't swallow it. She must think of something better."

"I don't see how she *can!* And, depend upon it, Hildebrand will come in, having no notion that he's very deaf, just to make matters worse!"

"Oh, is Hildebrand deaf?" he asked, interested.

"Yes — that is, no, you know very well he isn't! Oh, dear, I ought to have said I *was* a Wetherby! What's to be done now? *One* thing I am determined on! I won't meet him again! What shall you tell him?"

"I can't imagine," he said frankly. "It will depend on what Amanda may have told him."

"You may be obliged to tell the truth."

"I may, but I shall do my best to avoid the necessity."

"Yes, pray do! It is such a very complicated story, and I daresay it would quite exhaust you to have to explain it all to him."

His lips quivered, but he replied gravely: "And then we might discover that he hadn't believed a word of it."

"Yes, very true! Good God, he is coming!" she cried, springing out of her chair. "I can't and I won't face him! I should be bound to ruin everything by saying something bird-witted — you must know I should!"

"Yes, but I own I should dearly love to hear you!" Sir Gareth said, his eyes warm with amusement.

"How can you be so unfeeling? Where can I hide?" she said, looking wildly round.

"Slip away to your own room until he has gone!" he advised.

"I can't! The stairs are directly opposite this door! Oh, heavens, Gareth, only listen to him! How dreadful if he were to expire on the stairs! Though it would be a great stroke of good fortune for us, of course. But one cannot wish it to happen — unless, perhaps, it would be a merciful release for him, poor man! I shall have to get behind the curtain. For heaven's sake, Gareth, think of something to say that will satisfy him!"

The little bedchamber did not boast a wardrobe, but a chintz curtain had been hung across one corner of the room. To Sir Gareth's deep delight, Lady Hester plunged behind it, amongst his coats, just as Chicklade, who had aided the footman to push and haul Mr. Vinehall up the narrow stairs, opened the door, and announced the visitor.

Sir Gareth composed his countenance admirably, and greeted his father's old friend with every proper expression of gratitude and pleasure. It was some moments before Mr. Vinehall, deposited in a chair beside the bed, could recover his breath. His exertions had turned the red in his cheeks to purple, but this gradually abated. He waved his solicitous attendants out of the room, and said: "Gary! Well, by Jupiter! It must be a dozen years since I saw you last! How are you, my dear boy? Not in good point, I hear. How came you to break your arm? Lord, I should have recognized you anywhere!" He barely gave Sir Gareth time to answer suitably before he was off again, dropping his voice confidentially, and saying: "I'm glad I don't find that young lady with you, for I shouldn't know what to say to her, upon my word I should not! I wouldn't have put her out of countenance for the world, as I hope you know!"

"I am quite sure you would not, sir," said Sir Gareth, feeling his way.

"Ay, but it was not a very gallant way to behave, and I could see she was put out.

Well, no wonder, for there was I blundering along, and Trixie's girl tells me she is devilish sensitive!"

"She has a great deal of sensibility," admitted Sir Gareth cautiously.

"Ay, I daresay, and there I was, bringing home the evils of her situation to her, like a regular blubber-head! I should have known how it was as soon as that pretty chit said she was your other sister, but it never so much as crossed my mind. As soon as she was gone, Trixie's girl told me, and, I give you my word, Gary, I was never more thunderstruck in my life! God bless my soul, I should have said your dear father was the last man on earth — why, even when he was cutting a dash in his salad days I never knew him to be in the petticoat-line! Ay, and I was as well acquainted with him as any man. I declare I can't get over it! You acknowledge her, I see?"

"Quite — quite privately!" said Sir Gareth, only the faintest tremor in his voice.

"Ay, very proper," nodded Mr. Vinehall. "Was your mother aware of her existence?"

"Happily, no!"

"Just as well. She wouldn't have liked it. Nasty shock for her, for she doted on your father. Well, well, poor George, he managed to keep it dark, and you needn't fear I shall spread the tale about. Couldn't, if I wanted to, for it's seldom I see anyone these days. You'll know how to tell the poor girl she don't have to fear me. It's a sad business. Taking little thing, too; got a sweet face! What you should do, Gary, is to find her a respectable husband."

"I shall do my best to, sir."

"That's right: you're too like your father not to do just as you ought! But tell me, my boy, how do you go on? How is Trixie? That was a tragic thing, Arthur's getting himself killed."

He remained for some twenty minutes, chatting in a rambling way about old times and old acquaintances; but he had evidently been warned by Amanda that he must not stay for long with the invalid, for he soon pulled out his watch, and said that he must be off. He could not rise unassisted from his chair, but his attendant was waiting outside the door, and came in answer to his husky bellow. After grasping Sir Gareth's hand, and adjuring him not to leave the district without coming over to see him, he went ponderously away, and was soon heard cursing Chicklade genially for some piece of clumsiness.

Lady Hester emerged from her hiding-place, her cap now wildly askew. Sir Gareth lay back against his pillows, watching her, a question behind the brimming laughter in his eyes.

"Gareth!" said Hester, in an awed voice. "You *must* own that Amanda is wonderful! I should *never* have thought of saying I was your natural sister!"

He was shaking with laughter, his hand pressed instinctively to his hurt shoulder. "No? Nor I, my dear!"

Suddenly she began to laugh too. "Oh, dear, of all the absurd situations — ! I was just thinking how W-Widmore would l-look if he knew!"

The thought was too much for her. She sat down in the windsor chair, and laughed till she cried. Mopping her streaming eyes at last, she said: "I don't think I have ever laughed so much in all my life. But I must say, Gareth, there is one thing about this new story of Amanda's which I cannot like!"

"Oh, no, is there?" he said unsteadily.

"Yes," she said, sober again. "It was not well done of Amanda to make up such a tale about your father. For he was a most excellent person, and it seems quite dreadful to be slandering him! Really, Gareth, you should have denied it!"

"I assure you, he would have delighted in the story, for he was blessed with a lively sense of humour," Sir Gareth replied. He looked at her, a glimmer in his eyes, and a smile quivering on his lips. "Do you know, Hester, in all these years I have held you in esteem and regard, yet I never knew you until we were pitchforked into this fantastic imbroglio? Certainly Amanda is wonderful! I must be eternally grateful to her!"

CHAPTER SIXTEEN

Sir Gareth, slowly winning back to strength, knew very well that it behoved him to send word to his household that he had not been kidnapped, or snatched up into thin air, but he preferred to let the world slide for just a little longer. It would never do, he told himself, to let his servants get wind of his whereabouts, for ten to one they would allow their tongues to wag; or, worse, Trotton, already strongly suspecting him of having taken leave of his senses, might arrive at the Bull, in an excess of zeal, and the unshakeable belief that his services could not be dispensed with. It was really quite impossible to explain to them what had happened; to tell them not to mention his whereabouts to anyone would be to invite an extremely undesirable curiosity. After all, he was known to have gone into the country for several days, and it would probably be thought that he had prolonged his visit, or perhaps formed the sudden resolve to go from Brancaster to stay with one of his numerous friends. Trotton, of course, would expect to find his master in Berkeley Square when he reached town, and would undoubtedly suppose that Amanda had again given him the slip. Well, that couldn't be helped, and at least Trotton wouldn't be anxious. He did toy with the idea of writing to his brother-in-law, to enlist his aid in running a nameless Brigade-Major to earth, and even got as far as starting a letter to him. But it proved to be rather too exhausting a task. One sheet of literary composition was enough to make his head swim; and when he read over what he had written, he tore it up. Warren would undoubtedly think he had run mad. So he told himself that in all likelihood no one was worrying about him at all, and gave himself up to lazy enjoyment.

Hester was similarly unconcerned. The Widmores must believe her to be with her sister Susan; and even if some chance presently revealed to them that she was not at Ancaster she did not flatter herself that they would feel any particular concern. They might wonder, and conjecture, and they would certainly think it odd of her; but the chances were that Almeria at least would assume that having rejected Sir Gareth's offer she had left Brancaster to escape the recriminations of her family.

But Sir Gareth and Lady Hester underrated their relations. By ill-luck, Lady Ennerdale had occasion to write to her brother, and the contents of her letter made it abundantly plain that her children were all in health and spirits, and that so far from enjoying Hester's companionship she supposed her to be at Brancaster. Exactly as Hester had foreseen, Lady Widmore instantly informed her lord that Hester had taken a crackbrained notion into her head of setting up house on her own. Not a doubt but that was what she was meaning to do: idiotish, of course, but just like her. All this upset over Ludlow's offer had irritated her nerves: my lady had thought her manner very strange. But then she was always tottyheaded!

Lady Hester had been right, too, in thinking that her brother would not succumb to anxiety; but she had underestimated his dislike of scandal. Lord Widmore, had she gone to live with one of her sisters, would have raised not the smallest objection, for no one would have wondered at it. But people would wonder very much at it if an unattached lady left the shelter of her father's roof to live alone. To make it worse, she was not yet thirty. What, he asked his wife, would people think, if ever it leaked out that Hetty had tried to escape from her family? She must be found, and brought to her senses — unless she was all the time with Gertrude, or Constance. It would be excessively like her to have said Susan, when she meant Gertrude: he would write immediately to both his other sisters.

In London, a far greater degree of anxiety was felt than Sir Gareth had anticipated. Trotton did indeed assume that he was still chasing Amanda; but he was very far from accepting this solution to the mystery with equanimity. Devotion to the master he had served since his boyhood, coupled with jealousy of Sir Gareth's butler and his valet, prevented him from taking them one inch into his confidence; he told them that Sir Gareth had said he might break his journey at a friend's house; but he was deeply perturbed. Sir Gareth was behaving in a way so utterly at variance with his usual calm and well-bred self-possession that Trotton seriously supposed him either to be going out of his mind, or to have fallen desperately in love with a chit of a girl who would make him the worst wife in the world. Trotton had no opinion of Amanda. A bit of muslin, that's what he had thought she was at first.

Then it had seemed that he had been wrong; and although he didn't believe more than half of the things he had heard her say to Sir Gareth, there was no denying she hadn't gone with him willingly. Dicked in the nob, Sir Gareth must be, to make off with a girl who was trying all the time to escape from him! High-handed too: he'd never known him act like it before. A nice kickup there would be, if her father, or maybe her brother, got to know about all this bobbery! It behoved anyone who held Sir Gareth in affection to make a push to rescue him from the consequences of his folly, and Trotton held him in considerable affection.

So, too, did his sister. Mrs. Wetherby saw her adored brother set off for Brancaster, and had very little hope that he would meet with a rebuff there. When, at the end of a week, he had not returned to his house in Berkeley Square, that little died: he would scarcely have remained so long at Brancaster if his suit had not prospered. She expected every day to receive a letter from him, announcing his betrothal, but no letter came. She could scarcely believe that he would not have informed her of it before admitting the rest of the world into his confidence, but she, like Amanda, began to study the columns of the *Morning Post,* and the *Gazette.* She found no mention of Sir Gareth's name; and it was at this point that the conviction that something had happened to him took strong possession of her mind. Mr. Wetherby kindly and patiently proved to her how unlikely it was that any disaster could have befallen Gary of which she would not have been apprized long since, but he might as well have spared his breath. No, she said, she had not the remotest conjecture of the nature of the accident which she supposed to have occurred: she just had a Feeling that all was not well with Gary. Mr. Wetherby, well-acquainted with her Feelings, recommended her not to be on the fidgets, and dismissed the matter from his mind.

But not for long. It was recalled by a chance meeting at his club with an acquaintance who let fall a scrap of information which, the more he considered it, seemed to him of sufficient interest to recount to his wife. It was curious: not alarming — in fact, the inference to be drawn from it would probably do much to banish Trixie's blue devils — but it did make one wonder a trifle. It was not important enough to occupy a prominent place in his memory; he remembered it when he was in the middle of telling Trixie about young Kendal, whom he had run smash into as he was coming away from White's.

"Not that I knew who he was, for although I daresay I may have seen him when he was a child I don't recall it," he said reflectively. "However, Willingdon was with me, and at once introduced him. You remember Jack Kendal, Trixie? Fellow that was up at Cambridge with me — came in for a neat little place in Northamptonshire, and married some Scotch girl or other. I went to his funeral about five years ago," he added helpfully, perceiving a slight lack of interest in his wife's face. "Poor fellow! I didn't see much of him after he got married, but he used to be a close friend of mine. Well, this boy I was telling you about is his second son. Well set-up young fellow, though he don't favour Jack much: got sandy hair, like his mother. Queer chance, my meeting him like that. Which reminds me!" he said, digressing suddenly. "Knew I had something to tell you! Cleeve was in the club today, and he happened to mention Brancaster."

"Brancaster?" said Beatrix quickly, her interest immediately roused. "Did Lord Cleeve know — did he give you any news of Gareth?"

"No, no, nothing like that! But from what he said it seems Brancaster is down at

Brighton. He spoke of having dined with him in town the day he came up from Brancaster Park. He went off to join the Regent the next morning. What struck me as odd was that, by what I was able to make out, he must have left Brancaster the day after Gary arrived there. That is, if Gary held by his intention of going first to the Rydes. Said he meant to spend a couple of days with them, didn't he?"

"Yes, certainly he did, and Gary would never break an engagement of that nature! Then Gary cannot be at Brancaster! Warren, it must surely mean — though I find it hard to credit it! — that Lady Hester rejected him!"

"Looks like it," agreed Warren. "Brancaster's a ramshackle fellow, but he wouldn't go off to Brighton if he had Gary staying with him in Cambridgeshire. I thought you'd be interested."

"Thankful!" she declared. Her brow creased. "Yes, but — Warren, if Gary left Brancaster over a fortnight ago, what can have become of him?"

"Lord, I don't know! Daresay he went on to visit some of his friends. To get back to what I was saying to you about young Kendal —"

"He would not have done so without writing to me! He must have known how anxious I should be!"

"Anxious! Why should you be anxious? Gary ain't a schoolboy, my dear! I own it ain't like him to go off without telling anyone where he was bound for, or how long he meant to be away — but for anything we know he may have sent word to Berkeley Square."

"I shall call there tomorrow morning, and ask Sheen whether he has had any news of his master," said Beatrix in a determined voice.

"No harm in doing that, but mind, now, Trixie! — if he hasn't written to Sheen, Gary won't thank you for kicking up a dust, so take care what you say to Sheen! Well, about young Kendal! I invited him to come and take his pot-luck with us tomorrow. Jack's boy, you know!"

She was frowning over the mystery of her brother's continued absence from town, but these words successfully diverted her mind. "Invited him to dine with us tomorrow?" she exclaimed. "Good gracious, Warren, could you not have invited him to White's? Pray, how, at such short notice, am I to arrange a suitable party for his entertainment, with London so thin of company? And

Leigh gone off to stay with the Maresfields, too!"

"Leigh? Lord, Trixie, Kendal ain't a scrubby schoolboy! He's four- or five-and-twenty, and has seen eight years' service besides! What should he have to say to a whippersnapper like Leigh? As for company, you need not put yourself about, for I told him he would meet none but ourselves."

"Oh, very well!" she said. "I must say, though, that I should think he would be heartily bored!"

"Nonsense! He will be mighty glad to sit down to one of your dinners, my love. He has been putting up at an hotel these past few weeks, and I'll be bound he'll welcome a change from chops and steaks. He told me that he's been kept kicking his heels in town by those fellows at the Horse Guards, while the military doctors made up their minds whether he was fit to go back to his duties or not. Got a ball in his shoulder, and was sent home on sick furlough some months ago. He's a Light Bob: 43rd Regiment."

The vexed look vanished from her face. It was tiresome to be obliged to entertain a stranger at this season, when she was on the point of shutting up the London house for a couple of months, but no officer from the

Peninsula need doubt his welcome in Mount Street. "Oh, was he in Spain? I wonder if he ever met Arthur? Of course he must dine with us!" she said cordially.

Nothing could have been kinder than her greeting, when Captain Kendal was ushered into her drawing-room on the following evening; but what she had learnt at Sir Gareth's house that morning had destroyed all desire to entertain even a Peninsular veteran who might have been acquainted with her brother Arthur.

Sheen had received no commands from his master, since Trotton, more than a fortnight ago, had delivered a message that Sir Gareth expected to be at home again on the following evening. He had not come, and Trotton had disclosed that when he had parted from him, Sir Gareth had said that he might, perhaps, visit my Lord and Lady Stowmarket, which was no doubt what he had done.

Two pieces of disquieting intelligence were conveyed to Mrs. Wetherby in this speech. The first was that Sir Gareth should have sent Trotton home; the second, that he should have said he was going to stay with the Stowmarkets. It was very unlike him to prefer post-chaise travel to driving his own horses; and none knew better than he that the Stowmarkets were away from home. There was some mystery attached to his movements, and the more Beatrix thought about it the uneasier did she become. She betrayed nothing to Sheen, however, merely desiring him to tell Trotton, when he should see him, that she wished him to wait on her in Mount Street.

Nor would anyone have guessed, watching her as she sat chatting to Captain Kendal, that at least half her mind was occupied in turning over and over the problem of Sir Gareth's disappearance.

Captain Kendal was a rather stocky young man, with sandy hair and brows, a square, purposeful countenance, and a pair of very direct blue eyes. His varied career — for he had seen service in South America, before joining Sir John Moore's expedition to Spain — had given him an assurance which made him appear older than his twenty-four years; and his manner, which, although perfectly unassuming, was very decided, indicated that he was accustomed to command. His private fortune was small, but there seemed to be little doubt that he would succeed in his profession. Young as he was, when he had been wounded he had been Acting Brigade-Major. He was not very talkative, but this seemed to arise from a natural taciturnity rather than from shyness; and from having been with the army abroad ever since he had left school, he had none of the social graces that characterized the young man of fashion. He had not been acquainted with Major Ludlow, but in spite of this Beatrix liked him. The only fault she had to find with him was that his mind was cast in rather too serious a mould for her taste.

It was not easy to draw him out on his personal affairs, but he was ready enough to talk of military matters, or of any interesting things he had seen on his travels. Beatrix, enquiring about billeting arrangements in Spain, won far more from him than Warren, asking questions about his family, or his ambitions.

"It's several years since I had the pleasure of meeting your mother," said Warren. "I hope she's well?"

"Very well, thank you, sir," responded Captain Kendal.

"Does she still live in Northamptonshire?"

"Yes, sir."

"And — now let me see! How many brothers is it that you have?"

"Only one sir."

"Only one, eh? But you have several sisters, I fancy."

"I have three sisters."

"Three, is it?" said Warren, persevering. "And your brother — he was married not so long ago, wasn't he?"

"Two years ago," said Captain Kendal.

"Is it as much as that? I remember seeing the notice of it. Well, well! I suppose he must have been a schoolboy when I saw him last. I was used frequently to visit your father, you know, and was once pretty familiar with your part of the country. Lately, I don't know how it may be, but I have very seldom been in Northamptonshire. I daresay, however, that we have several acquaintances in common. The Birchingtons, for instance, and Sir Harry Bramber?" Captain Kendal bowed. "Yes, I was sure you must know them. Yes, and I'll tell you who is in town, who is quite a near neighbour of yours! Old Summercourt! But I daresay you knew that."

"I didn't know it, sir. I am, of course, acquainted with General Summercourt."

"Friend of my father's," said Warren. "I met him today, at White's. Breaking up a trifle, I thought. Not like himself. But I only had a couple of words or so with him: he was in the devil of a hurry — only dropped into the club to see if there were any letters for him. Said he couldn't stay, because he must call at Bow Street. Seemed an odd start to me. Not getting to be a trifle queer in his attic, is he?"

"Not to my knowledge," said Captain Kendal, staring rather fixedly at him. "*Bow Street,* did you say?"

"Yes: I couldn't help wondering what took him there. He was looking a trifle hagged, too. Nothing wrong, is there?"

"To my knowledge, nothing whatsoever," replied Captain Kendal, a crease between his brows.

Warren began to talk of something else, but after a few minutes the Captain said abruptly: "I beg pardon, sir, but can you furnish me with General Summercourt's direction?"

"I didn't ask where he was staying, but I fancy he usually puts up at Grillon's when he's in town," replied Warren, looking an enquiry.

The Captain coloured slightly. "Thank you. If he is in some trouble — I am pretty well acquainted with him — it would be civil to call upon him!"

Nothing more was said on the subject, but Beatrix received the impression that the casual piece of information let fall by her husband had arrested Captain Kendal's attention more than had anything else that had been said to him.

Not long after dinner, when the gentlemen had joined Beatrix in the drawing-room, the butler came in, and, after hesitating for a moment, went to where his master was sitting, and bent to say, in an apologetic and lowered tone: "I beg your pardon, sir, but Sir Gareth's head groom is below. I said you was engaged, but he seems very anxious to speak to you."

The words were intended only for Mr. Wetherby's ears, but Beatrix's hearing was sharp, and she heard them. She broke off in the middle of what she was saying to her guest, and demanded: "Did you say Sir Gareth's head groom? I will come at once." She nodded to her husband, and got up. "I left a message in Berkeley Square that I wished Trotton to come here. Captain Kendal will excuse me, I am sure, if I run away for a few minutes."

"I beg pardon, ma'am, but it is the *master* Trotton has come to see," interposed the butler, catching Mr. Wetherby's eye, and exchanging with him a meaning look.

"Nonsense! It is I who want to see Trotton, not your master!" said Beatrix, not blind to this by-play.

"Stay where you are, my dear," said Warren, going to the door. "I'll find out what

Trotton wants. There's no occasion for you to put yourself out."

She was vexed, but to engage in a dispute with him in the presence of a guest did not suit her notions of propriety. She resumed her seat, and said, with rather a forced smile: "Pray forgive us! The thing is that I am in some anxiety about my brother, whose groom it is who has just come here."

"I am excessively sorry!" he said. "I collect he is ill? Would you like me to go away? You must be wishing me at the devil!"

"Indeed I am not! I beg you won't think of running away! My brother is not ill — at least, I don't think so." She stopped, and then said, with a little laugh: "It is very likely nothing at all, and I am refining too much upon the event. The fact is that my brother went into the country on a visit more than a fortnight ago, and although his servants were in the expectation of his returning four days later, he *didn't* return, or send any word, so that I cannot help indulging a great many foolish fancies. But you were telling me about the *fiestas* in Madrid: do continue! How pretty the candles set on all the window-sills must have looked! Were you quartered in the town, Captain Kendal?"

He answered her, and she led him on to describe such features of the Spanish scene as he had thought memorable, an expression on her face of absorbed interest, suitable comments rising mechanically to her lips, and her mind almost wholly divorced from anything he was saying.

The circumstance of Trotton's asking particularly to speak with Warren rather than with herself was not reassuring; a chilling fear that some dreadful news was presently to be broken gentle to her by her husband began to creep into her heart; and only her good breeding kept her from jumping up, and following Warren.

He was gone for what seemed to her to be an ominously long time, and when he at last came back into the room he was wearing the expression of a man who did not wish his wife to suspect that anything was wrong. It was too much; she exclaimed sharply: "What is it? Has some accident befallen Gary?"

"No, no, nothing of the sort! I'll tell you about it presently, but there's no need for you to worry your head over it."

"Where is Gary?" she demanded.

"Well, I can't tell you that, but you may depend upon it he's perfectly well and safe wherever he is. Trotton parted from him at Kimbolton, so I daresay he may have gone off to stay with Staplehurst."

"Kimbolton?" she repeated, astonished. "What in the world took him there, pray?"

"Oh, well, that's a long story, and of no interest to Kendal, my love!"

"If you'll allow me, sir, I'll take my leave," said the Captain. "Mrs. Wetherby must be very anxious to learn more. I would have gone before, only that she wouldn't suffer me to!"

"I should rather think not, and nor will I! Sit down, my boy!"

"Oh, yes, pray do!" Beatrix said. "Is Trotton still in the house, Warren?"

"Having a heavy-wet in the pantry, I expect."

"Then, if Captain Kendal will excuse me, I will go down and speak to him myself!" she said. "I don't stand on ceremony with you, sir, but I am persuaded you will not care for that."

"I should rather think not, ma'am!"

She smiled, and hurried out of the room. The Captain looked at his host, and said bluntly: "Bad news, sir?"

"Lord, no!" said Warren, with a chuckle. "But it ain't the sort of news to blab to his sister! The groom's a silly clunch, but he had that much sense! From what I can make out, my brother-in-law has picked up a very prime article, and has made off with her the lord knows where! He's never been much in the petticoat-line, so his groom don't know what to make of it. Told me he was sure Ludlow had gone out of his mind!"

"Oh, I see!" said the Captain, with a laugh. "No, that's not a story for Mrs. Wetherby, certainly!"

"Trust Trotton to turn her up sweet!" said Warren confidently. "Catch him giving his master's secrets away! Devoted to him, you know: been with him since Gareth was a lad. The only wonder is he told me. Don't suppose he would have, if my wife hadn't summoned him to come here. The silly fellow's in the deuce of a pucker: thinks his master's heading for trouble! Funny thing about these old servants: never can be brought to believe one ain't still in short coats!"

"No, by Jupiter!" agreed the Captain. "Like my old nurse, who is persuaded I got hit because she wasn't there to tell me not to get in the way of the nasty guns!"

"Exactly so!" said Warren, laughing heartily. "I told Trotton I never knew a man more able to take care of himself than Ludlow, but I might as well have spared my breath. I shall have to discover what tale he's fobbed my wife off with, or I shall be bowled out."

But when Mrs. Wetherby came back into

the room he soon found that this would be unnecessary. She was looking so much amused that he was surprised into exclaiming: "What the deuce did Trotton tell you to set you off laughing?"

She threw him a saucy look. "The truth, of course! Did you think I couldn't get him to tell me the whole? Pooh! How could you be so nonsensical as to suppose I should be shocked, as though I were a schoolroom miss? I was never more enchanted! When I had despaired of ever seeing the *old* Gary again, doing such daring things, and being so gay, and adventurous! *How* I wish I could have seen him snatching up this beautiful girl in his curricle, and driving off with her! Of all the absurd starts! Depend upon it, he sent Trotton home because he was off to the Border with his Amanda! Did Trotton tell you what was her name? Isn't it pretty?"

"What?" ejaculated Captain Kendal.

She was surprised, for he had fairly shot the word at her, but before she could answer Warren intervened, saying in a displeased voice: "You are talking nonsense, my dear, and allowing your romantic notions to run away with you. The Border, indeed! You may be sure there is no question of *that!*"

"Oh, you are thinking of her trying to escape from him, and his chasing after her, and finding her in a cow-byre, or some such thing!" she said laughing. "My dear Warren, how can you be so green? No female in her senses would wish to escape from Gary, least of all a girl who was found in a common inn, entirely unattended!"

"You will be giving Kendal a very odd idea of your brother if you lead him to suppose that Gary would for a moment contemplate marriage with such a girl," Warren said repressively.

She was aware that her natural liveliness, exaggerated as it was by relief, had betrayed her into raillery that was beyond the line of being pleasing, and coloured, saying "I was only funning, of course! It cannot be more than a — well, a charmingly romantic interlude! — but it will do Gary a great deal of good, so you must not expect me to pull down my mouth, and preach propriety, if you please!"

After his one startled exclamation, Captain Kendal had not again unclosed his lips. They were indeed tightly gripped together, in a way that suggested to his hostess that he was tiresomely prudish. There was a stern look in his face, and an expression in his eyes which quite startled her. He might disapprove of her vivacity, but why he should look murderous she was at a loss to understand. She stared at him; he lowered his eyes; seemed to make an effort to suppress whatever emotion it was that had him in its clutch; and said curtly that it was time he took his leave. He would not stay for tea, but he said everything that was proper before shaking hands briefly with his hostess. Warren accompanied him to the front-door. "My wife, when she is in funning humour, talks a great deal of flummery," he said. "I need not ask you not to repeat her nonsense, I know."

"You need have no fear of that, sir!" said Captain Kendal emphatically. "Goodnight! And thank you for a — very pleasant evening!"

A bow, and he was gone. Warren went upstairs again to scold his wife for having shocked her guest, and to read her a homily on the evils of a long tongue; but he was himself a little puzzled by the Captain's behaviour.

Captain Kendal, meanwhile, hailed the first hackney he saw, and bade the jarvey drive him to Grillon's Hotel. While this aged vehicle lumbered on its way to Albemarle Street, he sat rather rigidly upright, clenching and unclenching one fist, and frowning straight ahead. Arrived at Grillon's, he demanded General Summercourt in a voice grim enough to make the porter look rather narrowly at him.

The General was discovered, seated at a desk in a small writing-room. There was no one else in the room. The General looked up, and when he saw who had come in, his face hardened, and he said: "You, eh? And just what do you want, young man?"

"I want to know what took you to Bow Street today, sir!" the Captain replied.

"Oh, you do, do you?" snapped the General, exploding into the wrath of a much harassed man. "Then I will tell you, you damned, encroaching jackanapes! Thanks to you my granddaughter has been missing from her home for more than a fortnight. Read that!"

Captain Kendal almost snatched the sheet of writing-paper that was being thrust at him, and rapidly read the lines written in Amanda's childish hand. When he came to the end, he looked up, and said fiercely: "Thanks to *me?* Do you imagine, sir, that Amanda took this step with my knowledge? That I would permit her — By God, if that is the opinion you hold of my character I do not wonder at your refusing your consent to our marriage!"

The General glared at him for a moment. "No, I don't," he said shortly. "If I had, I should have come to you and *choked* her whereabouts out of you! But if you hadn't come making up to her, putting ideas into her head, egging her on to defy me —"

"So far from egging her on to defy you, I have told her that I will not, while she is so young, marry her without your consent, sir! And she knows I mean what I say!"

"Yes! And this is the outcome! I am to be forced to consent! Well, you may be sure of this, Neil Kendal! — I will not! *Damme,* I will not!"

"I collect, then, that you haven't put a notice in the *Morning Post,* sir?"

"No! I have put the matter in the hands of the Runners. They have been searching for her now for a se'enight!"

"And she has been missing above a fort-night!" the Captain flung at him. "Taking it mighty coolly, are you not, sir?"

"Damn your impudence, I made sure she was hiding in the woods! She did so once before, when she couldn't get her own way, the little puss!"

"Call off the Runners!" said the Captain. "*I* can tell you more than they appear to have discovered, and pretty hearing it is! *Where* Amanda is I don't know, but *whom* she is with I do know!"

"For God's sake, Neil, what do you

mean?" demanded the General, turning pale. "Out with it!"

"She is with a fellow called Ludlow — Gareth Ludlow — who came upon her in a common inn, where, I know not, and bore her off to Kimbolton. I have been dining tonight with Ludlow's sister, a Mrs. Wetherby, and what I heard in that house — My God, I don't know how I contrived to keep my tongue still!"

"Ludlow?" the General said numbly. "Bore her off? My little Amanda! No, no, it isn't possible! Tell me the whole, damn you!"

He listened in silence to Captain Kendal's succinct recital, but it seemed as though he had hardly taken it in, for he sat looking blankly at the Captain, repeating uncomprehendingly: "Abducted her — trying to escape from him — found in a *cow-byre?*" He managed to pull himself together, and said in a firmer voice: "It isn't possible! She's nothing but a child! Did you discover from these Wetherbys —"

"Exactly what I have told you! They knew no more, and you may be sure I asked no questions! They suppose Amanda to belong to the muslin company: a *very prime article* was the term used by Wetherby! Upon no account would I have said one word that might lead them to the truth!"

"It isn't possible!" the General said again. "A man of Ludlow's quality — Good God, in whatever case he met her he must have recognized at a glance that she was a child — a gently-bred child, and as innocent — Why the devil didn't he restore her to me? Or, if she wouldn't tell him what her name was, place her in the care of a respectable woman?"

"Yes, *why?*" said the Captain harshly. "That is a question he will answer to me before he is much older! What kind of a man is he?"

The General made a hopeless gesture. "How should I know? I'm not acquainted with him. A man of fashion: he belongs to the Corinthian set. Handsome fellow, with a fine figure, rich enough to be able to buy an abbey. He's not married — I fancy there was some sort of a tragedy, years ago. I've never heard any ill of him: on the contrary, I believe him to be very well liked. But what's that to the purpose? If she has been all this time with him — by God, he shall marry her! He has compromised her — my granddaughter! — and if he thinks —"

"*He* marry her — ! We'll see that!" interrupted the Captain grimly. "Now, sir! The first thing you must do is to call off the Runners, so that we may get through this damnable business with as little noise as possible. I'm off to Kimbolton in the morning, and if I can get no news of Ludlow there I'll try a cast or two. But something I must learn: he cannot have passed unnoticed in so small a place. If you like to leave it in my hands, very well! If you prefer to accompany me, better!"

"*Accompany* you, you insubordinate, insolent young dog?" exploded the General. "What right have you to meddle in my affairs? Don't think I'll consent to let you marry Amanda, for I won't! *My* granddaughter to throw herself away on a penniless cub in a Line Regiment? No, by God! *I* am going to Kimbolton, and I desire neither your aid nor your company!"

"As you please!" shrugged Captain Kendal. "I shall be leaving at first light, and no doubt that would not suit you. I beg you will not neglect to send a letter to Bow Street. We shall meet in Kimbolton! Goodnight!"

Chapter Seventeen

At very much the same time as these stirring events were taking place in London, Lord Widmore received letters from his two youngest sisters, and learned from them that with neither had Lady Hester sought shelter. As he had by then argued himself into a belief that she could have gone nowhere else, the tidings came as a severe shock to him, and caused him to exclaim unguardedly: "Gertrude and Constance have not seen Hester since we left London!"

Until that moment, Mr. Whyteleafe had been left in ignorance of the true state of affairs, Lord Widmore being very much more circumspect than his sire. But Mr. Whyteleafe was present when the letters were brought up from the receiving-office, and this involuntary outburst not only arrested his attention, but caused him to demand from his lordship an explanation. He got the explanation from Lady Widmore. Her ladyship's disregard for appearances made her much inclined to treat the escapade as a very good joke, an attitude of mind which so much revolted her lord that it was with relief that he unburdened himself to the chaplain. Mr. Whyteleafe's reactions were all that they should have been. He changed colour, and uttered: "Not at Lady Ennerdale's! Not with Mrs. Nutley, or Lady Cookham! Good God, sir, this is terrible!"

Lord Widmore, looking upon him with approval, decided to admit him into his confidence. As a result, he learned for the first time of the existence of Hildebrand Ross. Until that moment no one had told him that the person supposedly sent by Lady Ennerdale to escort her sister on the journey had been other than a servant. He now discovered that Hester had gone away with an unknown young gentleman of undoubted gentility but suspicious aspect, and exclaimed: "She has eloped!"

But Mr. Whyteleafe did not think that Hester had eloped. Mr. Ross, although sufficiently depraved to utter unblushing lies to a man whose cloth should have commanded his respect, was scarcely of an age to contemplate marriage with a lady approaching her thirtieth year. Mr. Ross, he feared, was no more than a go-between.

Lady Widmore, laughing in a very vulgar way, asked who the deuce was there for Mr. Ross to go between, but she was not attended to. By rapid stages Mr. Ross became an infernal agent, employed either by a secret and obviously ineligible lover, or by a daring kidnapper. Lady Widmore, declaring that she was in stitches, said that any kidnapper who thought to wring a groat out of a family that had not a feather to fly with must be so bottleheaded that even such a goosecap as Hester would be able to escape from his clutches. In her opinion, Hester herself, more sly than any of them had suspected, had employed Mr. Ross to assist her to slip away from Brancaster without exciting surprise or opposition. She recommended her husband to subject his butler to a rigorous inquisition. If anyone knew what kind of an undergame Hester was engaged in, she said, he might lay his life that one was Cliffe, whose maudlin affection for Hester had often put her ladyship out of all patience.

Lord Widmore failed to elicit any information from Cliffe, but Mr. Whyteleafe was more successful. Cliffe, already anxious and more than a little doubtful of the wisdom of his having abetted Hester, crumbled under the powerful exhortations of the chaplain.

He was brought to realize that his mistress's reputation, nay, even her life, perhaps, was at stake, and, weeping, he gave up the only piece of information he had. He told Mr. Whyteleafe that he had recognized the post-boy in charge of the chaise that had borne Lady Hester away as one of the lads employed at the Crown Inn at St. Ives.

From then onward Mr. Whyteleafe assumed command. In a manner calculated to convince the trembling butler that he had aided Lady Hester to commit an indiscretion which must plunge her entire family into a ruinous scandal, he laid a strict charge of silence upon Cliffe. Almost as impressively he pointed out to Lord Widmore that no whisper of the affair must be allowed to reach the ears of any but themselves. Together he and his lordship would discover, at St. Ives, the destination of that post-chaise; together they would track down the fugitive. No coachman or postilion should go with them: they would set forth alone, and in the curricle which the Earl kept at Brancaster for his use when in Cambridgeshire. "And I," added Mr. Whyteleafe, recollecting that Lord Widmore was a very indifferent whip, "will drive it!"

Meanwhile, in happy ignorance of the hostile forces converging upon him, Sir Gareth was making a recovery upon which his medical attendant never ceased to congratulate himself. It would be some time before his wound would cease to trouble him (a circumstance due, Lady Hester had no hesitation in asserting, to the shockingly rough and ready methods employed in the extraction of the bullet), and still longer before he could hope to regain his full strength but the progress he made was steady; and it was not long before he was able to persuade his several nurses to let him leave his bed, and try what the beneficial effects of fresh air would do for him. A small orchard lay behind the inn, and, as the weather continued to be sultry, one golden day succeeding another, it was here that he spent his days, in an idyllic existence which not even the ill-humour of Mrs. Chicklade could mar. That stern moralist had never been convinced of the respectability of the party she was called upon to serve; and when she saw the parlour chairs carried into the orchard, together with a table, and all the cushions the inn could yield, and further discovered that her misguided spouse had consented to carry meals there, she knew that her worst suspicions had fallen short of the truth. A set of heathen gypsies, that's what Chicklade's precious ladies and gentleman of quality were, and let no one dare to tell her different! But Chicklade said that he knew the Quality when he saw it, and while the dibs were in tune the visitors might eat their dinner on the roof, if that was their fancy. As for the morals of the party, it was not for him to criticize an out-and-outer who dropped his blunt as freely as did Sir Gareth.

So Mrs. Chicklade, appeased by the thought of the gold that was flowing into her husband's coffers, continued to cook three handsome meals a day for her disreputable guests, and startled her neighbours by appearing suddenly in a new and impressive bonnet, and a gown of rich purple hue.

As for the disreputable guests, only Amanda was not entirely content to remain at Little Staughton. Sir Gareth had his own reasons for not wishing to bring his stay to an end; Lady Hester, tending him, sitting in comfortable companionship beside him under the laden fruit trees, valued as she had never been before, was putting on a new bloom; and Hildebrand, inspired by the rural solitude, had made a promising start to his tragic drama, and was not at all anxious to return to a more exacting world. He had got his horse back, too, yielding at last to a command from his adopted uncle to stop being a gudgeon, and to retrieve the noble animal without more ado. He still slept on a camp-bed set up in Sir Gareth's room: not because his services were any longer needed during the night-watches, but because there were only two guest-chambers in the inn. Sir Gareth was thus kept fully abreast of the drama's progress, the day's literary output being read to him each night, and his criticisms and suggestions invited. No qualms were suffered by Hildebrand: he blithely assured Sir Gareth that his parents, believing him to be on a walking-tour of Wales, would not expect to receive any letters from him; and as for the friends he should have joined, they would think only that he had changed his plans, or had been delayed, and would doubtless overtake them.

"Well, wouldn't you like to?" Sir Gareth asked him. "You know, I am really very well able to manage for myself now, and I don't want you to feel yourself obliged to remain here on my account. Chicklade can do all I need."

"Chicklade?" said Hildebrand, revolted. "What, let him tie your cravats with his great clumsy hands! I should rather think not! Just as you have taught me how to tie a

Waterfall, too! Besides, Aunt Hester and I have decided that when you are well enough to travel to London I am to go with you, to take care of you on the journey. What's more, if Amanda should take it into her head to run away again *you* cannot chase after her, Uncle Gary! And while I am in the vein, I do think that it would be a pity to break the thread of my play. Should you object to it if I just read you the second scene again, now that I have rewritten it?"

So Hildebrand was allowed to remain, although Sir Gareth did not think that Amanda had any intention of running away. Amanda, for once, was at a stand. It had never occurred to her that her grandfather would fail to obey her directions, and how to bring added pressure to bear on him was a problem to which there seemed to be no solution. Time was slipping by, and it might well be that already Neil was under orders to rejoin his brigade. She had not quite reached the stage of capitulation, and still exhaustively scanned the *Morning Post,* which Mr. Vinehall obligingly sent to the Bull each day; but Sir Gareth was hopeful that by the time he was adjudged to be well enough to travel he would have little difficulty in persuading her to accompany him to London. Nothing would prevail upon her to disclose her grandfather's identity, but she had begun to toy with a scheme whereby not her grandfather's hand, but Neil's, might be forced. Did not Uncle Gary think that if he believed her reputation to be lost, Neil would marry her out of hand?

"It seems most unlikely," he replied. "Why should he?"

She was sitting on the ground, a half-made cowslip ball in her hands, looking so absurdly youthful as she propounded her outrageous scheme, that he was hard put to it to maintain his gravity. "To save my good name," she said glibly.

"But he wouldn't be doing anything of the sort," he objected. "He would be giving you quite a different name."

"Yes, but if you lose your reputation, you have to be married in a hurry," she argued. "I know that, because when Theresa — when *someone* I know lost hers, which she did, though I am not perfectly sure how, someone *else* I know said to my aunt that there was nothing for it but to get her married immediately, to save her good name. Well, if you stay all alone with a gentleman you lose your reputation *at once,* so if I pretended Aunt Hester and Hildebrand weren't here, wouldn't Neil feel that it was his duty to marry me, whatever Grandpapa says?"

"No, he would be more likely to feel that *I* must marry you, and you wouldn't like that, you know."

"No, of course I shouldn't, but you could refuse to marry me, couldn't you? That would put Neil in a fix!"

"Yes, indeed!" agreed Hester, with unruffled calm. "But I believe that he would think it his duty to challenge Uncle Gary to a duel, and although Uncle is much better, he isn't strong enough to fight a duel. You wouldn't wish him to overtax himself."

"No," Amanda said reluctantly. "Well, Hildebrand must be the one to do it. Hildebrand! *Hildebrand!*"

Hildebrand, lying on his stomach at some little distance from them, his fingers writhing amongst his disordered locks as he wrestled with literary composition, vouchsafed only an absent grunt.

"Hildebrand, would you be so obliging as to pretend to compromise me, and then refuse to marry me?" said Amanda cajolingly.

"No, can't you see I'm busy? Ask Uncle Gary!" said Hildebrand.

This was not encouraging, nor, when he was brought to attend to what was being said to him, did he return any more satisfactory answer. He recommended her not to be silly, and added that she didn't know what she was talking about.

"I think you are uncivil and disobliging!" said Amanda roundly.

"Oh, no, I'm sure he doesn't mean to be!" said Hester, looking round for her scissors. "I expect — oh, there they are! However did they come to get over there? — I expect he did not quite understand. Really, Hildebrand, you will only have to refuse to marry Amanda, and surely that is not much to ask?"

"Oh, I don't mind doing *that!*" he said, grinning.

"You are an unprincipled woman, Hester," Sir Gareth told her, at the earliest opportunity.

"Yes, I think I am," she agreed reflectively.

"There can be no doubt of it. Are you really proposing to allow Amanda to regale her Brigade-Major with this abominable story she has concocted?"

"But I can see no harm in *that,* Gareth!" she said, vaguely surprised. "It will make her wish to go to London, besides giving her something to do in planning it all, which she *needs,* you know, because since the calf at the farm was sent off to the market it is really very dull for her here. And the Brigade-Major cannot possibly be foolish enough to believe the story. Anyone must see that she hasn't the least notion of what it means to be compromised."

"And having said that, do you still maintain that she should be permitted to marry the fellow?" he asked.

"It depends on what he is like," she replied thoughtfully. "I should wish to see him before I made up my mind."

Her wish was granted on the following afternoon. Sir Gareth, half asleep under a big apple-tree, with Joseph wholly asleep on his knee, became drowsily aware of a menacing presence, and opened his eyes. They fell upon a sandy-haired, stockily-built young gentleman who was standing a few feet away, grimly surveying him. Contempt and wrath flamed in his blue eyes as they took in the splendour of the frogged dressing-gown, which, since his coats fitted him far too well to be eased on over his heavily bandaged shoulder, Sir Gareth was obliged to wear. Interested, and mildly surprised, Sir Gareth sought his quizzing-glass, and through it inspected his unknown visitor.

Captain Kendal drew an audible breath, and pronounced in a voice of awful and resolute civility: "Am I correct, sir, in thinking that I address Sir Gareth Ludlow?"

"Sir," responded Sir Gareth gravely, but with a twitching lip, "you are!"

Captain Kendal appeared to struggle with himself. His fists clenched, and his teeth ground together; he drew another painful breath, and said in measured accents: "I am sorry, sir — *damned* sorry! — to see that you have your arm in a sling!"

"Your solicitude, sir," said Sir Gareth, entering into the spirit of this, "moves me deeply! To own the truth, I am sorry to see it there myself."

"Because," said Captain Kendal, through his shut teeth, "your disabled condition renders it impossible for me to deal with you as you deserve! My heartfelt wish is that you may recover the use of your arm before I am obliged to leave England!"

"Good God!" exclaimed Sir Gareth, enlightenment dawning on him. He lifted his quizzing glass again. "Do you know, I had quite a different picture in my mind? I wish you will tell me what your name is!"

"That, sir, you will know in good time! You will allow me to tell you that what I learned at Kimbolton brought me here with two overmastering desires: the first to bring you to book, and the second to shake the hand of the boy who tried to rescue from your clutches a girl whose youth and innocence must have protected her from any but an unprincipled villain!"

"Well, I am afraid you can't realize the first of these very proper ambitions," said Sir Gareth apologetically, "but there's nothing easier to accomplish than the second." He sat up, and looked round, disturbing Joseph, who stood up, sneezed, and sprang off his knee. "When I last saw him he was in the throes of dramatic composition, over there. Yes, there he is, but not, I perceive, still wrestling with his Muse."

"What?" said Captain Kendal, taken aback. "Are you trying to hoax me, sir?"

"Not at all! Wake up, Hildebrand! We have a visitor!"

"Do you imagine," demanded the Captain, "that I am the man to be taken-in by your shams?"

"I am sure you are not," replied Sir Gareth soothingly. "You do seem to leap a little hurriedly to conclusions — but, then, I don't know yet precisely what it was you learned at Kimbolton."

"Why," the Captain shot at him, "did the chambermaid find your *ward's* door locked? Why did your *ward* think it necessary to lock her door?"

"She didn't. I locked the door, so that she shouldn't escape a second time. Yes, come over here, Hildebrand! Our visitor wishes to shake you by the hand. Let me present Mr. Ross to you, sir! This, Hildebrand, unless I much mistake the matter, is the Brigade-Major."

"What, Amanda's Brigade-Major?" exclaimed Hildebrand "Well, of all things! However did you find us out, sir?"

"For God's sake, have I strayed into a *madhouse?*" thundered the Captain. *"Where is Amanda?"*

"Well, I don't know," said Hildebrand, looking startled. "I daresay she has gone down the road to the farm, though. Shall I go and see if I can find her? Oh, I say, sir, I wish you will tell me! — *will* she be obliged to wring chickens' necks if she goes to Spain?"

"Wring — no!" said the Captain, thrown by this time quite off his balance.

"I *knew* it was all nonsense!" said Hildebrand triumphantly. "I told her it was, but she always thinks she knows everything!"

"Neil!"

The Captain spun round. Amanda had just entered the orchard, bearing a glass of milk and a plate of fruit on a small tray. As the shriek broke from her, she dropped the tray, and came flying across the grass, to hurl herself on to the Captain's broad chest. "Neil, Neil!" she cried, both arms flung round his neck. "Oh, Neil, have you come to rescue me? Oh, how *splendid!* I didn't know *what* to do, and I was almost in despair, but now everything will be right!"

The Captain, holding her in a crushing hug, said thickly: "Yes, everything. I'll see to that!" He disengaged himself, and held her off, his hands gripping her shoulders. "Amanda, what has happened to you? The truth now, and no playing off any tricks!"

"Oh, you wouldn't *believe* the adventures I have had!" she said earnestly. "First there was a horrid woman, who wouldn't have me for a governess, and then there was Sir Gareth Ludlow, who abducted me, and next there was Mr. Theale, who said he would rescue me from Sir Gareth, only he was so odious that I was obliged to escape from *him,* and after that there was Joe, who was *most* kind, and gave me my dear little kitten. I wanted to stay with Joe, though his mother didn't seem to wish me to, but Sir Gareth found me, and told the most shocking untruths which the Ninfields believed, and went *on* abducting me, and locking me in my room, and behaving in the most *abominable* way, in spite of my *begging* him to let me go, so that though I *truthfully* never meant Hildebrand to shoot him, it quite served him right — Oh, Neil, this *is* Sir Gareth! Uncle Gary, *this* is Neil! — Captain Kendal! And that's Hildebrand Ross, Neil. Oh, Uncle Gary, I am excessively sorry, but I threw your glass of milk away! Hildebrand, would you be so obliging as to fetch another one?"

"Yes, very well, but you needn't think I'm going to let you stand there telling bouncers about Uncle Gary!" said Hildebrand indignantly. "He did *not* abduct you, and as for telling lies about you — well, yes, but you told much worse ones about him! Why, you told *me* he was forcing you to marry him because you were a great heiress!"

"Yes, but I had to do that, or you wouldn't have helped me to escape from him!"

The Captain, a trifle stunned, released his betrothed, and turned to Sir Gareth. "I don't understand yet what happened, sir, but I believe I have been doing you an injustice. If that's so, I beg your pardon! But why you should not have restored Amanda immediately to General Summercourt, or at the very least have written to inform him —"

"He couldn't!" said Amanda proudly. "He spoiled *all* my plan of campaign, and he carried me off by force, but he couldn't make me tell him who I was, or Grandpapa, or you, Neil! I *did* think he would win even over that, because he meant to carry me off to his sister, in London, and discover your name at the Horse Guards, only he wasn't able to, because, by the greatest stroke of good fortune, we met Hildebrand, and Hildebrand shot him — though that wasn't what he meant to do, of course."

"There is a great deal about this business I don't understand, but one thing is plain!" said the Captain, sternly eyeing his beloved. "You have been behaving very badly, Amanda!"

"Yes, but I *had* to, Neil!" she pleaded, hanging her head. "I was afraid you would be a little vexed, but —"

"You knew that I should be very angry indeed. Don't think you can cajole me, my girl! You may reserve that for your grandfather! He will be here at any moment now, let me tell you, for he was following me from London, and I left a message for him at Kimbolton. Do you know that he has had to call in the Bow Street Runners to find you?"

"No!" cried Amanda, reviving as if by magic. "Uncle Gary, did you hear that? The Runners are after me!"

"I did, and it confirms my worst fears," said Sir Gareth. "What a pity, though, that you have only just learnt that you are being hunted! You could have made up an even more splendid story, if only you had thought of it."

"Yes, I could," she said regretfully. "Still, it would have been much better if Grandpapa had done what I told him to."

"No, by God, it would not!" said the Captain forcefully. "And if you imagine, Amanda, that I would have married you, had the General been weak enough to have yielded to such a disgraceful trick, you much mistake the matter!"

"Neil!" she cried, her eyes flying to his face, and widening in dismay. "Don't — don't you *wish* to marry me?"

"That," said the Captain, "is another matter! Now, you come into the house, and make a clean breast of the whole, without any more excuses, or any of your make-believe nonsense!"

"I wouldn't! You know I wouldn't!" Amanda stammered, flushing. "Not to you! Neil, you *know* I wouldn't!"

"It will be as well for you if you don't," said the Captain, inexorably marching her off.

Hildebrand, watching with dropped jaw,

turned his eyes towards Sir Gareth. *"Well!"* he gasped. "She — went with him as meek as a nun's hen! *Amanda!"*

It was some time before Captain Kendal emerged again from the house, and when at last he came striding through the orchard he was alone. Lady Hester, who had been sitting with Sir Gareth for some little while, blinked at him, and said: "Good gracious, Gareth, how *very* odd of Amanda! I quite thought he would be a *heroic*-looking young man, did not you?"

Captain Kendal, reaching them, bowed slightly to Hester, but addressed himself to Sir Gareth. "I hope you will accept my apologies, sir. I don't know how to thank you enough. I got the whole story out of her, and you may be sure I've given her a rare dressing. You must have had the devil of a time with her!"

"Nonsense!" Sir Gareth said, holding out his hand.

The Captain gripped it painfully. "You didn't handle her right, you know," he said. "She's as good as gold, if you don't give her her head. The mischief is that the General and Miss Summercourt have spoilt her to death, and as though that wasn't enough, she's been allowed to stuff her head with a lot of trashy novels. I can tell you, it fairly made my hair stand on end when I heard the stories she's been making up! But the thing is that she hasn't the ghost of a notion what they really mean. I daresay you know that. I hope you do!"

"Of course I know it! My favourite is the one about the amorous widower — though I must own that the latest gem, in which Hildebrand is to play the leading role, has rare charm. Now you must let me introduce you to my natural sister, Lady Hester Theale!"

The Captain shook hands with Hester, saying seriously: "I am excessively sorry, ma'am, and I beg you will forgive her! I was never more shocked! I shall break her of these tricks, you may be sure, but in some ways she's no more than a baby, which makes it devilish hard to explain to her why she mustn't make up faradiddles about being compromised, and the rest of it."

Lady Hester, casting a look of mild triumph at Sir Gareth, said: "I told you it would depend on what he was like, and I could see you didn't believe me, only you perceive that I was right! Captain Kendal, don't listen to *anything* that *anybody* may say to you, but just marry Amanda, and take her to Spain with you. It would be too bad if you did not, because she has been to a great deal of trouble over it, besides learning to wring chickens' necks, and being exactly the sort of wife you ought to have, if you should happen to be wounded again."

"Well, I don't want her to wring chickens' necks — in fact, I won't have her doing such things! — and I'd as lief not have her by, if I were to be hit again — though I'm glad she'd the sense to stop you bleeding to death, sir! — but, by Jupiter, ma'am, if *you* think that's what I should do, I will do it!" said the Captain, once more shaking her by the hand. "I'm very much obliged to you. It isn't that I don't know she'd do much better with me than with her grandfather, but she *is* very young, and I don't want to take advantage of her. However, if you think it right, the General may go hang! Hallo! That sounds like his voice! Ay, here he comes — but who the devil has he got with him?"

Lady Hester, gazing in a petrified way at the three figures advancing towards her, said faintly: "Widmore and Mr. Whyteleafe! *Just* when we were so comfortable!"

CHAPTER EIGHTEEN

It was immediately apparent that although the three gentlemen bearing down upon the group under the apple-tree had arrived together at the Bull, this had not been through any choice of theirs. All were looking hearted, and Lord Widmore was glaring so hard at Summercourt that it was not until Mr. Whyteleafe ejaculated: "*Sir Gareth Ludlow!* Here — and with Lady Hester?" that he became aware of the identity of the figure in the brocade dressing-gown. Since not even his wildest imaginings had pictured Hester in Sir Gareth's company, he was so dumbfounded that he could only goggle at him. This gave the General an opportunity to step into the lead, and he was quick to pounce on it. Brushing past his lordship, and annihilating Mr. Whyteleafe with the stare which had in earlier days turned the bones of his subordinates to water, he strode up to Sir Gareth's chair, and said, in a sort

445

of bark: "You will be good enough, sir, to grant me the favour of a private interview with you! When I tell you that my name is Summercourt — yes, *Summercourt,* sir! — I rather fancy that you will not think it marvellous that I have come all the way from London for the express purpose of seeking you out! I do not know — nor, I may add, do I *wish* to know — who these persons may be," he said, casting an eye of loathing over Lord Widmore and the chaplain, "but I might have supposed that upon my informing them that I had urgent business to discuss here, common civility would have promoted them to postpone whatever may be their errand to you until my business was despatched! Let me say that these modern manners do not commend themselves to me — though I should have known how it would be, from a couple of cow-handed whipsters as little able to control a worn-out donkey as a pair of carriage-horses!"

"It was not my chaplain, sir, who was driving down a narrow lane at what I do not scruple to call a shocking pace!" said Widmore, firing up.

"The place for a parson, I shall take leave to tell you, sir, is not on the box of a curricle, but in his pulpit!" retorted the General. "And now, if you will be good enough to retire, I may perhaps be allowed to transact the business which has brought me here!"

Mr. Whyteleafe, who had been staring at Hester with an expression on his face clearly indicative of the feelings of shock, dismay, and horror which had assailed him on seeing her thus, living, apparently, with her rejected suitor in a discreetly secluded spot, withdrew his gaze to direct an austere look at the General. The aspersion cast on his driving skill he disdained to notice, but he said, in a severe tone: "I venture to assert, sir, that the business which brings Lord Widmore and myself to call upon Sir Gareth Ludlow is sufficiently urgent to claim his instant attention. Moreover, I must remind you that *our* vehicle was the first to draw up at this hostelry!"

The General's eyes started at him fiercely. "Ay! So it was, indeed! I am not very likely to forget it, Master Parson! Upon my soul, such effrontery I never before encountered!"

Lord Widmore, whose fretful nerves had by no means recovered from the shock of finding his curricle involved at the crossroad in a very minor collision with a postchaise and four, began at once to prove to the General that no blame attached to his chaplain. As irritation always rendered him shrill, and the General's voice retained much of its fine carrying quality, the ensuing altercation became noisy enough to cause Lady Hester to stiffen imperceptibly, and to lay one hand on the arm of Sir Gareth's chair, as though for support. He was aware of her sudden tension, and covered her hand with his own, closing his fingers reassuringly round her wrist. "Don't be afraid! This is all sound and fury," he said quietly.

She looked down at him, a smile wavering for a moment on her lips. "Oh, no! I am not afraid. It is only that I have a foolish dislike of loud, angry voices."

"Yes, very disagreeable," he agreed. "I must own, however, that I find this encounter excessively diverting. Kendal, do you care to wager any blunt on which of my engaging visitors first has private speech with me?"

The Captain, who had bent to catch these words, grinned, and said: "Oh, old Summercourt will bluster himself out, never fear! But who is the other fellow?"

"Lady Hester's brother," replied Sir Gareth. He added, his eyes on Lord Widmore: "Bent, if I know him, on queering my game and his own!"

"I beg pardon?" the Captain said, bending again to hear what had been uttered in an undertone.

"Nothing: I was talking to myself."

Hester murmured: "Isn't it *odd* that they should forget everything else, and quarrel about such a trifle?" She seemed to become aware of the clasp on her wrist, and tried to draw her hand away. The clasp tightened, and she abandoned the attempt, colouring faintly.

Mr. Whyteleafe, whose jealous eyes had not failed to mark the interlude, took a quick step forward, and commanded in a voice swelling with stern wrath: "Unhand her ladyship, sir!"

Hester blinked at him in surprise. Sir Gareth said, quite amiably: "Go to the devil!"

The chaplain's words, which had been spoken in a sharpened voice, recalled the heated disputants to matters of more moment than a grazed panel. The quarrel ceased abruptly; and the General, turning to glare at Sir Gareth, seemed suddenly to become aware of the lady standing beside his chair. His brows twitched together in a quelling frown; he demanded: "Who is this lady?"

"Never mind that!" said Lord Widmore, directing at Sir Gareth a look of mingled prohibition and entreaty.

Sir Gareth met it blandly, and turned his head towards the General. "This lady, sir, is the Lady Hester Theale. She has the misfortune to be Lord Widmore's sister, and also to dislike heated altercations."

His lordship's angry but incoherent protest was overborne by the General's more powerful voice. "Have I been led here on a fool's errand?" he thundered. He rounded on Captain Kendal. "You young jackass, I told you to keep out of my affairs! I might have known you would lead me on a wild goose chase!"

Captain Kendal, quite undismayed by this ferocious attack, replied: "Yes, sir, in a way that's what I have done. But all's right, as I will explain to you, if you care to come into the house for a few minutes."

A look of relief shot into the General's eyes; in a far milder tone, he asked; "Neil, where is she?"

"Here, sir. I sent her upstairs to wash her face," said the Captain.

"Here! With this — this — And you tell me all's *right?*"

"I do, sir. You are very much obliged to Sir Gareth, as I shall show you."

Before the General could reply, an interruption occurred. Amanda and Hildebrand, attracted by the sounds of the late altercation, had come out of the house, and had paused, surprised to find so many persons gathered around Sir Gareth. Amanda had washed away her tear stains, but she was looking unwontedly subdued. Hildebrand was carefully carrying a brimming glass of milk.

The General saw his granddaughter, and abandoned the rest of the company, going towards her with his hands held out. "Amanda! Oh, my pet, how *could* you do such a thing?"

She flew into his arms, crying that she was sorry, and would never, never do it again. The Captain, observing with satisfaction that his stern instructions were being obeyed, transferred his dispassionate gaze to the chaplain, who, upon recognizing Hildebrand, had flung out his arm, pointing a finger of doom at that astonished young gentleman, and ejaculating: "*That* is the rascal who lured Lady Hester to this place, my lord! Unhappy boy, you are found out! Do not seek to excuse yourself with lies, for they will not serve you!"

Hildebrand, who had been gazing at him with his mouth at half-cock, looked for guidance towards Sir Gareth, but before Sir Gareth could speak Mr. Whyteleafe warned him that it was useless to try to shelter behind his employer.

"Oh, Hildebrand, is that Uncle Gary's milk?" said Hester. "What a good, *remembering* boy you are! But I quite thought I had given the glass to Amanda, which just shows what a dreadful memory I have!"

"Oh, you did, but she threw it away!" replied Hildebrand. "Here you are, sir: I'm sorry I have been such an age, but it went out of my head."

"The only fault I have to find is that it ever reentered your head," said Sir Gareth. "*Is* this a moment for glasses of milk? Take it away!"

"No, pray don't! Gareth, Dr. Chantry said that you were to drink a great deal of milk, and I won't have you throw it away merely because all these absurd people are teasing you!" said Hester, taking the glass from Hildebrand. "And Sir Gareth is *not* Mr. Ross's employer!" she informed the chaplain. "Of course, my brother-in-law isn't his employer either, but never mind! It was quite my fault that he was obliged to be not perfectly truthful to you."

"Lady Hester, I am appalled! I know not by what means you were brought to this place —"

"Hildebrand fetched me in a post-chaise.

452

Now, Gareth!"

"You misunderstand me! Aware as I am, that Sir Gareth's offer was repugnant to you, I cannot doubt that you were lured from Brancaster by some artifice. What arts — I shall not say threats! — have been used to compel your apparent complaisance today I may perhaps guess! But let me assure you —"

"That will do!" interrupted Sir Gareth, with an edge to his voice.

"Yes, but this is nothing but humdudgeon!" said Hildebrand. "I didn't lure her! I just brought her here because Uncle Gary — Sir Gareth, I mean — needed her! She came to look after him, and we pretended she was his sister, so you may stop looking censoriously, which, though I don't mean to be uncivil to a clergyman, is a great piece of impertinence! And as for *threatening* her, I should just like to see anyone try it, that's all!"

"Oh, Hildebrand!" sighed Hester, overcome. "How *very* kind you are!"

"Good boy!" Sir Gareth said approvingly, handing him the empty glass. "Widmore, if you can contrive to come out of a state of what would appear to be a catalepsy, assemble the few wits God gave you, and attend to me, I trust I may be able to allay your brotherly anxiety!"

Lord Widmore, who, from the moment of Amanda's arrival on the scene, had been standing in a spellbound condition, gave a start, and stammered: "How is this? Upon my soul! I do not know what to think! This goes beyond all bounds! That is the girl you had the effrontery to bring to Brancaster! So it was to take her to those relations of hers at Oundle, was it, that you went chasing after my uncle? Not that I believed it! I hope I am not such a gull!"

"That girl, sir," said Captain Kendal, dropping a restraining hand on Sir Gareth's shoulder, and keeping his penetrating eyes on Lord Widmore's face, "is Miss Summercourt. She is shortly to become my wife, so if you have any further observations to make on this head, you may address them to me!"

"Widmore, do *try* not to be so silly!" begged Hester. "I can't think how you can have so little commonsense! It is quite true that I came here to nurse Gareth, for he had had a very serious accident, and nearly died; but also I came to be a chaperon for Amanda — not that there was the least need of such a thing, when she was in Gareth's charge, but although I have not a great deal of sense myself I do know that persons like you would think so. And I must say, Widmore, that it is very lowering to be so closely related to anyone with such a dreadfully *commonplace* mind as you have!"

He was so much taken aback by this unprecedented assault that he could find nothing to say. Amanda, who had poured the tale of her odyssey into her grandsire's ears, seized the opportunity to address him. "Oh, Lord Widmore, pray excuse me for having been so uncivil as to run away with your uncle without taking leave of you and Lady Widmore and Lord Brancaster, or saying thank you for a very pleasant visit! And, please, Uncle Gary, forgive me for having been troublesome, and uncivil, and telling people you were abducting me, which Neil says you didn't, though I must say it *is* abducting, when you force people to go with you. However, I am truly grateful to you for having been so kind, and letting me have Joseph. And Aunt Hester too. And now I have begged *everybody's* pardon, except Hildebrand's," she continued, without the smallest pause, "so, *please,* Neil, don't be vexed with me any more!"

"That's a good girl," said her betrothed, putting his arm round her, and giving her a slight hug.

"Amanda!" said the General sharply, as she rubbed her cheek against Captain Kendal's arm. "Come here, child!"

The Captain released her, and her grandfather bade her run away and pack her boxes. She looked mutinous, but Captain Kendal endorsed the command, upon which she sighed, and went with lagging steps into the house.

"Now, sir!" said the General, turning to Sir Gareth. "I am satisfied that you have behaved like a man of honour to my granddaughter, and I will add that I am grateful to you for your care of her. But although I do not say that you are to blame for it, this has been a bad business — a very bad business! Should it become known that my granddaughter has been for nearly three weeks living under your protection, as I cannot doubt it will, since so many persons are aware of this circumstance, the damage to her reputation would be such as to —"

"Dear me, didn't she tell you that I have been here all the time?" enquired Lady Hester.

"Ma'am," said the General, "you were not with her at Kimbolton!"

"I beg pardon, sir," put in Hildebrand diffidently, "but nobody saw her there but me, except the servants, of course, and *they* didn't think anything but that she was

Uncle Gary's ward. Well, I thought she was, too!"

"What you thought, young man," said the General crushingly, "is of no value! Be good enough not to interrupt me again! Ludlow, I am persuaded that I shall not find it necessary to urge you to adopt the only course open to a man of honour! You know the world: it has been impossible to keep my granddaughter's disappearance from her home a secret from my neighbours. I am not so simple as to suppose that conjecture is not rife amongst them! Or, let me add, that your zeal in pursuing her sprang merely from altruistic motives! She is young, and I do not deny that she has some foolish fancies in her head, but I don't doubt that a man of your address would very speedily succeed in engaging her affections."

"Believe me, sir, you flatter me!" said Sir Gareth dryly.

"Ludlow, am I to *demand* that you should do the only thing that lies in your power to protect my granddaughter's reputation?"

"I begin to see that in blaming the circulating libraries for the extremely lurid nature of Amanda's imagination I have been unjust," remarked Sir Gareth. "You will permit me to tell you, sir, that you are being absurd."

"Not absurd!" struck in Captain Kendal. "Ambitious!"

Lord Widmore, who had been standing wrapped in hurried and constructive thought, suddenly made his presence felt. "Quite absurd! Laughable, indeed! Miss Summercourt — pooh, a schoolgirl! I venture to say that her youth is protection enough! You may be easy, General: I give you leave to inform your acquaintance that she has been visiting Lady Widmore at Brancaster, should you think it necessary to put out some story to satisfy the curiosity of the vulgar. But my unfortunate sister's predicament is a different matter! *She* is not a child! I do not say that the blame for her having been mad enough to come here is to be laid at your door, Ludlow, but I must deem you grossly to blame for her continued presence here! I would not have believed that you could have been so careless of her reputation had I not been aware of what passed between you at Brancaster. I cannot do other than censure the means you have thought proper to employ to induce my sister to give you another answer than the one you received from her not so long since, but no other course is open to me than to tell her that she has no choice but to become your wife!"

"Kendal!" said Sir Gareth. "Be so good as to act as my deputy, and kick Widmore out! Try if you can find a midden!"

"Yes, pray do!" said Lady Hester cordially.

"With all the pleasure on earth!" said the Captain, stepping forward in a purposeful fashion.

"Hold!" commanded Mr. Whyteleafe, in such throbbing and portentous accents that every eye turned towards him. "His lordship is mistaken! *One* other choice lies open to Lady Hester, which I dare to think must be preferable to her than to be linked to a fashionable fribble! Lady Hester, I offer you the protection of *my* name!"

"*Two* middens!" said Sir Gareth savagely.

"No, because I am persuaded he means it very kindly," intervened Hester. "I am so much obliged to you, Mr. Whyteleafe, but it is quite unnecessary for anyone to offer me the protection of their names, because Widmore is talking nonsense, as he very well knows. And I shall be still more obliged to you if you will take him away!"

"You do not mean to *remain* here!" exclaimed the chaplain, in horror.

She did not answer, for she was a little agitated. It was Hildebrand who said hotly: "She needn't scruple to do so, because *I* shan't leave Uncle Gary, and I will take very good care of her, I assure you! That is to say, I should, if he was the sort of person you think, but he is not! Uncle Gary, let *me* throw him out!"

"No," said Sir Gareth. "You may instead help me out of this chair! Thank you! No, I don't need any further support. Now! You have all talked yourselves out, I trust, for *I* am going to say a few words! First, let me make it plain to you that I have not the slightest intention of allowing myself to be coerced into offering marriage to either of the ladies whose reputations I am alleged to have damaged! Second, I have not, in fact, damaged anyone's reputation. It would be hard to imagine how I could have done so during the time I have been in this inn, and as for the one night at Kimbolton, your granddaughter, General, passed as my ward, as Hildebrand has already told you. Let me add that in no other light have I at any time during my acquaintance with her regarded her. So far from having, as you seem to think, a *tendre* for her, I can think of few worse fates than to be married to a girl who is not only young enough to be my daughter, but who has what I suspect to be an ineradicable habit of flinging herself into the arms of the military. I suggest, if you feel her fair name to have been smirched in the eyes of your neighbours, that you lose no time in getting her out of the country. No doubt Captain Kendal will be happy to assist you in achieving this object!"

"Thank you: I will!" said the Captain briskly.

"Nothing will induce me —" began the General.

"Just let me say what I have to, sir, if you please!" interposed Captain Kendal. "I have hitherto acquiesced in your resolve not to allow Amanda to become my wife while she is still so young. Our attachment is of pretty long standing, but the force of your objections was fully realized by me. I shall not expatiate on that head, because this prank she has played has made me change my mind. It is quite obvious to me, sir, that neither you nor Miss Summercourt has the smallest control over her, and if I don't take her in hand now she will be utterly ruined! She doesn't play these tricks on me, so you needn't be afraid she'll get into mischief when I have her in Spain: I'll see to that! And you needn't be afraid, either, that she won't be happy, because I'll see to that, too! I should wish to marry her by special licence, with your consent. If you continue to withhold your consent, I shall be obliged to postpone the ceremony until we reach

Lisbon. That's all I have to say, sir." He perceived his betrothed coming through the trees, and called: "Here, Amanda, I want you!"

"You know, General, I am quite, quite sure that Captain Kendal is just the man for her," said Hester persuasively.

He groaned. "To be throwing herself away on Neil Kendal! It is not what I wish for her!"

"Throwing herself away?" said Sir Gareth. "My dear sir, that young man is clearly destined to become a Marshal!"

"Young Neil?" said the General, as though such a notion was new to him.

"Certainly! If I were you, I would give in with a good grace. If you could incarcerate her until Kendal has left the country, I should be astonished if I did not hear next that she had stowed away on a vessel bound for Spain."

The General shuddered. His granddaughter, having been informed, very kindly, by her strongminded lover, that if she was a good girl, and did as she was told, he would marry her after all, and take her to Spain, first embraced him fervently, then flung her arms round the General's neck, and ended by hugging both Lady Hester and Sir Gareth for good measure.

It was fully an hour before the Bull Inn sank back into its accustomed quiet. The General's party was the first to leave, and if he was by no means reconciled to his grand-daughter's engagement a suggestion made by his prospective son-in-law that he should accompany the bridal pair to Lisbon had undoubtedly found favour with him.

Lord Widmore lingered, alternately commanding and beseeching his sister to return immediately to her home. In these exhortations he was joined by the chaplain. Lady Hester listened to them with patience, but although she said she was sorry to vex her brother, she remained gently determined not to desert her patient. Lord Widmore then declared that since she was of age she might please herself, but that for his part he washed his hands of her.

"Oh, do you?" she said. "I am so glad, for it is what I have longed for you to do for *such* a time! Pray give my love to Almeria! I must take Gareth his medicine now: excuse me, please!"

Sir Gareth, left alone in the orchard to recover from the exhausting effect of his guests, watched her come towards him, carrying his medicine. "I am glad you haven't left me to my fate," he remarked.

"Oh, no! Such nonsense! Here is this *evil-*

smelling dose which Dr. Chantry says is what you should take."

"Thank you," he said, receiving the glass from her, and pouring its contents on to the grass.

"Gareth!"

"I have had enough of Dr. Chantry's potions. Believe me, they taste worse than they smell! Hester, that brother of yours is a sapskull."

"Oh, yes, I know he is!" she agreed.

"I meant what I said, you know. I don't think myself bound to offer you the protection of my name — did you ever listen to so much fustian? I'll swear I never did! — because the suggestion that I have compromised you is as ludicrous as it is nauseating."

"Of course it is. Don't let us talk about it! It was so stupid!"

"We will never mention it again, if you will give me your assurance that you have no qualms. Look at me!"

She obeyed, with a tiny smile. "Gareth, it is *too* foolish! How can you ask me such a question?"

"I couldn't bear to think, love, that you might consent to marry me for such a reason as that," he said quietly.

"No," she answered. "Or I that you might

ask me for such a reason as that."

"You may be very sure I would not. This is not the first time I have asked you to marry me, Hester."

"Not the first time, but this is different — I think?" she said shyly.

"Quite different. When I asked you at Brancaster I held you in affection and esteem, but I believed I could never be in love again. I was wrong. Will you marry me, my dear and last love?"

She took his face between her hands, and looked into his eyes. A sigh, as though she were rid of a burden, escaped her. "Yes, Gareth," she said. "Oh, yes, *indeed* I will!"

ABOUT THE AUTHOR

Georgette Heyer was born in London, England, in 1902. From the beginning of her career, her talent was obvious — she sold the first book she had ever written. Over the next fifty years she wrote nearly sixty romance and mystery novels. Celebrated for the wit and humor in her novels, renowned for the historical accuracy and vivid portrayals of various time periods, she is said to have single-handedly created Regency romance as it is known today. Scores of authors credit her as inspiration for their own careers — and millions of readers eagerly collect every one of her novels.

New York Times bestselling author **Linda Lael Miller** started writing at age ten and has made a name for herself in both contemporary and historical romance with over fifty published novels to her credit. Her bold and innovative style has made her a favorite among readers. She currently makes her home in Arizona.